TIGER

By Polly Clark

FICTION

Larchfield

POETRY

Kiss

Take Me With You

Farewell My Lovely

A Handbook for the Afterlife

TIGER

Polly Clark

riverrun

First published in Great Britain in 2019 by riverrun
An imprint of

r

riverrun

Quercus Editions Limited
Carmelite House
50 Victoria Embankment
London EC4Y 0DZ

An Hachette UK company

A CIP catalogue record for this book is available
from the British Library

Hardback 978 1 78648 542 7
Trade Paperback 978 1 78648 541 0
Ebook 978 1 78648 544 1

10 9 8 7 6 5 4 3 2 1

Typeset in Monotype Fournier by CC Book Production

Printed and bound in Great Britain by Clays Ltd, Elcograf S.p.A.

For Lucy,
my fierce, beautiful daughter

Prologue

Russian Taiga, Winter 1992

Oy, moroz, moroz . . .
Oh, frost, frost! Don't freeze me . . .
. . . My wife is of the jealous kind . . .
Oy, moroz . . .

A S HE SANG, DMITRY knotted the snare rope tight around the tree base. No matter how drunk he was, he could make a faultless bowline knot – one that tightened when pulled, but could be easily released. Swaying now, Dmitry paused in his song as he surveyed his work. A snare is a thing of beauty, he thought. Elegant, brutal, simple. Around this small clearing, formed by a fallen Korean pine tree, he had laid four snares.

This was the last. With a little brushwood and snow, he covered the metal ring with its coil of steel wire and plate for the tiger to stand on. Then he swept the area clean of footprints.

'Careful, Yana!' he said to the peach-coloured terrier sniffing round the fire. 'Hope you were watching where I put them.'

> My wife, such a beauty,
> Awaits my return,
> Awaits in sadness.
> I'll return home at sunset, embrace her . . .
> *Oy, moroz, moroz . . .*

Returning to his seat made from a stump, and his bottle, Dmitry did not pause in his singing – or rather the saw of breath across the polyps of his larynx – until the flames of the campfire sank and freezing air began to jump. It was like tens of Jack Frosts, leaping and landing, but, instead of a brush for his designs, each carried a khanjali blade, like the deadliest of Cossacks, slashing at the skin.

Yana, as always, refused to climb on to his lap. There was very little room, with Dmitry's belly bulging towards his knees, and by this point in the day Dmitry's breath was fiery with spirits. He patted his lap, wanting her warmth to delay the moment when he'd have to go and get more wood. 'Come on, girl!' he urged, but she twirled a little distance away. 'Humph,' said Dmitry, lighting a cigarette, taking several seconds to align flame and tip.

Dmitry was a man with a plan.

He was going to be rich.

'Very soon!' With these words, Dmitry hauled himself from the stump, grabbed his axe and weaved his way heavily through the snow into the trees.

'*Oy, moroz, moroz*,' he sang. 'Don't freeze me . . .'

Yana bounced after him, ears like blinks, her snout aloft like a flare. The snow was just that bit too deep for her.

Dmitry carried an armful of branches back to the fire. Splashing the flames with vodka, he took a warming swig himself, then strode a few admiring times around the shelter he'd made. It was a pathetic structure, consisting of a piece of rusted corrugated iron which he had found poking from the snow. He'd leant the iron against the immense fallen trunk and piled twigs and brushwood on it, weighed with branches, then he'd chopped more branches to block the end, creating what was basically a crawl space. It was woefully inadequate against the elements, but he was not going to be here long. The plan demanded only virility and courage, and these were Dmitry's finest qualities, eclipsing any practical deficits. And he had Yana to keep him warm. The dog regarded the shelter suspiciously.

A few metres ahead hung a deer carcass, purple and immobile, slowly freezing into rock. It was bait for the tiger, but he was having to eat from it himself now. He hacked a piece off, holding it in the fire while it hissed and dripped, then he chewed and swilled it down with vodka. He chucked a piece to Yana.

3

'Come on, tiger!' he yelled into the thickening dusk. Silence banged after the words. Dmitry sat down, facing the deer carcass, with his gun cocked and ready on his lap. Yana rested her snout on her paws, beside the fire.

Dmitry didn't like to be alone. In the village he always had company, someone with whom to toast his forthcoming wealth. The vodka made Dmitry's goal seem easily attainable, but did make the details hazy. Also, he was tired. Waiting for a tiger was hard work. And, staring into the dark, examining it for signs of the beast — well, it turned a man's attention into a worried dog, tied to a pole. Ducking, blinking, darting. The vodka hammered at his wakefulness.

Eventually, Dmitry yawned and scooped Yana up, her hind legs flicking with displeasure, and lowered himself with a grunt into the shelter. It was lined with brushwood, and he had a pine branch thickly endowed with needles and twigs to pull over the doorway. Inside the tiny space, man and dog rustled for comfort. Dmitry's breath soaked the air with alcohol. Beside him was the rifle, loaded, ready to go.

It was of course better to be awake when trying to kill a tiger. Dmitry conceded this, but if being awake was not possible, then he could rely on Yana. Dogs can hear a tiger from some distance. She would bark, wake him, and he would grab the rifle, burst out of the shelter and blow the tiger's brains out. The tiger would be caught in a snare, which would make the whole thing easy.

4

Then the only consideration would be whether to skin the tiger there and then, or drag it back to the village, where he would have help, but would have to share his earnings. It depended, of course, how big the tiger was. If he were to capture the king tiger – well, it would be immense. He'd heard the king could weigh as much as 400 kilogrammes. It could be four metres long without even including the tail. He could afford to be generous. These were exceptionally soothing thoughts, even through the cold, and Dmitry passed out peacefully, gripping the dog to his chest. Yana whined and gave up.

When he woke, Dmitry was so stiff and numb that he wondered briefly if he was dead. Yana was gone from his arms. He cursed as he pushed the branch from the entrance and stuck his head out. 'Yana!' he yelled across the snow. Branches fell from the shelter as Dmitry wriggled his bulk free, stumbling on to the churn of footprints outside.

'What the fuck?'

A smear of blood with a scrap of peach-coloured fur lay a little way beyond the shelter. Dmitry spun round. The deer carcass also was gone. His fire was completely destroyed. And pressed in the snow all round the shelter, right up to it, were copies of the king tiger's unmistakeably enormous pad, with its constellation of toe prints.

Dmitry could feel his lungs blistering. The sun was hard and blank, like a god turned away. Hurrying to the snares, unease lurched in his gut. One, two, three, untouched, unsprung – and then, oh! The last one sprung, snow everywhere, a smattering of blood. And . . . what . . . ?

The steel rope that had clenched the tiger's paw lay chewed. The tiger had *chewed through the steel rope.*

How the hell had it done that?

Dmitry wrestled his gun from the shelter and fired it. 'Tiger! Fucking tiger! Coward!' How could it have come right up to the shelter, taken Yana and the deer, and not woken him? And, if he was so soundly asleep, why didn't it kill him? Did it not know he was there?

Of course it knew he was there.

Through his hangover, shock registered, like a rock hitting the bottom of a well.

He was trapped here, two days from the village, with no dog and no food. And a tiger that could chew through steel rope and seemed to have a plan.

Dmitry scanned between the trees for the tiger's tracks, saw them heading deep into the forest. They were speckled with blood. Following them would leave him vulnerable on all sides. No, he was better here, with his fire, his gun and his snares.

The vodka bottle was miraculously still upright.

With a trembling hand, Dmitry unscrewed the cap and steadied himself with a long draught.

Man with a plan.

The tiger would be back. (But when?)

He just had to be ready.

He looked across to the bloodstain. Yana must have wriggled free from his arms in the night. The tiger must have stayed downwind, snapping her up before she could even bark.

Useless fucking dog. Better off without her.

He cleared his throat and tried to focus on the day. The familiar shakes that arrived every morning now made the axe fall from his grip. There was a different quality to them this time. Something else, not just craving for alcohol, was making his hands tremble. But he was not afraid. No, siree. This tiger had made a big mistake.

'A big mistake!' he yelled, but his voice snapped at the end, like a brittle twig.

Should he move the snares? He decided against it, instead devising a programme to break the day and keep himself awake. Time to find another deer, or something to eat. He would stock up on wood. Dmitry gulped another drink and stared defiantly into the forest.

'I'm here! You fucking pelt!' he yelled into the trees. The vodka had warmed him up now, and he was exhilarated. The king tiger. What a prize. It should have killed him while it had the chance. It wouldn't get another.

PURPOSE. IF ONE WORD could express the king tiger's sweep through the trees towards Dmitry's camp, this was it. The king was enormous, passing this quality on down his line to his daughter, and so extravagantly beautiful that he seemed to have burst from another world. Yet there was not a wisp of waste upon him. Every hair was the right length, every stride absolutely adequate to the demands of the moment. Should he need to break into a sprint, he could cover the ground at seventy kilometres an hour, but there had been barely five times in his life when this was necessary. To sprint opens up possibilities for prey; it's almost an admission of failure. Boar can twist through the trees with the fluidity of the wind. Once speed is unleashed, it's all the tiger has. Before that moment, he has purpose, incarnated as stealth.

The king had never hunted a man before. Most of his vast territory lay beyond the reach of them, encompassing a huge tract of untouched taiga. Also, the king knew about guns. Their ability to injure and destroy from a distance had travelled deep into the consciousness of every forest animal, to become in some way genetic, like knowledge of the rivers and the best places in the forest to find the pine nuts that were, like plankton in the ocean, the source of all life. The king understood the truth that lay behind the gun: men were fleshy and defenceless aliens, who tried, but failed, to master his kingdom.

It was approaching dusk, two days after the king's initial visit to Dmitry's camp. The delay in his return would have disorientated the hunter. The shelter was poorly placed, surrounded by dense woodland that afforded the tiger total camouflage.

The tiger slid through the gloom, like a shark.

If we were to have the misfortune to encounter the king at this moment – misfortune because it would be the last thing we would ever encounter – we would be paralysed with wonder that a creature so immense and bright, before whom all creatures fled, was possessed of such oceanic stealth. In the king tiger, the majesty of the forest became corporeal. The sun and moonlight, the stars and shadows, the complexities of striations and ancient rings upon the trees, the shadings of snow and earth – the king swept all these into his shape. To encounter him was to witness a fundamental truth: all natural things are incarnations of each other.

All, that is, except human hunters. Flimsy, ill-suited to the forest, they were incarnations of nothing. The king understood this about them, and this honed his approach. The hunter exists outside nature. He *changes* nature to suit himself. He burns it, chops it, digs it, destroys it. He disguises his own weakness with things he has made: snares, traps, guns. He fills the forest with copies of himself, as in the teeming village where recently one of the king's tigresses was taken and killed.

As the king approached Dmitry's camp from the back, he made no sound at all. Had he made a sound, it would likely have been drowned out by the hunter's wailing song, which faded as night closed in and Dmitry's resolve to stay awake weakened. 'Tiger!' he called periodically. 'Come here, you fucking coward!'

The snare had cut the king's paw and he had bled, but fortunately the temperatures mitigated against infection, even

9

as they slowed healing. If this was summer, the wound would have been infested with maggots within hours. The snare was really only adequate for a boar. For the largest cat on earth, it was an annoyance.

The tiger's tail flicked as if propelling him through dark waters. It flexed to balance his tilt through the trees.

How could something so massive make no noise?

When the forest manifests as a tiger, the transformation is perfect. Noise is an imperfection, and it has no place here.

The hunter was poking the fire, mumbling to himself. The rifle was in his hand.

It was pitiful, really, that the hunter did not understand that the king tiger owns everything in the forest. He *is* the forest. To maintain a territory of such immensity, every transgression must be avenged, boundaries must be ruthlessly enforced. This was essential to keep the king in his place at the apex of existence.

The tiger's skull, looming now behind Dmitry, would fill a man's arms. His magisterial face took on the stillness of a god.

Here, the king tiger left the magnificence of the shark behind. Here, he left behind every creature on earth.

If you take something of mine, I will come for you.

That is dominion.

The king crept over the log.

Dmitry was not a sensitive man, and what senses he had were dulled by years of vodka consumption. What remained was sentiment. Dmitry was a very sentimental man. He was weeping fat, inebriated tears now. For his dog, for his mother, for the prostitutes whose names he never knew.

It was as if the log offered itself to the king tiger. It seemed to lower itself, as the beast slithered silently over it.

A tiny sigh. A lump of snow, breaking.

Dmitry stopped sobbing.

He turned on his stump.

Perhaps he was the luckiest man on earth. For time stopped for Dmitry. The king tiger opened his jaws, fangs splitting the dark like lightning. There was no time for fear. No time for Dmitry to raise a gun. No time for anything at all. Just an eternity of gazing into the face of the divine, experiencing in his blood and in every cell of his body the true natural order.

Part One

FRIEDA

One

I T WAS BOUND TO happen that one day I would consume too much at work, and my façade would drop, and it would all be over. I had become exceptionally practised – the pharmaceutical-grade morphine ever-so-carefully pilfered, sham-ordered. Using in my favourite toilet cubicle, out in the animal house, where no one would notice anything. The syringe out of its packet, carefully disposed of in the animal-house rubbish, and the swift pinch to the skin. Then *rest*. It was the rest I craved. With the tiny, carefully calculated dose of morphine, I could rest *while I was working*. It seemed not to have much effect on my ability to interpret statistics, even less on my snapshots and meticulous notes on the bonobo facial expressions, which I homed in on with the cameras from inside the studio.

Also, something about me in my resting state seemed to calm the bonobos. The elderly matriarch, Zaire, would wander up close to me as I leant against the bars of the sleeping area. I wasn't meant to be there during the period of a study, because being too present, too close to the bonobos, of course altered the results. Just as in physics, where the act of observation changes the behaviour of light, making it become waves or particles, as if to please the viewer, so it is the same with the bonobo and the researcher who makes her observational status known. But I loved Zaire, and she loved me, and towards the end of this period of resting at work, I began not to care so much about what I should or should not do. It was important not to be caught, but even that grew less pressing. I went further, and began to creep into the enclosure at night, to lie on the column of hay bales, always taking care to be out of the range of the C.C.T.V. The bonobos would sit nearby, chattering among themselves. Zaire would often come and sit beside me. She rested her hand on my arm once, and had I not been so numb I would have cried when she did that. I had no fear when I was resting. It was fear that I was taking a rest from.

Often, during my secret resting sessions in the enclosure, I stared up at the black of the night sky. Were the bonobos interested in the stars? I wondered. Was it a matter of curiosity to them that, some dark nights, their familiar sky exploded in these countless pinpricks of light? Bonobos are intelligent and emotional in a way that humans can relate to and measure; they have a system of relationships that we might describe as a culture. They do a lot of deep thinking. They have self-consciousness too. Did they wonder what would become of them in the future? When they saw their old or sick companions fall ill and die, did they wonder what happened to them?

I would argue, when the time came for such desperate arguments, that my rest trips into the enclosure had caused me to stumble on to something that was a vital part of our research. My discovery was that bonobos dealt with death as a group, with a kind of ritual. Such behaviour had not been observed before; the wild environment, deep in the Congo, is hard to access, and research into captive bonobos was relatively new. This was a revelation similar to what had recently been discovered in elephants. The territories of elephants are vast in the wild, and conditions impossible to replicate in captivity, so that their complicated mourning rituals had remained hidden for a long time.

One of the bonobos was ailing. It sometimes happened this way, that the animal was born knowing it was in the wrong place, that its body was wrongly situated, that it was ruled over and defined by another creature. Such individuals never thrived. They could not shake off the truth that dogged them, that their life was somehow not real and not their own. Sometimes they developed actual illnesses, they were sickly and frail. But, even if they did not do this, they were runtish and lost from the beginning, and always, it seemed to me, waiting for the end, when the truth of their experience of themselves and the truth that resided somewhere in the world, in the starry sky perhaps, would be reconciled.

This was Dembe, a young female bonobo, great-great-niece of Zaire. She had taken, lately, to sitting in the dark, as if at the entrance to the underworld. The others had taken to leaving her there, no longer pulling her back into the group. Like a busy human crowd streaming past a beggar, she had moved to the margin of what the group could contemplate without unacceptable awkwardness. For the project, we were interested in what this signified. Dembe showed no visible distress, not that the C.C.T.V. could pick up, anyway, but when I was resting in the enclosure, I sensed something more. Lately, I had become possessed of a prey animal's radar and was unable to resist the assault of fine emotional details. These were mostly unprovable, rendering me more like a dazed pilgrim recounting a vision than a scientist. Resting in the enclosure, I noticed the way Dembe's eyes developed a distant quality, that was nevertheless quite peaceful, as if she were observing the group from behind glass. Her own mother, Kia, seemed to have forgotten about her, and mostly had her back turned. I knew she had not forgotten. Some feelings are unbearable. You have to turn your back on them. You have to *rest*.

Dembe had died soon after, simply closing her eyes in the shadow, slumping a little against the wall, becoming in moments an effigy of herself.

The bonobos seemed to know instantly that the death had occurred: a frisson went through the group, they called among each other, and Kia moved to the front and went close to her daughter. Her son, smaller and younger than Dembe, wheeled around her, grinning with square white teeth. From my resting place on the bales, I could feel their mood. *Sticky. Violet.* Goose-bumps rose across my arms and chest.

Next, Kia picked up a wooden vegetable box that her son had been whirling round his head, and threw it at the C.C.T.V. (from underneath, so that she was not filmed doing so – clever), shattering it. There was only my account of what happened next, which was so extraordinary, which no camera would have captured properly anyway. It was unfortunate that, by then, I was an unreliable witness.

They carried the body to the centre of the enclosure, clearing space around it. Dembe's body lay dark and indistinct, like a waterlogged spider.

Again the sensation of their mood swam over me, raising the hairs on my skin. It was as if their feelings were leaching out of their open mouths and adhering to each other. I felt in my gut a sensation like a heavy old gate, or perhaps a mill wheel, breaking through rust in a downward action. There is something metallic about grief. Dembe's life had oxidised, and all of us, we could feel that, we could taste it, like iron in blood.

Now they ran round the enclosure, finding items to cover her with. A piece of sacking, broken planks, some branches. They were burying her. This is not unknown among species in the wild: bears, for example, will cover the bodies of their dead with soil. Why they do this is not clearly known. But no one had observed this among bonobos. Zaire swung gracefully towards me on her heavy knuckles and hovered beside the bales. The others followed, the males a little more aggressive, pulling at the bales I was lying on. Eventually, Kia's young son pushed me a little, his eyes like flashes from a knife. His hand, already the size of mine, pushed against my shirt like a ferret.

More than anything, this wordless circling (wordless, but not without its grammar; the working-up to violence has a strict grammar, which some are born knowing how to read, and some born to write) reminded me of those pubescent gangs I used to run the gauntlet of, those boys who were already men enough to know that they were entitled to something of me, the space I walked through, as a precursor to the interior of my skin, which I had supposed was my own. I was afraid, and I carefully rolled off the bale. They ran towards it, shrieking, ripping it to shreds, then they scattered the hay over Dembe, until she was a mound in the centre of the enclosure, a haystack, a pyre. Who knows what they would have done in the wild, or if someone – me – had offered them a lighter.

I had no lighter. I had nothing but the clothes I was standing in, my keys and pass, and a soreness in the crook of my elbow. They let me be, the mood grew sticky again, and they gathered in the corner of the enclosure furthest from the body. They huddled close, chattering. Kia wailed – bonobos cry – and a wave of exhaustion brimmed around me such that I simply had to curl up on the tiles and sleep.

This was how they found me in the morning. I was blamed for shattering the C.C.T.V. I was blamed for the body covered in bedding. No one was interested in my witness statement. It was, of course, the last straw, because while I thought I had been managing my rest periods successfully, it appeared I had not, and my colleagues – especially Cosima, the self-righteous PhD student – had been observing me for some time.

I argued passionately to the Institute H.R. and the head of department that the animals trusted me, that I saw things that the C.C.T.V. could never pick up, that my abilities were unimpaired. Admittedly, the theft of morphine and taking it at work was gross misconduct, I couldn't argue with that, but, but, *but* . . .

Professor Charlie Grace, my head of department and mentor, looked stricken at the meeting to inform me of my fate. I observed him curiously. His confusion was like my childhood watercolours when they got all mixed up from their little squares and the whole palette became a scramble of brownish purple, that nevertheless seemed to shriek its former incarnation from each square. The H.R. woman, Gina something, wore lipstick that seemed to turn blue as she spoke. We were in a claustrophobic 'interview pod'. I tried to argue my case. The two planks of my argument were:

1. My work had not been affected.

2. This was the most contented and normal I had been since the unbearable events.

At this point, I was unaware of the full dossier, compiled

by Cosima, of my misdemeanours. My record in research could not be disputed. I was, and here I could not help a small, tender smile tiptoeing across my face as I looked at him, Charlie's favourite. I was simply doing what I had to do in order to rest. I was, of course, extremely sorry and it wouldn't happen again. I would find alternative sources of help, of course. We could all agree that stealing morphine and shooting up at work was unacceptable.

I didn't add the cry from my heart: *But I am the best I've ever been!*

Nor the truth that clawed like a mole round the darkness of my brain: *Morphine glued the scales back on my eyes.*

I knew my love affair with the blissful narcotic would have to end. I thought, deep down, Charlie must be sympathising.

But his confusion and his cool were very alarming.

They both listened to my well-articulated argument, and did not hear my well-suppressed truth. I sat back, aching. I added, 'My God, though. What they did with Dembe. It was astonishing. Charlie, we should look into it more. Bonobo expressions of grief.'

No one said anything. Charlie did not look at me. The discomfort in the interview pod was like nitrogen: inert, unbreathable, killing me.

Gina gave a cough that rippled her satin blouse. 'Our difficulty, Dr Bloom, is that the gravity of this offence circumvents any normal disciplinary procedure. We know that you have struggled since the . . . your . . . incident. At Professor Grace's insistence, we have overlooked other breaches, because he assured us that you were on the mend, and reminded us – quite rightly, of course – of our duty of care. And, of course, we all hold you in the highest regard and affection.'

Metallic eyeshadow a shade brighter than her irises orbited her eyes. It was very disconcerting. Her face seemed as big as the solar system, and I was gazing at two Saturns with their gaseous rings. I felt no affection from her, nor regard, of any height.

'But, you must see, the nature of what happened last night has to mean instant dismissal. You have not only committed an illegal act on the premises, but you have compromised our security and the results of the project. We like to think we can accommodate creative people and their eccentricities –' here, Gina's appalling smile revealed that she considered herself a fine example of a creative eccentric – 'but it's gone too far. You need help. Institutional help.'

I gawped at Charlie. 'Charlie?' I said.

My dear friend and mentor inhaled deeply and addressed his knees.

'I'm sorry,' he said.

Outside, he said, 'If you want a reference, I'll do it for you privately. Let me know how you are.'

I said, 'Can I go and see the bonobos? Say goodbye to Zaire?'

He shook his head. 'They won't let you back in, Frieda.'

I liked to believe his eyes were wet as he hugged me and

received my pass on its lanyard. He insisted that it was wrong to exit my career on the bus, so I stood awkwardly in the car park while he ordered a cab. When I got home, I rang him to clarify what had just happened. I almost asked, *Has the worst happened?* But of course the worst had happened already; nothing else was even close to being the worst. I didn't really know how to categorise being sacked for gross misconduct from the job I loved in that pantheon; it was like organising my C.D.s in the order of how much they meant to me, when the house had long blown up.

Two

'LOOK INTO HER EYES,' Charlie instructed long ago, right at the beginning, when I was just a student at the Institute. 'When you look into the eyes of a bonobo, there is "someone home".'

I had done so, bending awkwardly at the glass where Zaire had come to meet me. All researchers were separated from the apes to protect them from our germs and to avoid distortion of our research. A human cold could turn into pneumonia in a bonobo. Zaire's heavy-lidded eyes were set wide apart in the hairless recess of her face, and she had her head tilted back, seeming to consider me. I began to talk, but Charlie stopped me with a hand on my shoulder. 'No need to say anything. Just look.'

Her eyes were animated with an intelligence that made me feel quite nervous. I submitted to her gaze, not attempting to fill the space between us with words or interpretations, but trying instead simply to be present. Her face was relaxed and her lightly pink lips parted. In response, I felt a smile spread over my own features.

Zaire got to her feet and terminated the interview with a great cackle. She spun on her knuckle and bounded out of the enclosure. Charlie smiled at me. 'See?'

I did see, and it made me uncomfortable. It was not measureable. It was intuitive, and frankly strange. I was glad of the glass between us, the unambiguous difference between us, and I was even more glad that our studies were all about *their* communication with each other. I had a clear sense that life operated much better with these divisions in place.

Bonobos have only been recognised as a species separate from chimpanzees since the 1970s. Smaller, rarer, and temperamentally opposite to their violent cousins, bonobos are the only apes who have significantly mastered English words, concepts and sentences. This ability has been demonstrated most famously by the internationally renowned bonobo Kanzi, who picked all these things up by being around human researchers who were teaching his mother. Bonobos live in a matriarchal society, and are highly sexed and also very gentle. They are the only primates apart from humans to have sex face-to-face and for pleasure.

I joined the project at the Institute for my PhD. This was to study, over generations, the communication of bonobos, its auditory and bodily patterns. Unlike academics who had worked with apes before, we were not focused on trying to teach them our language and ways of speaking, but to try to decode how information and knowledge were passed among a group and down the generations. My own area of research became focused on the 'peeps' emitted by baby bonobos, which, on analysis, seemed very like human baby preverbal noises, being often context-free – that is, not related to a particular need or emotional state.

Among the questions we sought to answer were: Did the apes pass on the skills and information they had learnt in captivity? Was their ability to make tools innate, but the specifics of what tools might be made dependent on their environment and their communication with each other about that environment? Did they, indeed, have what we might term a language? The experiments we devised offered them new ways of interacting, to see if these would become adopted group-wide and passed down. For instance, we taught Zaire (via television) to make a ham sandwich – a food she really enjoyed. Would she pass the skill on? (Answer: no, but she did make more sandwiches to share.)

All this was done by quiet observation via camera and from behind the glass. To record the baby 'peeps', I set microphones around where the bonobos were nursing, and I analysed the range and type of the sounds, and the detail of the context in which they were emitted. It was painstaking statistical and observational work, to which I had contributed the ten years of my career so far, and it necessitated no physical contact, no relationship. We sought not to complicate our results with inter-personal relationships. This was what discredited the attempts to prove that bonobos could learn human language: the researcher had become so close to the bonobo that interpretation became something more cloudy.

Watching films of Kanzi made me feel sad. Genius at adopting an alien culture, he seemed demeaned, even as he excelled. Knowing concepts, being able to signal a sentence on his message board, did not give him more agency. He seemed more isolated and dependent on his human companions, reduced to a highly accomplished performer in our world, and an incomprehensible alien in his own. I was fascinated instead by the bonobo world, which, to me, even in the amputated version we allowed them at the Institute, was immensely complex.

Other work of the project included documenting the minute and fleeting changes of expression across bonobo faces and recording particular vocalisations. Once, during a quiet after-noon, I had played with speeding up and slowing down the recordings, and heard, to our amazement – I had called Charlie in and he had stood, dumbfounded – the words *orange*, *baby*, *Frieda*, clearly spoken, picked up by the bonobos and repeated through their completely different vocal system at a much higher, distorted pitch. They used the words much more flexibly than their real meanings allowed. *Frieda* did seem to be a recognition of my name, but also was addressed to any female in the group. This became another strand of our study, another example of how these highly intelligent creatures used any aspect of the environment as a tool for themselves.

The world of the Institute and the bonobos was my world. And I excelled: I won funding and became tenure-tracked. Charlie and I talked about how we might expand the project's work to look at the unexplored notion of interspecies communication, which he felt was so powerful. I preferred the clear bubble of the research we were already doing.

Inside the certainties of scientific research, it was clear where I fitted, and where everyone — individual bonobos included — fitted in, too. If, however, we became creature facing creature, with no rules of engagement, no familiar landscape, I was unsure how I would function. If you have grown up, as I had, *outside a family unit* — how coy that looks, but I was always ashamed to say the word *orphan* aloud, even to myself — the correct way to be in the world has likely never been taught. The project gave me a framework, inside which I could learn, contribute and be connected. If pressed, which I never was, I'd have said I'd had no childhood. I was a blank slate of the wrong kind, and how askew it could have all gone. The lives of people like me generally veered away from order, from success, as if that original depth charge of loss set off a gradually swelling tsunami of consequences, which in the end could not be resisted. I knew I was lucky. How many people like me find a place where they can belong and thrive? I was grateful every day for my simple life, its answerable questions.

But then, one day, the ordered world as I knew it was smashed apart, and I was expelled into chaos, reaching out wordlessly to another creature as I fell.

POLICE INCIDENT REPORT

CASE NUMBER: 12748PX
ATTENDING OFFICER'S NAME: Carey Munro
LOCATION: Spikers Subway, Parkerton, London
DATE AND TIME: 08.08.10, 00.57 a.m.
EVIDENCE: Shattered mobile phone (Exhibit 1). Skull fragment (Ex. 2). Orange wool hat, bloodied (Ex. 3). Wallet (Ex. 4). Photographs taken at the scene (Ex. 5).

The Parkerton borough of North London lies north-east of Haringey. It has a mixed population, with communities of Polish, Romanian and Turkish immigrants, and also many students and other young single people who have moved out of the centre for affordable housing. There is a high proportion of single people in private rented accommodation. There are several streets of large residential homes collected around the Momentum Park. There is a council estate at the northern boundary. There is a moderate incidence of drug-related crime, concentrated in the council estate and the residential area. The borough is not served by a Tube line, but is well connected with buses. The various communities are settled and mostly harmonious, with their own shops and streets that they have gravitated to. It is not a high crime area overall.

Spikers subway runs under the small Greenblatt roundabout, at the western boundary of Parkerton. Greenblatt roundabout used to be the transport hub into the area, but has been superseded by the bus terminus, further into Parkerton, which also has a shopping centre. This is where the main subway is located. Spikers subway does not have C.C.T.V. It is usually quiet, especially at night; the bus terminus is where most people disperse from. It is not well maintained, nor well lit. On the night of the incident, there was a storm with torrential rain, which caused some flooding on the main road, resulting in the late bus terminating early.

I was called to this incident at 00:45 on Sunday morning, 08.08.10, from where I had been patrolling the residential area around Momentum Park. It was raining heavily. I arrived before the ambulance, which was delayed due to the flooding. The victim was lying beneath an unlit street light, curled up on her left side, twenty feet in front of the subway entrance, in a pool of blood (Exhibit 5.1). The blood was spread by the rain down a slight incline in the concrete and was pooling at the blocked drain, some ten feet beyond. The concrete was cracked and overgrown. There were weeds growing out of the cracks. The victim had fallen on to a clump of foxgloves sprouting from a ridge. There was nobody in the vicinity. A call to 999 had been made from a phone box at the other end of the subway, but the person who made the call had gone, and also refused to leave their name. I immediately called for backup. The scene was very dark, lit only by a dim ceiling lamp within the subway and a street light thirty feet away. There were other lights in the subway, but they were all broken. The external tiles of the subway were chipped and broken and there was extensive graffiti on the walls inside and out. The street light beneath which the victim lay was long smashed. I took photographs.

The victim was female and was breathing but not responsive. She was white, with shoulder-length dark hair in a ponytail. The ponytail was held with a black velvet scrunchie, sodden with blood. She was five feet, five inches in height, and of slim build. Her eyes were closed. I lifted an eyelid and the eye rolled upwards. Mascara was running down her face, washed by the rain. She wore no jewellery, neither earrings nor rings. Her ears were not pierced. She had blue eyes and freckles over her nose and forehead. She had a slight over-bite and pronounced cheekbones. I could smell alcohol on her breath. My torch showed she was wearing a navy mac and, beneath it, a dark green evening dress, clear tights and black high-heeled shoes. She was extremely wet. A phone was smashed twelve feet away (Exhibit 1). In her right mac pocket was a wallet with an Oyster card and a bank card with the name Dr Frieda Bloom. There was no cash in the wallet. There was nothing to show her age, which I estimated and was later confirmed as thirty-three.

There was no sign of a struggle or an attempt to run: her shoes were still on, though the right one was only attached at the toe. Her hands were around her head, as if she had grasped her skull as she fell. I checked under her mac and palpated for further injuries without moving her. I checked her ribs and pelvis and her back. She seemed to have two injuries: the one causing the blood flow was to her head, on the side against the ground; the other, found when I lifted her head, was to her hand on the left side – a deep graze across the knuckles, with dirt from the concrete pressed in it.

I shone my torch on to the head injury. Parting the mass of blood-matted hair I discerned a fracture, consisting of a deep dent, approximately two centimetres wide, consistent with a blow from a hammer. The effect on the skull of such a blow is like a rock on to ice, with cracks radiating from the central wound. Feeling these beneath my fingertips, I judged that this was a wound serious enough to be life-threatening. Blood was streaming from it. I pressed my hand to the hole, in order to stem the bleeding. At that moment, the victim opened her eyes and looked at me. I said, 'Frieda, I'm a police officer. An ambulance is coming. Stay with me.' She tried to push my hand away and replace it with her own. I told her my name and repeated that an ambulance was on its way, but she did not respond. She did, however, begin to cry, as if pain was just registering, but then her eyes rolled back again and she lost consciousness, and did not regain it while on the ground.

At 01:12, the ambulance arrived and relieved me from my position of holding her head. At 01:15, officers Adam and Methuen arrived and taped off the scene and began to erect canvas over the area to protect it from the rain. I accompanied the victim in the ambulance to Whittington A & E, and later to intensive care, to continue my investigation.

Three

SURELY NOT EVEN CHARLIE thought I had left the building without taking something to keep me going through what would happen next – or, rather, what wouldn't happen. My need to rest – deeply, and soon – was inflamed by the realisation that all was indeed over, that I really had been fired from my job, the only thing that gave meaning to my life. I swallowed a tiny spoonful in the toilet of my flat (why did I always use in a toilet, even when alone? A few minutes' recognition of the addict I was, perhaps) and then went out into the garden, approaching a state of rest. It was a small city space, shared by all the residents, and was completely neglected, due to the residents being penniless young professionals or penniless old people. But there was evidence of it having once been a real garden in the shrug of the compost heap, the dock-overrun wildflower patch. What was impressive was that it contained a tree. No other gardens in the area had a tree. It was a yew, neglected and immense. How the neighbours hated it, with its ancient mass shrivelling their lawns, its obscene darkness.

But I loved it. I had spent many summer afternoons dozing against it during my long recovery from the attack, eventually wearing the trunk shiny and making a shallow hollow in the earth at its base. I returned there now, sinking down, drinking in the soft must of the soil. Sunlight sprinkled through the spiky leaves.

In my jacket pocket was something I always carried with me: a tattered card, folded in four. On the front was a grinning chimp (Charlie had been unable to find a card featuring a bonobo, at short notice) and inside, around the message *Get Well Soon*, were the signatures of all my colleagues.

The card had been pinned above the bed during my weeks in the I.C.U. When the I.C.U. nurse slipped it into my hands, I laughed at the image – the first laugh of my new consciousness.

Charlie had signed the card with an illegible squiggle at the bottom. No message. But there was a full stop after his name, oddly definite, making an indent in the card, as if a message had contracted into itself and become a singularity. For a long time, my vision was quite blurred, and I found myself gazing at the point after his name. I could not read, nor say much without exhausting myself, but the dot after Charlie's name transfixed me. It was both *something* and *nothing*. My sense of my own size had become loose from its moorings; I had become like Alice in Wonderland. Sometimes I felt huge as a corpse, sometimes shrunk to a single blood corpuscle. Sometimes I was tiny enough to rest upon the edge of that dot and look into its microscopic abyss, and in those odd, visionary moments, I felt I was within touching distance again of meaning, intention, even comfort. And then I would pull back, like an animation speeding from the subatomic to the universal, and my withered eyes would burn. It was just a signature, and the dot after his name was not a statement of presence, but of absence.

Above Charlie's name, those of everyone else, with little love hearts (from Cosima) or encouraging messages. I loved to look at these names because this was everyone who was with me that evening, before everything changed forever. It was a dinner Charlie hosted to celebrate winning funding. The inside of the card was like a jumbled-up table plan from a wedding, that the couple might take out from time to time to remember. And I wanted to remember. I wanted so much to stay in *before*. The Institute, the bonobos, Charlie, my work . . . They were a life I'd made for myself. It was beautiful.

In *before* there was no *why*. The *why* was more crippling than the actual bodily aftermath, which was the fragility of my skull and the blood vessels within it. Shifts of doctors had solemnly informed me, with scans to back it up, that I must never put my body under strain. I could have a brain haemorrhage at any time. For this reason, I must never attempt to have children. This was desperate information that I struggled to accept, but, still worse, the *why* metastasised through my thoughts, hardening into a great mass of the unanswerable.

Why did I get so drunk that evening?

(I was happy?)

Why didn't I wait for a taxi, as Charlie told me to?

(An ending I didn't want?)

Why did Charlie let me go home alone?

(*I can't come with you, Frieda*)

Why did my attacker choose me?

(—)

Examining it under the tree, I realised the card no longer comforted me. Perhaps exactly like a wedding table plan, stumbled on by one of the couple, now divorced, its reminder of another life was too painful. Not that I felt pain when I was resting. I floated above it, with detached interest, like a bird observing a raft heading for white water, with a human – me? – spreadeagled on top, clutching the drenched ropes.

I tore the card up.

Immediately, I began to panic, searching through the pieces in the dust, turning them over and over, searching for one name.

Thoughts spilled over the racing edge of my mind, a panicky tumult of silences I longed to break, truths and lies that I no longer knew the difference between:

I've been sacked; I'm addicted to morphine; I'm distraught because I can't bear to leave the bonobos; I'm very afraid; since the attack, I can feel the bonobos' feelings; we are connected, we are *kin*; a door of perception has opened; I'm doing really well; the attack is something I am over; I can move on without justice; the research is going really well and I am untouched emotionally; I'm going to be all right—

Then, 'Oh!' as I found it, the scrap of card with Charlie's signature upon it. How shrill I sounded, shrill and slow-motion at the same time. How a caterpillar would sound if it could talk. I tucked the fragment into my phone case. It was all that remained of my life before, like a piece of ash from a forest fire.

One of my neighbours was advancing across the lawn towards me. It was Danda, the chain-smoking retired Anglican vicar. The toboggan of my thoughts collided with a drift, jolting me into clarity.

Danda sat down opposite. Her taupe wrinkles opened into a beige smile. She had a lovely gravelly voice. 'Something happened?'

I realised I was leaning against the tree at quite an odd angle. I hauled myself straight. 'I've been fired.'

Her grey eyebrows curled gently upwards. 'I'm sorry to hear that. Not entirely surprised, though. Do you want a smoke?' She held out the box. I didn't smoke, but when Danda offered, I always said yes. I took two. When she offered the lighter, I shook my head and put both in my pocket.

Danda was looking at me closely.

'I was fired once, you know. Well, as fired as you can be in the Church of England. I was subjected to cheap biscuits at an awkward meeting where no one said anything. And then the bishop gave me a new parish.'

'Why were you fired?'

'Gossip. Went around being a woman vicar who smoked and didn't judge enough. The new parish was much better. Inner city. Everyone was too busy having a horrible life to judge me. They actually came to me for comfort. Me! Unbelievable. I stayed there till I retired. Best thing that happened to me, being fired. What did you do?'

'Shot up at work.'

Danda had a laugh like stones dropped in a bucket. 'Yep, well, that would do it,' she said. Then: 'Shall I call someone for you? Your parents, maybe?'

I felt terribly confused, the way light sometimes got confused in the evening: little moons burning in hollows; dark bodies lumped on exposed areas of road.

'I grew up outside a family unit,' I mumbled.

At the Institute, my disconnected life had become integrated, like a molecule. But that was all gone now. Whether I uttered the word or not, from now on, *orphan* was going to hover around me like some kind of fucking hornet, making everyone who saw me recoil.

Danda said, kindly, 'I don't understand what you mean.'

I said, 'My parents died in a car accident when I was five. Only my boss – my former boss, my ex-boss – even knows they are dead. I've been in foster homes and care homes. I haven't had to say this for years and years. There's no one to call. I must seem angry, but I'm not. I just haven't been an orphan for a long time. And now I am again.'

I looked up, it seemed, into the hard gaze of a bird. For a terrifying second, I was located inside myself, in all my fear and pain.

Danda said, 'Why don't you come in? I'll make us some dinner.'

I shook my head. Suddenly, I was incredibly tired. As my rest wore off, exhaustion often set in, followed by jitters.

'Thanks for the cigarettes.' I got carefully to my feet, steadying myself on the yew's trunk, waved cheerily to Danda and set off to the flat.

Inside, I poured myself a drink, some rather dusty port, which was all I had in the house. Morphine had lately rather superseded alcohol. Then I waited drowsily on the sofa for something to happen. My skin was deliciously warm from the sun.

Twilight draped the walls and the floor; the street lights splayed into the room. I did not move for a long time. What would happen if I did nothing at all? If I simply stayed here, on the sofa, doing nothing?

I gazed at the evidence of a life, before and after: the room's piles of *New Scientist* and books, its geological layers of dust, and then the curtains I had inexplicably made myself, by hand, in one fevered night when I thought I would never sleep again, when it seemed clear that safety had to be made, over and over, with tiny stitches, all through the night.

Maybe I should go to bed. It was, after all, the end of the day. I dragged myself into the bedroom and peeled off my clothes. In the poor light, I caught sight of a pale, bony woman, with hair that was wispy on one side, as if it had stopped growing. Our eyes met. Her pupils were so huge I could not see the colour of her irises.

I lit one of the cigarettes Danda had given me. It tasted like old bad news in my mouth. Nevertheless, opening my lips carefully, I blew a perfect smoke ring. The bony woman in the mirror did the same. Mine rose, wobbling like sound, all the way to the ceiling. Its expansion was beautiful, slow as a mushroom cloud. The other Frieda's smoke ring vanished at the edge of the mirror, leaving her gazing beyond the frame.

Four

FOUR WEEKS LATER, I stepped off the coach in front of a white-painted stone arch that marked the entrance to Torbet Zoological Park. I was deep in the Devon countryside, and about to start a new job as a zookeeper. Charlie had got me the post at this small, privately owned zoo. The owner was a relation of a friend's friend and they didn't ask too many questions. They always needed someone to keep the wheelbarrows moving.

'Are you finished with the morphine?' Charlie asked down the phone, when I rang, begging for his help. I was going mad without my job. I thought about Zaire constantly. Not even the stash of ampoules I had stolen from the Institute could keep me steady for long. I needed my career back. Nothing else would do. When I rang Charlie, I expected him to say he was working on getting me back on to the project.

'Of course I am finished with the morphine,' I lied. I had

been stretching out the ampoules I'd taken, softening the blow with diazepam obtained from the G.P., who didn't argue when I turned up needing something to calm me. What really needed to be done would take far too much time, but the G.P. was a very nice person and willing to do something.

'I'm not depressed,' I insisted. 'I've been suffering terrible anxiety since my . . .' I hated to do this, but needs must: 'My *attack*.'

She knew all about the attack. There was no need to go through it all again: the operations; the long rehabilitation. The bald dent on the side of my head that I managed to cover, just, but which was starting to be revealed by further hair loss. I could rely on no one wanting to discuss it at all.

She nodded warmly.

'Since the attack, I can't sleep. I lost my job. I just need . . . some rest.'

And so I got my rather stingy supply of diazepam, which she told me I would have to return to renew, and some super-strength prescription codeine as well, because, when the ampoules finally ran out, the aches were going to be terrible. I filled the considerable gap with the strongest effervescent painkillers I could get over the counter, and renewed my interest in vodka. So, when Charlie said down the phone, 'Are you finished with the morphine?' the fact that I answered with a lie was not, in my view, reflective of the deceitfulness of the addict; rather, it was a shorthand for the truth. I was *finishing* with the morphine.

By the time I went back to the Institute, I would be squeaky clean. The ampoules were almost gone, and I had my backup weaning system in place.

Charlie agreed to see what he could do. A few days later, he rang to tell me about my new job. I was so stunned, my mouth sagged over the mouthpiece as if I'd had a stroke and it was there to catch my drool.

Thank you, Charlie. Just the thing. Wow, how did you manage that? So grateful. I'll pack tonight. Start Monday week, you say? I'll be there. Great news.

Charlie emphasised he would not mention my drug problem to my new employers, as long as there was no longer a problem to mention, as he put it. By the time I arrived at Torbet Zoo, I had been clean from morphine for nearly a week. Inside my overalls, bought to show my willingness to embrace my new life of manual labour, I seeped with chilly sweat. My brain felt like sandbags, hefted from ear to ear. Beneath my brown wool hat, bought to hide my bald spot from my new colleagues, my scalp slurped like glue.

Beyond the arch was a cabin, with a man's head at the window, a quite extraordinarily pointed head, with a weird fuzz of hair, like a Chinese mountain. This was Frodo, I was about to learn. Was it like a boarding school where everyone had their nickname? I wondered what mine would be.

Frodo observed me with saggy eyes from over his *Socialist Worker*.

'You are?'

'Frieda Bloom.'

Frodo's face opened into a shocking twist of features. He was smiling, I realised. 'You're the new one, aren't you? You've to go to the office, meet Penelope.' He opened the sliding window and craned out, revealing a constellation of moles down his scalp and beneath his collar.

'You need to follow that road up there,' he said, indicating the single-track road wending up the hill. 'If you leave that case, I'll get one of the lads to bring it up.'

The case contained my vital supplies.

'No, you're all right. I'll just go slowly. It has a wheel . . .' Which it did, although it was buckled.

Frodo returned his head to the cabin like a bird in a Swiss clock. Ahead, I spotted a bend in the road and some bushes. If everything got too much, I could pause there and reward myself with some codeine.

Though my limbs felt like jelly, something else slipped into the furrows of my mind, those rigid channels which had reduced me to a series of reactions and needs. The smell of damp leaf mulch, animals and their bedding, their skin and fur – and the fresh air itself. These things refreshed me, like water pouring into dry earth. The Institute had been an enclosed, air-conditioned space; we only really went outside to observe the bonobos in the outdoor enclosure. The sensations now were a surprise, and not unpleasant. I pulled my case along on its bent wheel, leaning into the slope. My pulse banged in the cracks of my head beneath my hat; sweat began to drip; my windpipe tightened and I wheezed. But it was strength I had forgotten I possessed.

Penelope had cropped orange hair, heavy square glasses and a grey complexion livened by some well-matched auburn lipstick. She was curator of Torbet Zoological Park. She peered at me beneath my rucksack, with my squeaky case, then stepped out from behind her desk, revealing an ensemble made of what looked to be very thick beige felt. She shook my hand and said, 'Charlie told me a lot about you. You sound right up our street.'

I hoped my hand wasn't too slimy in hers. 'Hello,' I said.

She pulled a huge hanky from her felt pocket and sneezed voluminously into it. 'I'm allergic to wool.' She pointed at my hat.

My hands went to it. There was no way it could come off. I wasn't ready for the lowered voices, the alarm, the pity. Stepping back to give her room, I babbled, 'I'm so sorry. I've had an operation. I need to keep my head warm.'

Penelope said, through her hanky, 'Don't worry. It's not just wool. It's feathers, fur, pollen. Really, this is the last place I should be. I'm trying exposure, you know, rather than mainlining antihistamines and falling asleep.'

She took a deep, exaggerated breath through her swollen nostrils. 'It's hard work – you know that, don't you?'

I nodded. 'I'm stronger than I look,' I said. At the Institute, the cleaning-out of the animals and the general labour was performed by the students – such as Cosima – and technicians. I had done my share, back in the day, but then, on qualification, wore my white coat and used my brain, not my body.

'Your boss – Charlie Grace, at the Institute – well, you have a friend there. He pretty much said you hung the moon,' said Penelope. 'This place has a lot of misfits. Torbet, the owner, of course – you'll meet him at the end of the week, at the Siberian tiger evening – you know about that, don't you? He draws oddballs in like a magnet. They're the only ones who will follow the regime.'

Penelope sneezed again and waved a taloned hand. 'Please understand,' she said through the hanky, her eyes streaming behind the glasses. 'By *oddballs*, I mean everyone here. Me included. It's a *good* thing. Here. To be not run-of-the-mill . . .' She shook her head in frustration with herself.

I said, 'I've read about what you do here.' Charlie had told me that, although Torbet Zoo was the delight of one eccentric, it had some good, if unconventional, breeding programmes going. I had done some research, discovering that Torbet Zoo advocated a policy of keepers going in with the animals. I had read about John Aspinall's work and it seemed dementedly dangerous to go into an enclosure with a tiger or a gorilla, but the practice did markedly improve breeding rates. Probably, this was because it enriched an otherwise dull environment. Latterly, in my resting periods at the Institute, I had done this myself, and this was how I had made my own discovery about the bonobos and their grieving ritual. I sighed at the memory that this discovery would never be followed up, exactly because of how I had made it.

Penelope's nicely coloured lips curved. 'Yes. We go in with the animals. Large, small, deadly, cuddly. Torbet believes that keepers and their animals should have a close relationship. Obviously, there's a risk with that.' She moved back behind the desk and produced a form. 'I forgot this. It's a waiver. You need to sign it.'

I looked at the form, dense with legal type.

She was gazing at me with an almost maternal fervour. 'It does go awry sometimes. Mostly when a keeper gets a bit over-confident with the tiger. This is an attempt by Torbet to make you aware of the risks in advance.'

'I see.'

Taking a pen from her proffered hand, I rested the form on my knee to sign. Just as I was about to, she said, 'Just to clarify, you won't go in straight away. We're not irresponsible. Crazy, but not insane, if you see the difference. Anyway, Morris will make the decision.'

'Morris?'

'He's the head keeper of the monkey section. That's where we'd like you to go.'

'Will I be working with the bonobos?'

'Yes. Charlie told me that they're your favourites.'

Smiling, I signed the paper and handed it to her.

Penelope swept it into a drawer, then held up a bag. 'Two sets of Torbet Zoo overalls. What size feet are you?'

'Five.'

She rifled in the corner and dropped a pair of boots into the bag, then handed it to me. She placed in my hand a key with a tiger fob so big it occupied my whole palm.

'You know we have a Siberian tiger coming shortly?'

I didn't know.

She scratched her eyes behind the glasses. 'We are kick-starting our breeding programme. You must talk with Torbet at the tiger evening. Everyone will be there. We are telling the friends and members all about it and – of course – trying to raise money. I believe Torbet will be doing a slideshow.'

With a final flourish of her hanky, smearing lipstick on to her teeth, Penelope said, 'Start tomorrow at eight a.m. Morris will show you everything you need to know. You'll know him when you see him. John Lennon lookalike, the Yoko years.' Her eyes had disappeared into crimson slits; nevertheless, she smiled. 'So welcome. The lodge is that way.' She pointed out of the window.

Charlie had arranged for me to live on site, in the lodge, a down-at-heel baronial building on the other side of the park. Several of the keepers lived here. I think he hoped it would make me feel welcome, and stop me feeling lonely.

On each side of the avenue where I now trundled my case were posters advertising the impending arrival of the new tiger:

a snarling close-up, with the legend, Coming Soon: Lord of the Siberian Forest. Ahead of me was a signpost that indicated the monkey house, down the hill, and birds, big cats and zebras in a range of other directions. It was overwhelming to be surrounded by so many animals when my expertise was so narrow.

My views on conservation were uncontroversial, I thought. I had been content to keep the bonobos all their lives at the Institute: captivity for a greater purpose had never troubled me. Torbet Zoo, by my understanding, was more on the menagerie end of things than trying to be a serious contender for conservation efforts. Charlie had told me (I think to improve its scientific standing in my mind) that it had been part of a successful reintroduction programme of a small brown lizard, whose name I could not recall. The work we had done with the bonobos was not to do with their conservation directly, but about improving our understanding of them and adding to our knowledge. Perhaps there would be scope to do some research here. Perhaps it wouldn't be so bad.

I found myself in a corridor with numbered doors, the surface of one obscured by a giant poster of a tiger. There was a narrow flight of stairs at the end and I followed the steps as they curled upwards, reaching a small landing with just one door. It had the number four on it, my number, and, opening it, I found myself in a tiny circular room, painted white. I was in one of the turrets of the building and the room had a hexagonal ceiling and one thin window. The window was mullioned and leaded. There was a small single bed, a table with a hotplate, a chair and lamp, and a wardrobe. With a barely suppressed squeal of delight, I dropped all my luggage on the floor. I opened the window and fresh air and the sounds of the zoo drifted in.

Below me, the capybaras were sunbathing. Their gold backs shone, and one ambled across the enclosure in an attitude of complete contentment.

I grabbed my phone and texted Charlie: *I have a turret!* Then I walloped several codeines and a diazepam, because I was starting to ache, and I lay down in my clothes on the bed and fell into the first peaceful sleep I had known since the attack.

Five

THE GIBBON'S MELLIFLUOUS WHOOP vibrated in my ears. It was morning and I had slept the clock round. The garish scatter of my belongings against the sunlit white hurt my eyes. I did my morning reconnaissance of aches and cravings and found that my head was heavy but not painful, and it was just the daily sing of blood in every crease and follicle of my body. It was always there, the ballad of my addiction. I made my calculation. Codeine would soothe the blunt saw of my nerves, and I would keep my diazepam with me, just in case. There was a lot of *just in case* in my life now. Need, bodily or emotional, or both, could ambush me at any time. But I was now on the verge of being late, so I hauled myself out of bed, dressed quickly and ran through the morning sunshine to the monkey house, to meet Morris.

Waiting in front of the glass like a visitor, I almost wept at the fetid gloom of the bonobo enclosure, its hard, chipped tiling.

That they should have bonobos at all was quite something, but the environment was barer than at the Institute. Most zoos had chimps, the fighters and masturbators of the ape world. The public didn't enjoy the lack of spectacle of a peaceful, matriarchal grouping, the lovers not the fighters.

A man loped out of the prep room, curly black hair poking from beneath a baseball cap emblazoned with *TORBET ZOO PARK*, with a tiger motif and the legend *Embracing Conservation*. This was not Morris. There was no John Lennon resemblance. He caught sight of me like a fox would catch sight of me – a startle, with round eyes – and then he came and stood over me, like a cowboy in a film.

'First day?' He spoke with a London accent that seemed to me affected rather than born, and looked to be younger than me, by maybe five years. His skin was thick, while still youthful, like a young rhino, and his face was one that demanded from me a decision about whether or not I liked it. I decided that I did. Taking his hand, it was warm. Of everything, his warmth was what I felt most powerfully in those brief, wordless moments. It sent a shock through me, seemingly charged with meaning. I drew my hand away.

'I'm Gabriel Torbet,' he said. 'Morris will be along soon. Come in.' When I told him my name, he caught it between his lips, turned it over like a sweet. 'Frieda . . . Frieda.'

I trooped after him, feeling weirder and younger than I was. His legs disappeared beneath the edge of his zoo jacket, as if he had no buttocks. From the back, he was like one of the savannah grazers, an eland, or perhaps even a giraffe, all joints and extensions. I wondered, then, what it must be like to be tall like that.

A corridor ran round the building, behind all the enclosures. Here were bonobos, then drills, then, in the smaller monkey cages, the capuchins, the macaques, Dianas, lemurs.

The corridor led to an observation area not accessible to the public. We looked down on the bonobos from a balcony. It was wet outside, and the bonobos had elected to stay in their inner enclosure, preferring the knocking on the glass and the shrieks of the visitors to the rain.

The poverty of the space contrasted with the careful design at the Institute. A scattering of sawdust on the floor. A metal climbing frame occupying about a third of the area. Some pallets, wooden boxes and a rope. No bales, no hammocks, no levels or hidden corners. I began to tell Gabriel about Zaire and the Institute, but stopped myself. The bonobos seemed happy enough. They were quiet, moving for the most part naturally around the enclosure. Almost all the females had the wildly swollen backsides that showed they were in oestrus. Bonobo females have a much longer fertile season than other apes. They clearly found it awkward and painful to sit, so they strolled around the pen or languished like Victorian ladies in the straw. As female bonobos often do, they presented themselves to the males in blatant sexual invitation, in exchange for food the male might be carrying, or to settle some skirmish or other, or for no reason at all. There would be a brief friendly coupling and then the two would resume foraging or wandering.

Gabriel shook his head. 'They are shagging all the time,' he said. 'I mean, literally. We get parents complaining.'

I said, 'It's their way of solving problems . . . Chimps use it for dominance.' How prim I sounded. But this was how we all discussed bonobo sex at the Institute. We didn't call it *shagging*.

The largest female, certainly the alpha, was on her back, legs splayed, calling to a nearby male. He sauntered over and the two of them engaged in full face-to-face intercourse, right in front of a group of school children. As they finished, the female emitting a loud squeal, she reached out and took an orange from his hand. He did not object, and wandered off. The teacher's voice wobbled through the building, 'Come on, kids!' She wafted their faces ahead of her, like so many jostling balloons, blank and directionless.

'The females have orgasms as well,' I said. 'An orgasm and an orange. Not bad.'

There was a silence.

'What I don't understand,' said Gabriel, 'is how he can let her rule him like that.' His words prickled my skin, like radiation from my phone.

'They're getting a new tiger,' he went on. 'I was a tiger keeper, but they moved me down here because I left a slide open and he nearly escaped. You know they let us in with the tigers, don't you? You just have to be careful with the slides.'

He sighed, his attention drifting back to the scene before us. 'I just think it's bad for the children. They should bring the chimps back.'

'But chimps fight all the time! And they masturbate in front of the children.'

He grinned. 'Yep, they do that. It's true.'

'So?'

'Old-lady apes fucking anything that moves? Come on. Chimps are funny. This is like taking your kids to a porn flick.'

'If more kids saw this, perhaps they wouldn't grow up thinking like you.'

The effort of this exchange made me reach for my diazepam. Knowing the pack was there calmed me down.

Gabriel's eyes fixed on mine.

'Chimp behaviour is more natural,' he said.

'It's all natural! What's natural, anyway?'

'You're talking shit,' he said.

I felt the colour rise in my cheeks.

'*I'm* talking shit?' He said nothing and so I carried on. 'These apes are one of the rarest animals in the world. But hardly anyone studies them. They're not in zoos – because of people like you! Because of *you*, with your macho crap about chimps and tigers, bonobos are dying out!' My voice was very shrill now. Gabriel scratched his cheek casually and said nothing.

'It's a matriarchy. It's stable,' I went on. 'There is hardly any violence. We should be modelling ourselves on them. And, instead, all you can say is, "They're having too much sex." You make me sick.' We glared at each other in silence beneath the cobwebby rafters.

At that moment, two female bonobos began to cuddle and fondle each other, right in front of us. Gabriel sighed. 'I became a zookeeper to work with the tigers. I've loved tigers since I was a little boy. I have a son – guess what he's called? Yep: Tiger. I'm Torbet's son, and it's pretty shit, working for your own dad, but I put up with it because I am brilliant with the tigers.'

The two females paused in their fondling and started eating some melon pieces, vocalising warmly and exchanging them.

He went on, 'I built up a really strong relationship with the male, Lyric. It takes a lot of time with a tiger, to do that. It's not like this . . . chatting and shagging.'

I had never heard anyone say such a thing. 'What do tigers do that's so marvellous then? Killing? Roaring?'

Gabriel considered me carefully. My blood was jangling in my body again, a horrible cacophony of needs. Gabriel shook his head, pushed himself away from the rail and walked off.

'This is complex behaviour,' I called after him. 'Is that what you can't handle?'

He turned sharply, came back and loomed over me. He was so much bigger than I was. If he chose to push me, I would tumble down into the enclosure. If he hit me, he'd knock me out. I faltered back and raised my hand.

'Oh, for fuck's sake! Put your hand down. I'm trying to tell you something.'

I lowered my hand doubtfully, heart pounding.

'It's not that I think bonobos aren't important. It's just . . .' He paused and gathered his thoughts. 'Have you ever been in an enclosure with a tiger?'

'No,' I said.

'Okay. Well. You need to bear in mind that they can kill you with one swipe.' He lifted his hand. 'Retractable claws. If it unsheathes them and slashes your stomach, your guts will fall out, there and then.' He looked at me for my reaction. My face remained blank.

'In the wild – I mean *real nature*, and I'm afraid what these guys are up to isn't that – there are two things that matter: predator and prey. And a tiger knows himself to be the top predator. He's called the king for a reason. You know, on the tiger's face, on his forehead, is the Chinese character for *king*. Did you know that?'

He was very animated now. He kept looking at me to check I was taking it in.

'And what you have to do, the central skill of being the tiger keeper, which is not easy, which takes fucking ages, is you have to gain his respect.'

I rolled my eyes. 'Oh, come on,' I said.

'What? Don't be so fucking ignorant. In the wilds of Siberia, there's no time for any of this group dynamics bollocks. It's you and it's him, and there is every chance he'll kill you, just because he feels like it. You have to find a way past that, you have to connect to that wild spirit.'

I folded my arms. 'This "group dynamics bollocks", as you call it, is the most sophisticated society known in the animal kingdom.'

'Still chatting and shagging. And it's not successful, is it?'

'It's habitat loss that's making them extinct. Oh, for God's sake.'

After a brisk silence, he said, 'Look – any damn fool can go in there with the bonobos. Not much to learn. Turn to left: chatting. Turn to the right: shagging. You call it complex, I call it bollocks. But, to go in with the tigers, you need skills. If you can stop babbling long enough, I'll tell you what they are. Okay? They may let you do it, one day.'

I didn't say yes, being speechless, but my consent was not necessary.

'Right, then. The basic rule is that you must never act like prey. So, when a tiger plays, it likes to rest its paws on your shoulders, like this.' Unexpectedly, he pressed his arms over my shoulders. Shadows closed round me. I was barely an inch from his chest. Instantly claustrophobic, I pushed him away.

'Aha! You don't do that, or out come the claws.' He raised his hand in a claw shape. 'And out come the guts!'

'This is stupid.'

'No, it isn't! I'm saving your life. Now, this time, don't

struggle.' He replaced his arms on my shoulders. 'Keep still. Don't go limp. Don't start talking. Don't give him a hug. He is not your friend yet.'

My heart echoed in the tiny dark space, hot with my breath.

'Are you scared?' he asked. The words boomed against my lips. Sweat broke out down my back. I thought I was going to choke.

'No,' I whispered.

'Well, you should be,' he said. 'But you have to hide it. The way to get out of the hold and keep his respect is to back away, moving his legs off you as you do so. You can talk, if you want, but keep it low and, you know, don't say stupid stuff. No babbling because you're scared.'

A deadening memory slammed on me like a lid. The dark of a subway. My hands soaring to the blaze in my brain. If something wants to kill you, it will.

With a cry, I wrenched myself free from his arms and strode away.

'Never turn your back on a tiger!' He caught up with me and pulled me round to face him. 'That's the second time you've been killed in five minutes. Wait –' he leant in – 'are you . . . crying?'

'No!'

He stared at me, uncomprehending, as the two female bonobos started up some friendly squealing below us.

'Your idea of nature is fucked!' I cried. 'Look at me! Dead

twice in five minutes! This is . . . *boring* and *one-dimensional* and I hate it!'

A long moment passed. 'Suit yourself,' he said.

He walked away. I grabbed the rail and leant against it, my legs suddenly weak. What point was there in my fury, shrivelling already into sadness? I gulped a diazepam and imagined Gabriel on fire. It didn't help. After a few steps, he turned and called, 'Morris will be along in a minute. You won't take my advice on gaining a tiger's respect, but you'd better listen about Morris. He's got standards like you wouldn't believe. He will eat you *alive*.'

Six

ORRIS WAS MY HEIGHT, and his face was more than two thirds brown hair, like an arid planet covered with dead seaweed. It was decorated with wire-rimmed glasses. He appeared silently, as if he had floated, and beckoned me to follow him. Gratefully, I escaped Gabriel. In the humid prep room, I extended a hand to my new boss. Instead of taking it, Morris indicated a tangled mound of carrots, cabbage and assorted fruit. Then, a tiny pink area within the beard and moustache opened, revealing sharp teeth and a severe whisper: 'This all needs to be chopped. Don't take too long over it – there's all the cleaning-out to do. Think you can do it in half an hour?'

I nodded, letting my hand drift back to my side, untouched. Chopping. How hard can it be? Morris muttered, 'Don't listen to that bloody Gabriel. Doesn't have a brain cell in his head,' and strode out on his flamingo-thin legs.

Humming to myself, I took up the knife and started chopping and shredding, placing the different items in separate piles. The time passed quickly and I stood back proudly when he slid open the door, some half an hour later.

It was impossible to read Morris's expression behind all the hair, but there was no mistaking his utter fury and contempt as he picked up a handful of the chopped carrots and whisper-screamed into my face, 'Would you eat this? It's not even clean!' and threw the handful on to the floor.

Dismayed, I now saw what he saw: awkward shapes, straggly bits, a horrible lack of care. The strip light suddenly felt like it was burning my skin, and I wished I could back into the corner. Morris felt unpredictable, as if his fist might suddenly dart out and hit me. I orientated myself away from him, hiding my arms behind me. But I could not tear my gaze away, and this seemed to inflame him, as if it was defiance. Trembling with unaccountable rage, he whispered, 'If you can't even chop a fucking carrot, you're useless to me. Do you understand? Useless.'

'It's true, I'm sorry. I've never chopped a carrot. I was taught to slice them lengthways into batons. And I always peeled them rather than washing *and* peeling, which always seemed so inefficient. But that was in another life.'

While speaking, I had edged out of range, my eyes still fixed on his. I said, 'Will you teach me?' and managed a hesitant smile, which he faced down with a myopic stare from behind the immaculate lenses.

With an enormous sigh, Morris took a knobbly carrot off the pile and scrubbed it vigorously under the tap, using a brush, which he ostentatiously waved in my face. Then he lifted the knife from my hand and, with the lightning speed of a top-flight chef, chopped the carrot into regular-sized chunks, each about the size of a fingertip. The chunks glistened cleanly on the board. He swept them into a bowl, handed back the knife and said, 'Honestly. *Batons.* Fucking hell.'

The vegetables eventually chopped correctly, it was time to clean out the cages. Each monkey species had an inner and outer cage divided by the corridor where we now stood. Outside and inside were linked by a tunnel under the corridor. The inner cages, many decades old, were lined with tiles and each was accessed through a steel door, unlocked with its own key. The strip light gleamed on the walls and every movement echoed with frantic shadows.

Morris peered through the barred window of the first door, pulled on a rope to lift the slide, and made a squawk that sent the capuchins galloping into the tunnel. He then lowered the slide to stop them coming back in. 'You have to count them outside,' he whispered. 'And only then lower the slide. You will chop one in half if it's still down there.' He stared at me, as if not certain I was taking this in. 'Chopping the monkeys in half is bad. Okay?'

I nodded, no longer taking for granted, as I had with the food prep, that any fool could operate a slide without chopping a monkey in half. All these operations and skills looked familiar, but actually had to be learnt fresh.

'Bucket,' said Morris, pointing along the corridor. 'Hose. Disinfectant. Broom. Scrubbing brush. Shovel. Can you work out what all those are for? Or do I have to show you?'

I would have preferred a demonstration, for I was not at all confident that everyday objects were what they seemed. But I knew that uncertainty would not be well received. I tried to read the movements of his body, trying to discern his story, but it really did seem as though he had none. Instead, I copied the very slight incline of his head and restrained my arms behind my back. I had an inexplicable longing to touch the hair and beard. Was he warm beneath them? And the boxy chest, with its plain shirt beneath the regulation jumper — would I feel a heartbeat? The sense of nothing from him at all but vigorous contempt began to frighten me a little.

'I can do it,' I said.

With a flourish, Morris reached into his back pocket and brought out a toothbrush. It was worn, but extremely clean. He held open the cage door for me. The interior was bushy with twigs, all the way to the ceiling. I had to duck beneath them. Morris turned over a wooden crate, stood on it and mimed scrubbing a twig with the toothbrush.

'They get absolutely covered in shit,' he said. 'They must be scrubbed.' He looked down, like an owl in a tree. Was he waiting for a reaction? It was hard not to have one. There were *thousands* of twigs. It was an impossible task. 'You have twenty cages, ten each side. We do ten before lunch, and ten after. So don't spend all morning on this one.' He handed over the toothbrush. 'I'm going to send all the animals outside on my way out. Do not let them in until I am back.'

Now that he was gone, and I was alone in the tiled cage, toothbrush in hand, a small thrill began to flicker. I unwrapped the hose and switched it on, listening to the calls of the monkeys outside. The ugliness of the cages seemed to soften. Care had gone into choosing and arranging the branches. There were puzzles filled with food hanging from the ceiling, nets and sacking for the monkeys to swing on and hide behind. I ran my fingers over the walls, felt them slick with damp.

A bang sent me reeling backwards. Dozens of schoolchildren were hammering the glass and making ape impressions. Their hot breath misted the window. The pane vibrated with the force of their fists. Slipping on the slimy floor, I collapsed into the door. It clanged shut, the keys still in the lock on the other side, and I was alone, imprisoned in my cell, in full view of the shouting children. I reddened on the floor, the hose soaking my overalls.

An octopus can disappear into a space as small as its own eyeball. Octopuses have been observed carrying two halves of a coconut shell, nested together for ease of transport; when frightened, they sit in one half and pull the other half over themselves, like a lid. A squid can match almost any background colour instantly. How I longed to have such abilities. I shrank into the corner of the cage, trying to obscure myself behind some sacking. Savages. I hated them. They didn't care about the animals. Their fingertips smeared crisp fat and sweat across the glass. Their movements were a meaningless babble, like an out-of-control machine.

Wanting to frighten them, I pinched the end of the hose so that the water came out as a rock-hard jet, and directed it at the window. It clattered against the glass and, gratifyingly, the brats screamed in alarm, their faces obscured by the swirls of water. I crept forward, the hose focused on the window. In hysterical waves, the children reared back. Then an adult, whose bald head and thick glasses appeared briefly, called out to them, and they shrank away.

Silence was restored. It was then that I saw, crouched a few feet away, an enormous spider. Clearly some tropical species, probably brought in with the fruit, it was so big I could see its mandibles working. Its huge bent legs suspended its shiny body high enough above the tiles to cast a shadow. It was tensed, as if it might simply leap into my face.

I was a different person now from Frieda Bloom in her white coat. I turned the hose on to a spot near the spider, which curled into a soggy golf ball. It was quite an undertaking to get it into the drain by use of the water stream alone. It required bouncing the jet off the wall behind the spider to unseat it. It recovered briefly and raised itself, as if to run, but I calmly splattered it against the tiles. With an expert swirl, I washed the remains into the drain.

What now? With nothing to direct the hose at, I let it go back to its previous slow run, dropping it in the corner. Retrieving the toothbrush, I decided that I should at least try to make headway with the cage before yelling for help to get out. I climbed, as Morris had done, on to a box and began with the highest branches. He was right: they were slimy with spattered faeces. There was so little room to manoeuvre that the twigs scraped my face, spat drops of it into my eyes. Then I heard a burst of laughter in the doorway, and there was Gabriel.

'Did you know you were locked in?' he asked, dangling the keys from his finger. From my vantage point, I was a couple of heads taller than him and it was a giddy, strange feeling.

'Thank you,' I said, wriggling my way out of the branches, wiping the shit from my eyes. 'I think we got off on the wrong foot earlier,' I added.

Gabriel shrugged and gazed around the cage, jangling the keys.

'Oh, man – Morris is going to kill you.'

'Why?'

'Because the cage is filthy and you have nine more to do.'

'Does he mean it? This toothbrush thing?'

Gabriel smiled, a slow, glorious smile that had not been part of our previous encounter. 'I told you. He is mental about his standards. On my first day, he screamed at me so hard I thought he was going to have a stroke. Waved his knife around like some fucking goblin. I thought he was going to cut my knee-caps off.'

'What did you do wrong?'

'Disagreed with him.'

'At least I didn't do that.'

'Well, it won't save you. You are dead meat if we don't get this done.'

'Dead meat?'

'Fired. The end. Do you know how many of you he has got through?'

It had not occurred to me that it was even possible to be sacked twice in a month.

'Look, you have got to hurry up. I'll help you this once . . . because this –' he held up the keys – 'is an unfair handicap.' He laughed again. 'You are useless, though, aren't you? How did you end up here again?'

'I . . . like bonobos.'

He shook his head. 'You look like you couldn't even lift a toothbrush, never mind get ten cages done. Have you been ill?' This last question was thrown from the corner of his mouth and his entire body language showed the struggle between his curiosity and any significant draw that might be made on his empathic capabilities.

'I was in hospital for a while. But I'm better. Totally. It maybe doesn't look like it, but I'm really very strong.'

He nodded. 'Okay, bonobo girl, I'll start at the other end and meet you in the middle.'

When Morris returned at twelve noon, he stiffened like a pointer catching the scent of game, for there was peace, there was order, but everything, somehow, was not as expected. Gabriel had long gone, saying nothing as he left for the canteen, but making it possible for me to be in the prep room, wiping down the surfaces. Morris said, 'Where's my toothbrush?' and I handed it to him with a smile and took myself off into the fresh air. But my body still ached from the hard labour, the freakish standards, the sense that I belonged elsewhere.

Seven

WHEN NOT ON DUTY in the monkey house, my first week was spent exploring the zoo. My argument with Gabriel drew me in particular to the tiger enclosure. All the cats were housed in a long, meandering row, with a glass front for display to the visitors. It was old-fashioned, with little space. Despite what looked like grim conditions, the cats did breed. Part of the reason was that they were all – except for the tiger, which is not a pack animal – housed in a group, and being part of a family group is the main determinant of well-being in captive social animals. In addition, the interaction between cats and keepers seemed to benefit all.

It was like a bizarre police line-up. Here, violence was contained safely around me, where I could observe it from all angles, at my leisure, where I could feel pity for it. I was at liberty, while those who could kill me were not. At the end of the line was the tiger enclosure. This had been extended and was going to be a showcase enclosure for the zoo. The new Siberian tiger would live here. Currently, the only occupant was Lyric, the male of whom Gabriel was so fond.

I stopped outside Lyric's enclosure. He was massive and heavyset, with distinctively black ears, each with a white spot on the reverse. On his forehead, the dramatic hieroglyph, which Gabriel had told me was the Chinese character for *king*. He was pacing the bald greenery of his paddock with a passionless vigour. Lyric had been bought from an Eastern European circus as a young male and had settled in well. His mate and their cubs had been transferred to other zoos and he was ready for a new partner.

Perhaps my enjoyment of parading my freedom past these imprisoned cats was like that of those women who wrote obsessively to men on death row, who married them and touched them through slats in bullet-proof glass. Did they feel safe, as I felt safe, so close to what could kill me? Did this make me attracted to violence? Had my experience perverted me? A delicious calm settled over me as Lyric swung round the legs of his platform, in his familiar routine.

I'd read that a tiger kills its prey either by biting its throat, to suffocate, or the base of the neck, severing the spine. Death is swift and, more to the point, fearless. People attacked by tigers who have survived (a small club) report a calm descending as the cat mouth envelops the throat. Shock takes over. Fear is a surprisingly slow-travelling emotion. It must have time to arrive first, or it is useless. 'Fight or flight' no longer applies once the fangs have pierced the windpipe. Something else must come into play, something that allows life to meet death with some kind of equanimity, with clarity. Anything else is a waste of energy, and nature abhors wasted energy.

When the man at the subway attacked me, battering a hole in my head with a hammer, there was a dazzling moment, which seemed to be not composed of time at all, that went on forever. I too was not afraid in that moment. My eyes strived to connect with the man and the – what was it? Hammer? Spanner? – because I understood, in that fragment, that I was going to die, and no one wants to die alone. I had travelled from invisible to fantastically visible, an obstacle so enormous I had to be extinguished, and my assailant was both cause and witness. Never had I been seen so clearly, never reckoned with so profoundly. Like the deer with its throat in the tiger's jaws, there was no time for fear, only the roll of my eyes, seeking him out. I never did see him, though. He was never caught.

As these thoughts turned over, the side door, only for keepers, opened, and Gabriel stepped into the enclosure. I sank back into the shadows. How had he got keys to get in? We all only had keys to our own section. He glanced round, checking he was not observed, then did something with his radio – was he turning it off? He laid it, and his keys, by the gate – this was a sackable offence for anyone who wasn't Torbet's son – then he walked boldly into the centre of the paddock and called to Lyric. The tiger stiffened, turned, a black ear cocked forward, then he sprang, in a way I had not seen any of the cats do in their cages. It was a movement reserved for the final moment of capture of prey, the stride and bounce that meant a tiger could cover dozens of metres in a second or two. Gabriel faced him, his arms out and wide, his body completely open to Lyric's approach. One long leg was slightly back, bracing him against the full body onslaught: it was essentially a catch position, but less for a ball than for a comet.

Lyric landed his forelegs on Gabriel's shoulders with full force. His vast jaws opened over the keeper's face, pausing just an inch or two away. My hand leapt to my radio; this was indistinguishable from an attack. But Gabriel was still standing, though the force of Lyric's arrival had sent him backwards. His arms circled the tiger's head, and he rubbed Lyric's ears and ruff, as if he were simply a large, friendly dog. Lyric's dinner-plate paws batted Gabriel's shoulders with shocking gentleness, his claws retracted. Gabriel turned his face to offer Lyric his cheek and I saw his smile. Any expression of warmth he had shown me was as nothing to this. His unmediated joy radiated to my hiding place, and my fingers crept from the radio to the glass.

Gabriel sank to his knees, all the time chattering to Lyric with the abandon of a small boy. Lyric pushed him on to his back, pinning his shoulders and nuzzling, open-jawed, at his throat. It was horrifying. The tiger's only apparent concession to play was *not* to slash with his claws, was *not* to bite, and he seemed to make this decision over and over in each given moment. I could not understand what was satisfying to Gabriel about this encounter, except perhaps the thrill of the dangerous line they were so close to crossing. Bonobos quite simply had a *range* of behaviours and modifications: they didn't just turn a behaviour on or off. Perhaps I was not appreciating the consciousness required for the world's largest cat to control that predator switch. If *on* and *off* demanded immense mental and physical energy, perhaps the tiger was as evolved as the bonobos, with their range of less deadly behaviours.

I shivered in my hiding place.

It was getting late. The longer Gabriel remained here, with Lyric making his excited, guttural play-noises, like a motorbike revving, the more likely it was that a keeper on lates would walk by and he would be found out. He seemed to think of this himself and changed the way he spoke to Lyric. He slowed his speech and moved his arms between the tiger's forelegs, easing him off his shoulders, exactly as he had described to me.

Rule one: when playing with a tiger, *do not struggle*.

Having created a little space for himself, Gabriel rolled on to his side, which dislodged Lyric from him. Keeping one hand in contact with the tiger's face, and his voice soothing, he drew up his knees and pushed himself free. He had been so enveloped by the tiger's body that his emergence on to the ground, clumsy and blinking, seemed like a kind of birth. Lyric rolled on to his back, just like a domestic cat, writhing in excited pleasure, but the instant that Gabriel jumped on to his feet, Lyric also sprang upright. The game wasn't over for him: he thrust his paws once more on to Gabriel's shoulders. But the keeper was ready: he did not ruffle the cat's face this time, and said firmly, 'Get down, Lyric. Time to go.' He performed the manoeuvre again, loosening the tiger's grip, and then moving calmly backwards.

Rule two: *never* turn your back on a tiger.

Lyric circled the keeper. Gabriel was a tall man, and Lyric's muscular shoulder rippled at the height of his hip. Lyric threw back his immense head with its fiery ruff and roared, his fangs glittering. Gabriel backed steadily towards the gate, bending to pick up his radio and keys as he did so. His limbs were relaxed; nothing in his expression betrayed any apprehension.

Rule three: *never* run from a tiger.

He fumbled with the gate's bolt, slipping himself out and closing it again, just as Lyric decided he was not finished yet, and hurled himself at the gate. The entire frame shook and rattled. Lyric's claws gleamed, unretracted.

Gabriel threw, high over the gate, a whole raw chicken. It slumped on to the grass a few feet away from Lyric, and the keeper was forgotten as the tiger pounced on the meat and demolished it in a single bite.

Gabriel would see me hiding here; it was best to set off walking and hopefully get away before he emerged. No one wants to think they have been observed breaking the rules. My head ached, both with the extraordinary scene I had just witnessed and the relief that it had not been me in there.

'What are you doing here?' He stepped out in front of me.

'Nothing . . . I—'

'Were you watching me?'

'I didn't mean to. But then, once I started, I couldn't stop. I thought he was going to kill you.'

'Lyric would never hurt me,' Gabriel said. 'But, technically, I shouldn't have been in there. I borrowed the spare keys.' His gaze challenged me to say something and, when I did not, he went on, 'When the new female arrives, they'll need me back. You see, I got casual, about the slides. Because Lyric and I understand each other, I got casual. My mistake. What is it they say? Mea culpa! But there's only so long a punishment can go on for.'

My lack of reaction pleased him. He folded his arms and smiled, relaxed. 'So, did you learn anything? You see what I mean, about how he plays?'

'I'm not sure I will ever think of it as playing.'

My eyes drifted over his body in the uniform, the sheer strength he exuded. He and Lyric together had been hypnotic – two powerful males, working out their relationship. Now, one remained in captivity, while this one was out and free.

Gabriel looked back into the enclosure, where Lyric had resumed his pacing. He said, 'This female can't come soon enough. He's going mad in there on his own. Anyway, you know what's happening now, don't you?'

'No . . .'

'The Siberian tiger talk! We're all meant to be going.'

We set off towards the main house, side by side. Gabriel kept dawdling, peering into the cat cages, making some mental note about the condition of the occupants. I began a line of conversation, only to find myself some way ahead. Gabriel was not going to accompany me in a normal sense, any more than a cat would. I gave up. 'See you there,' I called. He barely looked up.

In my overall pocket, my phone buzzed. It was Charlie. He'd texted me a photograph of Zaire holding an incredibly messy ham sandwich and grinning, her head thrown back.

Her eyes sent a thrill of sadness through me. I sucked down a codeine tablet. My finger touched her face.

What would it be like to be myself behind my eyes, like Zaire? If eyes really were windows to the soul? Her brown gaze was rich with meaning, like soil about to sprout shoots. But of course I knew what it would be like. It would be like being smashed in the head with a hammer. There was no reward for vulnerability.

I was joined by a scurrying shape, which turned out to be Frodo, whom I had not seen outside his cabin since my first day. 'Hello, Frieda!' he said, rolling his *Socialist Worker* up tight and whacking me on the arm with it. 'How are those monkeys?'

'I haven't killed any yet,' I said. 'Early days, though.'

All the parts of his face moved discordantly and a laugh squeaked out of his damp lips.

'And how is *Gabriel*?' He raised his tangly eyebrows meaningfully.

'What do you mean?'

He sniggered. 'You know what I mean.'

'Frodo, I have no idea what you're talking about.' We were approaching the front door of the lodge, where I was going to slip in, to clean myself up. Frodo hovered at the steps, shivering with the urge to express himself.

'Be careful! You don't know where he's been!' His gleeful voice echoed up the stairs behind me.

In the bathroom, I changed my uniform overalls for a clean set. My hands were shaking. I leant heavily on the basin, longing to sink down on to the floor with a bottle, to take all my diazepams at once, to do something, anything, to break the swell of panic.

The other Frieda stared back from the mirror. Her lips were tight, her skin was a sick person's skin. Poor Frieda.

I pulled off my hat and ran my fingers through the damp hair. There was no way to disguise the patch. I splashed my face with cold water and replaced the hat. When I got to the front door, Frodo, thankfully, had gone.

In the members' room, a table with glasses and bottles of wine was laid against one wall and, as well as twenty or so keepers and staff, there was double the number of smartly dressed men and women. They observed us with a mixture of apprehension and delight. By this time of day, most of us reeked of stale animal bedding and of the animals themselves. There was no doubting our authenticity, or the messy reality of zoo life.

I grabbed a glass of wine and sidled away from Frodo, who was grinning at me, managing to wriggle my way on to a chair beside Morris.

A man I presumed must be Torbet was fiddling with the projector and a slab-like laptop, an ensemble that did not inspire confidence about what was to come. The lights caught the feather in his hat and it gleamed a beautiful olive grey. He was a solid man, with short, meaty limbs at the corners of a rectangular torso, and wavy grey hair beneath the feathered cap. I noticed he was wearing a waistcoat, embroidered with tigers. He made me think of a Victorian showman, as if he was going to sweep aside a curtain and reveal to us some bearded conjoined twins.

Penelope turned from the row in front and beamed. 'Hello, Frieda!' she said, wiggling her red talons. 'How are you settling in?' She saw the hat, and immediately prepared herself with a hanky.

'Absolutely great,' I said. 'Morris is teaching me so much.'

Morris grunted. The knife of anxiety began its twist. I gulped the wine.

Torbet now burst on to the stage.

'Here we go.' Penelope smiled and rolled her eyes.

'Thank you to our wonderful keepers for delaying getting

back to your various homes, loved ones, pubs . . .' said Torbet. A gold signet ring gleamed on his chubby little finger. 'I'm so thrilled to welcome some of our friends and members to this little preview event. We are extremely excited about our new acquisition, a Siberian tiger, whom we are very confident is going to propel our breeding programme into a new league.'

The members' room was like a once-grand Victorian hotel. Flock wallpaper, stained and faded, covered the walls and dusty velvet curtains drooped over the windows. The carpet was scarlet, worn in places to a weary pink. The stage upon which Torbet now paced, his hands rubbing hungrily together, was simply a platform, one step high.

'As you all know by now, we are shortly going to have a new arrival at the zoo, which I am very excited about. A female Siberian tiger, coming over from Ukraine, whom we all hope will make a good breeding partner for Lyric.' He pressed a remote in his hand, and the projector coughed into life. A grainy map appeared on the screen, and he bounced to one side to remove his shadow from its centre.

'This, as you can see, is the Amur region of Siberia, so far east that even the Russians call it the Far East rather than Siberia. The Amur River is the ninth largest in the world, and this basin, here –' he pointed to a shaded area alongside the Sea of Japan – 'this is the last virgin forest in the northern hemisphere, an environment so rich, diverse and unexplored that we might safely think of it as a kind of Eden. This is the last surviving habitat of the Siberian tiger, and estimates are that there are about 500 tigers left here, in the wild. This is a stable population, but vanishingly small in terms of maintaining genetic diversity, and so we hope that our breeding programme will help to improve that diversity. We hope Lyric and our new tiger will produce many cubs, and perhaps one of these may one day be returned to the wild.'

A hand went up. It was Gabriel, sitting at the front. 'Why via Ukraine?'

'My contact in Ukraine is a dealer who rescued her from a private home in Moscow. Did you know that, in Russia, you can buy a tiger cub for a few thousand dollars? I don't know her origin before that. But we will make her welcome. We will get her breeding in no time, won't we?' He smiled at his son, but it was a strange, distant sort of smile that ended quickly. Gabriel slumped back in his seat. Torbet pressed the remote again, bringing up a photo of a Siberian tiger and cubs on a mountain top overlooking the sea.

'In the wild, the male, or king tiger has a territory of some 500 square miles, which he spends his life patrolling. Within this territory are the territories of up to five females. So, you can see how hard it is to sustain a large population in the wild, with the habitat being shrunk by logging and mining, and the tigers themselves poached for furs and Chinese medicine.

'I hope it's apparent how vital our work here at Torbet Zoo is. This will be our flagship breeding programme at the zoo, one which will resonate particularly with our friends.' At this, he turned and dispensed an incandescent smile upon the audience.

He pressed the remote again, the laptop blinked and the projector flicked out another picture, upside down. This was a picture of a tiny antelope.

'Oh. Can we . . . ? Oh, never mind. It's a sika deer, one of the main prey of the Amur tiger, and also the primary source of game for the indigenous people of the area, who are thrown into competition with the tigers for food.

'Like Lyric, our current male tiger, our new female will be fed weekly on food as close to this as possible. We are, as ever, very grateful to our friends at the various pony-trekking centres, farms and animal-rescue centres for helping us in this area. Once settled, we will of course be getting to know her, and offering her the kindness and affection that we are famous for, here.'

Gabriel put his hand up again, and when his father ignored him, he stood up and addressed the room.

'My name is Gabriel – I'm Torbet's son – and I will be rejoining the tiger section when the female arrives. My father has explained the situation in the wild, regarding the tiger. It may be helpful for the friends to know a little about the day-to-day care the new female will get, so you can understand the efforts we will be making to help breeding and to make our contribution to bloodlines. Also, we have completed the first phase of the new enclosure, which was, for the most part, funded by your generosity—'

Behind him, Torbet coughed. 'Thank you, Gabriel. And now I would like to ask Leyland, head of cats, to tell us more about the enclosure.'

The atmosphere in the room started to prickle. Morris mumbled something under his breath.

Gabriel pressed on, as if his father had not spoken. 'The first phase is the section where the new female will live. You will have seen it on your tour, earlier. It copies some of the best features of tiger enclosures in some of the best-known zoos. There's a raised walkway to appeal to the tigers' preference for high ground. Currently, Lyric, the male, is living in the remaining part of the old enclosure, where he will be able to see and smell the new female—'

'Gabriel! Thank you!' Torbet rested his hand on his son's arm and Gabriel wrenched it immediately away. 'We are going to hear from Leyland, now. But everything that Gabriel says, here, is exactly right. Thank you, son.' He directed a piercing look at Gabriel, who hesitated in the total silence which had fallen in the room. Emotion worked behind his face. Then he drew himself upright, as if in an inspection line in the army, and walked out of the room.

Without missing a beat, Torbet beckoned the head of cats on to the stage, flicking quickly to correctly positioned pictures of tigers in captivity. Leyland was clearly reluctant in the spotlight, and uncomfortable following on from Gabriel's interruption. He cleared his throat and began in a muffled Northern Irish accent:

'So, with the generous support of our friends, members and

85

the organisations they are connected with, the next phase of finance will see the walkway extend over a glass observation tunnel for the public. We will be keeping Lyric and the new tiger separate until they have observed each other and we can begin to introduce them. Thank you.' Leyland nodded awkwardly and shuffled back to his seat. A woman coughed politely somewhere at the back.

'Fucking shambles,' muttered Morris.

Torbet continued, with a majestic close-up of a tiger's snarling face. He checked the room to make sure attention had returned, nodding in satisfaction at the effect the massive image had. There were sharp intakes of breath across the room. I marvelled that a tiger's face could always do this, always produce awe.

'We all know, of course, that the Siberian tiger is the largest cat in the world, and occupies the last truly wild habitat in the northern hemisphere. The patterning of stripes on the face and body are as unique as a fingerprint, and – here's a fascinating fact – if you shave a Siberian tiger, the colours are tattooed on to the skin!' He grinned delightedly. 'We won't be doing this, of course, although –' and here he turned his beaming gaze on Penelope – 'we could perhaps offer tiger shaving to funders offering, say, over a hundred thousand pounds . . . ?'

Penelope gave a weary giggle, which morphed into a sneeze.

'Ah, well – worth a try.' Laughter coursed through the room.

The projector whirred again and a shot of a desperate-looking man, in the snow, with a rifle, appeared.

'Brace yourselves, ladies and gentlemen, for the most important – and terrifying – fact about the Siberian tiger!' Torbet grinned round the room. 'The Amur tiger is the only creature, apart from people, to nurture a grudge. If you try to kill one, and only injure it, it will devote its days to finding you and killing you.' Shock rustled through the audience, as if wealthy ladies were grabbing strangers' hands in fright. Torbet went on, 'The tiger will identify you by the smell of your blood and *stake you out*. Now, this poor soul –' he indicated the sorry figure projected behind him – 'he was a poacher, and he made the mistake of shooting a tiger and only managing to injure its foot. The tiger followed his trail, learnt his movements and, in the end, lay waiting outside his hut. It took two months; the tiger was so diligent, the poacher thought he had got away with it – he even boasted to his friends! But, two months later, he was found – well, these bits were found: a thigh bone and a single boot. Oh, and the handle of the gun, full of tooth marks.'

'Oh my God!' someone murmured.

Delighted, Torbet wrapped up with, 'Moral of the story: do not piss these beasts off. Thank you for coming. Please, have a drink and chat to our keepers about everything that's happening. Thank you.'

He strode off the stage, winking at Penelope, and headed straight for an elderly, well-groomed couple in the back row.

'What happened there, with Gabriel?' I asked Morris.

He shook his head. 'Torbet should sack him, but he can't, because it's his son. So he dumps him on me.'

'Didn't he leave a slide open? It seems so unlike him. So careless.'

Morris scratched some invisible surface of his face through his beard. 'That's what he told you?' His greasy locks swung as he shook his head vigorously. 'That's not why he's off the cat section. He slept with Leyland's wife! Total humiliation for Leyland. He was blatant. She was blatant. Until she left Leyland, and then he dumped her. It was terrible. Leyland hasn't got over it. Gabriel doesn't give a shit.'

This was the longest speech Morris had uttered since I arrived at the zoo. He immediately got up and left me. I looked round for Gabriel, and saw he had re-entered the room and was standing with some of the friends, talking intently. Leyland, meanwhile, had disappeared.

The keepers loitered in the room to talk to whichever friends wanted some tales of life with the animals. Zoo-keeping, particularly of the more glamorous animals, held a kind of allure for many people, and Torbet was keen to exploit this. It seemed to bring the best out in the keepers; Morris was now whispering animatedly through his beard to an attentive lady of great height and Aztec jewellery.

Penelope appeared at my elbow and steered me towards Torbet, who broke off his conversation to direct a full-beam smile at me.

'This is Frieda,' Penelope said, meaningfully. Torbet's face clouded a little as he took me in. He rubbed his chin and said to Penelope, 'Is this the bonobo expert?' She nodded, and he extended his hand enthusiastically. 'Frieda, now I've got my tiny mind around which of our wonderful team you are, I am thrilled to report that Morris tells me you are very good with the animals.' He addressed the elegant couple: 'Herbert, Marjorie, this is Frieda. She works with our monkeys. How are we doing with the bonobos, Frieda?' The couple smiled and bowed elegantly towards me, like a pair of giraffes.

'Very well,' I said. 'Could I suggest something?'

'Of course.' He leant in expectantly.

'Bales of hay and straw, to make platforms and tunnels – and also they sometimes like to rip up the bales . . .' I stopped. 'I'm only mentioning this because you asked me; I would have said it to Morris.'

'Morris?' Torbet boomed out across the room and Morris turned his lenses on me.

'Your new prodigy, here, just came up with a nice suggestion for the bonobos. Wanted to run it by you first.'

I shrank back towards the elegant couple, who parted slightly to let me stand between them.

Morris weaved towards us like a toasted tentacle. I repeated, 'Bales of hay and straw. The bonobos. They can . . . rip them up . . .' I trailed off. 'Climb . . .'

Morris nodded. 'I was thinking of that myself.' Then, without

further ceremony, he returned to the group he had been talking
to.

Torbet grinned. 'I think that's a great big *yes* from Morris,
don't you?' he said. 'Well done, Frieda!'

I was starting to sweat now. To calm myself, I visualised the
lovely diazepam waiting for me back in my room.

'Frieda, how is Gabriel doing?' Torbet asked. Concern
orchestrated everyone's eyebrows upwards.

'He rescued me on my first day,' I said. 'You've probably
heard from Morris that I'm still learning the practical skills. I
locked myself in . . .'

Herbert nodded gravely. 'Locked yourself in where?'

'The capuchin cage. Got to see things from their point of
view.' I smiled. 'Then Gabriel . . . he rescued me. But also,' I
went on, 'I knew nothing about tigers and he has taught me so
much. He gave me a demonstration of how to go in the enclosure with them.'

'How completely thrilling,' said Marjorie, looking around
the room for Gabriel. 'Maybe he might show me, as well.'

Torbet said, briskly, 'Frieda, that is so excellent to hear.
Listen, when the new tiger arrives, please will you come and
see her? Do you think you will have time?'

'Of course,' I said.

Penelope gave me a surreptitious thumbs up.

Mumbling goodbye, I pushed my way out of the crowd, into
the cool evening. There, I broke into a run, trying to get to the

lodge and my small white room as quickly as possible. There, I would phone Charlie, swill some pills. *Rest.*

A hand on my shoulder, pulling me to a stop. Gabriel directing me determinedly out of the dusk and into a small alley. He angled me against the wall.

'What were you talking to my dad about?'

'The bonobos. I had a suggestion—'

'I heard you talking about the new tiger.'

'He just said I should come and see her when she arrives.' Then I added, 'Morris told me about Leyland's wife.'

'That's none of your fucking business,' he said.

My eyes fixed on the dirt marks on his jacket, from Lyric's paws. Blood beat in my head. If he'd asked me then, *Are you scared?* I'd have whispered, *Yes.*

'You told me you were taken off because of a slide.'

'Are you calling me a liar?'

'I don't know. Are you?' I said.

Instead of replying, Gabriel kissed me. When I say *kissed*, I mean that he impressed a roar into me. I had not been kissed in an extremely long time. But this was not even how I remembered kisses, which had tended – in memory, at least – to be more curious about the being on the other end of them.

This was an angry bite. I flailed with no time to think. This was a kiss that smothered thought.

'Whoa, Gabs, *mate!*'

He jerked away. Shapes. Men.

Gabriel said, with a grin that caught what little light there was, 'We were just chatting. Weren't we, Frieda?'

I nodded, uncertainly, my face flaming.

'Wait up,' he called to the group, and, without saying goodbye, loped up to them. His voice faded into theirs, a rough burst of laughter.

Wiping my mouth, I found that my hands, and then my whole body, were trembling uncontrollably. I sank down against the wall.

Zaire. Charlie. How I missed them.

Most of all, though, morphine.

Eight

THE ARRIVAL OF THE new Siberian tiger, two weeks later, meant the zoo had to be closed to visitors. Assembled on the tracks at the rear of the tiger enclosure were Torbet, Gabriel, Penelope and Carter the vet, whose matted beard drew the eye, as if a bird of paradise might emerge from it. All of them but Torbet had an air of solemnity about them, as if the weight upon those tasked with this job was very great. The zoo owner could barely contain himself. He shuffled, grinning, from foot to foot, looking at Penelope as if for approval. Keepers were filing up to the tiger enclosure from all over the zoo.

I had been mending ropes in the bonobo enclosure – they loved to untwist the splicing, and I had become adept at re-twisting it and coming up with better knots at the ends – when Morris knocked on the glass. 'They've brought the new tiger. You're wanted.'

I knew better than to ask if Morris would be coming. He turned away and got on with some fiddly repairs out at the back. When I was gone, he would probably pull out a book and read.

Up to now, my thoughts had been about finding something about the bonobos that I could pass to Charlie, and perhaps get my job back. I was quite hopeful this might work out, because here I could go in with them, now that Morris had cleared me as being not completely incompetent. He had adopted several suggestions of mine, including the bales of hay and straw, and had also strung hammocks across the corners, which the bonobos loved to doze and sway in. He brought out his own hefty notebook, full of tables and notes and sketches, and tossed it into my lap one day when I was sitting on the margin of the group. He made a noise through his beard, and said, 'I've not had time to do much, but this may give you some background.'

It wasn't anything like the project, though. There was no way of kidding myself that it was. Finally, it dawned on me: it wasn't *all* bonobos that I cared about. It was Zaire, and her group. And it wasn't Morris I wanted to impress – it was Charlie.

An articulated lorry was pulled up outside the tiger enclosure. Its walls vibrated with groans. Like a roadworks, there was a lot of standing around with no visible progress. The delay was due to a tunnel being constructed to connect the back of the truck and the enclosure, so that the hatch could simply be lifted and the new tiger could bound into its new home. Thick scaffolding and metal railings were studded together, then covered with stainless steel sheets. Gabriel and others were busy with it, along with numerous men I didn't recognise.

Since he had kissed me, Gabriel was avoiding me. Not in a way I could understand (and was considering myself), by perhaps changing his shifts, but by striding past me without looking at me, or by leaving rooms when I entered them, or by ending conversations in the canteen when I appeared.

He did not look at me once as he worked. The wish that he would was morphine-like in its pull – so strong, it caught me unawares.

There it was, the searing ache in my sternum. *Look at me.*

The only consolation of a life without morphine was the insight that, if I could resist that, I could resist anything. I ground my fingernail into my gum until the pain pulled me back into the present moment.

Excitement buzzed round the crowd of keepers. No matter that tigers have no facial expression that I can decode, that they are not social and therefore do not have a language or a grammar for me to analyse – nevertheless, to be this close to one was a privilege, even if it was not one I had sought. One of the men pressed a control and the back of the truck, and whatever cage door was inside, opened smoothly.

The entire truck shuddered on its wheels as something truly powerful leapt from its confines. A gasp rose from the keepers, the steel clattering like a rickety fairground ride. Thankfully, the tunnel was short, because, if the tiger had been determined to knock it down, it would have done so. Autumnal colours exploded into the enclosure as the tiger jackknifed inside and hurled itself against the glass.

'My God . . .' murmured Torbet.

All of us stared into the enclosure, open-mouthed. For the creature that had galloped in and flung itself at us was not the creature expected.

The tiger tore off across the paddock and jumped at the perimeter fence. Fifteen feet high and electrified at the top, it shook with the force, and she tumbled back, staggering to her feet. Dazed, she turned to face us.

She was emaciated. Her paws and head were enormous compared to the skeletal poke of her body beneath its patchy hide. Her lips drew back into a snarl as she regarded us clustered at the window. She had her full complement of teeth, but something had happened to her face: one side lacked bulk, and I realised she only had one eye – the right eye was a dark hollow.

Nevertheless, this broken face fixed us with a cold, furious stare. Her whole body, which was some six feet long to the tip of her tail, heaved with the force of panting.

'What the fuck is *that*?' Gabriel murmured.

She had the remains of a creamy-russet mane around her head, and a creamy underside. It was just possible to imagine her vanishing into a snowy forest. Her hide, patchy as it was, still broke her form up like bad reception in the foliage.

Torbet heaved himself into a wheelbarrow to raise himself above the crowd.

'She's in slightly worse shape than I expected.'

'Hey, Lyric, come check out the missus!' someone shouted.

Torbet looked stricken. 'Yes, we'll be talking with the dealer. In the meantime, we've got to keep her away from the public gaze and concentrate on building her up.'

A slide opened and a carcass sprawled into the enclosure. The tiger circled it and snarled, her face fixed on us.

Penelope said, 'She's not going to eat with us all watching.'

'Okay, people, let's leave her be.' Torbet waved his arms. 'Let's cordon off this side and give her some peace.'

The keepers began to file away, muttering to each other.

'You okay?' Penelope asked me.

'I'll get back to the monkey section,' I said. 'Morris will be wondering where I am.'

'Ah, yes. About that,' Penelope said. Out came the taloned hand, resting on my arm. Torbet was nodding at me. He was the only person I had so far encountered who reminded me of the apes we were related to. He had a springy exuberance about him and made an odd vocalisation in his throat when he was nervous. He was doing it now.

Penelope said, 'We've been thinking about how best to get the tiger settled in, and we think that you, Frieda, should join the team up here for a while.'

'Me?' I asked.

97

Gabriel appeared at my other side. 'But Morris will be short-handed with us both gone.'

'Ah,' said Torbet. 'No, you stay with Morris for now. He needs you, Gabriel.' His face flushed as he spoke.

Gabriel stared at his father. Confusion occupied his face like protesters in a road.

'But this is *my* job,' he said. 'You said that when we got the new tiger—'

'I said we'd *see*. Son, there will be a time when we can have you back, but it's not yet. Leyland . . . well, he won't have it. He just won't. And Frieda's very good, very gentle with the animals, and now that I have seen quite how fragile our new tiger is – well, I think it's her abilities we particularly need—'

'I've no experience of tigers. I'm good with bonobos, that's all,' I interrupted. 'I . . . think Gabriel would be better doing this. He's the expert.'

Beside me, Gabriel seemed to have turned to rock.

'It's not experience we're looking for just now, Frieda. It's something else.' Torbet turned to me. 'Jobs at the zoo are a bit like offers of employment from a U.S. president. I hope you're not going to turn down the opportunity to be of service?' He smiled, but in his eyes the unease swam. 'Gabriel, I'm working on Leyland, but it is his section, and he has the final say. He's been talking with Morris, as have we, and really everyone is very keen that Frieda start us off here.'

Gabriel began to speak and stopped. He looked bewildered,

and something worse moved across his face, a sadness that sank into his features, making him look much older. Then he said to his father, 'Leyland has taken this too far. You need to tell him I'm coming back.'

Torbet shook his head. 'I can't do that, son. You caused complete chaos, destroyed two lives, and clearly you're not even sorry. Leyland has been a loyal keeper and friend for twenty years. I'm afraid I'm with him on this. You're back here when he says so.'

Gabriel fixed me with a stare of such hatred that the urge to do something, anything, to salve him was almost overwhelming. I felt pinned like a moth between them, unable to breathe, until Gabriel, with a snarling expression at his father, tramped away.

'I'm not sure this is a good idea,' I said.

Penelope patted my shoulder. 'It's a brilliant idea. Morris really rates you, you know. And, as you know, he hates virtually everyone! Look – you can see what Gabriel is like. Just ignore him. This is a fantastic opportunity for you.'

Torbet nodded in agreement, his strange noise bubbling in his throat. He watched his son striding furiously down the road and bit his lip, before seeming to shake himself out of it, and saying to me, 'Morris told us that you have given everything to understanding those bonobos. That's what we are looking for. I mean, who could do such things? To such a creature?'

We were silenced by the roar that rose from the inner house. It was like a torrent of water blasting rocks ahead of it in a subterranean cavern. It had the shape of an owl hoot, a two-syllable *Ow-OO*, but the shape was filled with such ferocity that all the birds exited the trees, and I was sure every creature in the zoo had retreated into a dark corner. The male, Lyric, answered, and for a few minutes the sky rumbled as the two tigers made contact. I stared at the space stretching between me and the sound. It was the last place I belonged, the last place I wanted to be.

When the sound abated, Torbet continued, irrepressible as ever: 'Wow! We are going to turn this tiger into the sleekest, most contented – one-eyed – tiger in the world!'

I smiled; it was impossible not to. He leant into me, intently. 'I want to be kept up with everything, okay? I think she's going to need you more than we ever thought, Frieda.'

Nine

'THIS WAY,' SAID LEYLAND.

His 'office' was a small annexe added on to the tiger enclosure. It had an unvarnished table with a kettle; a sink and tap; and a leather armchair, worn through to the horsehair, the remaining leather buffed to a flimsy shine. There was the keys rack and, against the wall, the rifle, with the ammunition in a separate drawer, whose key hung on the rack. It was imperative to keep a rifle away from its ammunition, Leyland explained. If they were together, it was inevitable that the gun would go off. And you needed to be ready, and pointing it at the right thing, when that happened.

I fidgeted, examining the space. No booze. No fags. A small shelf of books – a mixture of manuals, including an out-of-date zoo-keeping handbook, and paperbacks about big cats.

Then my eyes fell on what must be the tranquilliser gun.

Oh, Jesus. My heart leapt into my throat as my eyes scanned the walls for the equivalent locked box of . . . what? Barbiturates? Succinylcholine? *Morphine?*

I knew a bit about succinylcholine, and it did not interest me. In fact, I hoped that was what was in the locked box – where was the locked box? – because I would not be tempted. It's one of the older tranquillisers, which causes the animal to be paralysed but fully conscious. This can be vital for large wild animals, who can react badly to anaesthesia and be hard to rouse afterwards. It metabolises quickly in the body, with no side effects – except the psychological torment caused by paralysis. I had seen it used just once, on one of the bonobos at the Institute: an adult male who became deranged and violent after trapping his fingers in a slide. The effect, I imagined, was like waking up during an operation: a hellfire of being unable to move while feeling everything. His eyes stared blankly as the researchers descended at high speed, checked his wound, dressed it and manoeuvred him into the sleeping area to recover alone. Behind that blank gaze, I knew terror was galloping through his brain. No, I wasn't tempted by that one bit.

Leyland followed my gaze. 'Yes, the tranquilliser gun. Used in different emergencies.'

'And you keep that loaded?' I asked.

Leyland stared at me. 'Of course not. We have pre-loaded cartridges of various things. You'll have to understand the difference and learn how to use them.'

'Can I see?' Saliva roared to my mouth. I hated myself.

'Sure.' Leyland took a key off the rack and went to a box behind his chair. Inside was an array of loaded darts.

'And they are . . . ?' I asked casually.

'Succinylcholine, here—'

'Yes, I know about that one.'

He scanned his finger across the labels while I thought my heart would burst. 'And ketamine-Valium.'

'No opiates?' I trilled. The box gaped before me like a forlorn box of chocolates, not the favourite sort, abandoned.

'Haven't you heard of morphine madness in big cats?'

I shook my head.

'Opiates excite them. The opposite of what you want. This ketamine combination has them out in five to ten minutes, but they lose aggression well before that.'

A tiny window, wreathed in cobwebs. A small electric heater. Clearly, Leyland spent a lot of time here. Alone. He knew his stuff.

'So . . . you don't use M99? I read it was for large zoo animals.'

'Etorphine? It's an opiate. A thousand times stronger than morphine. That's for the hoofstock. You know, if a vial of that stuff breaks and it touches your skin, you'll die. We have to have the antidote right there. More trouble than it's worth, in my opinion.'

I nodded, unable to speak. Was I disappointed or relieved?

I had not been harbouring any plans to steal morphine, but to have turned up on the one section where none would ever be available was a shock.

'Okay, on to the real thing.' Leyland picked the bullets out of the drawer, put them in his pocket, opened the rifle and laid it over his shoulder. 'Whatever Torbet says, you're not going in that enclosure until you know how to shoot.' His skin was lizard-wrinkled, and his eyes so alert I almost expected them to move independently, like a chameleon's.

My head swam with hallucinogenic sorrow. I could not concentrate on Leyland's words. It was impossible, now, to prove I was over my addiction, even to myself. I had nothing to resist. And now all my ampoules were gone, I would *never see morphine again.*

'Are you all right?' asked Leyland. 'You're sweating.'

'Yes, I'm fine. It happens sometimes.' I dug my nails into my palm. 'Let's go,' I said. Leyland's cabin seemed to have jaws, bearing down on me.

Leyland set off up the hill at a pace that belied his age and crumpled appearance. I trotted to catch up, passing the emu enclosure, oddly placed near the carnivores. Dead centre stood the emu, motionless on one leg. Its enormous lashed eyes gazed out sideways at who knew what.

Soon, we reached a rough area at the top of the zoo site, with an improvised firing range. There was a wooden prop on which to rest the rifle, and a number of targets at increasing distances. With the briskness of an expert, Leyland set the rifle up. It was too long and heavy for me to aim without support. He squinted down the sights, then took the bullets from his pocket and slotted them into the rifle, clicked it together again and rested it on the frame.

'Now, look along the top and align the notches beneath the ring, and get the target in the ring.'

'Is there no telescopic thing?'

'No telescopic thing. It's an old rifle, but if you can shoot this, you can shoot anything. This is the real deal.'

I arranged myself on the stool and Leyland showed me how to brace the rifle against my shoulder and to lay my cheek gently on the barrel.

'There'll be a kickback,' he said. 'So be ready. Take your time. And then squeeeeeze that trigger. Reckon you can do that?'

Reeling already beneath the rifle's sheer size relative to my own, I said nothing. The wood was warm against my cheek, the metal cool. It was immediately apparent that aligning four things – two notches, a ring and a target – was more like balancing a goldfish bowl of water containing an intricate puzzle. It was not only difficult, it was perhaps impossible, because the rifle throbbed against my shoulder, and I could feel Leyland standing silently behind me, having *no expectation* of success.

I remembered then – as the target wobbled into the ring and out again, as the notches set themselves free of each other and poked into the ring, like pins in a balloon – how I sat for hours watching Zaire cradling her niece, documenting the minute and fleeting expressions across both their faces, missing no detail, so that I would know them again when they appeared. And how, when we were studying the infant peeps, I played the sound over and over to engrave the pattern on to my memory, to compare it to others, to add it to my lexicon, and how that act, of precise listening or watching, had sometimes caused my mind to open out into an endless white plateau of calm, my concentration sharp as the very edge of the crest of a wave. In that calm, I had been able to do anything, I had been able to distort time itself and make more time. Time became malleable, plentiful. The narrower my focus had become, the more that time and space seemed to open out to me. And, after the attack, it had become harder to find that eye of concentration, but I had still found it, or perhaps it had been the morphine making me believe so.

I fired the rifle and fell back.

'What do you think?' I gasped from the floor.

Leyland shrugged. 'I think you hit it, maybe.'

We crossed the field to the first target. Leyland let out a great laugh. 'Look! Right on it!'

And, indeed, I had hit the target. I had even brushed the edge of the bullseye.

'Well, that's a first!' Leyland pulled out his phone and took a picture. Then waved me beside the target and took one of me standing next to my triumph. He slapped my shoulder with a huge and genuine grin. 'You haven't shot before? This is very good. Very good.'

I smiled. It caused an ache not dissimilar to the ache of the rifle, using unfamiliar muscles.

'We'll be practising that as often as possible. If you can shoot, you can help with darting, with all kinds of things. As well as being able to defend yourself.'

We practised a few more times, to prove it was not simply beginner's luck, and we both had a definite spring in our step as we went back to the office. He took out the ammunition, locked it in the drawer, laid the rifle against the opposite wall.

Picking up the tranquilliser gun, he said, 'Now, this *does* have a telescopic sight. But, if you've mastered the rifle, that's a doddle.' He held it out to me. 'See?'

I took it from him, raised it to my eye. It was slim and light. Everything was blurrily large in the sight. Nodding, I handed it back. My mind wandered to the ketamine-Valium combination. Would it calm me . . . or just send me down a tiger-sized k-hole of dissociation from which I would never emerge? More importantly, would it ever be worth stealing? I had lost everything because of morphine, but at least for a while it had been worth it. Emotion barrelled through me even at the thought of it, like the name of an old lover suddenly called out. I blinked hard, to press the normal world back into my brain. Leyland replaced the gun on the wall.

'The work, here, with the tigers – it's not like what you've been doing, because the animal you're dealing with is different. It's solitary, noble, a king. Loneliness is not something it understands. It understands concentration, intuition and confidence. It is master of all these. And, if you can master them too, then you will be safe in there.'

Leyland's office was connected to an observation area with a balcony. The new tiger was pacing the boundaries of her enclosure with a deliberation that seemed relaxed until you saw the precise repetition of each turn, the placing of each paw in the print that had gone before.

'We've called her Luna,' Leyland said. 'Russian for *moon*. She's got that crescent under her face. When her condition improves, she'll be magnificent.'

We stood in quiet admiration.

Leyland added, 'We've got to enrich this environment. You can see, she's stressed, she's not come to terms with this at all. I want you, when you're not cleaning out, to start mapping this route, to observe her; try to deduce something about her. I want it all documented.'

I looked at him, delighted. 'You want me to study her?'

'I want to know some things I don't know. It's the only way we're going to make this work.'

Excited, I clutched his arm.

'I want her cleaned out, of course. And the others. The job is basically shit shovelling, as you know. But I want this as well. Let's talk about what you've found in a week or two.'

'I don't want to go in, though.'

He laughed. 'No, you're not going in there for the foresee-able. It will be good for her to get used to your presence, though. Just seeing you out here as often as possible. Get her accustomed. Now, I'm off to the pub. You stay for a bit. Watch her.'

It was drifting towards evening now; the crowds were thin-ning. Luna's side of the enclosure was cordoned off to help her settle in, and so no visitors troubled her. I had no notebook with me, but I could at least get a sense of her, my new charge. The almost-forgotten delight of preparing to observe swept over me.

Luna made her way along the far end of the enclosure, her coat rubbing over her ribs. Despite her emaciation, she carried her head high. She did not stop to explore anything, revealing that she had already given up on the enclosure having any kind of stimulating quality.

I was unobserved. I was trusted with the keys, the weap-onry and the most dangerous cats in the world. Something overcame me and I ran swiftly back to Leyland's office. Passing the tranquilliser box with barely a glance, I lifted the rifle from its place, snatched the keys from the rack and unlocked the drawer. Bullets. I wanted to feel that power again; I wanted to be in control. Even if Leyland would not understand, even if I were to get in trouble, I simply had to chase that feeling one more time, ramp it up. I slung the rifle against my shoulder, as he had done, exiting swiftly to the balcony.

Back at my spot, I slipped the bullets into the rifle. I pressed the wood to my shoulder and my cheek to the barrel. Squeezing my left eye shut, the notches were hands and the ring a moon. Into this space, Luna rose. My breath condensed on the barrel's metal as her bony flank rippled through the sight, fragment by fragment. I moved the gun along her body, sweat breaking out under my jacket. Carefully, I edged the sight towards her head. My finger rested on the trigger as her dented, majestic cheek grew immense. Her great amber eye flashed in the ring.

She vanished. Frantically, I moved the sight around to get her back, but she was gone. I lifted my head from the barrel. She had evaporated to the other side of the enclosure, where she stood watching at a safe distance. So, she knew a gun.

And she knew I was not a good enough shot to reach her.

Not that I was ever going to shoot. Was I?

It was the knowledge that I could.

I could destroy something, if I chose to.

I didn't want to destroy anything, did I?

I, Frieda, with the bashed-in head and the haystack hair and the limbs like sticks.

I was dangerous.

Ten

THERE WAS A BENCH I liked to go to, right at the top of the hill. It overlooked the entirety of Torbet Zoo, and the various paddocks and sections were laid out before me. My mind was the kind to seek patterns, and I liked to rest my eyes upon those created by the enclosures. It was a little like the auditory printouts I had pored over at the Institute, looking for consistencies that would tell me something of what the bonobo infants were trying to communicate. Facts, patterns, numbers . . . These were what brought one understanding. Or so it had been. My previous hold on the cool truth seemed to have slipped away.

There were few animals up here, at the far reach of the zoo. A lot of our 'dull' animals were kept here – the rare antelopes who bred extremely well, or those in need of isolation.

I was here now because the eland had made a run for it. The eland is like a rehearsal for a giraffe: not so tall, nor gorgeously patterned, but with the same elongated neck and long-lashed eyes. Torbet's eland was rather neglected up here, as she had been donated before a suitable enclosure was found or constructed, and her paddock was barely more than a square of worn grass with a single tree, grazed to the limit of the eland's reach, and a solitary pole holding a hay net.

The eland (her neglect extended to her having no name) was aggressive and bright, and she had escaped. She had accomplished this by studiously ignoring a weak spot in the fencing, so that no one else noticed it either. So much of the infrastructure at Torbet Zoo was bodged and broken, often rotten, held together by goodwill and the D.I.Y. skills of the keepers, and part of the neglect of the eland was the underestimation of her desire for a better life and her intelligence in obtaining it.

The eland had bided her time and, this morning, had destroyed the fencing at the moment that it really was rotten enough to collapse with one kick. While no one was around, she had escaped into the open fields and woodland that surrounded the zoo, gorging on the leaves remaining on the trees. She enjoyed hours of freedom before her absence was discovered. Radios summoned the keepers and we trooped up to bring her freedom to an end.

Once she was tracked down to a clearing in the woods, we crept in and formed a line to herd her gently back to open ground and her enclosure. The difference in her, now she was free, was startling. The sun was gold bars on her coat as she rested her hooves high against the tree trunk, reaching with her long tongue to pull the twigs into her mouth. Her platypus ridiculousness vanished now that she was in at least an approximation of her world.

As we advanced through the trees, the contentment evaporated from her gaze and she set off at an awkward trot. Her tail bobbed white through the undergrowth. Panicking, she collided with bushes and trunks, bouncing away from them, the whites of her eyes gleaming. Pity for her filled me; I hoped she might find a way to break free entirely and lose us, this raggle-taggle posse of guards. But, if that happened, where would she go? She was wrong, she belonged nowhere.

At last, she broke out of the wood into the open field. Her gallop was fiercely alive. Her neck waved as she ran. From our line, Gabriel broke free, chasing her. His baseball cap blew off as he gained speed, his eyes fixed on the eland. She was far ahead of him, and it seemed impossible that he should reach her, but all of us were transfixed by his catlike ease of movement. His fingers closed to make his hands like blades, cutting the air, and his stride was enormous, each step now almost like a leap in itself. The eland was not built for stamina, so was slowing, darting like a rabbit in an attempt to dislodge him from her trail.

Now was the moment Gabriel made the big cat calculation. As she bounded past him, trying to double back, he launched himself at her heels. It was a pure and savage kind of flight that I had never seen a human being perform.

He collided with his target. He grabbed her rear fetlocks, and brutally pulled her down with a thump, then scrambled to get a better hold, sitting heavily on her shoulders. He held the graceless neck as far back as it would go, while she grunted and her eyes rolled and foam erupted from her mouth. I found myself with a length of rope in my hands, tying makeshift hobbles around her hocks. Her neat hooves cycled away from me, but Gabriel leant over and pressed them together while I tied them. The rope slipped in my hands, the ends worming their way out of the knots. The eland became simply a set of feet to be tied, and, under Gabriel's gaze, my determination hardened.

This was what Gabriel had told me that very first day: that nature consisted of predators and prey. I had protested at the time, had continued to protest, but now this truth was undeniably laid out before me. Nature is strength and speed and power, and is filled with bids for freedom that never succeed. I wanted to align myself, somehow, with the winning side. Otherwise, what was my fate? This? Hobbles done, I patted the eland's flank and Gabriel rolled off her, keeping a tight grip on a rope around her neck and with his fingers nipped inside her nose. This hold, I had read, can reduce a grown bull to a huffing subordinate.

Together, we helped the eland up and led her, shuffling, to her paddock. Keepers were hard at work hammering new planks on to the fencing and checking any weak spots. While they worked, the eland was tied to a post. Her eyes shone like huge droplets of water. Her neck sagged.

Instinctively, I went to stroke her, but she shied away from me, her eyes rolling in panic, ropes tightening.

'Leave her be,' Gabriel called. 'She'll strangle herself. Silly cunt – her, not you,' he added with a grin.

AS THE WORK FINISHED, Gabriel announced, 'A party! The lodge!' and, at clocking-off time, the keepers headed there noisily, a few peeling off to go home to families. I had heard about the lodge parties, how they went on all night and everyone was invited. It was the first opportunity I'd had to get to know anyone outside of work. There would be booze. Perhaps it might even be fun.

As well as the corridor of individual rooms, and my own turret, there was a large sitting room and a communal kitchen. I had rarely been in them when others were there, preferring to cook something on my little hotplate. I now understood why Gabriel did not live with his father in the main house. His relationship with Torbet was broken beyond repair.

I threw my filthy, ugly uniform in the corner of my room and hunted in my drawer for something I might wear to a party. There wasn't a great deal to choose from. I had one dress, which had been included when I was packing as it scrunched up small and was also very cheerful. It was roses on a cream background and had not been worn in more than two years. I slipped it over my head, remembering how I had always liked that it seemed to say something about me in advance of me having to speak. *This girl is cheerful. You will enjoy talking to her.* Out of the pocket fell something else I had not worn in all that time: a lipstick. I scooped it up and went into the bathroom.

The lipstick was warm in my hand. Bringing it along from my old life was an expression of hope. *Hopeful.* Saying the word aloud made my lips round in the right way to run the applicator over my mouth.

Then I removed my dirty work hat and, after confirming the sad plight of my hair, replaced it with a pretty blue one bought just in case there should ever be the right occasion.

The other Frieda looked better than she had in a while. The dress was lovely. The hat framed my face, a pleasing halo of blue. There were only trainers to wear on my feet, so the whole effect was going to be a little disjointed. But it was cheerful and it was hopeful. I nodded at my reflection and joined the party.

There was a tired piano in the corner of the room, and no sooner had the first of us arrived than Morris arranged himself on the torn stool and began to pound out some unexpectedly danceable rock ballads. His head bobbed like an anemone in a current. He did not smile or talk to anyone. When I offered him a drink, he ignored me.

I settled myself on the sofa with a cold beer, squeezing away with determined blinks my fantasies of disappearing into a vial of ketamine and Valium, up at Leyland's cabin. Gabriel compiled a mauve punch from whatever was in people's rooms and set it with a flourish on the coffee table. Winking at me, he was gone before I could respond, not that I had a response. He moved from group to group, laughing, the natural order restored – and, with it, his confidence.

Crisps appeared on the little coffee table. Morris played without let-up, segueing into some Abba tunes, which he riffed on with virtuoso flourishes. Music, it seemed, was how he expressed his sense of humour, and any other non-hostile emotion. He was playing everything from memory, his spindly fingers by turns pouncing like spiders or scurrying the length of the keyboard.

I fixed myself a pint glass of vodka and Fanta in the kitchen. Slipping back into the sitting room, I felt the first smooth lift from the alcohol, my aches seeming to float from the fibres of my muscles. I gobbled some crisps, standing awkwardly by the sofa, which was now occupied. Morris vacated the piano without warning, grabbed his jacket and left. A youth I faintly recognised – penguins? – tapped an iPad and a lively playlist of unfamiliar music blared from two enormous speakers. The pint of vodka and Fanta was gone. I'd have to get another. The kitchen had taken on the appearance of an adult party imagined by a child. Packaging and soft drinks, crisps and torn slices of white bread and cheap cheese were over every counter. There were cans of beer, empty and bent or full and warm, bottles of spirits and sweet wine, and then the other drinks, dredged up because that was all there was: the Cointreau, the Baileys, the peculiar mixers.

More vodka, this time with some nameless, flat cola out of a crackling litre bottle. My head was spinning now. The air erupted with party poppers and whoops. When I closed my eyes, my eyelids buzzed. The youth connected the iPad to some kind of lighting system, and the sitting room flashed orange, blue, red. It was only then that I noticed the glitter ball hanging from the centre of the room. It had been there all the time, waiting to become the sparkling centrepiece.

Someone pushed the furniture back against the walls. The room was packed with more people, people I didn't know. They must be other staff, from the shop and catering, or perhaps the keepers simply rang round when a party was in the offing. Gabriel emerged from his room, dressed in a T-shirt and jeans, and began to dance with Kizzy, the willowy girl from the kiosk. I sucked on my drink and tried not to watch him. But, if I did not watch him, there was nothing to watch. He was the only beautiful thing in the room.

Gabriel's arm was looped over Kizzy's shoulder, hers were clutched around his back, running up and down it as they yelled at each other. It was her face, kaleidoscoped in the dark, that demonstrated the hard fact of his beauty. Longing strained her features. He could do anything he wanted to her.

I stepped back into the shadows, gripping my drink. I was now desperately afraid. The lights beat across my dress, great red pulses, as if I had been shot and then whipped back in time to the second just before it happened. I was pinned between the need to escape and the need to walk across the room and pull off my dress and stand naked in front of him. Now I had thought it, I became afraid that I would do it, as if I was at the top of a tall building, drawn to throw myself off. I began to talk to myself, sternly, like a doctor, one who would be able to give me a pill for the surges of electricity that were numbing my lips, shooting my eyelids wide. I begged my drink, my imaginary doctor, God himself to place me somewhere safe, anywhere, next to Charlie, next to Zaire, somewhere, anywhere with a pane of glass between me and whatever it was that was going to overwhelm me. Gabriel bent to kiss Kizzy, and I spun away, gasping.

I was now in front of a wall of C.D.s, and I examined them, but it was too dark and I realised I was just staring at them. Time passed. Someone appeared and poured mauve punch into my glass. I drank it. Then there was a frisson in the air, laughter, and Gabriel appeared from his room, Kizzy hanging off his arm in a camisole, her hair messed up. He was wearing her T-shirt, with the Playboy logo on the front. It was too small for him and his midriff was bare. His shoulders had ripped the fabric at the arms. His body had destroyed her T-shirt, yet still it clung to him hypnotically. It was as if the girl herself was in tatters around him. He disentangled himself from her and went alone into the kitchen.

One moment I was staring at C.D.s, the next I had travelled in my cheerful dress, with my hopeful lips, to a spot right in front of him. I was amazed by my lack of control, how I could read danger as accurately as a deer in range of a tiger, and yet propel myself right into its path.

Gabriel was surveying the dismal array of drinks remaining. His hands ran over the labels as he tried to focus. 'What the fuck is ginger wine? Where's the vodka!'

I placed my hand over his. In the tiny second before he whipped it away, I felt his warmth, the bolt of meaning.

His hand as far from mine as possible, he looked down at me, as if for the first time. He leant in so close I thought he was going to kiss me again. My chin even tilted towards him.

'What the fuck is the matter with you?' Gabriel slurred. Then he pulled back, taking in the audience which had appeared in the kitchen.

'Nothing,' I said. 'Nothing is the matter with me.' Silence weighed around me like rocks. Confused by having misunderstood everything so thoroughly, I felt dizzy and unreal. It was as if I had stepped through a door to what I thought was, say, a swimming pool, and instead found myself about to be dropped into the river, to check if I was a witch. Strangest of all, the man tying the stones to my wrists and feet was the most beautiful creature I had ever seen.

How I longed for Charlie to steer me carefully away, but he was not here to do that and never would be. How I wished I was lying on the bales next to Zaire, but I never would be again. That world was gone. No one, not even me, was going to save me from whatever happened now. My own legs had carried me here to Gabriel. My own body had betrayed me.

'I wanted to say, I'm sorry about the job. I didn't ask for it. I—'

Gabriel's huge hand leapt out and snatched my hat from my head. He pulled it on to his own. Then he flung open the cupboard beside him, unscrewed a jar of jam and smeared red over his mouth.

'I'm sorry about the job!' Gabriel imitated me in a falsetto. A gasp ran through the others watching.

My hands flew to my head in an attempt to hide my hair. My words fled, like rats: *stop following me, stop popping up wherever I am, leave the tiger and me alone.*

I was rewarded by a sudden, agonising blow between my legs. Gabriel's fist rammed with such force that he half lifted me on to the counter. I cried out in pain.

'That's what you want, isn't it?' he hissed into my face. His eyes were sparkly blue around a dark centre. Horrified, I searched them for some kind of meaning, but found none. My hat that I loved so was stretched to breaking over his black curls. I could smell the jam, just inches from my mouth.

'What the fuck even *are* you?' he said. The disgust in his voice sealed me into his question. I had no answer.

He pulled his hand away and I fell against the counter and crumpled on the floor. The keepers were staring at me. No one came to pick me up. Gabriel pulled off my hat, rubbed the jam from his mouth with it and threw it at me, before pushing through the keepers, back into the sitting room. I curled up with my head in my hands and tried not to place my hand over the pain. A low moan escaped my lips.

'Oh my God! Get out of the way, you fucking ghouls!' Leyland kneeling beside me. A knobbly hand circled my arm gently. 'You're coming with me, Frieda.'

'No . . . no,' I mumbled.

'You're coming,' said Leyland.

The music was even louder, the kitchen was empty. I got to my feet, picked up my sticky hat, pulled it back on. In my confusion, I didn't know what to do, how to exit the room. Leyland propelled me gently down the corridor, the music fading behind me.

It was dark outside. I began to sob, leaning against the keeper as he led me down the stone steps and to the waiting tractor.

'I've not drunk anything, I'm on lates,' he babbled kindly. 'I was planning to shift some planks left over from the construction. Or, actually, just sit up the top of the hill for a while. Gabriel . . .' He shook his head. 'Shall we go to the police?'

'The police? Jesus, no.' Shame engulfed me.

'He's out of fucking control.'

'I shouldn't have . . .' I wasn't sure what I shouldn't have done, except all of it, every single fucking thing, especially giving in to the terrifying feelings.

Leyland said, 'Nothing ends well with him. Come on. Up you get. I've got a flask of coffee in the front, there.'

The tractor revved and diesel enveloped us. We drove up to the firing range and Leyland pulled over.

I sipped the rough, sweet coffee, and felt my head clear a little. We sat in a gentle silence. After a while, Leyland said, 'How's that coffee going down?'

'Good.'

Leyland said, 'You know that monster fucked my wife.'

I didn't want to say that Morris had told me.

Leyland brought out his phone and scrolled through photographs, before alighting on one of a young woman with a cheerful smile. 'That's her – Gail,' he said, turning the screen to me. 'She's a lot younger than me. Wife number two. I got it right, second time around.'

'She looks very happy,' I said.

'We were happy.' He scrutinised the picture, expanding it with his fingers. 'Although, maybe she was fucking him when this was taken.' He was silent, lost in the photograph. 'She denies it, of course. She says they started up after this.' He looked over at me, lit by the glow of his phone. Despair dragged at his kindly features. 'What do you think?' he asked.

'Do I think she was seeing Gabriel when this was taken?'

'Yes.'

I took the phone from him and looked carefully at Gail. 'I think she looks too happy to be seeing him. You've just seen what he's capable of.'

Relief flickered across his face. I realised that what I had taken for impassivity was a mask of sadness. 'He's an absolute fucking monster,' he said, again.

I returned the phone, unable to speak.

Leyland went on, 'She's only with me because he finished with her. She packed her bags, you know, went to the lodge. My wife begged Gabriel. Right there, in front of everyone. Begged him to keep seeing her. What am I supposed to do after that?' He turned to me. 'Really. I'm asking. What am I supposed to do?'

'Leyland, I don't know,' I said.

The blow between my legs ached. There was going to be a lot of bruising. Through the blanket of numbness, a flame of anger. I put my hand on Leyland's arm. 'Keep him off the tigers. It's the only thing he really cares about, anyway. Not being with them is driving him insane.'

'It is, isn't it?' He smiled with new energy. 'And you getting his job makes it worse. That's behind what he did to you tonight – you know that, don't you? It's my only pleasure in life now, denying that fucker access to the tigers. But I'm sorry you've got caught up in it.'

'I think something would have happened, anyway,' I said.

'Women love him, don't they?' Leyland said. 'What's that all about?'

My mind flashed back to my frightened pleading with myself in the darkness. 'You know, he said to me on my first day that all there is in nature is predators and prey. They're entwined together. Desire and fear. I think he was even trying to warn me. About what he is.' I finished the last of the coffee. 'It's sick, really. Your wife and I, we forgot what we are.'

Leyland said nothing for a while. Then, gently: 'I don't want you to think my battle with Gabriel is all there is to you being on this section. You are good with the tigers. As good as he ever was.'

We looked at each other in the dark. Leyland went on, 'You know, Gail and I, we should have moved away. A fresh start. But I can't leave them – the tigers. It was maybe our trouble, anyway – me being here all the time. This work, it's all I know. It's my life. I'm trapped, in a way.'

'I understand about devotion like that,' I said. I almost told him about Zaire and the Institute, but stopped myself. Suddenly, I wanted to walk, to be alone, to gather my thoughts. I rested my hand on his arm. 'Let me off here, would you? Thank you. I'm fine now. I need to walk around and get some air.'

'Are you sure?'

I swung down. 'See you tomorrow, Leyland,' I said.

He revved up and the tractor rolled off.

I thought I would go down to the bonobos, but instead I made my way, a little unsteadily, to the tiger enclosure. High above me, the sky was bright with stars and a perfect sickle-shaped moon. The gibbon gave a last whoop before settling down for the night. And then I was alone at the glass. I scanned the shadowy enclosure for the tiger. I wanted to see her, desperate to understand what it was about this creature that could make a man love her more than his wife, or make another man deranged to be kept from her.

Her face suddenly before me.

I stifled a scream.

I took a deep breath, stood my ground, put my fingers up to the glass.

Her glowing eye scanned me, unblinking. The moon caught its retina, made it burn red, and cast the broken side of her face in shadow.

In that moment, we each examined the other as if we were looking at ourselves in a mirror. Could she see my broken face?

When I thought of Gabriel, I was afraid.

When I looked at this tiger, I was not.

Unlike with the bonobos, I could not place the mood that emanated from her. It had a language so foreign, it seemed that I would have to start over. Whatever transpired between us would be completely new.

My mind was icily clear now. In a blink, I found myself at the door to Leyland's shed, lifting the stone and removing the key to the padlock. I let myself in. How I longed to be free of pain, to feel what I really felt, to slide out from under my own wrongness and sleep. No sooner was I in the musty interior than the tranquilliser box was in my hand.

Luna came into my mind, and I thought, When they kill you, there is no fear.

I replaced the box, instead grabbing the spare keys for the

tiger enclosure. Fumblingly, I let myself into the side door. No one knew where I was, and no one was concerned. Instead of feeling bereft, there was a wobble of freedom.

I stepped into the enclosure, making sure Luna could see my shape, lit by the moon. Hers was bulked out by shadows, and it was impossible to tell if she was gathering herself to spring. Gabriel's voice filled my head. Not the strange, cold voice of a few hours ago, but that voice from the first day, explaining how not to be prey. It is important to greet a tiger noisily: let it know you are there, signalling friend and not victim.

'Luna . . . *Luna* . . .' I called, in a sing-song.

She paced in front of me, back and forth, never taking her one terrible eye off me.

My heart banged my ribs. I forced stillness into my rubbery limbs.

Back and forth, back and forth. She panted a little. In the poor light, every movement caused a cascade of shadows that seemed to follow her like a cape, or like crows.

At the bottom of each breath, a different sound, a growl.

Calm flowed strangely in me, like an almost-frozen river. Fear slipped away, leaving a space within me; and it seemed as though she began to occupy that space. The pad of her paws reverberated in my chest; the fleshy smell of her seemed to occupy every crevice and cavern in my body.

A cloud drifted across the moon and I could no longer see her. I put out my arms – just in time, because she jumped up, pressing those great front legs across my shoulders. I stumbled backwards but did not fall.

It felt nothing like it had when Gabriel had shown me. The fear that had overwhelmed me then felt small and petty, a shrill chewing on the edge of this . . .

. . . *grandeur*. She could kill me with a swipe or snap – and who knew whether her claws were retracted or not. But I was in the arms of a creature that defied limits, whose deigning to be close to me was overwhelming.

'Luna . . . Luna . . .' I whispered. Even as my legs threatened to buckle, we fitted together. Our hearts were inches apart. The heat from her belly simmered through my dress. Her whiskers dawdled like wire across my cheeks, her breath unexpectedly sweet-edged.

When I turned my face, I saw the glint of her incisor. Her jaw was open, a few centimetres from my cheek.

Not even when I prepared my syringe with morphine had I sensed death so within reach. I was warmer than even morphine had made me. Did I want to die? Such a question belonged in another place now. But this embrace, with its tunnel of her jaws the only exit, was utterly free of humiliation. This was what Gabriel had got wrong with his explanation of nature.

Her breath was hot as a crater. Her jaws grew even closer, swallowing the moon and all the stars. My longing to live was like a beautiful thing – a green field, my mother's remembered face – that I observed from this dark vantage point. It did not distress me to be unable to reach it. As her mouth descended, I felt only calm.

Her great black tongue dragged across me.

I cried out as it scraped a layer of skin off my neck. She was tasting me. Gabriel had told me that a tiger uses its extremely rough tongue to remove flesh from bones.

Having tasted me, she paused, chewing the air like a gourmet.

Blood is exciting to tigers. It's their signal that food has arrived. While not prone to a feeding frenzy, like sharks, nevertheless a bleeding injury is dangerous around a tiger. Why was she not reacting? I began to shake beneath her forelegs, expecting her to plunge her teeth into the wound.

With a desiccated sort of grumble, Luna pushed herself free of my shoulders. She circled briefly, and stood watching me.

Astonished, I kept very still. Blood trickled from the deep graze on my neck.

Dew soaked my dress. In the silvery light, the roses were like holes.

Aching with cold now, I was aware of every breath each of us took.

My blood did not seem to interest her. Growling gently, Luna moved slowly off into her indoor enclosure. I remained still until she was completely gone. Amazed, breathless, I pulled my hat straight and backed carefully out.

Eleven

A WEEK PASSED AND A letter arrived. I carried it with me all day, and, that night, could not sleep. Alone in my room, I scrolled through the contacts on my phone for the only one that mattered.

'Charlie?'

Rustling. His voice muffled with sleep.

'Frieda? What time is it?'

'Oh. I don't know. Two? Sorry.'

'Has something happened?' His clothes scratched as he stumbled out of bed. 'Hang on.'

His breathing came in puffs as he creaked carefully down the stairs. In my imagination, the stairs were cluttered with children's toys, the walls covered in family photographs. Charlie had mentioned that, at school, he was a good runner and had competed in school athletics competitions. I imagined a shelf with his childhood trophies, perhaps joined by those of his own children. It made my gut lurch, but I could not stop myself picturing it. I had never seen his house. We had been colleagues for so many years, yet I had never received an invitation to his home. I had met his wife only once, at an Institute Christmas party, when it was clear she did not want to be there. He had two children, a boy and a girl, their smiling faces in a frame on his desk. I was so ashamed of my longing. I went to great lengths to hide it. The thought of him bending to lift his child, of him kissing that child, of him saying *I love you* to his wife could drive me to morphine faster than anything.

'What's going on?' The sound of him settling into a chair.

'They've written to me,' I said. 'My case. They've closed it.'

'Oh, no.' A pause while he thought carefully. 'Are you all right?'

'I can't sleep.'

'What does it say?'

I read him the letter, stumbling over the detail of all that had not been found: witnesses, D.N.A. evidence, suspects. There were so many absences, and yet what had happened to me that night was the greatest physical presence of my life. I began to cry. On the other end of the phone, I could hear Charlie's shoulders stiffen and he cleared his throat.

'I guess we were half expecting it, after all this time, but you must be feeling terrible.'

'You'd given up?' I protested. 'You never said so. Should I complain?'

'Two and a half years, Frieda. It seems very thorough. I'm not sure what you could complain about.'

'That they haven't caught him! My life, ruined! That I am left with a dent in my head, and a job I don't want in a fucking zoo!'

'You're bound to be upset. It's not the news we hoped for.' He shuffled around. 'Are you keeping off the morphine?'

'Yes. I go in with the tiger instead.' I wanted him to be outraged on my behalf. Unreasonableness swelled in me, like the discordant bubbles of foam around a rock in a stream. 'She jumped up on me. Licked me and scraped all the skin off my collarbone. It's only just healing. They say, when a tiger is going to kill, you don't feel fear. And it's true. I wasn't afraid. I'm afraid of Gabriel.'

I had kept Charlie updated with cheerful texts and phone calls, but these had stopped after the party.

'Ignore him.' I heard the soft exhalation that Charlie made sometimes when preparing to consider a funding application. He wasn't outraged on my behalf. He was reasonable.

'You don't know him, Charlie,' I said. 'He . . .' I struggled for the right words. How could I explain what had happened? If only Gabriel had just punched me, like he would a man who'd taken his job, Charlie would have understood and not blamed me. Gabriel's questions, which were not questions, but brandings – *That's what you want, isn't it? What the fuck even are you?* – how could I bring those into a conversation with

Charlie? Even uttering them would change me in his eyes. My life with Charlie was an innocent life, and I was seized with the need to return to it.

'Charlie, I . . . want to come back.'

There was a long silence on the other end of the phone. 'Oh, Frieda,' he sighed eventually.

'What? Why can't I come back? I'm clean. I've stuck it out. I miss it at the Institute. I miss . . .' I couldn't finish. 'How is Zaire?' I continued.

'Oh, her daughter is pregnant. Due in a couple of months.'

'Her daughter, Nana?'

'Yes, Nana. Well remembered.'

'Of course I remember. And I know they remember me.'

'They do. I showed Zaire a photo, the other day.'

'A photo? Of me?'

'Yes, in the interests of science, you know.' He laughed softly. 'And Zaire, she pointed right at you, and she vocalised.'

'A happy sound? Or sad?'

'Hmm. Curious, I think.'

'Why didn't you tell me?'

'Because, Frieda, it would have upset you. I shouldn't have told you now, except that I . . . Well, it's two in the morning and my guard is down.'

'You said I could contact you any time. You said you were there for me.'

'And I am. It's just . . . It's just that it was gross misconduct,

Frieda. I don't think you're coming back from that. I don't think you can, not even if I advocate for you all day, every day.'

'Have you replaced me?'

I could hear his slow smile. 'You're irreplaceable.'

'You have, then.'

'No, of course not. We have a PhD student. Don't know if she'll even last. She's not awfully good, to be honest.'

I bit my lip, to halt the despair that lingered at my throat. 'And you?' I said. 'How are you?'

'I'm okay, thanks . . . but, Frieda, it's nearly two thirty. Let's pick this up tomorrow, when we've both had some sleep.'

'Charlie, I need to talk to you. I have to talk about what happened.'

A long silence.

A sound in the background. A woman's voice. 'Charlie?'

'Frieda, I really can't do this now. I'm sorry. Let's talk in the morning. Just coming!' This last, out into the room, away from me.

'No! If you hang up on me, I will keep ringing and ringing!'

'For Christ's sake, Frieda.' But he didn't hang up. I could feel the phone away from his ear, his big, patient face solemn with apprehension.

'Why didn't you come back with me that night? I thought we were friends.'

'That's not fair.' His voice was different now. It had a quality of realness. It scared me.

134

'What's not fair?' My voice rose. 'After all our years together, after everything, you couldn't just do that one act of friendship.'

'You were never interested in my friendship.'

'What do you mean? I'd never have left you, if you needed me.'

Charlie always considered his replies. I admired it, the way, in the funding committees or other interminable meetings which nevertheless had to be attended to, because otherwise an academic could see himself sidelined, his department starved of cash, he would lean back, tent his fingers, sometimes rest his chin upon them. He never hurried. It made the speaker feel important. I didn't admire it anymore. It was a stalling tactic, a way of getting me to say too much. I bit my lip to prevent me saying anything more, or crying, until he had replied.

'Frieda, you were such a funny, strange thing, turning up at the Institute, all those years ago. I'd never met anyone like you. So clever, and an animal freak, like me. There was a moment – several, in fact.'

'Moment? What moment?'

'If you'd wanted me, you could have had me. The way things have turned out is a reflection of what you want.'

'That's fucking rubbish,' I snapped. 'How could I possibly want how things have turned out?'

'I mean, it's a reflection of what you want that we are not together – in the sort of relationship that would have meant I would have walked you home.'

I was like a beagle, mad for the scent. It was like lust, my need to get to the truth.

'Let me get this straight, then.' How I hated my voice, horrible with calm. 'I'm only entitled to some basic human decency if we're in a relationship? It was pouring with rain, fucking midnight and no transport—'

'You could have got a taxi, Frieda. I'd have waited with you. What must you think of me, to say these things? I don't think human decency – nor, for that matter, friendship – is expressed by going miles, in the opposite direction to my home, on the bus, when you could have got a taxi. I am devastated by what happened to you, I think about it every day, but it's not my being there that would have changed it – it's you, getting a bloody taxi! What does it say about . . .' And here he paused, checking that he was still alone. His voice dropped. 'What does it say about your view of me, about your view of friendship, that you would demand that I cross the city, away from my children, on a bus, in a storm, to your house, instead of getting a taxi? Why did you do that, Frieda? It's left me wondering what the hell I actually am to you. Just a bloody escort?'

I ignored his question. 'We've been side by side for years. I had no life apart from you and Zaire. You've known . . . you've known . . . you've carried the fact around with you all these years that . . . that I love you.' The words were out. My cheeks burned in mortification and fury.

Someone, I think it was even Charlie himself, had said to

me that you should never ask a question to which the answer might be no. That was the manager in him, the secret of his endurance, the risk calculation that meant he was a success with funding applications, and with life. I, however, was out of that calculated world now. I had lost everything.

Into the planetary silence which had opened up down the phone, I went on:

'Do you love me?'

He was rattled now. The calculations turned in his brain. I could feel them. If he hung up, I *would* keep ringing. And if he ignored me, I *would* get the next bus down there and I *would* see his home. I would finally see his children, the toys on the stairs, the photos on the walls. I would see for myself how Charlie had a family, a life, a future – everything I'd lost. We would all be confronted with what had happened to me. This was entirely the wrong mood in which to declare love, but what did that matter? It was just the truth, now, that mattered.

'You know I do,' he mumbled.

'But then, if you love me, and I love you, why has all this happened?'

Blood fizzed in my head. A bizarre pumping hope that I had never felt before. As if this declaration might turn back time. What I would give to turn it all back.

'Frieda, moments *pass*.'

'But . . . I love you and you love me,' I repeated uselessly.

'Yes.' An exasperated pause. 'But things change.'

'Why didn't you say something?' I sobbed down the phone. 'Why did it have to be me?'

'Frieda, *Dr Bloom*,' he spoke firmly, as if to a child. 'Not everything is a fairy tale. I'm not a bloody prince who's going to rescue you from a tower. I'm just, you know, *me*, a pretty ordinary bloke, working at the Institute, with a wife and two kids. There was a chance for us – yes, there was – and neither of us took it up. So, I'm thinking we made other choices. You, as well as me.'

'You know what, Charlie, a lot has happened to me in the last couple of years. But I think this may be the worst thing of them all. Fucking well . . .' The words were like thorns in my mouth. I couldn't believe I was ending that whole lifetime, that I was leaving that life behind.

'Frieda—'

For the first time in the entire history of our relationship, I hung up on him, and I threw the telephone across the room, and I wished with all my heart that my attacker had finished me off.

Loneliness gripped me around the chest. My own breath seemed somehow hot and enveloping, as if it was coming from outside. The night was cavernous and strange, as if it was a tiger lowering its jaws around my throat. I lay inside it, eyes open, until it was over.

When the morning finally came, I dragged myself up and left the lodge briskly, head down, to get past everyone, simply to get to my place at the stores – and then get out on my rounds and fill the chasm of myself with work.

Sickly sweet air swirled in icy clouds as I yanked open the door of the walk-in fridge. This was where we stored the meat. The skinless corpses swayed on their hooks. They had dull, flayed faces and sunken, glazed eyes, and slowly turned to reveal the shocking hollow of their bodies. I hauled a purple corpse on to my barrow, having long given up on wearing gloves to protect my hands from the dried blood, congealed fat and stink of the mortuary. Everything at the cats section was about death, it seemed. Prowling, predation and death.

Except that Luna had sat by me that night, and had not attacked me. I was still working that out, how I had embraced a predator and emerged unharmed.

Just then, Gabriel came striding down the drive, with an enormous smile on his face. He knelt down on the tarmac and opened his arms. A little boy cried, 'Daddy!' and tore up the drive into his arms. Gabriel swung him round and lifted him effortlessly on to his shoulder. In my amazement, I stopped dead. This must be Tiger. A woman appeared and handed Gabriel a holdall. This must be his ex, bringing their son for a visit. She stood and talked to him as he wheeled the boy on his shoulders. How strange it was to see him with a child, as a father.

The flesh rolled, glistening, in the barrow. If running was possible, I would have bolted past them, but I was held back by the slow fact of pushing a dead body. The little boy, a small, haughtily tousled creature, who was twisting his fingers proudly through his father's hair, did not glance my way. As if in slow motion, the woman turned to observe this spectacle of a blood-stained keeper pushing a corpse up the hill. Through the corner of my eye, I glimpsed a denim jacket and a cute hat embroidered with flowers. Her hair streamed down her back. She did not stop in what she was saying; I caught a soft, insistent voice.

Gabriel and the woman did not touch each other. They did not need to. Their past conversations and arguments and intimacies entwined them so completely I could almost see them, like scarves or gentle ropes.

I pressed on up the hill. The weight dragged at my muscles, but I could not show this. If I allowed certain thoughts to take hold, it would be impossible to continue. What I had was a job. It was all I had. I was the tiger keeper. Perhaps I did not have a great deal of fellow feeling for my charge, but that did not matter. In my barrow was her breakfast; it was my duty to give it to her, and I was going to perform this duty. In doing so, and in enduring the privations and hardships that it entailed, I was offered a small respite. I was part of something, I belonged to something. This and only this got me past the little family group. It was breaking up now, the woman waving goodbye to the little boy and turning to leave.

Luna was waiting at the glass when I appeared. Her hearing was impeccable, and her one eye was wide and clear, taking in everything. When she saw me, her face concertinaed in a hiss. I found it so hard to reconcile the hostility that radiated from her with the cuddly twitch of her teddy-bear ears, and, frankly, the sheer beauty of her head. In the weeks since her arrival, she had filled out handsomely. Was this what men thought about cold, beautiful women, why they turned them into haughty princesses in fables? It was impossible to be sure of any consistency. Gentleness shown at one moment could vanish the next.

I tipped the carcass into the flesh cell. When I had shut and locked my side, I pulled open the slide so that Luna could drag the meat away, foolishly not securing the slide rope when I called for her. A bomb of orange and black detonated against the door. I screamed, but miraculously did not drop the slide, which would have cut off her tail. Gasping, I wrapped the rope safely round the hook. Her claws, and then her fangs, poked through the barred window in the door. Her eye stabbed me with its void.

Then she turned her attention to the carcass, dragged it out and set upon it as if it was going to escape. Oh, she was hungry. She gobbled and gnawed, and it seemed that, gradually, there was some pleasure creeping into the noises she made. I watched as she ate, unable to turn my attention to the other tasks in hand. She looked at me, at one point, from the hole she had made in the body. Her jowls were covered in blood; tendrils of meat hung from her jaws, but where, perhaps, I might have found it monstrous, I suddenly felt hunger growl in my own belly, an overwhelming physical appetite that almost bent me double.

It sent me haring down the road to the kiosk, not caring if Gabriel or anyone saw me. I was in the grip of something. I had some money tucked into the pocket of my overalls, which I thrust at Kizzy, the kiosk girl. 'Four Mars bars, please, and –' I checked the coins in my hand – 'crisps, salt and vinegar. Three packs.'

Wordlessly, she took the money and handed over the snacks. I carried them back to the inner house, where I locked the door from the inside and leant against the bars, to be as close as I could to Luna. I crammed the Mars bars into my mouth, followed by the crisps. Chocolate melted down my face, augmented by the delicious salty crunch of the crisps, and I could not suppress a moan of pleasure. I had not felt such abandonment to hunger in so long. My hunger had been something to suppress, to bury beneath other satisfactions, like morphine. Luna growled and moaned as she stuffed her skinny body with meat. She was oblivious to me, and, for a while, I to her, as we each satisfied ourselves without restraint.

Afterwards, I lay on the floor. There was a rush to my head of, I guessed, sugar. My eyes were heavy as a cat's. Luna was still eating; a tiger can eat for hours, making the most of a carcass that may well be their last for days. I rolled on my side and watched her. In this half-sated state, she appeared more like an overgrown house cat and less like a monster.

I called her name, my hand against the bars. Ears twitching, blood across her face, she turned her eye to me and licked her lips. 'What is it, Luna?' I asked. 'What is it you want?'

There was nothing in her expression that showed she

remembered being near me. Nothing of her gentleness. In fact, I began to doubt that it had even happened. I had not been in with her since that night, though I had spent many hours watching her, taking notes, as Leyland had asked me to.

She sneezed, and, to me, it sounded like a laugh. Tell me what she wanted? Reveal anything of herself to me? That would never happen. I saw a crow, then two, twirling high above her in the trees. In the wild, the crows follow the tigers, hoping for a meal.

Time to get on. There was cleaning-out to do. I gathered together the tools. As I was leaving the inner house, I saw Gabriel at the enclosure's front window, with Tiger on his shoulders, and dropped the fork.

Gabriel was pointing Luna out to the boy, telling him, 'She was born in the wild. She's a true wild animal. Daddy looks after her – and the king, over there.'

The animation drained from his face as he caught sight of me, but his eyes challenged me to contradict him in front of his son.

'That's right,' I said to the little boy, in a brittle voice. 'Your dad is a tiger keeper.' I glanced at Gabriel, but there was no thanks in his eyes. They gazed at me with empty resentment.

All I had in my life was this, the fact of my role at this little zoo. I would have liked to say it aloud – *I am the tiger keeper* – to a little boy, and have him be interested and delighted. I nodded to them both, and I walked on past.

*

AS I FACED THE fridge for another load of meat, someone called, 'The mice are here!' With a grudging murmur, the keepers gathered round the long wooden prep table placed in the centre of the stores yard. Once a week, the van arrived from the laboratory. Keepers were unloading high-sided trays and stacking them on the table. Shadowy movements could be seen within the plastic containers.

Gabriel appeared, in his uniform, the child gone. I had not yet been in the stores yard when the mice arrived, and I took my place nervously. With practised indifference, Gabriel shunted the boxes down the table, so that we all had one within reach. I recoiled as I saw each box was teeming with mice scrabbling desperately towards the rim. Without further ceremony, without even interrupting their conversations, the keepers reached into the nearest box, lifted a mouse by the tail and smacked it, head first, on the table edge, throwing it, twitching, into a heap in the centre. The yard echoed with the sound of mouse skulls against wood, and the smell of fear and blood drifted down the table. Hesitantly, I reached into the nearest box and picked up a mouse; it writhed at the end of its tail; horror snagged in my throat.

'Stop staring and smack it,' said Gabriel.

Closing my eyes, I brought my arm down. There was no smack, only a whoop from the keepers and, when I opened my eyes, I was holding a tail in my fingers. The mouse had become detached and was running around blindly under the table, a red-streaked flurry across the cobbles.

'Mine!' called Gabriel, holding back the others, as if about to take a free kick. He crept around the table as the mouse finally came to its senses and made a run for it. In an action that seemed to take ages and ages, Gabriel turned to look at me. 'Kinder, this way,' he said with a wink, and then, stretching his great crane leg, he squashed the mouse with his vast zoo boot.

He raised his arm victoriously to cheers, and, as discreetly as I could, I exited through the plastic sheeting and ran to the staff toilets, where I retched into the bowl. A brown torrent of chocolate poured from me. There were so many things I had grown accustomed to. Spiders, snakes, dark spaces, blood. But not this. The endless cruelty that seemed to follow Gabriel, wherever he went.

Twelve

WINTER HAD ARRIVED, AND, when the gibbon gave his morning whoop, I woke to a blank window, the world outside white. Skin-paring cold hovered in my little room and I wriggled away from it, into the pocket of warmth beneath the quilt. When I looked down at the bedclothes there was now a noticeable shape, not just the slight interruption to the flat surface there had been previously. I had gained weight and muscle in the months since my arrival.

With a deep breath, I leapt out of bed. The white floorboards chilled my toes. Frost etched the windowpanes, and the capybara enclosure was like a cake moulded with icing, the hut encrusted. There were no tracks; everything was brand new. I pulled on my uniform quickly, eager to get outside.

My barrow, that morning, contained only straw, shovel and fork. It was not a feeding day, so the main job was cleaning-out.

This work was just as strenuous: a bale of straw is as heavy as a pig carcass, and the fork and shovel were the old-fashioned sort, with solid wood handles and thick steel ends. My heavy boots crunched behind the barrow, the cold searing my skin through my thin gloves. But, in this moment of perfect, unbroken snow, with my blood pumping easily through this newly strong body, what I had was enough.

When I was definitely alone, I pulled off my hat to cool down. Unexpectedly, I felt *tumbling*. My hair had grown and thickened, but not, alas, over the scar. My disappointment was drowned out by the din coming from Luna's enclosure. Replacing my hat, I hurried to the window. She was behaving as I had never seen her (nor any cat) behave, leaping in the snow, racing and bucking like a cow released from a byre after the winter. She lapped the enclosure effortlessly, snow billowing round her. Of course, Luna had experienced no snow since her arrival, and who knew for how long before that.

Luna was, for the first time since arriving here, utterly happy. She yowled as she leapt, more of a bark than any sound a cat would make. She pounced and galloped. How wonderful it was to see her so exhilarated in something of her home.

After watching her for a while, I let myself into the sleeping area to start work. Slip the fork into the bedding and shake the droppings free, tossing them into the barrow. Lift and shake the remaining bedding. Shovel away any dirty or wet sawdust beneath. Break open a bale of sawdust with the fork, by stabbing.

Square off the thick, comfortable layer on the concrete floor, which otherwise would be punishingly cold, then pile on the straw. More straw flung on the platforms where she liked to spread out. All of these actions were second nature to me now.

Luna finished her acrobatics and stood panting in the centre of the enclosure. She clearly wanted to play, she wanted company, and so I let myself into the space, making sure the radio was switched on and the gate bolted. The snow was energising, and she was more beautiful than ever, stood in something resembling her element. The gold and brown, which seemed so incongruous for a snowbound creature, broke her shape up, and the soft off-white of her belly faded her into the snow. She was miraculous.

'Luna, come to me!' Her ears twitched, and the great head turned with a gold stare. I opened my arms and stood still. She sprang towards me, covering half the distance between us in one leap, her great front legs on my shoulders, her huge jaws gaping at my head. I wrapped my arms around her neck in the way she liked. Her thick winter coat roiled beneath my fingers. Rancid carnivore breath gushed over me, her face closing on mine like the approach for a kiss.

Gently, but heavily, she pressed me to the ground. Snow crunched beneath my back, a chilly contrast with the hot blanket of Luna's belly. Sweat beaded my face, as if expressing my body's confusion. Luna nuzzled me with her whiskery cheek. The gentle tigress was back now.

Was it . . . tenderness? With both hands, I stroked Luna's

heartbreakingly lovely face, running my hand over the broken, blind side. Snow and the trees reflected in her enormous eye, and it was as if I was seeing into her memory of a different place. There was 'no one home', in the way I understood, but perhaps my seeking of this was what had kept me from her for so long. Her gaze held a kind of wordless expanse of herself, as if I was looking into a Siberian landscape. It held no fear, nor pity, but at the edges it faded to a kind of twilight that reminded me, in that second, of Kia turning her back on the death of her daughter, Dembe. Suffering, turned away from; suffering kept at the margin of the pristine expanse that is survival.

As the magnificent tigress shifted upon me, there was a sensation through my body – not quite pain, but an ache.

And then a sensation of warmth – wetness – between my legs.

I connected my returning strength, my burgeoning health and the ache in my belly. This must be menstrual blood. After two years of being so thin that I had no periods, my fertility had returned at this moment.

A shiver ran through Luna and she stiffened. I wanted to get up, to investigate this almost forgotten function of my body, and to clean myself up before anyone saw me. The tiger shifted on me, squeezing the breath from my chest. Gently, I began to ease myself out from under her. But, like a kitten with a trapped mouse, she slammed her forearms down on each side of me, pinning me in the centre. A bolt of pain sliced down my arm and a scream balled in my gut.

Luna opened her mouth in a pant, tasting the air for what felt like an age. Then, she sprang to her feet, and we both saw the spots of blood seeping through my overalls.

'Luna!' I called cheerily, through the agony of my arm, which was certainly broken. I rolled myself upright, making sure not to turn my back, not to look like prey. I was confident, at least, that my blood would not interest her much, as it had not before.

But, oh, something had happened to Luna. She plunged her nose into the reddened snow, then into my crotch, inhaling the smell of blood, and, when she lifted her head, something was gone, something had changed. Her eye had emptied; it was a predator eye. With horror, I saw her claws were extended. She tensed her entire body, snarling, sizing me up. I reached for the radio with my good hand, fumbled it, dropped it in the snow, reached to grab it again—

Luna sprang upon me, knocking me to the ground. Snow crushed into my hair and mouth. The huge claws punctured me like a tyre, each bringing its own little spurt of blood. Her jaw opened at my throat and the great incisors descended. The sky was white behind the dazzling black of her mouth. Why had my blood suddenly had this effect on her? Was she going to kill me? But I loved her. She loved me.

Blackness. Luna's boiling fury. Crows. Then *Gabriel*, dragging me through the snow. 'Get out!' he screamed in my face.

Luna was scrabbling on the ground, a pitchfork waving from

where Gabriel had stabbed it into her side, right to the hilt of the tines. He must have approached on her blind side, and thrown it. I snatched the radio from the ground, screamed into it as Gabriel backed away from the tiger, his arms wide to block me.

Never had I seen such rage in any creature. Not in the man who attacked me; his was a practical violence. Luna had become the beast she truly was. My legs buckled, drenched in blood, my arm dangled limply. With a paralysing roar, Luna launched herself at Gabriel, who was obstructing her path to me. (Why did she want to hurt me so? I did not understand.) He landed on his back with Luna gaping at his throat. He stretched vainly for the fork, to pull, to twist, anything. I tore it from her side, leaving a drooling wound and thrust it into his hand, then backed towards the gate.

'Hurry!' screamed Gabriel, as he held Luna's jaws millimetres from his face with the fork. Sensing me leave, Luna raised her terrible head and hissed at me. It was a sound I would never forget.

I threw the bolt across and ran the few steps to Leyland's shed. Gasping and dizzy, I stared for endless microseconds at the rifle leaning against the wall, and then at the tranquilliser gun.

Kill her with the rifle? My hand went towards it, but then swerved at the last and gripped the tranquilliser gun. Shooting her with bullets would not kill her outright, I was sure. I could not balance the gun well enough to aim confidently, and any injury would madden her further.

Luna. Nothing that was happening was her fault. I did not

understand why she had turned on me – but whatever the reason, it was not her fault.

Gabriel. Terror flattened my image of him until it was like a sheet of ice, blazing in the sun.

I made my decision and wedged the tranquilliser gun under my broken arm, gabbling and drooling in pain. Throwing open the box of darts, I grabbed the ketamine-Valium, loaded it and fled the room.

Shouts. Engines.

Resting the barrel of the gun on the balcony, I took aim. Agony twisted through my arm. In the telescopic sight, Luna's flank streamed with blood.

'Give it to me!' Leyland reached for the barrel.

'Fuck off, Leyland! I'm doing this!' I pushed him away with my good arm.

'Frieda – now!'

'I fucking mean it, Leyland!' I briefly swung the gun to face him. 'Get away!'

He backed away, his face alive with sweat. 'Do not fuck this up!' he yelled.

Luna knew what I was holding. She pulled her lips back and snarled, and if there is any sight on the earth meant to frighten a creature to the point of a heart stopping, it is that sight. Ears flat, teeth and gums bared, and a gaze so focused, so full of alien hostility that it can never truly be reckoned with, never understood, never known.

The gun was light, but nevertheless wobbling hopelessly on my broken arm. Sweat bit my eyes. Luna stared at me, and how I ever thought that I could have been anything to her, I did not know. Something in me had turned us into enemies. Maddened by the pain in her side and the threat I now posed, she leapt, from a standstill, right at me. I fired, not even knowing if I would hit her or not, screaming as the crows wheeled above me. Everything had changed. Everything was wild. I was nothing but a broken and bloodied creature myself.

Leyland's voice: 'She's down! Come on!' The boots of keepers, drowned out by the clang of pain, and the force of my longing not to pass out, not to abandon the battlefield of everything I loved.

Part Two

TOMAS

Thirteen

TOMAS HAD HAIR DYED a convincing brown, and a moustache that pleased him. A tattoo of a mermaid rippled up his ribs and across his back, and he wore a chain round his neck. He would never take this chain off because it had belonged to his grandfather and it had a tiger tooth as a pendant. On his cabin wall was pinned a photograph of Liz Hurley, ripped from a magazine. The photo had Hugh Grant grinning next to her, and sometimes he considered ripping the stupid streak of piss out, but that would spoil it somehow – they were holding hands and he'd have to rip off her arm – and, anyway, Grant's presence did not diminish the pleasure Tomas, and his cabin mates, had taken in Liz Hurley's dress over many years.

When Tomas smiled, he revealed a gap between his front teeth, and he held the smile for slightly longer than you'd expect, given the life he'd led. He had not left this region of the taiga in many years, except once, not so long ago, when some American tiger researchers came and took him out with his father, in Khabarovsk. He wore his only suit and a tie, and food got caught in his moustache and he didn't know how to make conversation in a restaurant for such a long time, because he had never really been anywhere, and it was too strange to talk about how he built the *banya* for his comrades with his own hands, and how he went cold turkey on the vodka and hadn't touched a drop in five years, though all the men drank and he was the only one who didn't.

Anyway, all they wanted to talk about was Putin and how crazy he was, and Tomas hated this conversation. It made him feel quite violent, because Putin was strong, and foreigners did not understand that strength is important. *Russia*, he longed to say, or for his father to say, *is the biggest country on earth*. Here, in this noisy restaurant, with its Georgian food – he squinted at the menu, having never tasted Georgian food – they were fully seven time zones away from Moscow. *Such vastness needs a strong leader to keep it all together.* The words clanked around in his throat without emerging and he stared murderously at his father, who was nodding benignly, and, when asked for a comment (which was not often), simply said some bullshit about how he hoped the joint effort to save the tigers would mark a turning point in East–West relations.

Tomas's father, Ivan, was the boss of the reserve, and was diplomatic in a way that Tomas simply could not understand.

He knew his father felt about the fatherland as he did, but he seemed able – no, compelled – to finesse these thoughts. It was, in its way, as amazing to see as a tiger itself, how he made use of silence and deployed some mysterious quality that Tomas did not have, did not even want, to steal round the conversation and kill the conflict.

Tomas longed to interrupt their gabble to make something very, very clear: Putin had saved the Siberian tiger from extinction. He wanted to jab his finger into the face of the baby-eyed American girl who was shaking her head about Putin, to make this point: You're *researchers*, you're *conservationists* – there would be *no reserve*, there would be *no tigers* anymore without him. Putin, alone among Russian leaders, had taken the reserves seriously, enforced punishments for any killing of tigers, put his name behind the tiger conservation programmes, the global ones, even.

Furthermore, Putin's nationalism, his protectionism – the qualities these people were ridiculing – these had saved the Far East and its tigers from the free-market hell visited on the region by perestroika. Russian border controls in the 1990s were relaxed. Trade opened up. In the small peninsula of the Far East, surrounded by foreign powers, uncontrolled and illegal trade in logs and tiger parts prospered, all profits disappearing into China, Japan, Korea. Tigers were plundered, for and by the Chinese, almost to extinction. Putin had put a stop to all that. *Put that in your pipe and smoke it, you stupid bitch,* he longed to say, as he itched inside his suit.

These fucking Westerners. He even opened his mouth, but was cut off by Ivan smiling indulgently at the girl, who was, after all, young enough to be his granddaughter. He had passed her some vodka, murmured something about how astute, yet also how lovely she was, positioned himself somewhere between father and lecherous suitor. The woman had drunk the vodka, forgotten what she meant to say, and received Ivan's compliments, and hand, with befuddled amusement. Her colleagues, also young, also earnest, were charmed out of their self-righteous fury to the point where Ivan could get a few remarks in about how well the reserve was doing, how the tigers that used his reserve were thriving, and how it was a privilege to have these knowledgeable folks from America see his humble work. All this done without a word in common – Ivan had no English and the Americans had no Russian – requiring the delicate manipulation of the young interpreter from the university. She was technically fluent, but chronically shy, and, in the face of the wrong kind of banter, clammed up with burning cheeks. Ivan played them all, and this was what was enabling him, in these later years of his life, to do something potentially spectacular in the new Russia.

Under Putin, anyone who could scrape together the cash could set up a reserve. All over the taiga, the forest had been carved up into reserve-sized chunks and the owner of each could do as he wanted with it: sell licences for logging or hunting, which was profitable but very short term, or, as Ivan did, have a brainwave and decide to make a business out of saving tigers. This aligned itself with Putin's own desire to be the Tiger President, and to be seen as the saviour of the symbol of Russia.

Had Tomas been able to drink, to swallow some courage and show something of what he actually was, this is what he would have forced into the consciousness of these self-satisfied foreigners: the Russian genius was in adapting to reality, no matter how outlandish it might be, and, when it changed – as it eventually did, becoming pretty much the absolute opposite – sliding into that, as if it had always been that way too. Russians are strong. They are flexible. That is why Russia is the greatest country on earth, and why the greatest predator on earth survived here.

It used to be – and, of course, this was a matter of silence now, Russia being in a new reality – that the only value of the tiger was the massive one of its fur and organs, mainly for the Chinese market. During perestroika's time of plunder by others, there were no state jobs anymore, the Far East was an abandoned land and men had turned to the forest, the Mother Taiga, for food and income. The taiga went back in time – it was pioneer country, with local people rekindling skills from centuries ago and returning to a pre-industrial existence, even as they lived among the ruins of vast state industry. Poaching and illegal logging went on unabated as a means of survival for the Russians who remained. They were terrible times, communism and all brotherhood gone.

While they had not hunted tigers themselves, there had been occasions when Tomas and Ivan helped to load a logging truck, and a tiger carcass was hidden in a space inside. So, while now, all these years later, he could never utter a word about this practice, Tomas was quietly forgiving of his young and ruthless self. There was nothing to be gained by saying no at the time, nor dwelling on it in the present. The time they were in had to be survived by any means possible. Tomas was sure the tigers understood that. They were engaged in the same struggle.

And, anyway, the forest was endless, they had been sure of it. They could log for as long as they had to, catch whatever they had to, and it would all grow back, and when Russia came to her senses, as she undoubtedly would – and did, once Putin became president – everything would be all right. Ivan, it seemed, had been preparing all those hard years for the opportunity that finally came his way. He saved every kopek he was paid, and that, together with his pension, meant that, when the time came, he could buy the reserve for himself, for twenty-five years at least, and do something magnificent instead of just surviving.

Tomas was on the right side of something now. He had to hand it to his father, who had segued from the ruins of perestroika into this new time. Ivan was not a hunter; for this, he needed Tomas. He was a dreamer, a charmer, a salesman. He was grooming Tomas to take over the reserve when, as must happen before too long, he could no longer run it. As their eyes met over the table, however, Tomas could see the disappointment in his father's eyes that Tomas had none of these new modern skills, which, as much as tracking and hunting, were essential. Giving up the vodka had been hard enough, it had taken everything Tomas had. He didn't know how to do this other thing, this supine betrayal for the greater good.

There was something else these bloody Americans understood perfectly but never acknowledged. The President is like family. The only one who should laugh at him is the family. Even if you might agree, you don't let a foreigner laugh about your leader. A war could start that way. Not that Russians didn't make jokes among themselves. Tomas usually started the day in the cabin with a joke from his lengthy repertoire. But that's different. That's in the family.

That evening, a rare experience for Tomas of being out in the world, was a long-remembered agony that left him sure he would never leave his own place again. The wider world got him riled, and, quite simply, Tomas could not get riled anymore. Without the vodka to numb it, getting angry actually hurt, like a punch in the guts. You need to save that kind of thing for when it matters. The evening had been a long, sore challenge to not drinking. After five years, it got no easier. Tomas won at cards more, being sober, but the men did not trust him the same, and he seemed to spend a lot of time mediating disputes.

This was where he differed from his father: he loved the forest, and regarded it as his home. The forest does not plead its case, the forest does not lie. The forest asks nothing of you but respect. And the czar of the forest is the tiger.

THIS WINTER WAS THE hardest Tomas could remember. Metal shattered like glass. Once, when he was on another fruitless trail through the forest, checking the empty sable traps, one of the birches exploded in a deadly spray of wood and ice. It had to be at least minus thirty-five degrees Celsius for that to happen, over several days, so that the water in the trunk expanded and the body could no longer contain it. Fortunately, it was a distance off to the left and all that reached him were wood chips and gobbets of snow, as if the tree had spat on him. But it had frightened every creature within 500 metres as surely as gunfire, and so had destroyed most of his chance of bagging a deer.

The men of the camp were a disconsolate collection of former hunters and loggers, young opportunists, ageing bachelors who knew no other companionship, and former miners from communist times, when mining was a lucrative occupation, plundering resources was state-organised and there were jobs for all. Some, like Petrov, had been here as long as Tomas, or longer, and had survived at the camp through its many incarnations – as logging base, hunters' shelter, and now reserve – but even they were grumbling that this winter might finish off the boss's big dream, because they would all starve to death.

The *banya* was the sauna, the social point of the camp, and the only place consistently warm. From plans his father had drawn up, Tomas had built it, and it was his pride and joy. It was the strongest and best-made building in the camp, with three rooms: a changing room adjoining the stove, where the birch branches hung; the washing room, with basins and a tank heated by the stove until it was piping hot; and the sauna itself, with its smooth wooden benches. Each was meticulously carved by Tomas from half a log, arranged to surround the open part of the stove, on to which the men threw beer to create an intoxicating haze while they sat together and sweated out the mortifying cold and pains of the day.

'Come on, Tomas, your turn,' said Petrov, his paunch in thin layers like chickpea porridge poured from a ladle.

'Piss off. I've had a hard day.'

'You are *such* a boring fuck,' said Petrov. 'What on earth did that girl – Marta, wasn't it? – what did she see in you?'

Erik snorted with laughter and threw some water on to the coals. A cloud of steam hissed over them. Women were a subject of endless fascination to the men.

'What was wrong with her again?' Petrov said.

'She wasn't right for me,' Tomas said grimly.

As if he hadn't heard, Petrov said, '*And* she was blonde. *And* she was so into you, man.'

'Natural blonde?' Erik asked.

Tomas warned him to shut up with a look.

'Do you remember that impression she did of the boss?'

Petrov continued. He pulled his hair over to the side, in the manner of Ivan as a much younger man, and then said in a ponderous voice, with an extravagant hand action, 'Custodians! That's what we are! Every beetle is precious!'

'That's my father you're talking about,' Tomas snapped. But the truth was Marta's impressions of Ivan were unforgettably funny.

'I don't know what went on, there, Tomas,' Petrov continued, 'but I can't believe you chose this shit heap over her. I'd have been off like a shot. I mean –' and, here, he looked at Tomas intently – 'what does a woman have to do to get you? You're not even a fucking catch.' He shook his head and made a *sheesh* sound of exasperation. Petrov was one of the torments of the camp for Tomas. A huge, eternal, biting cockroach.

Through his laughter, Erik pointed to the room next door. 'Go on, Tomas. We're waiting.'

Tomas sighed and hopped on his burning soles out of the door and got himself a bunch of birch branches. The men swung round so that their backs and shoulders were to him, and, methodically, Tomas whipped them with the branches, not so hard as to draw blood, but hard enough to leave weals across the skin and elicit expletives and moans from his comrades. Sweat drooled down his back, rendering the mermaid tattoo wet, as if she had pulled herself from the sea. He knew, after all these years, quite how hard to do it to amplify the heat of the sauna and enliven the skin of these tired men, who otherwise

166

were never touched at all, for years and years, nor would be, until they died.

It was of no consequence among such long-standing comrades if being touched so, with women an incomprehensible and hurtful memory, caused the body to show its longing, and if a man relieved that longing, quickly, with his own hand. And nor did it mean anything, no weakness at all, provided it was never referred to, if a comrade reached over, stilled a friend's hand, finished the job for him. All they knew was self-reliance, dependence on no one; abhorrence of all weakness.

Some days — usually the days that had been the hardest, with the most to exorcise — the time in the *banya* ended with Petrov crying, 'Out into the snow!' Tonight was one such night and, as Tomas half-heartedly hit his own shoulders in the washroom, the others all tore out, from roasting to freezing in a second, throwing themselves into the burning snow, caterwauling like beasts in the forest, lost in sensation, the breath in their bodies temporarily knocked from its relentless parade towards nothingness. Tomas rinsed himself with cool water, longing more than anything for a drink, because he was thinking of the past now, of Marta, the woman who had been so devoted to him, long ago, and whose devotion he had refused — no, that he had pulverised, that he had crushed with no hope of return — and for what? On nights like this, with the men's drunken shouts ringing through the forest, he knew that he had wasted his life.

Fourteen

'T OMAS!' HIS FATHER'S VOICE echoed across the snow
into the cabin, where Tomas was already long awake. Erik
and Petrov were still asleep, one a dumpling beneath the brown
blanket on the narrow bed, the other an angular arrangement
of hollows and furrows, as if mud had flowed over sticks. Their
snores and farts filled the tiny space.

Tomas was brewing coffee. Since he had stopped drinking,
his head was desperately clear in the mornings. He hated it, this
clarity. Like the Siberian anticyclone, it was high and merciless.
Frost had decorated the windows overnight with astonishing,
intricate patterns. The colder the night, the greater the artistry.
He shone his torch across the black glass. He remembered how,
as a boy, he had revered Jack Frost, had tried to stay awake on
cold nights to catch him at his designs. His father had ridiculed
him, and had explained the science, taught him the word *fractal*.

Tomas had remained unconvinced. Perhaps part of him still was. After all, how could such regularity, precision, design occur simply out of thin air?

'Tomas! Wake up!' Ivan burst through the inner door, bringing shoals of ice with him. His eyes were livid, his hair full of snow.

'What is it?' Tomas looked round from the window.

'Come and see the email!'

'What email?'

'The Minister for Protection of Natural Resources! General Ussuri! He goes fishing with Putin! Tomas, you have to get a grip on all this before I die. It's so important! And his office has sent me an email to say he is coming here! They have heard of me and my reserve!'

Petrov and Erik had woken at the commotion, and now leant sleepily in the doorway.

'When's he coming?' asked Petrov. The calculation of extra work that would be required for this visit tramped across his tired features.

Ivan ignored him. 'Come to my cabin, Tomas. I must show you. And then we must get on with accounting for all the tigers. The Countess – you must go into the forest and get the camera traps set up so we have pictures of her to show him.'

Tomas finished his cigarette with one enormous, crackly inhalation, and, in a cloud of his own smoke, got his hat and coat and followed his father out. Ivan was still talking, his words chopped by the inner door, the middle door and then the heavy outer door, until they were muffled. His excitement blurred through the darkness as Petrov and Erik shrugged and put the kettle on.

Entering his father's cabin always made Tomas feel like a small boy. Flora and fauna were everywhere: peeling posters of tigers alongside framed collections of beetles, moths and flowers. It had always been so – long ago, at home in Khabarovsk, his father's study had been the same private space. At that time, his collections were of papers and journals and, for a while, ukuleles. Now, his father was bent over the aged laptop, muttering to himself. The laptop was never backed up, frequently broke, and housed every single photo taken of the forest and tigers, the camera-trap videos and his own records of tracks, laydowns, scat, all with their measurements. It was also the only computer in the camp and had a rudimentary and very weak connection set up that enabled emails to be erratically sent and received. It made Tomas nervous even to watch. Behind Ivan loomed his favourite poster, as big as a portrait of Lenin or Mao, of an old man with long silver hair and beard, with his hands open, as if in nurturing prayer, around a ginseng plant.

Custodians. This is what we are! Ivan liked to say. *And businessmen. But mainly custodians.* Ivan was humming to himself as he waited for the laptop to connect. 'This will be the making of us, Tomas. The General! Here! Look at this! Do you see that bit, there?' Ivan pointed with a trembling finger at the email.

'He wants to see how my use of the forest is working out! He wants to know all about our tigers, and look at that!' Ivan's hair was practically standing on end. 'He will be *reporting back to the President*.'

When – and if – this fabled visit would occur was not specified. But this did not intrude on Ivan's excitement.

'Everything has to be accounted for. And the Countess – we must have footage. We must know she is in the vicinity.'

As he spoke, he was fumbling again with the laptop, which started to wheeze. The fan kept breaking, as if the burden of keeping everything that mattered to Ivan at a suitable temperature was just too much for it. Last time it broke, a whole section of the hard drive had overheated and many photos were lost, but Tomas had managed to solder the fan back together. It was the only moving part in the whole machine and was therefore the only part he could do anything about. He had pleaded with his father to get another laptop, but Ivan had not.

Ivan was pointing once more at the screen as he replayed a video from one of the camera traps. These were set up where tracks or kills had been found, in the hope of capturing the tigers on film. Careful consideration of where the cameras were placed and how he set them, and how long he left them, had resulted in some of Ivan's pictures being printed in a national magazine. Putin himself had seen the photos, it was rumoured. A good photo of a wild Amur tiger brought instant publicity. And publicity was what was needed: the eyes of the world upon this corner of the Russian taiga, the secrets of its lord revealed, which would bring the attention rolling in, with visiting researchers and the money not far behind. This was Ivan's grand plan, executed with charisma, vision and complete impracticality.

'See this!' Ivan swung the laptop round so that Tomas could see the video. It was one they had watched many times, but still enjoyed. A huge tigress, whom they had named the Countess, was playing with her cubs. She picked them up by the scruff and tossed them to the side. They writhed on their backs in the snow and came bounding clumsily back for more. Ivan paused the video, as he always did, trying to pick out distinguishing features or markings on the cubs, so that they could name them. But they were too young and too fast. The film was from a year ago, in an easier winter, when berries, acorns and nuts had kept the boar and deer in the area. Tomas was not sure there were even two cubs with her anymore. It was so hard to keep a cub alive in these conditions. It was so hard to keep yourself alive.

'She is so beautiful,' sighed Ivan, and both men gazed at the Countess as she batted her cubs around and licked them. This was rare, astounding footage. The Countess was going to make them famous, Ivan was sure. She'd not been seen for a while now. Ivan got anxious if any of the tigers that used his reserve had not been seen for a while.

Ivan's finger hovered over the tigress's shining flank. 'If she were a woman, I would leave all this and go wherever she wanted,' he said.

'If she were a woman, I doubt you'd be out of bed,' said Tomas.

'Too true.' Ivan nodded wistfully.

The images never lost the capacity to amaze. A long time ago, Tomas had met some AWOL soldiers, adrift from their postings, and one had told him about how he'd once been sent to guard a submarine base, and there were the submarines, sliding by every day, and every single one gave him a shock. You never got used to them – the lightless black, the sinister threat. The tigers were like that, but it was a shock of beauty.

'So, let's plan your route,' Ivan said, moving to the huge, detailed map on the wall and rubbing his chin. The map showed Ivan's reserve, shaded in red, bordered on two sides by neighbouring tracts of land, similarly bought on a twenty-five-year lease. On one side, the area was used for logging, on the other, hunting of game. Ivan's reserve connected between these to the vast primary forest beyond, shaded green and with few landmarks. What had happened over the years was that the tigers in the primary forest had learnt that they were safe from the logging and hunting of their food in Ivan's area, and had started to include it in their territories.

Tomas was going to travel out of the reserve to set camera traps in the virgin taiga, where they believed the Countess had gone. It would necessitate him staying out in the forest for several nights. Ivan wanted more footage, always more footage. He would send it to other important men in the government and they would see the value of what he was doing.

He broke off describing the plan, to explain to his son again the enormous significance of this email. If the General liked what he saw and – here, he could hardly even articulate the words and almost squeaked – *reported back to the President*, this would definitely mean some kind of state support. Direct funding, trips to Moscow, trips abroad, meeting Putin . . .

While he was describing this bigger picture, and piling on the duties for Tomas, Tomas noted that he did not acknowledge it was his son's skills he was depending on. Every time Tomas interjected to say it would be better to take this route or that, that he could see from the weather now what it would be over the next day or two, Ivan was cross at being interrupted. They were gradually raising their voices, as happened so often between father and son, and Tomas knew the men would be outside listening. They would be wondering if Tomas and Ivan would be coming in for breakfast, whether to leave them to it or whether, like the children of warring parents, they should burst in with some distraction.

As it happened, Tomas was keen to be away from the camp. He grew tired of the men, the relentless sameness of the days there. He agreed the route with his father, left him with a nod, then packed his bag, collected his rifle and set off. It was a three-hour drive to the last accessible point on the logging trail, then a two-day walk into the forest, where there were no trails.

The moment he was alone, Ivan answered the email in a fever, taxing the intermittent line to the maximum by sending camera-trap photos of the Countess and her cubs to the General's office.

Of course, then there was no reply. But the email did exist — it was there in his inbox still — and Ivan was determined to be ready, at any cost, for the General's visit.

THE WINTER FOREST CREAKS but does not sigh. Sighing is for the city buildings, resisting captive urban winds. Here, trees shoulder time like a burden. There is no fight, only labour.

Snow plummeted from a branch as Tomas slammed the door of the truck, locked it and began his journey into the forest. He listened carefully, trying to judge if the fall had been caused by a deer or bird, or if simply the burden had grown too great. All sounds in the forest were vital information, but at this distance it was impossible to be sure.

To his surprise, directly in front of him were bear tracks heading into the forest; for some reason, a bear not hibernating. The tracks were slightly crusted around the edge of the oval heel, where the sun had melted them a little and they had refrozen. Tomas deduced that the bear had crossed the trail into the forest perhaps two days ago. Adjusting his pack and checking the sun, so he could know how much time he had before he must camp, he decided to follow them for as long as they were going in the direction he was. The beast probably had the best route worked out.

A short time after, tiger tracks appeared alongside the bear tracks – in space, but not in time. Each print was sharp, perfect: four points over a rising sun. The tiger had come upon the bear tracks and had decided, like Tomas, to follow. Each print had a scrape behind it, like the trail of a comet, the tiger just brushing the snow with its paw before pressing down. It made Tomas think of the joined-up handwriting they were taught at elementary school, the pointless little flourishes in front of and behind each letter, that did not, he believed then, add any meaning to the words. Tiger cursive . . . That's a different matter. It told him all he needed to know about the beast's nonchalance, its slow, devouring lope. He knelt and measured the pad. It confirmed what he knew at a glance: the pad was exactly ten centimetres, the pad of the Countess. However, there were no cub prints. He pondered the tracks over a cigarette. It was foolish to follow a tiger in the direction of travel; if the Countess realised she was being followed, she could easily double back and select Tomas as an easier meal than a bear. It must be that the Countess was hunting and had left her cubs behind, in a den. This would make her an even more hazardous proposition to follow. She was hungry, she had mouths to feed. She would do whatever it took to feed her cubs and would destroy anything that got in her way.

So, it was madness to follow, but the Countess was why he was here and he needed to get to whatever place would allow him to set a camera trap and obtain the footage Ivan needed. His father's voice urged him to continue. Ivan would always choose the 'big picture' over personal safety. Well, other people's personal safety. But, as it happened, on this, Tomas and his father were in agreement. This was a spectacular find, a never-before-witnessed forest drama unfolding in the snow. A tiger and a bear, both starving, both desperate. He wanted to be the one who found it, and told it. He would take pictures and notes and make sense of every aspect as the snow unscrolled to what must be its bloody conclusion.

The tracks weaved around each other, on and on. Tomas scanned the trees as he went for recent signs of deer or boar, but there were none. Aside from winter's harsh famine depleting the game, a tiger would clear the area of any animals who sensed its presence.

The bear was leading them gradually upland, winding round the foothills of the Sikhote-Alin mountains. Its destination was mysterious; it should long have been curled up asleep in a hollow. It was likely that it had been unable to set down enough fat to hibernate and so was condemned to trawl the barren forest for lower and lower returns. It seemed not to rest at all, perhaps sensing a tiger on its trail. The tiger, while not hurrying, showed an urgency in the long stride that barely faltered. Tomas knew that a Siberian tiger could cover long distances at a lope, not altering its pace, pushing on through deep snow for hour after hour.

The spliced trail crossed streams, rounded impenetrable areas of woodland, where the bear had scratched at the ground beneath a tree in the hope of a stray acorn, or sprayed the trunk. The Countess paused at each of these places too, the four paws drawing together as she sniffed for information, or covered the bear's scent mark with her own. Tomas rested where they did, taking measurements and sketching the positions of prints, noting the weather conditions and using his compass to determine the location. He had brought salted venison with him, which he chewed and swilled down with snow. In this way, the journey was made together: bear, tiger and man.

At the boundary of the known forest, there was a bivouac place, used by many trappers and hunters over the decades. As the light began to fade, he left the trail and headed there. On the way, he had a lucky encounter with a hazel grouse, those huge, silly birds that launched up from the ground like fat fireworks and almost seemed to hover in the air while you got your gun sorted and aimed. The noise of the shot, alerting any tiger to his presence, was a price worth paying to have some food. The temperature was already plummeting, and this would ensure a relatively comfortable night.

The bivouac was a temporary shelter made from trunks, woven branches and brushwood, and had been added to and improved until it was almost a cabin. It was big enough for one man to sit and to lie down, and needed only a few repairs to the sides. The last occupant, in the way of those who used the forest, had left some wood, matches and brushwood, which meant that Tomas soon had a fire going, just in front of the entrance.

The fire burned cleanly, and heat poured into the space. Beetles and flies, hibernating in the lichen filling the cracks in the walls, were confused by the sudden heat and, thinking the winter was over, buzzed around Tomas's face. The roof creaked beneath its tall layer of snow. Buildings became elderly in the winter: spines bent, brittle joints splayed, snapped. Wood talking to wood. Always the forest was talking, the living trees to the dead. The cabin was part of this laboured conversation, and it creaked and did not sigh.

Tomas roasted the grouse, being careful to dispose of all of the unused parts, incinerating the feathers and the gizzard in the fire so as not to leave blood traces outside the cabin. He had veered a long way from the tracks, but wanted to do nothing that would attract either tiger or bear to him.

He considered the day that lay ahead tomorrow. Beyond this bivouac site lay primary forest, with stands of oaks and cedars. The story of the bear and the tiger would play out among these ancient trees. What a battle it would be, when these two starving titans of the forest clashed.

He was at the mercy of tigers, alone here. It didn't do to relax too much. But he was exhausted; he wrapped himself in a deerskin from his pack, stoked the fire, and soon fell asleep.

Fifteen

How HAD HE MISSED these strange tracks last night, here, by the edge of the bivouac clearing? Tomas sank down beside them in the icy dawn. He was a top hunter, who missed nothing, but perhaps his age was catching up with him. Often, he woke to a frozen weariness, and it took him hours to break free. His judgement was occasionally not what it should be. He had also been so wrapped up in the pursuit of the tiger and the bear that he had not attended to his surroundings as he usually did at camp.

The tracks were about the same age as the Countess's tracks; snow had softened their edges, and the sun had further blurred them. But nothing could take away from Tomas's certainty that these were human, not animal. He was astonished, checking around the cabin in case there were more.

These were *boot prints*. Smaller than a man's, and a complete shape, with no cleft of a deer or separation between pad and toe. A set of regular shapes in the snow, quite wide-set: a creature with a firm stride. He thought *creature* because *woman* seemed too specific. What woman could live out here? Alone? There was a pause where the prints came together, one slightly behind the other, with the indentation of the toe a little deeper, half hidden, as if *she* – again, the image of a woman, impossible though it was – had been observing something deep in the trees.

As with all the animals he tracked, it was possible to discern the dimensions of a creature from the footprint: its approximate height, its proportions. The tracks were not very clear, but Tomas grew certain that *she* – the woman – was a little smaller than he, and slender, pressing less deeply into the snow than some of the deer who passed this way. Tomas was getting old, at forty-one years, and was lonely when he considered such things. He had not known a woman's touch for many years, nor been a father, nor been part of the world beyond this forest. And so he found himself scouring the snow for more of her: a fallen hair, perhaps; a handprint. Something that would bring the real-life woman into line with the one now firmly taken hold in his mind. It was like photos flung into the air, the images of her, turning to him now with a knowing smile, the cold pinching her cheeks.

Tomas set a camera trap pointing at the spot, including the shelter, in case she should stop there next time. His father would be furious at him wasting a camera trap on such a thing, but, well, he didn't have to know, did he?

And now he had no choice but to divert from his plan and follow these tracks, not those of the Countess and the bear, because how could he discover a woman in the forest and not find her? He packed up quickly and moved off after the tracks, but soon they, too, joined the trail of the tiger and the bear. There were spots of blood at one point, and he paused to examine them, trying to work out if she was injured. Her recklessness in following this tiger made his heart quicken. Perhaps, like all of them on this weary journey, she was hungry. The image of her starving and injured and just ahead spurred him on. Now, they were a group of four, each in their own trail of time, but inextricably bound together by the snow.

After a while, the trees opened out to a series of frozen streams. Here, in one of the many individual flurries that occurred in the forest, new snow had fallen, obliterating all the tracks. Tomas cursed, wandering up and down the banks, trying to see where any of the creatures might have crossed, but all had vanished, as completely as if they had never been. After more than an hour searching, he gave up on the trail, and slumped in frustration on a log to consider his next move.

At least the Countess was alive and hunting. What he must do now was to take a calculated guess as to where the bear had headed. The bear was leading this whole procession, and, if Tomas could imagine its destination, or even direction, this would bring him to all three. Finding the bear would bring him the Countess – and the woman. He ran through what he knew.

Throughout the journey, the bear had headed upland, into the mountains, pressing on into virgin forest. These supremely remote areas, hard to access, probably held the best chance of finding scarce game. The bear was growing weaker; this had been apparent from its frequent hesitations in the snow. He suspected the bear did not know yet that it was being pursued. Starvation would have maddened it and narrowed its focus. The ability to calculate risk would have gone, as would any apprehension that obtaining a sizeable meal in such a weakened state was a near-impossible task. This was perhaps the only salvation of extreme hunger: it completely stifled uncertainty. Failure of judgement was, in extreme situations, sometimes exactly what was needed. An almost supernatural belief in the possible overcame the starving animal, a refusal to countenance failure. It was often a creature's only chance to survive, creating opportunity through sheer force of will.

These calculations made, Tomas checked his compass and the sun, to orientate himself and to work out how much time he had before the light would be lost. He would press on, without the tracks, in the direction last seen, towards the mountains. He had never been this far, and did not know what he would find, but he could tell from the distribution of the tree types that the landscape was changing. He would travel in this direction for one more day and hope to pick up the trail.

He might be wrong, of course. And so, before he left, he wanted to see, one last time, the woman's tracks. Quickly, he retraced his steps to the little boot marks. There they were, impossible, and yet real. He knelt in the snow and took off his gloves, and laid his hand next to the print. It was hardly bigger than the span of his hand. For a moment, he imagined the boot that had made it, the slim ankle inside, the leg springing to make the next.

The hunter ran his finger round the edge of the mark. He would know it instantly whenever he saw it again. Loneliness was terrible – it tormented you with your choices, made you believe different ones would have been better. It made a man stupid, made him suddenly imagine that unravelling the past was possible and solace might be found in the fading outline of a footprint. The image pressed upon his senses, he set off on his decided path.

Tomas monitored his progress by the hard bead of the sun in the sky and frequent pauses to check the compass. The slow beat of his legs through the snow wearied him. He had to manoeuvre constantly over fallen branches and between trunks so close together that his jacket scraped and snagged and threatened to tear. Nevertheless, his progress was faster than in the summer, when the leaves grew impenetrable. All the time, he scanned the ground for a reappearance of the tracks.

'Fuck!' He flew, face down, into the snow and a branch fell after him, whacking him on the temple so that, for a moment, the white air and the dazzle inside his head were one and the same.

He staggered to his knees, checked his head for blood. Clean.

He stared round into the silence, gripping his rifle. He had walked straight into a sable trap, so expertly hidden that he had not seen it. Now that he looked carefully, this whole area was a mass of sable traps, a lethal spot indeed for any 'Russian gold', as they were known. Who could have done this?

A sable trap consisted of an extravagant scaffold of skinned branches, wide as a gate in some places, and yet cleverly disguised to be almost invisible. Forest animals notice even tiny changes to their environment. This, for the most part, protects them from poorly made traps and snares.

Tomas had constructed some much nearer the camp, but for two winters now the catch from them had been very poor. Sable were vanishing. His traps had languished and rotted.

But not these. These traps, perhaps six of them throughout this area of trees, were clean and in good order. They were designed so that, when the bait was hung, the sable scurried up and poked its head between the crosspieces to reach it, causing them to crash together, as they were poised to do, smashing the sable's spine without damaging the fur.

Tomas bent to examine the one he had blundered into. He replaced the branch he had dislodged, admiring how carefully balanced it was. On it was a tiny metal latch, which he reset. Usually, the workings on a sable trap were whittled dowels, in order to keep the wooden surface uninterrupted, but if it could be maintained and disguised, a metal latch was more reliable and hard-wearing. This latch had been carefully reinforced with wire, and rubbed with dirt to blend it in. It was miraculous. He was very proud of his own metalwork on the traps near the camp. There was a kind of artistry that was possible with metal. The most ordinary of objects could be made perfect. Form could fuse with function beneath the soldering iron, and Tomas's work was admired by the men, even as they ridiculed him for his excessive effort. This latch, however, was better even than his. He could see it had been broken at one time: it had been taken off, the rust removed at the break, the pieces melted together and then rubbed until the join was visible only to a master's eye. More amazing than this were the little holes that had been made around the join and the fine wire that had been woven between them, for strength, like stitches. These stitches had then also been melted and rubbed. Where once the break was a weak spot, it was now the strongest part of the latch. It was also staggeringly intricate.

Tomas stepped back to admire the whole mechanism. The skinned branches were carefully smeared with mud and leaves to give a green tinge. This encouraged the wood to dull and harden, without harbouring rot and insects. The branches often warped as they seasoned. The fall of them had to be adjusted, and this had been done meticulously. Tomas could see scrape marks where the branch had been filed back to straightness, and, at the end of one branch, the most beautiful piece of dowel work he had ever seen. Rotten wood had been cut out of the end; instead of starting again with a whole new branch, the piece had been painstakingly replaced, the joins softened to invisibility with earth.

Every trap was maintained to this same standard. Almost invisible to the untrained eye, they rendered this corner of the forest lethal for sable. However, none of the traps was baited. This suggested food was so hard to come by that even bait was human food.

Snow had fallen recently in this area, erasing tracks. But, as Tomas explored the clearing, he found one trap sheltered by a huge pine, and, around it, a small pocket of churned-up boot marks. *Hers.*

Craving for a drink seared through his nerves, as if the sable trap had slammed on his fingers. He had been close to bringing vodka with him as it was useful in the forest as an emergency antiseptic and for lighting fires, but he had resisted. Alone in the forest, he knew some thought would occur to him, gather momentum like a blizzard, and he would have guzzled the alcohol as if he had never been sober.

Was the woman tracking him? Though he had left her behind, though he was pressing on, here she was again – this time, presenting him with different evidence of herself. She was more than just ephemeral traces in the snow. She was a skilled hunter, and she was determined to have his attention.

As if he were blackout drunk, the woman, in all her ingenuity and recklessness, rose before him from the muddle of her prints. She manifested with visceral force, vivid as a vodka hallucination, so that he found himself moving towards her. She was bending to her intricate work, as if she were in one of the flickering films he'd brought down the satellite. He was so moved by her loneliness, her cleverness. Her breath misted from her lips. He could not see her face. She had an obstinate back. He was in love with her already.

It all played out before him. He was meant to save her from whatever harsh life she was eking out in the forest. He would take her home to the camp. He would love her. They would have children. They would be happy. He would do things right.

Longing gnawed at his brain. What was she? Some kind of ghost? Sprite? With a groan, he lurched forward, hand outstretched. He wasn't a drunk anymore, and now he understood what that meant. He was driven to know what was real and what wasn't, even as he wished more than anything to fall to his knees, grow sleepy in the snow, and watch her busy at her work until his eyes closed for good. His hand fell through her, against the trunk of the pine, creviced and ancient, and she was gone, vanished into her prints. Tomas leant against the tree and sobbed, with the abandon of a man who knows he is alone.

As the vision of her vanished, the memory of the other woman whom he had known long ago from her tracks came back to him. For surely this was what was happening, some kind of manifestation of what he'd lost? Sent to torment him, knock him off course?

To and from his door at the camp, Marta had come, winter upon winter.

The scratch of her form on the horizon, that grew real and warm as she drew closer.

Her boot prints, sometimes entwined with his, sometimes the only ones, the first ones of the day.

With a roar, Tomas kicked the snow, wiped his eyes with an ice-crusted glove. The forest was cruel. Cruel to a starving bear, leading it to believe it could triumph over circumstances. Cruel to him, deluding him with little prints, with the possibility of second chances. He tore himself away to continue his trek upland.

But he could not help himself, just one more time. He knelt and ran his finger tenderly around one of the prints. Then he touched it with his lips. They burned at the contact. Tomas was a hunter to his very core, and hunters know that tracks are all the hope there is. They bring everything into play. They change everything.

Sixteen

MARTA'S DEVOTION TO TOMAS took the form of walking the fifteen kilometres, unbidden, winter and summer, broiling heat or piled snow, from the village to the camp, to bring him vodka and cigarettes.

Her face was one of those big, plain-girl faces. It was easier to think of it like that, as if he hadn't liked it that much, as if it was a common face, one you might forget. As if hers were not the only one.

When Tomas arrived back from hunting or logging, in those days, he would find her sitting with the men, playing cards or finishing a joke that would have them snorting into their vodka. Her own laugh was unforced and raucous, like ice cracking into warm water.

Marta was not a natural blonde. She was a purposeful bottle-blonde. She had dark roots, because it was expensive to get it done too often. And your hair could fall out too, she told Tomas. This was one of the incomprehensible things about her, that only later he wept to have lost: she told him everything. Good-humoured words tumbled out of her, even when they were never caught by him, even when he was a complete and utter wall against her feelings. She couldn't help it. She kept telling him these details of her life, a cheerful commentary, like bright stitching on the frayed edges of an old coat.

She had a thing about Marilyn Monroe, perhaps because he'd said in passing that he did, and, in the village, she tried to re-create that look. She was going for sexy, but what came across was *love me*, and, though he never told her, he liked that more. She spent a lot of time on her appearance, disappearing into his cabin on arrival at the camp to tidy her hair and sculpt the thick brown eyebrows. There was no mirror in the camp, so she brought her own from home.

When he arrived back, any tiredness from her own journey was transformed by make-up, creating the potent mix of fakery and raw need that characterised her. He never said how much he had come to love this moment of arrival, the burst of laughter he would invariably hear from the kitchen, and then her face lighting up at the sight of him. *Lighting up.*

TOMAS PRESSED ON THROUGH the virgin forest, now, the sable traps receding in his mind. This memory of Marta greeting him needed to be wrenched out of the way, a boulder in front of a vantage point.

As he trekked, his gaze fanned out to examine the snow. It was tiring work, which demanded no distraction. A man could go blind from the earth's white stare, or he could start to hear sounds that weren't there. Overwhelmed, he could miss the clues that were.

Tomas's breath was like a wraith companion, in front and beside him. His legs swooshed quietly in the snow. In a land where tigers manifest without warning and food can become so rare as to be miraculous, a hunter's gut feeling is his greatest intelligence. In the forest, intuition is science. Like the bear, with its starving certainty, Tomas's conviction that the tracks existed played as important a role in finding them as his fiercely attuned senses.

A long, empty hour later, he was rewarded by a burst of prints rounding the base of a tree. Tomas swore at the miracle of them, rubbing his eyes to be sure. But they were not as he expected. Before him were the Countess's tracks only, with a lone cub following. After checking that there was no bear, and no woman, Tomas studied them carefully, to piece together the story.

The tracks were headed in the same direction as those yesterday, but were more recent. Tomas noted the cub tracks inside the Countess's tracks, as the youngster tried to ease its journey by travelling in its mother's wake. He searched the area around them for a second set of cub tracks, but found none. It seemed that the Countess had lost one cub.

All Ivan wanted was footage of the Countess, but, for Tomas, the probable death of a cub – for now, at least – was more important. Had it, for instance, been caught by a snare? Or simply died of starvation? Once again, Tomas decided to break from his chosen path. This time, he decided to follow the tracks backwards, away from the direction of travel. This meant that he would be travelling back in time, back into the story of the Countess and her cubs. Tomas took photographs, location notes and measurements, and began his journey into the past.

Where a stand of larches gave way to willows shrouding another frozen stream, Tomas stopped. Before him was what they called a 'lay-down', and this was a perfect one indeed.

The tiger, like any cat, took frequent rests, and lay down in the snow. If it stayed for a while, it would melt the snow around its body and, when it stood to leave, the snow would freeze to ice, creating a perfect mould of the underside of the tiger's body. In this case, the detail of the Countess's body was spectacular: perfect paw prints, haunch marks, the indentation of the snout, even the swish mark of her tail. The Countess had rested in the spot by the stream, and so had her single cub. Perhaps she had nursed it. They had churned the snow together, and then the cub, too, had rested, creating another mould, like a shadow of the mother's.

Tomas took a camera trap from his pack and fixed it to a trunk. It was unlikely that the tigers would return to this spot any time soon, but you could never know, and something had been interesting enough to detain them here. Then he carried on, firm against the direction of travel, back in time.

The act of going back in time through the forest inevitably brought Marta tracking back into his memory. Her regular emergence from the trees began, over the years, to carve out a space in Tomas, which was then filled by her, much as a river will erode the shape of itself, and it will bring silt from upstream and deposit it to change its outline still further.

Long after it was over between them, Tomas found himself checking the window for signs of her. The memory of scanning the blinding horizon of bone and feathers rang in the now-empty space inside him. He had no name for the pain. He had drunk heavily to drown it.

The Countess's tracks showed her progress through the forest: firm, determined, wasting no time. Her single cub had struggled to keep up. In order to hunt, a tigress must leave her cubs, which are a liability when hunting. Alone for long periods, the cubs were vulnerable to many dangers, especially if they wandered from the den. Was this what had befallen the second cub?

After a successful hunt, the tigress drags the kill to a safe spot and then returns to collect her cubs. Tomas believed he had come across this later point in the story. The Countess had made a kill – the bear, surely – and had dragged it to a safe place. He had intercepted the return journey of mother and cub to the drag site.

Ahead, he glimpsed a confusion of cub tracks in the snow. Among them, what seemed like burst berries; he realised it was blood only when he got close. Anxious now, Tomas examined the prints and recorded in his notebook that there were two cubs, at this point. One had leaked blood into every one of its prints. As there had been no blood when he came across the tracks of the Countess and a single cub, it must have been the injured cub who remained behind. He wondered what injury could have befallen it. A trap?

The whole area was alive with furrows and marks. Where was the cub now? Could it still be here? Tomas came to a standstill at the centre, coughing in the freezing air. Through the treetops, the sun gazed mercilessly down at him. He stood alone in a living whirl of something that was over. The bloody prints drifted further from the other tracks.

He followed them, though he was terrified, now, to do so. He knew, with a certainty like a rock in his gut, that he had been led to this desperate place in the lonely forest for a reason. He was going to be shown something that he had deadened himself against, and his breath came shallow and reluctant in the wake of the crimson prints. All the magic of the forest had drawn him here; the Countess herself had driven him down the trail of time. And now he came to a breathless halt as the terrible thing he had made Marta do so long ago rose before him like a sheet of ice . . .

And, oh, the body of a tiger cub, fallen in the snow. It was frozen rigid and its lips were drawn back in a rictus snarl, because a tiger never gives in, not even a cub, not even in death.

Seventeen

TOMAS KNELT BESIDE THE cub and ran his fingers over the poking ribs. Though small, the body contained all the magnificence of the adult male this cub would never become. The disproportionately large paws, to hold him above the snow as he patrolled his vast territory, were fully formed in miniature; the fangs, perfect and white, were bared in a snarl. His potential strength was visible even through wasted muscles. He was a tiny czar, whose nobility and mystery were demonstrated in the way he had resisted death until the last breath.

Tomas lifted the injured paw. A streak of flesh was gone, leaving a raw, licked area that was rotten. A snare, that the Countess had managed to chew off? Tomas palpated the cub's body, looking for signs of other injuries. It seemed that the foot injury had slowed the cub down and, in the end, he was unable to withstand the days, stretching to weeks, of hunger. This was what had killed him.

Tigers often had three, even four offspring, but in a harsh environment it was unlikely that they would all see adulthood. Did the Countess wait with him until he was dead? Or did she look at her other cub and decide between them, leaving this one to die alone in the snow?

Tomas stroked the cub's ruff and closed its eyes. He ran through a mental inventory of all the hunters he knew – who would have laid such a snare, so far out? Perhaps it had not been intended for a tiger, and had captured the cub because he was inexperienced, incautious, and probably alone when it happened. Of course, the snare could have been laid many miles away, the cub struggling on its lacerated paw for weeks. All that was certain was that the cub had suffered a slow, painful decline.

Wearily, Tomas photographed the body, took measurements, set a camera trap. He could not remove the corpse, for it was likely the tigress would follow the body of her baby if it was taken away. He would have to come back another time.

When he reported this death on his return, and his suspicion of a snare, there would have to be an investigation. This was why Ivan desperately resisted documenting any seriously bad news. This remote area of the taiga would be invaded, questioning would take place of every hunter within a hundred kilometres. These days, tigers could not be injured or killed by people without severe penalty. Investigations caused suspicion, bad feeling, and courted the possibility of tighter regulation.

These were not images that the General would want to see, that was for sure.

Ivan would be furious when presented with this evidence. Why, he would thunder, why had Tomas not simply pursued the Countess, as requested? Why go back in time to find the sorry end to a commonplace story of the wild? Death of tiger cubs was common, Ivan would insist, and speculating on the cause of death was a *waste of time*.

Good news. Footage. The Countess. These were what was needed if the reserve was going to prosper.

But Tomas couldn't leave. Not yet. He took out his axe and began to look for a suitable spot nearby to bury the cub. Not only was it unbearable that he should leave it abandoned above ground, as though it did not matter, it would also be scavenged swiftly, the moment he left the scene. As he looked, he lit a cigarette and turned over in his mind what his father would have to say, how the situation and the bad news would need to be handled.

THERE WAS MUCH TO be afraid of in the taiga, and Tomas had long been master of those risks. But fear of disappointing his father was something he had never mastered. There had been an ice field of distance between father and son all Tomas's life.

It had been bridged only by the beatings meted out by his father when Tomas was a small boy, and then later the longing to please, which grew in Tomas, like a kind of vestigial organ, uselessly converting his father's coldness into the son's adoration.

As much as disappointing Ivan was frightening, to please him was intoxicating. When pleased, Ivan's face broke into a brilliant smile; he had a rich laugh, like the thick sap from the maple trees. A boy, and even a man, could be forgiven for snatching at that laughter – and, with it, the sweet approval – smearing it all over his hands, all over his upturned face. The difficulty of pleasing Ivan caused Tomas to love him with a hungry fervour, like a rat in an experiment, pressing the lever for a reward it still believes in, over and over, unable to stop, even as it administers an electric shock to itself.

The catastrophe of perestroika in the Far East had ended both his father's career as a technician at the gold mine outside Khabarovsk and Tomas's opportunities to work as a welder and metalworker. After months of unemployment, during which time Ivan had made it clear Tomas was a drain on his dwindling savings, Tomas had the idea to travel into the ungoverned lands of the taiga. He'd heard it was possible to survive there, from first principles. He could adapt his practical skills to great effect, he thought.

In the end, the taiga would offer a lifeline to them both.

When Tomas first turned up at the camp, an exhausted stranger emerging through the trees in the impossible heat, the men had looked up from where they were cooking meat beneath a makeshift awning and watched every step he took towards them. They were considering robbing and killing him, there and then, Petrov later told him, but, with a glance between them, which Tomas saw, decided to allow him to approach and say his piece first. 'You had an honest face,' Petrov would wheeze. 'We thought you might be some use. *Then* we could rob and kill you!' There were so few strangers here that sheer surprise had saved his life.

He explained he was a skilled metalworker. For food, he would mend whatever machinery they needed mending. Perhaps he had inherited something of Ivan's persuasiveness, because they did feed him and he did make some repairs, within days also fashioning a radio receiver, wired into the men's kitchen. It received music channels from Moscow and, in particular weather, the English football league. This made him an instant celebrity in the camp and secured his position. The men crowded round the radio and listened to the matches. That same receiver, with some embellishments, was still there to this day, enhanced by a satellite dish that brought them flickering Russian news and war films.

Over the months following, Tomas learnt from the men the other essentials: hunting, fishing, foraging from the forest. He made himself the camp cook, doling out an increasingly acceptable boar stew, dredging up half-formed memories of what his mother had made when he was a child, before she died when he was ten. The men survived by hunting and logging, and, in good years, by the sale of sable pelts. Very occasionally, he could send a letter to Ivan, when the men were delivering logs to the port at Khabarovsk and remembered to stop in the city, and pick up a reply to a letter he had sent months before.

It was a letter that, two years later, brought Ivan to the camp. *I've told them you understand science,* Tomas wrote, *and you are good with letters and numbers.* This was what the men thought they needed – what they actually needed was leadership, and this was what Ivan would provide.

Tomas had gone proudly to collect his father, taking one of the trucks to Khabarovsk, getting his hair cut and buying new clothes in which to pick Ivan up. They had not seen each other in two years, but Tomas got the familiar lurch at the sight of the tall, charismatic man, with the full head of silvery hair. Ivan sat rigid and uncomplaining all the pounding way to the camp, and, when he stepped out to meet the men, he strode forward, spoke easy words of welcome to them, bestowed city vodka and cigarettes on them, and immediately seemed in charge.

Ivan designed the *banya* and Tomas built it. Most of all, he had vision. The logging operation was barely more than a couple of trucks, obtained by violent means. The men sawed and then drove logs down to Khabarovsk, where they could be sailed down the Amur River into China. Ivan managed to perform a negotiation with the Chinese representative at the port, and they were provided with a third truck as part of a deal. Then Ivan made sure the logs were delivered on time, to the correct place. When the actual boss was killed, some months later, by some logs tumbling off the lorry, Ivan was the natural successor.

TOMAS CLEARED SOME SNOW and set a fire going on the ground, just enough to soften it. Then, with his axe, he hacked a hole and laid the cub in it, and scraped soil and then snow over it. He hated to leave the cub, so alone in the frozen earth. He found it almost unbearable to turn away from that wild creature, just beginning its life.

Another image pressed into his mind. The past was mingling with the present, now, like rivers converging.

It was a different season – early summer. His father was watching the finches on the bird table, from his cabin window. To this day, Ivan rigged bird tables all over the camp. He loved birds and could watch them for hours. He would often continue to watch them, even as Tomas was talking.

The memory concerned itself very precisely with a particular moment. Tomas had just finished informing Ivan that Marta was pregnant. He was thinking he should marry her and move back to the city. Marta's father had a job in Khabarovsk. Construction. The Chinese were building a casino. He could put a word in for Tomas.

Ivan listened to this speech, all the while keeping his eyes fixed on the finches. He even nodded, Tomas remembered. His hand, in his pocket, jangled some keys.

So, Tomas went on, he would be leaving.

Starting a new life. With Marta. And a baby.

And then, his father turned from the finches on their table. It was this turning from the window, from the finches, that Tomas remembered most strongly. How it took a long time. How his father was changed, and the change was revealed in slow motion. As if someone had made a statue of his father and was turning it slowly to face him. And when, at last, this was accomplished, the look upon Ivan's face had taken Tomas's breath away.

Don't you dare, the look said. *Don't you dare leave me.*

Tomas was transported back to boyhood, standing before his father, awaiting a beating. As he lifted the cane from the stand, Ivan's eyes held within them a flash of vulnerability, which would only be accessible once the beating was over. Is this not what makes every beaten child compliant? The hope of love, after the fear and pain?

Minutes before, Marta and he had been excited about the possibilities in Khabarovsk. She had shyly pressed his palm to her belly. She had said, and he couldn't remember the words around it, she'd said, *Our baby.*

The keys jangled. Ivan turned back to the window.

I love you, Dad, said Tomas.

Ivan nodded.

Marta was waiting for him in the kitchen of the main cabin. She was looking forward to their new life. She'd put in the hours, the effort, and now she would have a baby and Tomas and a little flat somewhere in Khabarovsk. She did not understand, when he emerged into the kitchen, that everything had changed. She greeted him with a huge excited smile.

He said, *Too much to do here.*

He said, *I can't do this now.*

Marta said, *But, our baby.*

Tomas said, *You know what you have to do.*

No make-up could hide her astonishment. It was a depth charge, devastating her from inside. *I don't understand,* she said.

Here, Tomas tried to turn away from the memory, but he found, now, he could not.

She had leant over the table and slapped him across the face. She sat back down, unable to complete the gesture of defiance by storming out of the room. She wept in disbelief.

I'm sorry, he said. And he took out two glasses and filled them with vodka.

That was the end of their story. A mess. The girl being sick, so great was her shock. Then, fleeing the kitchen, out towards the trees. But she couldn't go home and tell her parents she was pregnant and would not be getting married. They would only insist on an abortion, anyway, or throw her out.

Tomas staggered from the table to go after her. What he would say, he didn't know. The yellow hair flying as she ran, the plain face hidden. He wanted to explain himself. He needed her to understand that he couldn't leave his father. He tripped over the table, picked himself up, weaved out of the cabin, but was intercepted by Ivan. *Go inside, Tomas,* his father said. *I will deal with this.*

Whatever he said persuaded Marta to let him help. Ivan drove her to the Udeghe village, where there were women willing to administer the herbs to cause miscarriage. The aborted foetus would be buried in the forest. No one would ever know.

Ivan commiserated with her, telling her Tomas was a forest man and she was better off with a city man who could give her what she wanted. He set her down a little way outside the village, for her to complete the journey alone, pressing notes into her hand.

On his return, Ivan smiled his heavenly smile and embraced his son. Tomas's head fell against his father's chest, and his father's heart beat against his cheek. Tomas may have wept – in fact, he was certain he wept – and his father held him throughout.

A few years after this, in 2000, Putin came to power, and Ivan was in the perfect place at the perfect time. The unbreakable team of father and son was on the rise. Even as Tomas spent each morning looking for Marta's form on the approach to the camp; even as he did not know what to do with her name, now that he could no longer utter it, but it remained on his tongue; even as an emptiness flowed into him that he could not identify, he did not question his decision. For, look what they had achieved.

But, now, the understanding of what he had lost blundered into him like a stranger falling through a blizzard.

Tomas never saw Marta again, though he heard she married a man who took her to the city, and maybe she had more children. Perhaps she laughed often and never thought of the forest, which is so without mercy that it will kill a beautiful thing on a beautiful day, and yet go on, indifferent. Ivan, though cruel, was right about his son. Tomas *was* a forest man. The taiga had given him a life. The taiga would not let him have another.

HE FOUND A ROCK and mounted it on the tiger cub's grave. The mound was so small. He took a photograph. He marked in his notebook where it was, its proximity to a huge cedar, its place beneath the trajectory of the sun.

Eighteen

TOMAS RETURNED TO THE Countess's tracks, stumbling through the deep snow in the direction of travel. It was time to find out where she and her remaining cub had gone. A storm was mounting, the sky had lowered and smashed plates of snow were winnowing down to the ground. The tracks were vanishing before his eyes, the great comet trails softening to nothing.

He coughed out gobbets of snow. Exhaustion dragged at his muscles. Tracking the Countess had become an impossible task. The deepening snow increased his gravity, slowed his movements to a mortifying suck through the white. No analysis was possible in the blizzard and soon he would lose his ability to find his way to shelter. He needed the sun, which had vanished, or the stars, if he could live through the night. He would soon be marooned in a deadly no-man's-land. This was not survival.

This was carelessness, of the kind he abhorred and, up to now, had skilfully avoided. On he persisted, imagining tracks where now there were none, on into virgin forest where he had never been before.

Beneath a huge yew, whose branches gave respite from the snow, he stopped and caught his breath. Tomas was deeply disorientated. Should he fire the rifle? It might scare tigers away, or it could let every creature know that he was here.

He cocked the rifle, peered through the burgeoning white. The snow tumbled in muffling layers, silencing history, possibility, intelligence itself. The only thing to do in such a storm was to find shelter and wait it out. But Tomas had missed that opportunity, the one that required him to turn sharply back to the bivouac site at the moment he found the cub, and now he was suspended out of time itself, trapped inside the white book as it turned its new blank page.

His inhalations tugged the downy snow into his mouth, freezing his tongue. Fumbling in his pockets, he pulled out a cigarette, flicking the old lighter that had been nearly empty for so long, whose tiny flame could put up no fight against the bitter wind. He crouched down to protect the flame, but it trembled and vanished.

Then, looking up in exhausted despair, he (definitely, *definitely*) saw a flash of orange. Breath snapped in his throat and he grabbed the rifle again. But the orange did not disappear; it was a glimmer through the trees. A squall of wind momentarily cleared a space in the sky, and he saw, he was sure, a swirl of black, faintly, like distant crows.

Fire.

There was a fire in the forest.

Flinging the sodden cigarette away, he headed upland towards the glimmer. It was as if a tiger had liquefied into the atmosphere itself. How could a fire have started in the middle of a freezing blizzard?

He bashed through bare saplings aggressive as spears. His legs were clogged with snow; he was wading through a frozen sea to reach a blazing land.

Now, he could hear it, the great gobble of the flames, the wind crying and the trunks screaming. The air blackened into smoke. Heat scowled through the snow.

A deer screeched past him. It was followed by other creatures dashing away from the inferno — a streak of wild boar, the russet flash of more deer. Where had these beasts come from? He saw the flames licking higher and higher up the trunks, taking hold, now, of the crown of, first, one tree, then the next, ignorant of the snow, the white simply fizzing away. Smoke pumped into the sky.

A ragged curtain of fire rippled across the slope. He stopped at the line beyond which he could not stand the heat, and peered through his hands. Could it be? Shimmering beyond the flames was a cabin! It had a wide clearing around it and was not on fire. But all it needed was a change in the direction of the wind and it would be engulfed.

Tomas pulled off his wool hat, drenched it in snow and held it over his face as he advanced. He tried to work out a route through the flames that would get him to the cabin. The line of the blaze seemed organised, as if the birch trees had been deliberately set alight. They would have gone up like flares, the flames leaping from crown to crown. His only route was to approach from the back.

Tomas gave the fire a wide berth, crashing through the dense brushwood. All the time, he was thinking of the inhabitant of the cabin – was it the woman? He burst through the undergrowth into smoky space and yelled, 'Is anyone here? Come out! Quickly!'

Ripping a hole in his hat, he drenched it again in snow and pulled it over his face. With the rifle, he spun left and right to cover himself as he backed towards the cabin. The rear of the building had no opening. He whacked the wall with the rifle and cried out again, 'Anyone there?'

When he peered round the corner of the cabin, he saw that the snow in front was black with blood and ash. In a red slick in the middle, the Countess lay sprawled, as if she had made a great leap. Tomas knew it was her, from the hours of footage he had watched. He lowered the rifle, dumbfounded to be this close to her. It was bewildering to see this immense creature – whose personality he knew, whose tracks he had followed, whose dimensions he could recite – right in front of him. She was a vast bloodied lump, ash dulling the glory of her coat.

Beneath her was a human form, barely visible. The stench of fresh blood overwhelmed him.

He could see almost nothing of the body, so thoroughly was it enveloped by the Countess. A leg stuck out, and, on the end of it, a boot. He knew instantly it was the author of those prints, seared upon his memory.

The Countess had been felled in mid-leap. Her great head was half shot off. Blood poured from another wound, but it was clear what had happened here. Someone had quite simply blown her brains out.

But how? Where was the gun, and how had she killed the woman, after this?

His skin prickled and he raised his eyes. Disappearing into the forest like a flash of embers – a cub. He would have doubted he had seen it, were it not for the brushwood swaying for a second afterwards.

'Drop your gun!' gasped a voice behind him. He heard a rifle click into life.

'Do it! Or I will kill you!'

Tomas flung his gun to the side and turned slowly round.

He raised his hands, coughing. The person edged forward.

He was astonished to see that it was a young girl. Though she was nearly as tall as him, her ash-smeared face had the softness of the very young, and he guessed she could be no more than ten years old. She was holding the rifle with an icy stillness that made him realise she was the architect of some, if not all of this, and might very well now kill him.

Nineteen

'I WANT ALL THIS PAINTED,' said Ivan, pointing at the cabins on the approach, and the *banya*. He had been unable to sleep and had gone out into the fiery cold of the dawn to walk the trail into the camp, and, looking at it with a visitor's eyes, he was appalled. It was not of a standard that the General could possibly endure. Paint peeled and faded beneath the harsh U.V. light, and had been patched with tar, or whatever other material was available, or just left bare. The corrugated iron roofs were rusted and bent beneath billows of snow. It did not look like a camp for tigers that Putin would want to fund, and that had to change immediately.

'What colour?' asked Petrov dully.

'We've only got black,' said Erik.

'Tomas has got the Hilux, boss, and, if we have to go to Khabarovsk for paint, that'll mean taking Petrov's shitty van, which will mean two days away.'

Ivan wasn't listening. He paced in front of the central cabin, rubbing his chin.

'And the shitters. The General can't crap there.'

'Where's he going to crap, then?'

'We'll have to build him his own. A good one. Painted. With a proper hole.'

Petrov raised his eyebrows. 'The ground's frozen, boss.'

Ivan turned on him in a rage. 'I don't care! Build a fucking fire on top and melt the ground. When the General is here, he is going to take a shit in a proper hole!'

The men did not reply, but looked sideways at each other.

Ivan strode round the edge of the cabin and turned back to the men. 'And another thing — no pissing against the cabins until he's been and gone. I'm sick of all this fucking yellow snow everywhere. I mean, it's twenty paces into the forest, so, if you really can't make it to the shitters, then go to the forest or piss your pants till he's been. We are not savages!' He marched into his cabin to check his emails.

Petrov sighed and took on the task of assigning the jobs. 'You and me on paint, Erik,' he said. 'The rest of you — the General's shitter.'

'Where does he want it, do you think?' Erik asked.

Petrov considered. 'Next to his cabin. When the General comes, he'll have the boss's cabin, I'm sure, and the boss will be bunking up with us.'

'Best not to ask him, anyway,' said Erik. 'Not the mood he's in.'

The men divided, and shuffled off to attend to the work.

How slow the laptop was, Ivan thought. It was agony checking his inbox several times a day. How he wished Tomas would return. Perhaps Tomas could improve the connection. He would certainly be good at the preparations. Increasingly, Ivan was spending his days checking the email for a reply, or the horizon for his son. Both were overdue.

Not that Ivan was worried. No, he wasn't worried, even though the route should have taken four days max, and Tomas had now been gone for seven, and the temperature every night was at least minus thirty degrees Celsius. He was annoyed, certainly, because he felt Tomas's absence in every practical way. As if it knew he was gone, the satellite dish had begun to play up, and the men got very restless if they had nothing to listen to. Ivan was keeping up with marking the latest tracks and kills on the map with the help of Petrov, who was, unfortunately, not very dextrous and his pen slipped as he made the marks (how can you slip, making a straight line against a *ruler?*), and he breathed heavily while he was concentrating, perhaps the beginnings of emphysema, and he found endless excuses to go and have a cigarette, and, basically, he sat there making a stellar job of not being Tomas, until Ivan thought he would scream.

No one suggested sending out a search party. No one

complained about the lack of reception. Erik had started to preface some statements with, *When Tomas is back*, or, *That's something for Tomas*. But things happened in the forest – in fact, it was the one thing that could be relied upon, that something would happen – and, in a life that did not include mobile phone reception, expectations of what would happen when, of punctuality, and of time itself were necessarily elastic.

No one was going to say anything until Ivan said something, and Ivan had decided – here, he banged the table next to the laptop as the connection whirred helplessly: 'Come ON!' – that he would not become concerned until two weeks had passed. At that moment, the connection died completely. Ivan stared aghast at the frozen screen. His concern for Tomas was suddenly promoted. He would send out a party in two days, if Tomas had not reappeared. This gave time for the paint trip to Khabarovsk, the new shitter and at least a start on the decorations.

There was, if he had been going to think about this, which he was not, a standard list of dangers which could afflict the hunter, alone, in the winter forest. These were: injury; getting lost; cold; tigers. Probably, these should have been in the opposite order, but Ivan did not like to think about tiger attacks. A tiger attack was terrible on a host of levels, that went far beyond the multifaceted tragedy of losing his only son.

There was no reason for a tiger to attack his son, except that it was the hardest winter there had been for a long time. Deer and boar had vanished from the forest within range of the camp. Tomas would be deep in the remote areas where the Countess would be hunting.

Ivan looked out of the window to where Erik and the other men were lighting a fire to melt the ground so that a hole could be dug. Ice crystals, which coated the windows in brand-new patterns every morning, were starting to fray a little, creating a lacy border around the scene. The men had got over their reluctance, as they always did, and were laughing as they worked. A thought occurred to Ivan, and he pulled on his coat and went out.

'Make sure it faces that way.' He pointed. 'I want the General to be able to see the bird table.' The men nodded.

Erik was on cooking duty, and it was a fourth consecutive day of the army soup, *balanda*, that was his specialty – and which definitely, this time, contained squirrel – that finally caused Petrov, hungry and weary from the long round trip to Khabarovsk, to burst out, 'Where is Tomas, boss?'

Ivan slurped his soup, making an involuntary wince as the fatty strings of rodent writhed down his throat. 'I think we could do with a hunting party,' he announced. 'I'm putting one together in the morning. Will you be on it, Petrov?'

'Of course.'

'And the party will head out into the primary forest, along Tomas's route. That way, you will meet each other quickly.

Some of you must stay to get things ready for the General, who could arrive at any moment. So let's decide in the morning.'

AS THE MORNING OF the tenth day since Tomas had left dawned, Ivan looked up from where he had been photographing the ice crystals on the window, unable to concentrate on anything else, and saw that the men had finished the General's toilet. It was a triumph: large, solid, painted yellow, with a glittering new corrugated-iron roof.

It smelled of new wood. It had a ceramic door handle, purloined from some kind of dish, and a tiny window facing the bird table. Ivan pulled the door open. A planed bench with a smooth hole greeted him, and, best of all, beneath the bench, a hole so deep he could not see the bottom. There was a toilet roll in one of the dispensers he had invented – half a plastic bottle, the paper pulled through the neck. Ivan felt quite emotional at the genuine care that had gone into the shitter. He doubted that the General would have a better experience in the Kremlin itself. And when the General had gone, it would be a pleasure to use it himself.

Shaking his head with the thought that these men continued to surprise him, that they were true comrades, he made his way back into his cabin, but was halted by headlights dazzling through the thin dawn.

It was the Hilux, bouncing up the track from the forest. Ivan stared, then hobbled towards it, peering into the gloom.

For, next to Tomas, on the passenger seat, was . . . a girl.

And there was some kind of crate or box on the back, covered in canvas.

He did not run down to greet his son, only stood, clearly visible. He was furious. And so glad, he could, if he were another man, in another country, have wept.

This was the only road into the camp, and by this route everyone had always arrived, like Marta, all those years ago, and like Ivan himself. A rare thrill in this isolated life was the approach of strangers or loved ones, or being that stranger emerging from the trees.

The truck swept into the yard, and out leapt Tomas. He was etched with filth and soot, splashed with blood, and stubble covered his face where the moustache did not reach. Without acknowledging his father, or the men, he went round the side of the vehicle and yanked open the door, helping out what was – it was now apparent, by the youth of her face and the flatness of her body – a child.

Tomas held the girl by her shoulder. She hung away from him.

'Everybody, this is Zina,' he said.

Zina stared round her. Though the whites of her eyes were visible, there was no fear, only a restless scanning for movement. Her upper lip was curled over her top teeth, in a snarl.

The men moved forward, transfixed, unsure how to react to this personage, who was clearly a child, but so tall and unrepentant that she inspired unease. Like Tomas, she too was bloodstained, and every fold of her skin, hair and clothes engrained with dirt and ash.

Ivan cleared his throat. 'Why is she here, Tomas?'

'I found her in the forest. She's been living there. She won't tell me how long.'

Ivan stepped forward, looked into the girl's face. 'What is your father's name?'

No reply.

'Your mother's name?'

A growl came from beneath the canvas and Ivan spun round.

'What the fuck is that?' he asked, striding round to the side of the truck and pulling at the tarp covering the crate beneath.

'Petrov! Erik!' Ivan called the men over to help him get the canvas off.

From inside the crate came a scrabbling sound, and then a roar shook the Hilux. Tomas felt his scalp tighten, and fear bolt up his spine. A tiger's roar at close range can paralyse a creature with terror. This was only a cub; nevertheless, she was so close and so urgent that the men all took a step back – except Ivan, who circled the truck.

'A tiger? A fucking tiger?' He stared at his son.

'It's a cub.' Fatigue was swallowing him, legs first, its swampy gape about his throat now. 'We need to use the dog pen. Petrov – get the dogs out.'

'But what the fuck have you done, Tomas?'

Tomas shook his head. 'I can't explain now. We have to get this cub into the pen. She's got a leg injury. Petrov!'

Petrov sparked into life and he and Erik went to clear the dogs out of their enclosure. They whined and scraped at the fence, already terrified. As soon as the gate was opened, they fled into the forest and barked hysterically from a safe distance. Hastily, Petrov scraped the bedding out from inside, laid some dried birch bark and brushwood down.

The others carefully lifted off the crate and apprehensively carried it into the pen. Growling and hissing emanated from inside. Petrov cut the ropes and swiftly stepped back, pulling the iron gate closed behind him. The cub sprang out, leaping round the few square metres of the pen, holding her injured leg off the ground. She was fantastical against the dull wooden frame and steel mesh. Already her muscles were defined beneath her coat. She covered the space inside the pen in a couple of paces, even with her limp.

Petrov and Erik swiftly inspected the pen for any weaknesses. Dogs were not inclined to escape, but a hefty young tigress was. Tomas pointed out a few places that needed reinforcement, and the men set to work with nails and soldering iron. All this was done quickly, without explanation. Men in the forest knew to deal with the crisis first, await explanation later. But, as they worked,

Petrov and Erik glanced, awed, into the cage. They had never been this close to a tiger in the flesh, and it was inexplicable to have got out of bed and, five minutes later, be securing such a beast in a pen.

Though the cub had travelled, immobile, for three days and was weak, this only increased her fury. She drew back her lips and hissed, exuding all the menace of a much larger tiger.

Ivan stared, dumbfounded, longing for a way to silence her. There was a logging settlement a few kilometres away that, conceivably, might hear.

Like the tiger, the girl was checking her surroundings for a means of escape. She blinked slowly, taking in the various buildings, the open areas between them. Her gaze settled on the men themselves and she frowned, as if overwhelmed at the sheer number of them. Just when it looked like she might bolt for the trees at the back, Tomas grabbed her arm.

'Come on, we've been through this,' he said. 'No one is going to hurt you.'

It didn't look good, half dragging a young girl into the kitchen's steam, pressing her into a chair. Ivan gawped from the doorway as Tomas swiftly fried eggs. Zina sat in paralysed alarm, her big amber eyes roving round the kitchen.

'Tomas, what happened?' said Ivan.

'The Countess killed the girl's mother,' said Tomas. 'I got there too late.'

'And is the Countess . . . dead?' asked Ivan, already knowing the answer.

Tomas nodded.

'Dammit!' Ivan hit the doorframe with his fist. The girl sprang away in alarm, and Tomas eased her back into her seat.

'What about the other cub?' Ivan asked.

Tomas scooped the eggs into a bowl, cut some chunks of bread. 'Dead,' he said.

'Oh my God. A woman and two tigers, dead? And a cub captured? The General is coming! Any minute!' He watched his son's back moving round the room. 'We'll be ruined.'

'Calm down, Dad. The girl has just lost her mother.'

Ivan's attention was swallowed up by his son, and the disaster he had brought home.

'The girl's mother shot the Countess. Trying to defend herself. She managed it, too, but it was too late for her. The other cub, a male, died of starvation. I brought the surviving one and the girl back. What else could I do?'

Ivan could not compute this information. He turned to the girl, who met his gaze emptily.

'Where is your father?'

Zina said nothing.

Petrov and Erik huddled in the doorway, staring. Ivan shooed them away.

'So, Tomas. The bodies. You left them?'

'Burned them.' Tomas placed a bowl of eggs and bread on

the table in front of the girl. She looked at it listlessly. 'You have to eat,' he said.

Zina fixed him with her large amber eyes. 'No,' she said.

'Who are you, girl?' Ivan cried, and Zina shrank back in her chair.

'Stop it, Dad! She's frightened, can't you see?'

Ivan pushed back from the table and slammed out.

'Don't mind him, Zina. He's worried about the tiger and about you. Eat the eggs. Please.'

Reluctantly, she pulled the bowl to herself and scooped the eggs into her mouth. They were gone in an instant.

Then she said, 'When are you sending me back into the forest?'

Tomas sipped his astringent coffee and shook his head. 'I think your days of being in the forest are over.'

Twenty

A FEW HOURS LATER, TOMAS burst from the cabin, screaming Zina's name. It was incomprehensible that she had gone. She had seemed to accept how things were, even giving him a small smile when he showed her the drawer he had cleared out for her. She said she was tired, so he had left her alone in his cabin to sleep. How stupid of him. When he checked on her a little later, the bed was empty.

Grabbing his rifle, he circled the camp to find her departure point. She had stuck to trodden areas within the camp, so there was no track for him to follow.

'No . . . No . . .' Pure panic bubbled from his lips as he ran up and down like a dog, searching for her entry point into the forest, his rifle battering his shoulder. Never had he longed to see a track so much in all his life. Never had he wanted something so much.

How far could she have got? The thin winter light was fading, and already it was harder to discern anything in the snow. Remorselessly, he searched, almost on all fours. He wouldn't have it. He wouldn't have her go.

At last, a short scamper of tracks taking an unexpected direction away into the forest. The tracks darted round the trees, taking tiger-like leaps over logs to break the trail. The light was so poor, he had to keep stopping to check, wasting valuable seconds. Air shivered over him; life was draining from the day. It was impossible that Zina could survive a night out here without shelter. For that matter, nor could he. Tomas had run out without his coat or his hat or his gloves, and now the cold attacked his fingers, his ears, his eyeballs.

'Zina!' The name clanged through the trees, its edge of anger shattered, leaving only desperation. He knew his voice would make her run away faster, but he could not help it. He had just got used to saying the name; he had just got used to having that word in his life. He could do nothing but scream it and hope that she would understand, and stop.

The tracks vanished. 'Zina! It's all right!' he cried helplessly. The problem was that she was more taiga person than he was. She was a huntress better than any of them; she was a forest spirit, easily able to outwit and outrun him. Perhaps she was, at this moment, watching his blundering uselessness, like a tiger. All he had in his favour was his desperate need to find her, that could not countenance failure.

He tried to think how she would think – for this, in the end, is how the best hunter, tiger or man, successfully catches its prey. Where would she think to head to? He imagined her, the tangled vines of hair swaying round the long face, the strong arms reaching ahead and tearing brush from her way. The amber eyes drilling ahead.

Her only thought would be to *get away*.

She would not be thinking of surviving the night, or finding food – that comes later. Like a fleeing sika deer – or any creature, mad with terror and loss – the only thought would be breaking the trail to escape immediate danger. Only then would she stop, panting, and realise that she was alone, without food or shelter, in the deep of the night.

Suddenly, Tomas knew. He must forget following tracks. He would never catch her if he attempted to follow this dance of prints, all made to delay him.

The decision calmed him, and he began to tread with certainty. Some distance from here, the forest thickened and the trees were full of bear nests. She would attempt to leave the trackable forest completely; he imagined her climbing one of the great oaks or limes and then curling invisibly, like a bear. She would let him wear himself out searching the wrong dimension, while the cold made her drowsy and she thought of her mother and rubbed her lynx-claw necklace for comfort.

The moon blazed through the trees. His ears strained for her. Nothing. He pressed on, even though, if he was wrong, he would certainly have lost her. On and on he went, with nothing to guide him but intuition and conviction about how her child's mind would work. How frightened she must be. How lonely.

Ahead of him, a branch cracked. He froze, raising the rifle as a shadow flashed through the trees.

'Zina!' He broke into a grinding run, the trees impossibly close, so that he bumped and scratched himself. He could not be certain it was her, but if it was not, and was a tiger instead, he decided he was ready to face it. But he needed it to be Zina and he pushed on, blood booming in his temples.

The shadow crumpled, flickered back up, switching direction to risk the illumination of the frozen river.

This is what a forest creature would do. If you could run fast, it was worth being visible for the clear access of the frozen surface. 'That's it, Zina!' he breathed to himself.

As she stepped on to the ice he saw that it was her, a tall, beautiful shadow on a brilliant canvas.

The river had a covering of snow over its icy surface, which gave her grip as she ran. He was behind her, now, gaining. 'Zina!' he gasped, but she ignored him, throwing herself into her clumsy stride. The ice creaked beneath their feet.

Only when he was a few metres behind did she turn to look, her face a sheet of fear.

'No!' she cried, zigzagging to escape him.

Tomas saw what he must do. Tossing the rifle to one side, he leapt for her, a great stride and bounce that he did not know he was capable of, that flung him with back-breaking force on to the ice. Somehow, his hands found her ankles and gripped them tightly.

Down she plummeted, crying out in grief. 'No, no, no!'

He clambered up her body, turning her over, so that he had her pinned beneath him.

'Zina, please, it's all right. I won't hurt you.'

'Let me go!' She squirmed and kicked. She was muscly as a snake.

Tears poured down his face as his full weight stilled her arms. 'I can't, Zina. I can't let you go.'

'Mummy! I want my mummy!' A great wail escaped her and she sobbed on the ice, the big pale face contorted.

'I know, I know.' He fell on the flat chest, in which the child heart banged.

'What do you want with me?'

Tomas's answer, almost impossible to articulate, struggled from somewhere deep. Afraid of crushing her, he eased off, and pulled her to him, trying to share his meagre body heat.

'You're just a little girl,' he said. 'And you're mine.'

Twenty-one

IVAN SAT IMMOBILE WHILE his emails loaded. Then, all the breath seemed to exit his body in one go.

'Next week!' he whispered, pointing.

The General would stay for two nights. He would like to track the tigers and discuss the programme, so that he could *compile his report*.

The blood drained from Ivan's normally ruddy cheeks. 'What are we going to do?'

'I will ring the Rehabilitation Centre,' said Tomas. 'They will take the cub.' Two hours' drive away, there was a clearing on a slope, with a tiny signal – enough to support a text or crackly phone call. The reserve had a single mobile phone, in a drawer – a flip phone, long out of general use. This was how phone calls were made, and consequently they were made only in cases of absolute emergency.

'How can we do that?' Ivan asked desperately. 'They will ask why we have a cub. And where is its mother? And on and on. Take it back to where you found it and let it go.'

'I can't believe you're suggesting that.'

Ivan rubbed his eyes. 'Tomas, you have fucked up so badly, I can hardly look at you. I sent you out for some footage. Footage! How could you do this to me? You knew the General was coming. Everything I have is in this reserve. If we are stopped, or starved of cash, it's not just the tigers that suffer – it's us. All of us – the men, too.' He shuddered in disbelief. 'All I can think of is that you did this on purpose. Trying to ruin me.'

Rage, which Tomas had known so intimately for so many years when he was drinking, began to swell in his gut.

'I fucked up? You're only here on this reserve because of me. You sit there behind your desk like a fucking giant tick, sucking the life out of me. All you care about is yourself.'

He had never talked to his father this way. He was not trying to please him. This was what hate must feel like.

'Tomas,' said his father, calmly and coldly, in a way that would normally have stilled his son. 'One day, you will need to grasp the bigger picture. We have twenty tigers who use this reserve. Or we did, until this disaster. I can't allow this – this *development*, this stupid dead woman in the forest, who clearly distracted you from the task in hand – to destroy the bigger picture. If I am not here, it will be loggers here. You know this is true. Take the cub into the forest and either let it go, or shoot it.'

'And what about the girl? I shoot her too?'

Ivan rolled his eyes. 'I don't know what to do about her. But she's not staying here, and that's a fact.'

Tomas leant over the desk, his knuckles whitening. 'You're wrong,' he hissed. 'I understand the big picture perfectly. The big picture is that you took advantage of me.' He reached out and grabbed his father's hair, twisting it, so that Ivan winced. It was frail, spidery hair now, and threads of it drifted on to Tomas's sleeve. He pulled his father's face close to him. 'I was stupid, I was a drunk. Back then. I let you manipulate me. I could have had a wife and a family, but you tricked me out of it. All these years, all I've had is *you*.'

'What are you talking about?' cried Ivan.

'You stood at that window, with your fucking old man poster and your beetles in their case, and you turned to me, and you scared me to fucking death, just like you always have. I *loved* Marta. I wanted that baby. Instead, I made her have an abortion. I fucking hate you.'

'Tomas, calm yourself. You may regret your decision, but the fact remains you made it. That's what makes a man, for God's sake! Standing by your decisions! Not this pathetic shit, blaming your father. If you'd wanted a wife and a baby and a flat in fucking Khabarovsk, you'd have done it. My only fault, Tomas, is that I know you. I'm your father and I know your heart. You love the forest. You never wanted to leave. I just gave you the excuse you needed.'

Tomas yelled in frustration and twisted his father's hair harder. 'I should fucking kill you. It's the only way I'll be rid of you.'

It was always dangerous to leave a beast – any beast – with nothing to lose. Gathering all his mental resources, Ivan said quietly, 'Tomas . . . please. I'm sorry. I shouldn't have said that. I see I hurt you, back then – though, I didn't mean to. But that is in the past. We have to think of now. Look at what we've made! We're so close to massive success.' Tears welled in his eyes. 'Everything we've worked for. The fucking General. Please.'

Tomas leant in closer. 'I am *not* shooting this tiger, and the girl is staying here. I am going to ring the Rehabilitation Centre. We are going to do the right fucking thing. Or I am. And if you get in the way, I will email the General myself and tell him what a lying cunt you are.'

Ivan's jaw fell open. He managed to nod, too shocked to speak. Tomas let him go and Ivan sat back, rubbing the spot on his head. Regarding his son cautiously, he said, 'Thinking about it . . . yes. Of course. We need to follow the protocols. To be a proper reserve, we need to follow protocols, have standards. I was making a start, out there, with the General's shitter!' He grinned weakly. 'How about this: as the reserve owner, I will deal with the Rehabilitation Centre. I will ring them myself. No emails, at this stage. I don't want things in writing, just now.' He looked at Tomas reproachfully. 'Perhaps I can make this reflect well on us. I don't know how yet, but . . . if you will let me handle the tiger with them, in my own way, let's agree that the girl stays here, with us. Okay? We will pass her off as a relation. Okay?' Tomas said nothing, and Ivan carried swiftly on. 'Tomas, do we have a deal?' He put out his hand.

The waning adrenaline left Tomas worn out. Worries about Zina swamped him. She had fainted when they returned, and needed to be watched over. He had put her in his bed to sleep, posting Erik and Petrov to guard her. Without vodka to fuel him, his rage became sadness and confusion. He shook his father's hand briefly and left the room.

Zina was fast asleep when he let himself into the room. Her tangled hair was spread out round her. He leant over and examined her face by the dim light. It had a rather feverish sheen, he thought, which was not surprising, after all she had been through. But her breathing seemed peaceful. Standing back to survey the scene, Tomas was glad he had not ripped Hugh Grant out of the poster above the bed, for the two actors looked kindly and happy, sort of like parents.

The bedroom needed one other adornment. Tomas went to a drawer and brought out, from beneath his sweaters, Marta's mirror. He breathed on its smeared surface and rubbed it with his cuff. The face which looked back at him, finally, did not displease him. It had purpose. It was the face of a man who was going to make things better than they were before. He propped the mirror on the cabinet by the bed. The space looked decorated now, suitable for a young girl. On his way out, Tomas

said to Erik and Petrov, 'That poster stays where it is. And . . .
no . . . looking.'

'Where are we supposed to sleep, then?'

'My father's cabin. I'll get you set up tonight. I'm sleeping
here, in the kitchen.'

Outside the Hilux revved. Headlights sliced through the
room as Ivan reversed out and drove off, into the forest.

'Don't worry about him. Come on,' said Tomas, and he led
the men to the cabin, where they made up beds for themselves
and shared a joke.

Ivan drove the two jolting hours to the signal site. Once
there, he cut the engine and rang the man he knew, who knew
a man in Vladivostok, who knew a dealer in exotic animals.
The dealer would come quickly for a tiger and would ask no
questions.

Twenty-two

THE DEALER'S TRUCK PROWLED up the camp access
road, a little before three o'clock in the morning. Ivan
was awake and waiting, as he had been for the last two nights,
nurturing the impossible hope that a tiger could be transported
from the camp without waking anyone. Emerging from the
van, the dealer resembled no one so much as the old man of the
forest in Ivan's poster, right down to his large graceful hands
and benign stoop. He had a sad expression and a silver beard,
and the watchful movements of a man used to subterfuge. A
wispy halo of hair glittered round his scalp. He climbed out of
the van and shook Ivan's hand, introducing himself as Oleg, and
then his assistant, a solid, barrel-chested woman in a balaclava,
as Nelly. 'My wife,' Oleg added, proudly.

The cub was pacing in the pen, as she did all day and night,
barely resting. Oleg shone his torch down her sinuous body and

spoke quietly to Nelly. Painted lips shone through the hole in the balaclava as Nelly responded in a high-speed whisper. Oleg nodded and returned to the truck, taking a tranquilliser gun from the back. He screwed a vial of something into the barrel and, while Nelly shone the torch, Oleg traced the cub's movement through the sight. Then, casually, he shot a dart into her flank. With an outraged yowl, the tiger bucked in the air. She hissed at them all and threw herself at the mesh, before tearing round the pen, collapsing after a few staggering circuits.

Ivan bit his lip. He glanced round to see if lights had come on.

Oleg and Nelly had the efficiency of butchers. Oleg prodded the cub, through the mesh, with a broom handle, to be sure she was unconscious, then, swiftly, he and Nelly let themselves into the pen and tied the tiger's legs together. Nelly brought a stretcher from the truck, and the two of them rolled the cub on to it. They staggered comically with the overflowing tiger to the back of the truck. A large crate was on the back and Oleg let down a ramp, then husband and wife dragged the lolling beast up the ramp, into the crate. The whole operation took less than twenty minutes, and all through it Oleg remained unperturbed. From a compartment in the front of the truck, he brought out a packet, which he handed to Ivan. It crackled like frost. By now, Nelly had secured the crate, fixed canvas to cover it, and was in the passenger seat, impassive as a stack of coats.

'No!' screamed Zina, running towards them, her face white in the moonlight.

The truck revved and spun away, down the track. Oleg was used to these messy conclusions and was always prepared to make a swift exit.

Tomas appeared after her, pulling on his coat. 'What the hell is going on?' he asked. He saw his father tucking the packet into his jacket and grabbed it from him. It was a stack of roubles.

Zina flew to the pen, searching it pointlessly, wailing into the darkness. Tomas stared at his father. 'What have you done?' he whispered.

THAT WAS SIX WEEKS ago. Now, Ivan was making his way slowly through the darkness in Petrov's van. The vehicle whined and shook, like a dog being dragged where it did not want to go. The Hilux was gone, along with his son and the girl. A winter's worth of snow towered on each side; very soon it would start to melt into torrents, as spring arrived. Ivan was travelling to the signal point. He made this journey most nights, now – now that Tomas and Zina had gone and he could not sleep at all.

In scenes too terrible to remember, Tomas had demanded the number of the contact, to trace the dealer. Ivan had given it to him, but of course it would not help his son. Ivan himself did not know who the dealer was, and the whole arrangement had been done at several removes. The little girl had wept and wept. This had disturbed Ivan. He did not know what to do with her grief. He did not understand its vehemence. He was both irritated and helpless before it.

The signal bars suddenly appeared at last on the phone's screen, and Ivan halted the truck. He rang his son, as he did almost every day. The call was never answered. Sometimes, he would leave messages. He said, *I did it for the best.* Or, *I meant well.* Or, *Call me, son. Leave me a message that I can pick up, here, tonight.* He sent texts. *How is Zina? Tell Zina this is her home.* There was never a reply, but Ivan was an optimistic man, and he came to the signal spot hopeful, every time. It was unimaginable that this rift could be permanent.

Surely Tomas understood why he did as he did? The General. The reserve.

The following week, the General had come, as planned. He found the camp organised and tidy, and appeared delighted by his private latrine. Ivan deluged him with old footage of the Countess and new footage of other tigers from the camera traps. He had sent Erik round the nearer traps, and they had provided impressive footage of other animals: a snorting huddle of boar, a lone sika deer standing, poised, in the moonlight, her eyes glowing like pearls.

The General was awed by all he saw and seized the opportunity to go tracking with Petrov. Petrov reported that he had taken notes of everything he had been shown. When they returned in the evening, the General enjoyed Ivan's tales of tigers, drank prodigiously and was gloriously indiscreet about

Putin's idiosyncrasies. 'That fucking Japanese dog of his,' he said. 'It has to come in the boat when we're fishing! It's huge now and he won't leave it with anyone! And it bites everyone, and steals the fish. "Mr President," I tell him, "this is not good for your image, for the world to see. The father of Russia, with his magnificent chest, pulling a two-metre pike from the river, with a fucking dog licking its balls in the background!"' The General wheezed with laughter. 'And he says to me, "Constantin, we are brothers, we are comrades, but if you ever refer to my Yume as a fucking dog again, I will kill you."'

The General laughed so much at this remembered threat on his life that it turned into a coughing fit. Ivan poured him another drink and laughed along.

'The President has a tremendous sense of humour,' said the General.

'You can definitely tell that,' said Ivan. 'From the photographs.' Changing the subject, he went on, 'The fishing in the Amur is unparalleled. And we also have some smaller places, only I know. Sturgeon, pike, we have them all. Next time you come, we will go. And if the President would like to come as well—'

The General had already moved on, remembering aloud other fishing trips, and the conversation turned to great fish both men had caught, and, later, an elk the General had shot.

It was a successful evening, and the General remained unaware of the yawning void in Ivan, caused by Tomas's leaving, two days before, taking the girl, and the Hilux, and the tiger money, and the number of the friend.

His fruitless calls made, it was time to return. Where the trail widened, he turned Petrov's van and rumbled back towards the camp.

The headlights of the truck speared the darkness. The ancient chassis rocked.

Then, a pair of eyes, ablaze in the lights. Ivan cut the engine, leaving just the lamps on.

In the middle of the trail, barely twenty metres away, two tigers were mating.

Though he spent his life documenting the lives of the tigers on his reserve, Ivan had never seen one outside a camera trap or a cage.

And no one at all had ever seen this.

He hadn't brought his camera. There would be no proof of what he had seen. He peered carefully at the tigers, trying to see which ones they were. The male was almost fully grown, unfamiliar. The female had a band of black across her forehead which marked her out as Lady, the Countess's sister – who, now the Countess was gone, might well have an improvement in her fortunes.

It was miraculous that, being discovered, they did not bound away. Except, as Ivan knew, or thought he knew, the tigers owned the forest. This, and every road, was theirs, and if they chose to mate in the middle of it, everyone would have to wait. The male bit the female's nape. The female clawed at the snow and yowled. It was a chilling, fairy-tale sound, which pinned Ivan to his seat.

An understanding ascended from his gut to his now-watering eyes, that this was the most majestic thing he had witnessed in his life, except for that day when his son was born, when, appalled and mesmerised, he watched a new life tear itself free of flesh and give its cry into the sky.

The female turned her head slowly, like a machine, and stared down the beams into the car. Her cavernous mouth opened in a roar. He could see the black of her throat, like a tunnel into the beginning of time itself. He could almost feel the burn of her breath. Inside the roar, he heard the shrieks of animals fleeing for their lives.

He turned off the lights and sat trembling in the seat. Then the tigers separated and leapt away, capes of darkness crushed with stars.

Ivan's heart jumped in his chest. Sweat beaded on his palms. He felt his own insignificance and his own weakness, and he was sorry. He was so sorry.

He had stolen Tomas's chance of a bigger life. He had held him back, all these years. From the first bloodied moment of his birth, Tomas was the most beautiful creature Ivan had ever seen. Ivan could not say he had not meant to keep the boy down, and close, for he had, but he was sorry for it, now. In the end such efforts were futile anyway: nature had a majestic force in one direction only – the future.

Ivan tossed the phone on to the passenger seat. What was needed, here, was not an old man's sentimentality. The van ground purposefully through the ruts towards home. When he got back, Ivan would begin the process of making the camp the diamond in the centre of Russia's tiger conservation efforts – and he would make his son the director. It was time he stepped back. It was time he marvelled at his son's brilliance with the forest, his boundless love for the life within it. Tomas was the only person on earth who would understand the vision Ivan had just witnessed, who would crave the telling and the retelling, who knew and loved the tigers as Ivan did. It was time for Tomas to take over, and lead the reserve into the future.

Part Three

EDIT

Twenty-three

THE FIRST TIME EDIT saw a tiger, she saw it die. She
had witnessed both dying and death before, and even
her own mother's corpse, briefly, before they whisked it away
beneath a shroud. A village life, isolated from the modern world,
meant that she regularly witnessed suffering and slow death
in animals trapped or shot for food, and in people injured or
sick and beyond reach of medical treatment. But none of this
prepared her for the sight of a captured wild tiger, hobbled and
jolting like a felled log on the back of the truck sweeping into
the village that day.

It was as if all the Udeghe stories of her childhood – the
songs and prayers she knew by heart, her mother's voice itself
– had become flesh and were about to be murdered before her
eyes. She was not alone in turning away with a great moan as
the truck screamed to a halt in the snow and the dogs leapt

from the back seat as if there was a fire. Even a tiger half-dead will terrify a dog. Edit retched all over her hands. The tiger's stripes glittered with blood. It was a young tigress and Edit could not understand why the clouds did not break apart and send lightning to burn them all up.

Her father fell out of the truck, flanked by Dmitry and Valery, two Russian hunters. Dmitry slapped him on the back and passed him a bottle of vodka. Edit's father was a well-known tracker, the best, and they had pressed him to help them find this beast, which was prowling too close to the village at night and had reportedly stolen a dog. It was a maneater, that was for sure, just waiting to happen. That's what Dmitry had said. It justified it, really — the capture. Soon, the fur would find its way into a rich man's house in the Party, and its bones and — had it been a male — its penis to China.

Valery held back a little, his eyes casting about apprehensively for Edit. Events had spiralled out of control and he knew that this spectacle was going to have a devastating effect on his chances. Valery was young and new to this region, having, like many others, drifted away from his army border posting that no one was backing up. You could lose yourself in the Far East throughout the 1990s. It was full of AWOL soldiers, as well as the unemployed from the mines and the factories, and the opportunists drawn by stories of the tigers — how, if you could kill just one, you'd be rich. In his case, he couldn't go back to anywhere, being a deserter. So why not stay, find a way to survive in the forest, this task made a little easier by the knowledge of all the game to hunt – and the Udeghe village, with its girls.

He admired Edit, with her frizz of black-brown hair and cheekbones that gleamed like polished maple. She had thick eyebrows, almost meeting in the middle, and she reminded him a little of his mother – a slim, angry farmer's wife. He'd wanted to touch her from the day he first saw her. He stared at her when he came to the village to drink and barter, and tried to communicate with his eyes how much he wanted her. Wasn't that how it was done? Wasn't that how a man told a girl that he wanted her?

Sometimes, during these staring sessions, he forgot himself and his eyes drifted to her form beneath the simple felt, with its attempt at feminine decoration round the neck. She frowned in confusion, confounding his view that the village girls were supposed to be warm and natural, tuned into his staring. He tried talking to her instead, clearing his throat as she passed, commenting on the state of the snow and the prospects for hunting. It was an attempt to reel her in from behind her startled gaze. He moved carefully towards her, talking gently, without ceasing, like a kind of charm. Unlike many other Russians now populating this forsaken corner of Russia, Valery had managed to finish school. He could present himself as a man of the world. All the way from the Black Sea he had come. He blurred the bit about being AWOL; he was a mercenary, he said, who had fallen in love with the forest.

It was Dmitry who had finally intervened to say that this was not the way to get Edit, and that, really, these girls were there for the taking. They were just village girls. He shouldn't take too long, or someone else would have her. 'And these native girls, they are beautiful until they turn twenty-five, and then . . . their animal nature takes over. They get ugly and practical, and, if you're not careful, you may have married her!' Dmitry, a long-sacked brewery worker from the decimated town further down the coast, was obsessed with bagging the king tiger, whose enormous fur and body parts would, he said, make him the wealthiest man in the Far East. He had latched on to the young Valery as someone who could applaud and help him in this mission; in return, Valery benefitted from his advice. When they were drinking in the village, Dmitry's glassy expression would turn both sad and ruthless as he whispered to Valery, 'You stick with me, lad. This forest is overflowing with tigers. We'll get the biggest of the lot, and you'll have so much money, every girl in this village will be begging you to screw her.'

The wintry sun caught the blood on the tiger's fangs as her mouth lolled open. There were ropes around her neck. This was how they caught tigers, back then: a good tracker to piece together the trail, and dogs to run ahead, and finally the tiger, moving away from the hunting party to a spot where snares or traps had been laid, where it would be disabled by a snare around the paw or the neck, or a steel trap around a leg. In later years, it was often a rifle snare, where a tripwire would trigger a gun to fire bullets, ripping a great hole somewhere in the tiger's body. The hunting party would catch up, aided by the expert tracker, and the job would not be over by any means, for a trapped tiger was the most deadly of all; it was possessed of supernatural strength, and never, ever gave in. Some tigers could absorb more bullets than the hunters would even have, so then the nooses would be brought out, and a man each side would strangle the beast between them, hitting it with rifle butts, stabbing it with their knives.

Dmitry and Valery lifted the tigress down and, in an appalling act of tenderness, they set her gently on her feet and led her, staggering, a man each side, to the centre of the village. Valery was overcome by shame. He hadn't envisaged this conclusion to his first successful tiger hunt. He knew that the Udeghes, or what was left of them, still revered the tiger. He did not even have to know their traditions to read the horror on their faces. And Edit – Edit! Hands over her mouth, her eyes wide, her gaze fell on him. What was it? Hatred? Contempt?

He had imagined, in so far as he had thought ahead at all, that, if they presented the village with a *dead* tiger, one that had been troubling them, and promised them a cut of the profits, they – that is, *Edit* – would be grateful. Perhaps even impressed. It was Dmitry who had taken the whole venture to a different level, seeking now to humiliate the beast. All the way back, in the truck, Dmitry had complained, in between drinking bouts, that the tigress was small and, in many ways, worthless, and sharing the profits three ways made the whole scheme a waste of time. 'I want that fucking king tiger!' he repeated, banging the dashboard with his fist. The tigress's value for Dmitry, now, was in the spectacle he could create for the villagers. A threat disguised as a good turn. Heavy with mortification, Valery put his head down and simply kept walking, waiting for Dmitry's show of strength to be over.

The tiger growled, pulling her lips back over her bloody teeth. By now, everyone in the village had poured out, silently, to see. Dmitry, actually a popular man, who sold them cheap cigarettes, called out, 'We've got it – the tiger that's been terrorising you. We're protecting you and your village.'

Edit's father slipped away through the crowd, his head in his hands. Edit was going to go after him, but was transfixed by this explosion that was taking place between the spirit and animal world. Though this was the first tiger she had seen in the flesh, tigers were not just dreams and stories: like the bears, they lived alongside the people in the forest, and their tracks were a common sight. Tigers were no longer openly considered sacred, because shamanism was officially dead now in Russia, but everyone knew, in their blood, that it was a catastrophe to kill a tiger. It was a misfortune even to *see* a tiger. It was only with Edit's grandfather, the last shaman, that they stopped laying offerings for the Lord of the Forest. Edit remembered this ritual as a dream fragment: the pyre of leaves, the haunch of a deer, or a hazel grouse, on top.

The old women were hiding their eyes and turning away, for

the sight of a god of the forest so brought down was, though they could not say so openly, a damnation. Who had told the Russians about the dog being stolen? Edit hoped guilt was chewing at their heart as this majestic creature from the fables of her ancestors, from the very recesses of her own heart, made its pitiful parade to the centre of the village.

We all know how this ends – with the beast poked and prodded into madness. The tigress snarled at the crowds, as if to find the one who betrayed her, her eyes seeming to search for Edit's father, and then settling on Edit. Perhaps this was what changed the course of Edit's life, turned her, as her father said, into a girl he no longer knew.

There would be no valuable tiger genitals from this specimen, for the parts of a female tiger had no value. The Chinese wanted wild male tigers (farmed tigers also had little value), whose potency would amplify their own. The pelt would have some worth, though it was smaller than a male's. This tigress was young and inexperienced, a relatively easy catch for men with dogs and rifles and Edit's father as a tracker. Edit wondered if indeed this was the one who had taken the dog, or if this was the one that they had managed to catch.

Where, only days ago, Valery had stared at Edit, trying his hardest to communicate, now Edit stared at him, in incomprehension. All communication was incinerated by this act that Valery, her Valery, had committed. She did not understand how he could have taken part in this. He was a Russian, given, and the Russian nature was to conquer and destroy, but this was not the side of him she had seen.

When the tigress was dead – which took a long time, because she absorbed Dmitry's blows and refused to die and had to be shot – Edit fled to the little cabin she shared with her father. She found him drinking by the stove, holding the shaman drum given to him by his father. Strictly speaking, he should not have had this. All relics should have been handed over to the museum. But, because he was so useful as a tracker, and one of those men who endures conflict without seeming to make it worse, it had been overlooked that he had the most powerful shaman tool still in his home. The membrane, a fine parchment of deer skin, was painted with a snake-like tiger. In the shaman's hands, the drum is the boundary between the spirit and the animal world, and the shaman himself is the communicator. Her father was weeping and Edit was not sure if it was for the tiger, or for the loss of his father, or for the terrible thing he had done. She silently took the vodka away, and curled at his feet and rested her head on his knee. His hand came out, as it always did, and stroked her hair, and he said, 'Be afraid of the forest, Edit. It is a dangerous place now.'

His daughter did not reply, but what she thought was – and she did not know where the thought came from, or how it even made any sense – *I will never suffer like that.*

After that day, the forest's silence became a deep and mysterious consideration. All the tigers were watching now – everyone talked about it. There would be revenge. There could not be such a terrible murder without consequences. But what form the revenge would take, on whom it would be visited and when it would occur was not known. There was no shaman anymore to consult on this, just whispered gossip among the villagers and private worrying.

A few days later, Edit was alone, in the early afternoon, on her way home from a spot at the edge of the forest where the last of the berries from autumn could still be found. The women made these into a bitter medicinal jam, which Russians liked to stir into their tea. Walking down the centre of a logging road, setting the daylight on fire, a tiger.

If a tiger needed to get somewhere, it always used the easiest route. Tigers were unassailable in their confidence that they owned the forest, and their tracks were often visible on the trails. The tigers themselves, however, were almost never seen.

Edit dropped her basket in shock and backed away into the trees, bowing her head. The tiger was truly enormous. Though this was only the second tiger she had ever seen in her life, Edit knew, with horrified certainty, that it was the king male. Revenge was coming to the village. It had come quickly.

She whispered a prayer, long remembered from her childhood, a prayer of appeasement to the god of the forest, begging it to pass her by and to stay away from the village.

She opened one eye the tiniest crack. The king's shoulder blades rolled like the wheels of a truck. He moved without hurry, and, despite his size, almost silently. Hot breath wafted from his lips as he drew parallel to her inadequate hiding place. This was the biggest creature Edit had ever seen, in her life or in her dreams.

Edit had no gun, because she was close to the village and, when they went to collect berries or even check the nearer traps, they did not take a gun. People and tigers went to great lengths to avoid each other. The villagers were always alert to the possibility of an encounter, but the forest was their home, and you don't take a gun on every trip around your home.

Her breath turned to wasps in her throat. She pressed her trembling lips together to prevent the gasp of fear emerging and giving her away. She knew that, of course, the tiger was perfectly aware of her and her feeble attempts to hide, because a tiger always knows you are there.

She lifted her fingers and hid behind them, this being the last refuge of the terrified. She could create a tiny place of safety, like that. She waited for the tiger to leap upon her, whispering her desperate plea, '*No, no, no.*' The silence of the forest rang in her ears, and when she finally let her hands drop and peeped through the blinding light, the track was clear. The tiger had vanished as surely as if she had never seen it at all.

Her basket lolled in the snow where she had dropped it, its wound of berries slashed across the white. Edit stared this way and that, and slapped her own body to be sure she was still alive. Had she really seen the king? She ran down to the trail and there were the tracks. Big as the span of a man's hand, they veered off into the forest on the other side.

But, before they veered off, the tracks showed the king tiger had paused, four feet standing still, to look into the forest where she cowered.

The tiger had seen her and spared her.

And where had it gone?

Edit left the fallen basket and tore back to the village, to her father. She would tell no one but him, because, if word got out that the king was this close to the village, who knew what would happen?

As she ran, her heart hammering, she wondered for what reason the king tiger had appeared, and then gone, sparing both her and the village.

It was as if the tiger was giving her a message, as if there was a bargain there that she had made, without knowing what it was.

SINCE THE KILLING OF the tigress, Edit had avoided Valery, wishing their attachment broken. He appalled her in every way. She knew that if a Russian wants something, you must give it to him, or he will take it anyway, and it will be much worse for you. Even so, she had turned her back on him every time he approached.

Valery could not rest until she had heard his side of the story. After trying and failing to explain himself in public, he had bided his time until she was alone, at dawn, on the very morning she saw the king. He grabbed her where she was strapping on her skis to go ice fishing.

'Let me go!' she cried, wrenching her arm free.

Valery jogged about inarticulately before her. He was wiry, rather than scrawny, and he liked that Edit's head fitted neatly into the bony dip of his chest. The prospect of this ever happening again was looking very distant, however. He was desperate to say something, his face contorting with the effort, his former charm deserting him.

He burst out helplessly, as she bent to tighten the leather straps on the skis, 'I needed money. It's why I helped kill the tiger. I wanted money, so I could marry you. I'm sorry about how it turned out. I wanted money so I could marry you.'

Edit said nothing, concentrating on the straps, which were meant for a man's foot and consequently were loose around her toes. It was only the toes that were held to the skis, so they would slide properly and the foot could manoeuvre, but too loose and you could twist your ankle, out there in the forest.

Valery had murdered something she revered, right before her eyes. He had forced her own father to be complicit. How could he even think there was anything between them anymore? She turned her back on him and set off on the skis. Her movements were utterly determined, her pack blocking all but the glossy back of her head.

It was infuriating to be silenced like this, Valery thought. She had to hear him out. She had to think about it properly. It wasn't as though he had planned the atrocity. It wasn't as though he would ever do it again. It wasn't as though he was a wicked man inside. And, in the end (although he was not planning to say this), it wasn't as though it really meant *all that much*. The villagers had come to terms with it. They still bought Dmitry's cheap cigarettes. Only the previous night, another girl in the village had made eyes at Valery. Life moves on. There were plenty more tigers.

While Edit was gone ice fishing, Valery went instead to her father. He apologised anew, pleaded his case and offered money. Three hours later, when Edit returned from the river, a set of three good-sized fish in her pack, she found her father awkwardly making Valery's case for him. The thing was, a man could only be made to feel guilty for so long, and then he would become angry, and she must capitalise on this moment, when he was genuinely remorseful, when he would do anything in his power to make amends. Anything except leave her alone, of course, for that was a consequence that could not be contemplated.

'You have a future to think of,' her father said. 'What has happened cannot be changed,' he went on. 'But we may be sure Valery will never do such a terrible thing again. I've spoken to him, and, as your father, I say that he means it.'

He did not say that he had accepted money from the sale of the dead tiger. Things that used to be true were lies. What used to be a lie was true. This was the Russian way, and this was where they were now. He did not say that his only aim now was to protect her by any means possible, because he loved her with all his heart, and this marriage to a remorseful Russian was the best future he could see for her.

She stormed out, dropping the fish on the table. She picked up a basket to go back into the woods.

And that was when the king tiger appeared to her, and only her, making his majestic way down the logging road, just as if it had been made for him, and she had backed away into the trees, dropping her basket as she went.

FLINGING HERSELF INTO HER father's surprised embrace, she knew what his interpretation would be. There would be no village childhood for her anymore. The tiger had come by, and the tiger had decided not to kill her. Her father took her hand in his and said, 'So, daughter, do you see what you must do? You're meant to be that man's wife. He's worked hard for you. You could do much worse. And, until you marry him, the brokenness will remain in the heart of the village, bringing great misfortune on you, and on all of us.'

It was not possible to refuse Valery anymore. He was so happy to have won her round. Her father was happy. The villagers were happy. No one spoke anymore about the killing of the tigress. Everything moved on. And if Edit looked sometimes at her husband and was afraid, without knowing why, it didn't really matter. Everyone knew that life was hard and dangerous, that a woman needed her protector, that not even a tigress was safe in this world.

Twenty-four

AFTER FIVE YEARS OF marriage, it was a surprise to Edit how much it was possible to forgive. This thought bloomed in her mind as she sat by the stove one evening, repairing moccasins by the small electric light. The Russians had rigged up a generator and re-electrified the village, and now the winter nights were – for the most part, when it didn't fail – a whole other realm of individual pursuit. Now, there was more to do of an evening than gather round and drink home-made vodka. The light sent them off to be families, each alone, and, within the family, whoever was nearest the light could have even greater solitude.

The space beneath the bulb was, although it was not said aloud, hers. If Valery was there and Edit approached with a book or her sewing, he would read the situation and get up. He would do this unostentatiously, so that Edit never felt she was obliging him to move. Such acts of consideration enabled a wife to forgive really quite enormous things. If combined, over time, with other things – like bringing home game and knowing how to salt it and roast it; like being able to be alone without drinking oneself into a stupor; like catching the light sometimes with a smile that made the breath scramble in Edit's throat – it seemed sometimes, on a peaceful winter's evening, that there was almost nothing that could not be forgiven.

There was something else that kept them close.

From the beginning, they told each other their secrets.

Both being young, they did not have many. In fact, Edit suspected Valery had perhaps made some up.

Edit's secrets were mostly thoughts. For instance, her thoughts about forgiving him and how difficult it was; her wish that he was not a Russian; her longing for something, for *more*. This last one proved a fertile ground for confession on both sides. By the stove, on the earth floor, where they spent a lot of time in those early years, he asked her to tell him about her longing for more. And she told him about something that had happened to her a few years before, when she was maybe fourteen, when the village got a new pony to help the old one with its labouring with the cart, and this pony was glossy brown, with a broad back and a mane standing up in a crest, and it had a young, fizzy energy. The smaller kids all played on it, trotting it round the village, bareback, with a halter. It was liberating to be off the ground, borne by another creature, but Edit wanted more. One night, she took the pony out of his yard and walked him carefully into the forest, hopped on his back and kicked him on, down the logging trail. The moon was high and full, and the trail was brightly illuminated, and the pony cleared his lungs in delight. He jogged, at first, destabilising her so she had to cling to his mane; then, as she squeezed him with her thin girl-legs, he broke into a gallop.

As her body absorbed the rhythm of his body, gathering pace, the warmth of his shoulder warming her as she moved with him, an excitement, previously only felt in her mind when she imagined what it might be like to be a free, wild creature in the forest, became something else, something located in her body, a ball of sensations spreading from her belly, down inside her legs and up to her heart and her lungs. Her face shone with sweat and her legs shook from gripping the pony so, but also from the convulsion that ripped through her, like a tiger *on the inside*, an explosion of inexplicable colour, a blur of gratification, rising up and out of her open mouth.

In that galloping moment – here, her hand went out to Valery's arm, because she wanted him to hear, she wanted him to know this – her body had *opened into happiness*. A phrase leapt from her lips as she fell forward, panting, on to the horse's neck: *I can do anything*. She had eased the pony to a halt, bewildered by what had happened. She took the pony out as often as she could, after that. 'It was freedom,' she told Valery. 'I couldn't get enough of it.'

Valery's craggy face opened in surprise, and the teeth, tired by cigarettes and a lifetime of poor diet, still created a handsome smile. And he giggled, which set her off too, and he told her about how, when he was a boy, he'd overheard a drunk farmer joking that there were few pleasures greater than sex with a melon that had been warming in the field. And, back in the old country, far away to the west and south, he had stolen into the field at night and cut a hole in a warm melon and put his penis in it. 'And do you know what?' He'd turned to her then, and it was clear he had never told anyone this, either. 'It was true!' It was the most flagrantly delicious experience his pubescent body had ever known.

When they were not confessing to each other on the floor, Valery returned to Edit another kind of escape. He had rekindled her interest in reading, from the one book he possessed, which he had brought from home, which he loved because it was from home. His mother had inscribed it. Edit read it often under the single bulb: *Russian Folk Tales*. How magical it was, and yet also, compared to the songs and the stories she knew from her childhood, how barren.

Edit had been taught to read as a little girl; it was part of learning to be Russian, part of becoming – what? One of the proletariat? The native girls were never going to ascend quite to that level, but while their parents worked in the quarries and the mines, a bereft-looking Russian teacher came to the village and taught the children about the greatness of Russia and how lucky they were to be growing up in this modern age. Learning Russian, abandoning an oral culture in favour of order on paper, was part of this progress.

Although their future was plainly quarrying and mining, or sitting by the electric bulb, mending, the Russian teacher persisted. There was a library with a few tattered books, mostly tracts and histories of Russia. Then, even that future evaporated, as the U.S.S.R. crumbled and industry vanished, and the bereft-looking teacher grew frightened and left.

By then, Edit knew only Russian, except the Udeghe words in the songs they still sang when together round the fire. Her father was worn out by the quarrying and was too tired to stop his language vanishing. He barely spoke at all, except in a pidgin Russian that stayed just this side of resistance. The books mouldered in the broken-down library, and everyone slowly forgot how to read. Reading was accepting that the Russian language was the only language; not to do so was a quiet assertion of freedom.

But Valery's book . . . it made Edit feel like reading. Its existence in her hands came about because of love.

DESPITE THE INTIMATE HOURS spent on the floor by the stove, Edit failed to get pregnant. This was not a problem for her, really, but it was a problem for them. They discussed it on the floor sometimes; Edit even said, 'I don't want children.'

But this was an incomprehensible state of affairs and they redoubled their efforts to change it.

She said, 'There's a tribe of my people beyond the mountains . . . Shall we go and join them?'

I want to be free.

But her confessions seemed to have developed a shocking quality, and Valery often did not answer.

A wife not producing a baby produced gossip. Probably, Edit was barren, or perhaps – and this was said only in whispers among other women – she had availed herself of the services of the old woman at the far end of the village, whose medicines were known to help unmarried Russian girls out of trouble.

One twilight in summer, Edit was outside her cabin, beating a rug, the flies stinging in her sweat-damp hair, when she looked up to see a Russian woman tramping quietly through the village, keeping to the side of the central track, her head bowed beneath a wide hat, bleach-blond hair poking out from under the brim. Her arms were solid and mud-streaked. The noise of the beating startled her and she raised her head. Their eyes met, Russian and Udeghe woman, one without a child, and one – Edit was sure, from the direction she was taking – soon to be without one. The Russian girl's eyes had blueish shadows beneath their brown centres. Her mouth was pressed into a determined line. The girl paused and tilted her head towards the far end of the village with a questioning look at Edit. Edit nodded and continued with her beating. There was often a

Russian girl making that journey, but it was not often that she was alone, and on foot. The eyes of the village bored into the girl as she made her way slowly through the dust and the flies. The next day, or the day after that, depending on how long it took the herbs to work, there would be a quiet exodus into the forest to bury the creature expelled – or to burn it, in winter. Edit wondered if the women craved something to remember the baby by. A leaf from whichever tree it was buried beneath or a strip of bark from the pyre. She did not know, because she had not fallen pregnant, knew nothing about that kind of love, and the mysterious woman with the blueness under her eyes gave nothing away.

She seemed so lonely, making this pilgrimage. Edit considered running after her, taking her hand, offering her a drink or some stew. But while an abortion was not illegal for the Russians (there was just a dearth of doctors to perform them – or any other procedure), it may as well have been for the villagers. A shadow was already over Edit; should she be seen consorting with a woman aborting her baby, it would be confirmation of some badness within her, which was likely contagious.

She glimpsed the woman a few days later, returning alone, her step heavy, her face expressionless. Women had abortions to be free, didn't they? It didn't look like the freedom Edit imagined. But then, without a baby, Edit was not free either. The weight of what was expected – demanded, even – of her body filled the cavern where a baby might have been. Watching the woman's receding back, her narrow, slumped shoulders, Edit wondered if it was simply the case that a woman was never free, and it was to do with something more than whether or not she had a baby. To be free, you have to be able to see it. You have, in a way, to know it a little, even before you get there. Edit was just like everybody else, only able to imagine a life that already existed, confusing rites of passage for acts of freedom.

She and Valery still talked. They had many floor-based discussions about when he would take her home, back to the collective farm, far away. When she complained of boredom, he did not take offence, but produced his *Russian Folk Tales* and reminded her of reading. And he told her of his mother, and how much he missed her, and how he wished he could know if she was well.

But these efforts by her husband no longer satisfied Edit. For she missed her homeland, even while she was still notionally in it. This hard, destructive truth grew between them and would, on that evening by the stove, make her drop her sewing when she realised the difference between forgiving him and loving him. All the people of her childhood were around her; she could still visit the favourite tree she'd known as a girl; the animals she knew still roamed in the forest. And yet, these precious things were like fragments of a broken shamanic bowl, shattered beyond repair. When she looked at Valery, she finally understood that it was he who had smashed the bowl of who she was, simply by being who he was. It was impossible for her ever to love him.

Edit was in an unspoken state of mourning for what they had lost – all of them were. She saw it in the faces of the old women, struggling with their Russian; in the menfolk, weary from the decades of hard work, and now lost without it. And, everywhere, the faces were Russian, now – even the little children, their native features rubbed out, the forest slowly erased from them. Valery was a good man. She forgave him everything. But this – and now her eyes brimmed with tears and she bowed her head to hide them – was the end of them, no matter how long they stayed married.

Valery looked up from where he was stoking the stove. The firelight played across his face. He rarely spoke first: she would catch him looking at her, wondering something. And the urge to speak, the pressing dissatisfaction would come into her mouth. She picked fights with him. She wasn't proud of herself, and the women warned her that it was a mistake. Valery was a good husband, providing well, under the circumstances, not going drinking all the time. It would be a mistake to lose him.

Catching his eye as he looked up made Edit suddenly furious. It was as if they had already had a protracted dialogue, and she had not just been thinking. She flung her sewing across the room and cried, 'What are you looking at? Can't I be alone for a second?'

Valery frowned, then flushed at the dishonesty of it. He knew very well that his staring – a habit he had never got out of, with Edit – was a kind of conversation, but one that allowed his wife no right of reply. So many things poured out of his eyes, he knew this. And she read them, but could not respond except by doing as she did now. So he did blame himself for the fight that was about to take place, but of course nothing but indignation betrayed itself in his expression.

'I wasn't looking at you!'

'You're always looking at me! Demanding something with your sad-dog eyes.'

And so the argument unrolled before them, both of them heartbroken to be having it, but having it nonetheless. Fighting became what they did, as sharing secrets had been, and they no longer told each other anything.

Escape, her constant dream, swirled about in her like a shaman tiger spirit that was not allowed to be contacted. It was no longer expressed, on the floor with Valery, or anywhere, and, gradually, like an unread story in a mouldering Russian book, it ceased to have life at all.

Twenty-five

FIVE MORE YEARS PASSED. How astonishing it was to Edit that this happened, just like in a fable.

There was an old Udeghe folk tale of a little girl, Elga, whose mother died, and whose father treated her as his son and made her a spear and a sledge and toy dogs and reindeer. He made her hunting clothes, and talked to her one day of how she might be a hunter in the forest. But the father married again and the evil wife was jealous of Elga and did her very best to destroy her. When the father was killed by a tiger in the forest, the evil wife stepped up her efforts, loading Elga with women's work.

Edit remembered this story from her childhood, her mother telling it to her. And how so much time passed in the story, simply marked by the phrase *years passed*. Little Elga was set impossible tasks, cried countless tears at her cruel treatment, and she lived in fear as *years passed*. How wise the old stories were, though the Russians did not think much of them, considering them slight and dreamy. How Edit wished she had understood that they were explaining to her the hard, true nature of time, and how it *passes*, and what seems to be intolerable becomes simply a feature of it, as if time had a face that observed her always and simply grew uglier and crueller.

There was still no baby. And she loved her husband no more than she had before. She had hoped that love might grow, despite her terrible apprehension of their situation, in the nest of goodwill and forgiveness they had created. But Edit knew now, as she sliced the brushwood and stuffed its rustling mass into her pack, that love for one's husband was like a spark from a flint. It is there or it is not there. It is intolerable to be tied to a man one doesn't love, and no baby, nothing to show for it, nothing to make sense of the bond. There it was, that notion of *intolerable* – and yet years had passed, and here she was, peacefully cutting the brushwood.

Valery, in the way of a man who is not loved by his wife and comes to know it, though the words are never spoken, had made his own adaptations. He no longer sought Edit's approval or affection. And he no longer felt the need to resist the vodka that was present everywhere in the village. Valery had made a modest success of life solely because he had realised that drinking stopped everything in its tracks and, like Edit, for the most part he resisted. But what was the point now? Dmitry had long vanished into the forest with his snares and his certainties. This place crushed dreams, and it crushed love.

Valery was an intelligent man, and though Edit's love was lost, he knew how to keep her attention. He set about inserting some uncertainty into their domestic arrangements, creating a tableau that was utterly compelling to his wife. With evening came a vodka bottle, and a single glass, which Valery placed upon the table. There they stayed, without comment, while the two of them ate. Edit wanted to ask why they were there, but she found, to her surprise, that she was afraid to. It was the flicker of fear she had felt years ago, when they first married: the momentary apprehension of what her husband was capable of. A wife needs to turn from that. It is not safe to think about that.

Of course, Valery knew this. Manipulation is the last refuge of the unloved. He caught Edit's eye, and she saw the still-young man she had married. He was not ruined. He was in control, he was worthy of love. But, in all seriousness, his stare proclaimed – for he still used staring as his main method of communication with her – *How long can I resist?*

And, when I capitulate, as surely I must, then it will be your fault. Because you did not love me, and you left me with no choice.

A special form of anxiety began to live in Edit, much as love might have done, and it created actions that resembled passion. Edit eventually lost her temper. She poured the vodka out on to the snow. She told Valery it must not come into the cabin again, but when Valery said, 'But, Edit, this is my cabin,' she knew she was beaten. The vodka and the solitary glass became a fixture on the table.

Eventually, on his name day, when he was maudlin about home, the moment came when Valery looked at his wife with the saddest and most wicked of smiles, and had his first shot.

That first night, she was furious – in a way that she perhaps had not been since Valery's mistake with Dmitry and the tiger, all those years ago. She was drawn into the scene, exactly as Valery knew she would be, and she threw the bottle away, screaming that didn't he know her mother had died that way, and she was not going to sit there in her own house and watch her husband drink himself to death. Valery, ill from the speed at which he had taken the shots, swayed into the little cubby-hole room with the bed, and fell upon it, retching, but not before he had told her to shut the fuck up or she would be sorry.

Now, the line had been crossed, so it was no longer if, but when he would have the next drink. And then it became, when would he stop? And Edit's fury began to freeze. Over time, it became a glacial compression of anguish and fear, in which other feelings died and remained only in trace, as fossils. Meanwhile, she collected the brushwood, and she mended the moccasins, and she went ice fishing and she gathered berries, observing all the while, with a kind of wonder, how years passed, even though life was intolerable.

In the story of Elga, the father gives the little girl a spear. Thwarted in her attempts to kill Elga, the wicked stepmother steals it and finally chases her in the moonlight, hurling the spear at her. The spear comes alive and turns around and enters the stepmother's left eye, exiting from the right, tearing them open and turning her into an owl. And Elga, with her one remaining wooden dog, carved by her father, which has come alive, escapes to the moon along the path of its light.

The story began to occupy Edit's mind. Its lessons about time were one thing, but this niggling gleam of escape and the saving power of the spear had another lesson, she was sure.

Her father bit his lip when she talked to him, poured himself a drink and gripped it, and said, really, she must try a little harder, although, with no child, he did not see how she could tame a man's behaviour. Edit noted that he had not given her any hunting toys when she was a child, and asked him why, but he looked at her with such weary impatience that she did not pursue it. Perhaps more time had to pass for matters to become clear.

Whether time had to pass or not, it did.

At last, Edit did what Valery longed for her to do. Because, if she did not love him, it might be forgotten by them both if she would drink with him. And Edit longed for nothing more than obliteration.

This time, it was her name day, and, in a concession to the importance of this occasion, Valery made some stew and placed upon the table a second cup.

'Your health, darling Edit,' he said, and toasted her.

And Edit sighed and held out her cup, which he filled, and

she swallowed what was perhaps only the third drink she had had in her life. It burned with a soulless tastelessness that licked at the glacier of her feelings. She had another, and another. Valery sang to her, and she laughed, and they gravitated to the space on the floor by the stove, and different memories came to her, memories of how it had definitely seemed that she loved him. She had wanted him, anyway, and now the vodka had warmed away her fear, she wanted him again. And as Valery kissed his wife on the floor, and she kissed him back, it was as if a tiny carved toy of a child came to life deep within her, just as in a fable.

In the morning, Valery woke first. He poured the day's first drink and took his place at the table. Looking down at his sleeping wife, he knew that he had lost her forever. He could fight her, he could frighten her, but she had gone and all that would happen is that years would pass. Time was a mountain that had sprung up when he wasn't looking, and his wife was a small figure going down the far slope. He poured himself another, because his destiny had finally become clear to him – and, oh, he had waited far too long to know it. Edit was somehow going to make it down that treacherous slope. She'd say it was to bring something, she'd be back soon; she'd say – had, in fact, been trying to say, for years and years – *Do you want to come with me?* But – and here he shook his head tearfully as he looked at her, with her hair all tangled, and the beautiful mouth fallen a little open – no, he was going to wait it out here, on the snowy ledge, with the sleepy cold, and watch her go in the path of the moon.

Twenty-six

JUST BEFORE EDIT'S LITTLE daughter cried, her mouth turned down at the corners, forming a perfect upside-down U. What made it so unbearable was that it was funny. Where she had learnt it, Edit did not know, for Edit herself had never cried in all their years in the forest. There was nothing to cry about. There was no time, and, anyway, didn't a person cry only when the present moment encountered the past and was wounded? She and Zina had no past. Through Edit's passing-on of Udeghe forest knowledge from her father, and the songs she made to reconstruct their adventures, they were building their own story. But their life was just the present moment, managed over and over. There was no gain and no loss of the sort to merit either ecstasy or grief. At least, this was how it seemed to Edit.

But Zina's face was now a white sky with a crack in it. Her

lips pressed together until they were drained of colour, and her large amber eyes reddened, like two alien suns. She stared at her mother reproachfully, as the corners of her mouth made their journey downwards. Alone, once, by a pool, Edit had tried it herself, but the shape was complicated by other movements in the face, wrinkles of skin, problems of knowledge, and the effect was neither comic nor expressive of anything.

Edit knelt down on all fours. 'Do you remember what the mummy tiger does?'

Zina nodded. Her curls, in places, had wound themselves into creepers.

'And what's that?'

'Grrrrr,' said Zina half-heartedly, making chubby claws out of her hands.

'That's right! Grrr. The mummy tiger goes "Grrrr" and catches something for dinner.'

Zina knew how this game ended. There was a tremble in the upside-down U; a tear overflowed and rolled down her cheek.

'Grrr,' she whispered.

'But, to catch dinner, the mummy tiger has to be very quiet, so the pig doesn't hear.' Using exaggerated steps, Edit paced around her little child. Zina's breaths wobbled from her mouth, and her eyes, following her mother, were magnified behind the bulge of tears.

'So, the mummy tiger goes out alone. She tucks her special, favourite cub —' at this, Edit gave her daughter a huge hug, swept her up and set her on the mattress – 'safely away, and then she goes out and grabs that pig quick.'

By now, the little girl was inconsolable. She sobbed in her mother's arms. It didn't matter how much of a game Edit made of this, Zina was cast into despair at the prospect of being alone. She had to remember not to touch the stove, not to go outside, not to touch the knives. She had to occupy herself alone, for many hours.

When she herself was a little girl, barely older than her own daughter, Edit remembered one night that was filled with terrible sounds coming from the other end of the village. She had run into her mother and father, at the back of the cabin, finding only her father sitting on the edge of the *k'ang*. He had gathered her up and said that the shaman, her grandfather, was trying to cure her mother of her illness. It had to be done at night, for secrecy's sake, and he must not be disturbed. It was a terrible sound, impossible to tell whether it was male or female. It was sobs and roars of pain, as shocking as the roar of tigers they sometimes heard in the night. She could not remember how the night had passed, except that she had stayed with her father. He had let her cuddle into him, and she had fallen, at last, asleep, despite her fear.

Edit only glimpsed her mother one more time, briefly – as a sunken, sleeping body, before it was carried into the forest to be buried. What stayed with her most of all from that time was that she was not alone. Her father had become bigger, it seemed, stronger, his smell of warm hide an endless comfort.

It was an agony to leave her daughter, when she herself had not been left, and every time she had to do it – once Zina was too big to carry and too small to help – there was this scene. Edit wondered, every time, how many years this would have to persist, how a tigress managed to leave her cubs when so small and not be afraid for them. And, also, the sheer terrible frustration, for, if they could not work this out, if it turned out that Zina could not be alone or Edit could, finally, not face this anymore, then this attempt to live in the forest would fail. It was a madness, anyway – what woman and child had ever survived here alone?

As Zina wailed and clung, Edit racked her brains for something that might offer a little girl solace. From around her neck, she untied the lynx claw that her father had given her when she left the village. It was to keep her safe, and to remember him. She sat down again in front of Zina and pressed the claw into the girl's hand. It was dark and glossy as a nut.

'Now, this claw is magic,' said Edit. 'You must hold on to it – it will always bring me home. As long as you have it, I will be drawn to it. My father gave it to me when we came here.'

Zina brightened. What child does not take comfort from the certainty of magic?

'If you rub the claw and close your eyes, you will be able to see me and what I am doing, on your eyelids. Shall I tie it round your neck? Or are you a big strong girl who can keep it safe in her hand?'

'In my hand!' Zina whispered. Then she thought again and

went to the cot where lay the stuffed toy her mother had made. It was soft, made of sable fur, with eyes made of bone, and a long fluffy tail. Stuffed with grass, it was intended to be a spirit creature, and its name was Kimunka. Zina had had this toy all her life.

'Kimunka will look after it!' Zina wrapped the necklace around the toy's neck, and quickly kissing her mother goodbye climbed into the cot, babbling to herself. She was impatient for Edit to leave so that she could enjoy the charm.

This had marked a turning point, for, when Edit returned that night, a deer slung over her shoulder, she found the little girl sound asleep, clutching the claw tightly. Edit woke her, and was greeted with one of Zina's enormous, strange smiles. 'I saw you in the forest,' she said. 'I watched you all day. You flew into the clouds and played with the birds.'

'You're right – I did,' said Edit. 'And I have dinner, now. Come and help me.'

She replaced the claw around her own neck, for safekeeping till next time, and lifted one of the two knives from her girdle. These were knives that all Udeghe hunters carried: a large hunting knife and a small curved blade that could be used for all kinds of fiddly jobs. She cut off the deer's tiny tail and gave it to her daughter, together with the curved blade. 'Have a go at skinning that. Keep the knife always outwards, like this . . . and concentrate. I will make another magic toy for you when you have the skin off.'

How miraculous it was to watch the three-year-old girl, who just this morning had wept with a baby's abandon, squat on her haunches in front of the stove and, with total concentration, work the knife with her delicate fingers. Something had shifted, transmuted. Zina was not a baby. She was now a female cub.

Edit was swift with the butchery of the deer. Nothing could be wasted from it. She drained its blood into a bowl and, with the big knife, swiftly disembowelled it into the snow. Some of the intestines could be used; what could not, was buried. The body was still warm, and steamed gently in the freezing air. She cleaned the cavity with snow. It was gory, horrible work, and Edit found the only way to deal with it was to shut down all her senses and retreat into total focus. Next, she skinned the beast; they needed new moccasins and her daughter needed a new jacket, having grown out of the last one in a matter of weeks. Much of tomorrow would be spent on this work, the repairing and making that could only be done when there was food.

The body butchered, Edit buried the pieces in a pit she had dug in the summer, which was now full of ice. The meat would remain frozen for as long as they needed it – although, they would get through it in a week, if she caught nothing else. She carried in a haunch and prepared it at the stove, first making pancakes from the blood she had gathered, then putting the meat on the open part of the fire to roast. Some strips of fat she rubbed with salt and hung up to dry. It was long, absorbing work. When she looked down at her daughter, she saw her grinning victoriously, a rather holey piece of hide in her hands.

When she had set off, all that time ago, with her baby strapped to her front and her pack to her back, she, similarly, had only the lynx claw and her undimmed fantastical imagination to propel her into the forest. She remembered it, of course, in every detail. Some details she could not allow to grow too sharp, because they hurt. Her father's face, for example, in the moonlight, as he walked with her to the first cliff, as they called the jagged wall of rocks that marked the end of the Udeghe reserve land.

The image of his face was blurred now, after nearly three years, but the emotion in his voice was seared on to her imagination.

Her father had handed her the lynx claw. 'It was your grand-father's,' he said. 'It will protect you.' He kissed Zina on her tiny cheek, and touched his hand to Edit's face. 'Don't forget me, daughter. When you get to the other tribe, I hope you'll tell them about us.'

'Of course I will.'

'And, who knows? Maybe these endless petitions we put into the government will get us our land back. Then you can come home.'

'I can never go back to Valery,' Edit said.

'If we get our land back, I don't care what he or any of the Russians say. They'll be trespassers, all of them!'

It was this notion of her taking her baby to join the

uncollectivised tribe over the mountains and beginning again that had motivated her father to help her. This goal had united them, where her despair at Valery's drinking had not. Edit wanted to escape her marriage; her father wanted the Udeghe people to survive. He would never have helped her leave her husband, no matter how much Valery drank, simply to vanish into the forest with her baby, *especially* not with her baby. However, when she gently drip-fed him the idea that she could be a vessel for all the fragments of shaman knowledge silenced in the village, that she could travel, like a seed, and perpetuate their line in a better place, he slowly began to take on the idea as his own. He began to believe that she would not be entering dangerous territory, a woman and baby alone, but going home. She and her child, returning the squandered Udeghe culture to where it should be and preserving it. Edit, too, believed in it as an escape – hadn't this very idea been the one she had turned over during all those years of marriage with Valery? It was a kind of escape that she could imagine: one that was actually a return home.

They did not dwell on the very real dangers that awaited her in the forest. For instance, should she be found on her journey by either Chinese or Russians, she would at best be brought back and punished; at worst, she would be enslaved and raped, her child stolen. In addition, there were tigers, and encephalitic ticks, and bears, and, in a few months, deadly cold. Instead, her father, over the six months or so that led up to the moment in the moonlight, had focused on teaching her everything he knew.

They met secretly, while Valery was out or asleep. And a whole new side to her father had revealed itself; he stopped drinking, the lines on his face eased, like paper smoothed by a hand. He showed her how to use the knives, how to make and use arrows, how to brew medicinal tea. He took her shooting, both rifle and bow, and made her practise until her body ached. He told her where she would find a hot spring, and where ginseng grew. She should, he instructed, take some ginseng roots to the tribe as an offering. And, all the while, he made her repeat the shaman chants, and pressed into her memory the laws of the forest as the Udeghes had always known them. Most of all, the tiger is *Amba*: the spirit of the forest.

One evening, she said to him, 'I am like Elga, now. You have saved me, and set me free.'

'You're not free. You have a job to do. A great responsibility,' he replied, but his cracked old hand squeezed hers.

On the last night, he helped her fill the pack, which contained everything she would need for the journey. He estimated it would take her three months to cross the mountains. He wrapped her body in a belt full of bullets, almost every bullet he had, and he included a tiny vial of the poison that, if arrow heads were dipped in it, could fell a boar. The pack had skins, vodka, pans, water bag, a bottle, needles, herbs, axe, saw, dried meat and fish, salt, tea.

What neither of them quite grasped, as they said goodbye for the last time, was that he had created a brand-new person.

This new person could make decisions on her own, for herself and her child. She would be making all the decisions, from the practical to the moral. He had thought of her as a mule, transporting their vanishing culture to safety, but he had made his daughter completely independent. She would become her own people.

THE DAY DAWNED HIGH-SKIED and fiery cold. Edit spent the morning working on repairs, while Zina tried to sew. She did not cry when she pricked herself, but gazed at the bead of blood with interest. Edit made a sister toy for Kimunka. Then they wrapped up and set off upland, to the hot spring. This was the secret spring that Edit's father had told her of, a source of warmth and salt that only the Udeghes and the animals knew. The Russians had so far never found it, locked as it was in an area of such densely packed trees that barely any light, even through the sparse foliage of winter, reached the forest floor. Even Edit had not found it for several seasons, coming upon it only by accident.

Zina – a different child from yesterday – did not totter or play. She walked carefully and firmly in her mother's wake, only bursting into a little song occasionally, when it could not be suppressed. After all, they had eaten and slept well, there was food tonight, and they would soon be warm by the hot spring.

The spring bubbled out of the base of a rock and coursed

down in steaming red and brown. It had a slightly sulphurous smell. Frozen steam coated the surrounding trunks and saplings with crystals of frost. Where the spring became a stream, the banks were trampled with the prints of many animals. Edit observed her daughter. When they had collected salt, she would see how Zina fared with keeping still, waiting for whatever might come to drink, and seeing her mother shoot.

They scraped the dirty salt into birch bags. When they got home, Edit would mix this with snow to wash it, and then dry it out on the stove. Clinging like a bear to a branch, Zina dangled above the stream, smiling in pleasure as the warm steam drenched her face, her fur hat dripping.

Edit lit a fire and roasted some of the venison from the day before. Rubbed with the salt, it was especially delicious. As she watched her daughter playing, she considered how it was that somehow they had never undertaken that journey over the mountains. They had reached the scrubby foothills, and there discovered the tiny broken-down cabin, unused for decades. It had been a good place to rest properly, after the weeks of travelling and bivouacking with a baby.

By then, winter was creeping closer, and travelling in the snow with a baby was impossible. Edit had got the stove working. She had chopped and stacked wood, had become skilled at hunting. The baby had grown exponentially; she was already toddling.

Edit had, without quite meaning to, created a home. In

addition, a thought had taken hold in her, regarding the tribe over the mountain.

Wouldn't she simply have to marry one of them?

Would they accept her child?

Wouldn't it be more of the same for her – but worse, because she could not blame the Russians?

And worse again because she had no father to protect her?

An arduous journey over the mountains to throw herself upon the mercy of strangers became less and less easy to undertake. Plus, there was the constant need to hunt and provide, which distracted from the preparations. One winter had turned into two, and, now, this little girl playing above the hot spring knew nothing else.

Zina was dangling from her knees in the steam, cackling like a crow. Kimunka jigged in her hands, his tail swinging.

'Do you want some meat, Zina?'

But the little girl was lost in the imaginary game. Edit put some pieces to one side for when she was ready and watched her daughter play.

When she had been planning her escape, there had been no question of leaving the baby behind. Valery was too far gone to care for her. Rather than frustrating her plans to leave, Zina's noisy, squirming form had given them new energy.

Truthfully, Zina had frustrated all subsequent plans. Edit would have travelled quicker without the encumbrance, and the baby had been a source of non-stop worry and inconvenience.

But Zina had kept her here, in this remote, plentiful space in the forest. The baby had prevented her completing the journey to the tribe.

Edit felt a warmth in her heart, then – a gratitude. Zina had destroyed her intentions, and, in so doing, opened up a new life.

Edit lay back against a trunk and closed her eyes. The warmth of the fire and the spring made her drowsy. The winter sun was like a gentle hand. Food, sleep, rest. This was a blissful moment, the kind that only the taiga could give. She knew to enjoy it, savour it, for something, some crisis, would happen soon. All was crisis in the forest.

Twenty-seven

THE FIRST PROBLEM WAS how to avoid setting off the dogs barking. That would be the end of everything, not just the five days it had taken them to reach the camp, but the five years they had successfully been living in the forest. Edit and Zina crouched in the thick undergrowth and considered what to do. The darkness was so complete, Edit could not see her own daughter beside her. The sky was overcast, with no moon. Their clothes stuck to their skin.

Insects bit and sucked, like vicious atoms. The night air wavered, the strange, eternal music of the dark. Zina scratched at the scarlet bites that had appeared on her cheeks, and one just inside her ear. Furiously swollen, they tormented her all day and night. Edit seemed to have an immunity to the worst of the irritation. Though she was covered in bumps and sores, they did not itch with the same intensity.

Several hours earlier, in the soupy heat of the afternoon, they had crept around the circumference of the camp, scoping out the buildings, trying to guess where ammunition, fuel and other supplies might be hidden. They had come to steal. All their bullets were gone, even though Edit carefully retrieved them from every animal she successfully shot. All the poison for the arrowheads was gone, and, even skilled as Edit was, feeding them both on what she could catch with a simple bow and arrow was becoming impossible. She had resisted for as long as possible, being unsure of the effect on Zina, or if she was old enough to undertake the journey. Finally, there was no choice.

After the reconnaissance, they had stopped to wait for nightfall in a shady hidden spot with a good view. They were camouflaged with mud smeared over their faces and arms. A woodpecker started drilling into a tree nearby. An enormous jay bounced along a branch above their heads and burst into song, loud as a cataract.

The shouts of men banged through the heat. Edit was transfixed. In five years, she had not heard a man's voice.

Zina's mouth hung open. She had never seen another human form apart from her own and her mother's. And, what was more, these were *men*, who up to now only existed in imagination.

'Are they my daddy?' she whispered.

Edit pressed her finger to Zina's lips. 'No. Remember – no noise. They must not see us. They will kill us.' Edit hated to scare her daughter, but had to stop all discussion. The little girl's eyes widened behind the finger. 'Men are as dangerous as tigers to us now,' Edit said.

Cedar bronze and stripped to the waist, the men went about the business of the camp, chopping logs, simmering stew on the outdoor stove, and sitting beneath a makeshift awning, smoking and playing cards, with the radio playing tinny music. They were all ages, with toasted skin loose around their frames or stretched over the drum of their bellies. They were sleepy in the heat. Zina, too, grew sleepy. Even fascination dulled when she could not talk about it, nor run down to the men and bring them into her world. Her eyes grew heavy, and she slumped against her mother's arm.

In her sleep, she swatted at her skin, like a cat kicking in a dream. Sipping warm water from her bag, Edit watched the camp.

A truck revved and disappeared in a black shimmer. The dogs stretched out in the pen or followed a particular master round the camp.

Close to the dog pen was a teetering construction, like a tumbledown watchtower. It was boarded on three sides, with a saloon door hanging off its hinges. A man of about her own age approached, hauling a plastic tank of water. He clambered up a stepladder and hefted the tank into place at the top. His skin shone with sweat, and, as he turned to angle the tank correctly, a mermaid tattoo on his side and back caught the sun.

The man climbed down the ladder and kicked off his sandals.

Then he pulled off his shorts and stepped into the cubicle. Edit was chewing the sweet base of a blade of grass. Her jaws slowed to a halt. The rickety door almost closed behind him, but not quite, leaving the edge of his body, his head and his calves visible. He reached up and unscrewed a valve, and water coursed from the tank, through a hosepipe, cascading down his neck and spurting from the corners of his eyes, like a cartoon grief. He directed the pipe into his hair and raised a hand to rub the coolness gently into his scalp.

His throat was exposed, and Edit's eyes rested on the Adam's apple, which moved as he swallowed. His movements were greedy, as if his skin itself was slaking a thirst.

He turned, and the slice of body that she could see shifted from a shoulder, a thigh, to the slope of a buttock. Water sluiced from it like a waterfall.

A beetle crawled over Edit's wrist and she batted it away, its iridescent carapace smooth as a fingernail. How she would love to be beneath that trickle of water, to be cool and clean. She peered through the shade of her hands at the fragments of the man's body.

The memory rushed over her, like a spring rising up from the earth, of Valery fucking her on the cabin floor. The memory was electrical in its details, sparking from one encounter to another. Longing came with it, like a cloud of biting insects. She had loved what they did. She had loved even the inexpert years, at the beginning. Valery had wanted her constantly, back then, and no matter how clumsily he reached for her, it was thrilling to be wanted like that. He was repeatedly bewildered by the complexity of her clothes, which seemed designed to thwart him at those times; he would fumble, almost weeping in frustration, until she took them off herself. That was how their married life began, with his unending, repetitive need for her.

But then, a simple physical desire, that was uniquely hers, arrived on its own.

And, when it did, he had been ready.

Edit found herself waiting impatiently for Valery to get in from whatever work he was doing, kissing him full on the mouth as he stood, startled, in the doorway. She woke him in the night, unable to sleep. She appeared when he was busy at the wood store, shyly taking his hand and guiding it under her dress.

Valery had responded with a kind of wonder to this development. And when, as began to happen, the fucking on the floor produced a change in his young wife, from girl into writhing, weeping, magical animal, his pleasure turned to awe, while retaining all the elements of pleasure, such that he believed he might die, and didn't care. And when, as also happened, they underwent the writhing transformation together, were each other's witness, Edit experienced it as perfect, soaring escape.

In her hiding place, this remembered delight became something else, burnished, like an old bronze knife. It hurt, even as she could not help turning it over and over.

She liked to watch him get up in the morning, moving naked

around the cabin, as unselfconscious in his body as this man she was watching now. But this man did not know she was there, whereas Valery had been unselfconscious *because* she was there.

She used to call him back, to the floor or the bed.

He would turn, with that smile.

Edit gasped, tears at her eyes. She covered her mouth, glanced down at Zina. The girl slept on.

An ache, long forgotten. She wished she could tell Valery, *Then, those years — I loved what we did.*

If only it could have been enough.

The man drained the tank and emerged from the cubicle. He shook the water from himself like a bear, and pulled on the shorts. He was good to look at, in the way that a glossy horse was good to look at, or an expertly stacked woodpile. She would have been content to look at him for a long time.

But did she see herself, on some floor somewhere, with him? Would her dreams tilt that way when they got home?

She didn't know how to untwist desire from memory. If you've known ecstasy with someone, like that, and it turned to sorrow, is it not a kind of reverse alchemy? Are you not forever left with lead, that once was gold?

'CAN YOU DO IT, little one? Can you come down with me, quiet as a fish?'

Zina nodded.

'Good,' said Edit. 'So, we go to that shed, there, where all the rifles are stacked, and we will find bullets there, I am sure. Have you got your pack?'

Zina grinned. This was getting exciting.

'Then we need to see if we can siphon some fuel out of the truck. And then anything else we can find. But we mustn't be there long. A few minutes, at most. And we must not make the dogs bark. So keep close behind me. Hold on to my pack.'

Zina obeyed and they made their way round the back of the camp, emerging at the far side.

The generator pumped and growled, and a light glowed in the kitchen. The men had retired away from the insects. Their shapes blurred in the steamy windows. Edit was carrying a long, dry branch. She crept to the truck, unscrewed its petrol cap and pushed the branch into the tank, holding it there for a few seconds to soak. Then she crept to the outdoor stove, where the men had been cooking, and lit the branch from the embers. She froze as a flame burst at the tip. In the shed Edit had observed earlier they scanned the shelves above the rifles.

Salt. Matches. Vodka. A plastic sheet. Nails. Pegs. Wire. Rope. Hammer. Pliers. Knife. Leather strap. Length of hose. Jars. Tape. It was a treasure chest. Edit's mouth watered as she gazed at the plenty of the shelves. So much time was spent making do with what they had brought from the Udeghe village and adapting from the forest. Edit wedged the taper in a gap in the wall and hurriedly piled as many bullets as she could into her pack. She arranged the boxes that were left along the front of the shelf, so it would not look as if any were missing, at first glance. Then, everything else. In a frenzy, she grabbed and picked like a crow at a tiger kill, until her pack was bulging. Just as she was doing up the cord, a glimmer caught her eye. A small, dirty square of glass, the size of a face, was tucked in a corner. A window! For the cabin! Excited, she wrapped the glass in a rag and taped it carefully to the top of the pack.

The final job: she took the hose to the truck, pushed one end into the tank and sucked the other, spitting out the diesel when it reached her mouth. Then she filled the old bottle she had. It did not drain the tank, and would not be noticed, but a bottle of diesel would be invaluable one day, she was sure. She tied it to the pack (with wire! Leather! So easy), grabbed the taper and looked around for Zina.

The girl had vanished. Edit spun on the spot, holding the taper aloft. She could not call, and did not dare cross into the path of the windows. Panic fluttered in her chest.

'Zina!' she whispered. The sound was drowned by the generator.

Edit crept round the side of the building. Peering into a glowing window, teetering on a stump used for chopping wood, was her daughter.

No matter that they were as dangerous as tigers, Zina had tasted the sight of people now. She would be like a hunting dog that has tasted game, or a tiger that has tasted human flesh. Nothing else would satisfy her.

Edit suppressed all her terror and outrage. She crept up to her daughter, rested a hand on her shoulder. The face that turned to look at her, bathed in the weak light, was radiant.

'They are laughing,' she whispered. 'They are big, like I am big.'

'Zina, we must go. We've stolen from these men and they will be angry if they find us. Now, quietly, follow me.'

The smile faded. Reluctantly, Zina stepped off the stump. Her mother lifted her pack on to her, stuffed with some lighter items. Then they retraced their steps, using the taper to light their way. It had become a dull glow, now, with a trail of smoke, but was adequate to get them into the forest.

Zina looked back at the camp, its lights now very small. 'I want to stay,' she said.

'It's not safe. Our home, with Kimunka – remember him? – is safe.'

'Can we come back soon?'

'When all we have here has run out, maybe we will come back.'

Zina sighed, the sound of someone much older, and took her mother's hand. And Edit led her away from men and habitation, and the flaying memory of how, at one time, there had been a connection between her and such a man, such a life. Her little girl would never know it for herself. This was an enormous, shocking thought. The passion of a woman and a man for each other was dangerous. It chewed up everything, every feeling, every organ, leaving time itself a mangled mess. It felt like freedom, but was a mirage, a cheat. Edit wanted, with all her heart, to protect her daughter. She wanted better, for Zina, than love.

Twenty-eight

THE COLD SWARMED AGAINST Edit's cheeks, buzzing into her lungs. Snow burst around their legs as they approached the frozen stream. Five years had passed since the expedition to the camp. At ten years old, Zina was already taller than Edit by four hands. She carried her chin high, her senses absorbing every detail. Her animal keenness tore at her mother's heart. Zina carried her own pack now, with an axe and her own ice-fishing rod with a fish-bone handle, which she had carved herself. It had an excellently strung sinew line, and several spare hooks.

They were so hungry. Edit thought of the hunger like an animal in her gut, pacing, growling for escape. Sometimes the animal was smallish, like a lynx; more often, these days, it was a bear or a tiger. It was bearable if she simply curled herself around the furious creature to soothe it to sleep. That was all she could do, for it was often impossible even to think clearly when she was this hungry. Starvation's roar trembled to the tips of her fingers. What was worse than this, what was truly unbearable, was to see the hunger in the face of her child. Zina was well practised in not showing any suffering; nevertheless, she could not hide it completely, for she was still a child, and had not grown the bark-like carapace over her appetites that her mother had. Zina did not cry, nor complain. Her long, thin face grew pale, the skin sank beneath the cheekbones, she chewed her lip.

This was the third year of a poor crop of pine nuts. Mast year – when all the trees seeded together, in a vast, strange communication – came every three or four years. This meant that, in the mast year, the ground would be deluged with seeds: acorn, pine nuts and others, which the depleted herds of deer and boar would not be able to consume totally. In this way, some seedlings would survive. The cycle of starvation and plenty worked for the tree population, but the year or two before the mast year, when the pine nuts and acorns were at their most scarce, were hard and terrible for all. But this was the coldest, harshest winter they had ever known.

Hunger had not halted Zina's relentless growth, however. Edit was alarmed at how enormous her child was becoming, filling out like a sapling setting down rings of wood. It was as if she had skipped a chain of evolution, leaving humans behind, to become like the carnivores in the forest. The forest's tigers and bears had to be enormous, to keep their surface-to-volume ratio low and, in this way, have a chance of staying warm. Like them, Zina was huge, yet stealthy. One could not help but feel awe at the sight of her. She was much more a creature of this place than her mother.

'Here it is, Mum!' The little girl pointed up at the larch tree bored with dozens of fist-sized holes. This was where the biggest beetle in Russia, a variety of the longhorn beetle, laid its eggs. The eggs would now be larvae.

Mother and daughter paced the circumference of the tree to assess the difficulty of felling it, and the arc of its fall. Chopping down an entire tree had become a lot easier since Zina had grown so strong.

Edit pulled her axe from her pack and swung at a spot a little way above the base. Zina joined in with her own, and soon the two established a rhythm of alternate swings at the trunk. The bang of the axes sailed far across the frictionless cold until the padded branches finally subdued it.

Zina delivered a powerful kick to the tree, which began its slow, regretful descent. They covered their ears against the splitting of the trunk and the almighty collapse of the dead tree, with its vines sprawled round it like jewels around a shaman. As it fell, it swept more branches off the trees about it, the birches and cedars and oaks, all snapping and tumbling in an explosion of snow.

The trees in the forest were packed so close together that nothing could fall completely flat. But Edit had calculated its trajectory well enough that holes were in reach. Now, they used a two-handed saw, which Edit had carefully sharpened the night before. Long practised, they made short work of the trunk. The lower section pounded to the ground, while the upper section sprang violently upwards. Even a dead tree is full of energy.

Next, Edit split the sections with the axe. As the halves fell apart, finger-sized burrows were revealed. Zina was expert in wriggling her fingers into the hollows and scooping the fat white larvae into the little birch-bark pouch, brought for the purpose. Each larva would make bait for a hook. She scooped ten into the pouch, while her mother split the remaining wood and stacked it at the base of the tree. They could collect it on the way back, for the stove; dead wood still burned.

This work done, and the morning still stretching ahead, they resumed their journey to the river. Their heads moved constantly, scanning the snow for tracks and the branches and sky for birds. The position of prints and the way that twigs around them were snapped or bent could tell much about what creatures had recently passed by, and where they were headed. Edit came to a halt and dropped to her knees. She had to be sure she was not hallucinating the possibility of food. It happened sometimes: the sheer cold oxygen of the forest, combined with hunger, could skew the mind, bring hope where hope was dangerous, where keen senses and patience had to be dredged up from the body's emptiness.

Wapiti tracks, *too old*. Twigs were snapped at the beast's

shoulder height. Its presence was confirmed by the way that bark had been chewed off a sapling nearby. Deer, in winter, turn to cambium, the sugary layer underneath the bark, easily accessed in young trees. Edit's excitement faded to a dull bang. The tracks had drawn close together as the wapiti paused to listen, and vanished as it bounded in another direction. Something had frightened it. They were *days* too late. They'd come into the story long after it was over, long after they could be part of it.

Edit shook her head at Zina and they pressed on. Mother and daughter were like two parts of a forest creature, moving in step. Their two gazes complemented and reinforced each other. Without Edit being able to pinpoint a moment when it happened, her daughter had become a gifted hunter.

'Wait!' Zina pointed to tiger tracks heading on towards the mountains. Edit knelt to assess them more closely. There were three sets. A mother and cubs. The mother's tracks were deep, but soft-edged. The group had passed that way perhaps three days ago. The sun had melted the edges, and night-time temperatures had frozen the print again. It was as if each day made a copy of the print, each copy becoming progressively less distinct.

Edit knew this was the big tigress, who, in the last couple of years, had begun to patrol this area. There were two cubs. One had spots of blood in its prints.

Edit reached for Zina instinctively, and mother and daughter stood motionless, taking in the scene. A tiger must be avoided at all costs. Especially a mother with cubs. Though the tracks were not fresh, this did not mean that the tigress was far away. It would be extremely simple for her to double round and come up behind them. If she decided that they were a threat – for, certainly, she knew they were there – this was catastrophically dangerous. Every creature in the forest was starving, now. And if her cub was injured, this could only mean she was more desperate still. Edit motioned to her daughter to move quickly on, put as much distance as possible between their presence and the tracks. The river was quite some way ahead.

Travelling through deep snow was tiring without skis, even though the felt trousers shed snow and the deerskin boots had a flat sole to try to spread weight, but at last the trees opened out on to a wide expanse of frozen river.

The river gurgled beneath a good couple of hands of ice. To make the hole, Edit dented the ice with the axe, then scraped a hole about a hand wide with her knife. Zina squeezed a wriggling larva on to the hook at the end of her fishing rod and squatted on her haunches beside the hole. Edit went to set up a couple more holes, moving softly across the ice, because fish can hear everything. Forest fish are clever. Everything in the forest has an awareness as penetrating as the cold itself.

Zina lay flat on the ice, on an old deerskin, peering into the hole, her face millimetres from the edges, very gently twitching the rod beside her cheek. This was Zina's own method: her face blocked the light from the sky, and she could communicate directly with the fish. She liked to whisper into the freezing space between sky and water. It looked odd, and it meant Edit's daughter got cold, but it often worked when other forms of hunting had failed. Periodically, Zina scraped the hole open again with her knife; in a bloodless healing process, the holes closed up with new ice every few minutes.

Edit observed her daughter proudly. Soon, Zina's skills would surpass her mother's. Edit marvelled at it, although surely it must end? How could they stay here when Zina was a woman, and Edit was old?

On the other hand, where could they go?

She turned from this thought, as she did several times a day. Edit baited her own hook and dangled it deftly in a hole, twitching it very gently, then holding it motionless. The cold, here, was more agonising than in the forest, where there were branches, vines and leaves to hold the air. Just above the ice, the air gnawed through the thick boots and trousers. Edit wiggled her toes, trying not to shift her weight and disturb the fish.

It was then that she was gripped by a strange sensation. *Heat.* It took a moment to register, so out of place was the feeling. It began in her chest — no, *on* her chest — on the skin beneath the layers of felt and fur, and it spread up her neck and into her face. A lava-like creep, that, it seemed, might cause her cheeks to steam. Sweat broke out across her body, and she longed, suddenly, to tear off her coat, to fling it away in order to quench this clawing flame that suddenly possessed her. Sweating in these temperatures was dangerous; the felt and fur breathed quite well, but any sweat remaining would rapidly cool, turn to ice and bring her body temperature down to dangerous levels.

Edit wrenched open her coat, pulled up the layers beneath and lay down flat on the ice. For a moment, she was afraid that the fire on her body would melt the river itself. The relief was gorgeous: ice and fire meeting on the shivering interface of her skin. She was the membrane between two worlds. They met upon her and blanked her mind. Then, the ecstasy was gone, and she realised she was shivering uncontrollably.

'Mummy!' Zina raised her arm. A very small fish was wriggling on the hook. Zina's big face was split by a brilliant smile, and tears spilled from Edit's eyes and froze sluggishly on her cheeks.

Edit picked herself up, pulled her clothes together and hurried over to her daughter. She dispatched the fish quickly with a rock and wrapped it in birch bark. It was not even a snack, but it gave them hope. 'Try for a couple more, and we'll eat them here. I'll start the fire; you keep the rods going.'

'Mum, are you all right?'

Edit's coat was still open, and her words had come out unevenly because of her shivering. 'Yes; I got cold, that's all. I will be fine when the fire gets going.' She set about gathering twigs, then she ripped some of the thin bark from the birch trees and laid it on top. Birch bark is the best kindling there is. In an emergency, you can set fire to the entire tree, which will go up like a flare. Edit's fire stones were carefully wrapped in her pack. She struck the stones until a spark caught the bark, which immediately flickered into life. Soon, a fire was roaring on the bank. Edit cleaned out the fish, cut it into a few sections and skewered it on to twigs, ready to roast over the flames.

Zina caught another fish, a few minutes later, wrestling it carefully to the mouth of the hole. When the fish realised it was caught, it could pull with tremendous force, much more than its body weight would suggest, and landing it became a kind of conversation between girl and fish, designed to wear the fish out. Simply trying to haul it ashore would result in broken sinew and the fish gone with the hook. Zina was very patient, and, in ten minutes, she had eased a long slender form on to the ice. It flipped into the air in its blind attempt to get back to the water, and mother and daughter leapt comically, trying to clasp it, until Zina threw her deerskin over it and, giggling, sat down on the edges.

Edit reached underneath, grabbed it by the gills, and soon had it cleaned out and added to the skewers. Zina returned to the holes and managed to land a couple more before giving up, the cold boring into them, like a beetle laying its eggs, to chew them up from the inside. Edit's mouth watered as she skewered all the flesh and quickly roasted it on the fire. They were giddy with the thrill of food, giggling and dribbling as they wolfed it down. They swiftly felt the energy returning to them. Zina grinned, pleased with herself. 'Should I try for more?' she asked.

'It's too cold,' Edit said. 'Let's try for a bird on the way home.'

As they gathered their belongings together, Edit thought again about what had just happened. What *had* happened? She felt fine now, felt herself. She was in tune with the actual temperature of the world outside. To be possessed by fire like that, counter to the physical facts in the world, made her apprehensive. Survival in the forest depended on being part of the forest; it depended on being at one with whatever was going on. That was camouflage, and camouflage was as necessary as water, here.

What happens when I am old? Round and round went the question.

Of course, Edit dreamed often of the village, longing sometimes with a visceral loneliness to see her father again. Also, when the winter was hard like this, she fantasised about eating food that someone else had caught. She thought of being with other people – although, it had been so long now that she thought she was actually afraid of other people. They were dangerous to her and Zina.

'Yes,' she said aloud, shaking her head. 'He will be dead, I am sure of it.'

Zina looked back, enquiring. 'You were thinking of my father.'

'No, I was thinking of *my* father.'

'Why did we leave them? My father and your father?'

'Oh, Zina, it's too hard to talk and walk through the snow at the same time.'

'No, it isn't!' Zina pulled on a branch over her mother's head and darted away, doubling over with laughter as snow cascaded down all over Edit's head.

Edit was furious. The snow slipped under her collar, sent breathtaking chills down her back. She squirmed as she attempted to sweep it out from under her clothes. 'Zina!' she cried, infuriated.

'Come on! Tell me about my daddy, and your daddy. And when are we going back to the village?' Zina skipped ahead, unburdened by the snow, by the past, or by the future.

Edit felt disturbed inside her own skin, as if she was a plot of earth that had been turned over and newly exposed. 'Now isn't the time!'

'Why isn't it? We have all the time in the world! Time is all we have!' Zina opened her arms and twirled round, then allowed herself to fall, star-like, into the snow. She was not prone to childish exuberance and Edit stared at her, somewhat at a loss.

'We can't ever go back there,' she said.

Zina stared up into the trees and waved her arms and legs in the snow, angel-style.

'Why not?' she said, upwards, into the clear, harsh sky.

'Because . . . because . . .' Edit did not have the words readily to hand. She rested against an ash trunk, pressed her fingers into its gnarled latticework. 'Because I *escaped*,' she said.

'What do you mean, escaped?' Zina sat up in the snow.

'Your father . . . couldn't take care of us anymore. He drank too much vodka. And so my father taught me all the things I know, and gave me all the tools we have, and we escaped. And now . . . we are strangers there. Both our fathers are dead, I'm sure of it. We would not be welcome.'

Zina said, 'I don't look like you.'

Impatience squeezed Edit's heart. 'You don't look like him, either,' she snapped.

'Who do I look like, then?' Zina cried.

'You look . . . like a spirit of the forest.'

'What do you mean? I'm human!'

Edit remembered the little three-year-old with the turning-down mouth, and realised she was still there in this almost-woman.

'You . . . are *more* than human, Zina. You are more than your father and I ever made together.'

Zina stared at her mother.

Edit went on, 'It's as if all the best and most powerful things in the forest – the tigers, bears, snow, sun – it's as if they have made you theirs. They've made you taller than any other child, and stronger than I am, when you're only ten. You're clever, in the forest, more so than even the Udeghe hunters in the stories. Sometimes . . . when I wake at night and see you sleeping, all curled up, you look like a tiger.'

'I'm *not* a tiger,' Zina said, thoughtfully, examining her hands.

'Zina, if we go back to the village, they won't see how wonderful you are. They won't see how special you are . . .' The words broke in Edit's throat. She bit her lip.

'What if my father is alive?' Zina said. 'What if he misses me? What if . . . What if . . . he's out in the forest looking for me, every day, calling my name, all these years?'

'He's not doing that, Zina.'

Her daughter started to shiver. 'But how do you *know*?' she cried. 'He could be searching for me. Why are the men as dangerous as tigers? They are human, aren't they? I have dreamed about the men in the camp since we went there. You think I've forgotten because you won't talk about it, but I haven't. I don't think they are dangerous. Why can't we go there?' The question hung, unanswered. Zina leapt to her feet. 'I think you want to keep me here in the forest to look after you when you are old, and you don't care about me at all.' She charged on ahead.

Edit stared after her. She trudged through the snow, no match for the furious ten-year-old. 'Zina!' she called. 'Wait!'

She finally got close enough to grab her daughter's arm and stop them both.

'Zina, you're too young to understand, but I have to tell you, anyway. Your daddy is dead. If he isn't actually dead yet, his soul is dead. He drank so much vodka, it destroyed his soul. He's not looking for you, because he can't. He is less than you, Zina, not more. It's very hard. You are special, he is not. I am not.

'In the camp, they will hurt you. Maybe not the first day, or the first year, but, in the end, they will hurt you. It would be like . . . putting a tiger in a dress and saying, "Here she is, an ordinary girl!"'

Edit saw with horror the little child, who was always some-where in her daughter's eyes, always accessible, turn away. She watched it happen, a dark shift in her daughter's gaze – the soft-ness, like a baby's face, gone; an empty space instead. Though they looked so different, they were, until this moment, deeply connected, as if they were reflections of each other. Now, the mirror had cracked.

Zina blinked, like a bear roused from hibernation. She looked outrageously out of place, a creature in the wrong Udeghe fairy tale.

'Zina, if I achieved nothing else with my life, I brought my daughter home. You belong here, in the forest, not with the stupid men in the camp, or the ignorant fools in the village. I couldn't make a life for you in the village, but I did bring you home.'

Zina pulled herself free and strode on. No matter the pain and the fury, they still had to hunt, and they had to get home before nightfall. Even with Zina's anger vibrating between them, they still had to work together.

Edit followed, struggling with a realisation. It was as if Edit had interrupted her mother, all those years ago, when she was telling her the story of Elga, to ask, *But, Mummy, why did Elga not go and find her father in the forest, and bring him back to life? That would be much better. A much happier story.* Indeed, but that happiness would have been like firing a rifle to scare away the terrible truth. The truth had to be reckoned with, always. It would only have vanished for a while, looping on ahead, and one day would be waiting there with cold, amber eyes.

STICKING OUT FROM THE trunk of a larch, just ahead, was the gnarled cusp of a *chunga*. It was a fungus that looked like a cancerous sore. Edit reached up and sliced a good chunk of it off, into her pack. At the very least, this could be brewed into tea and it would take the edge off their hunger, should no meat be found today.

The snow between the trees was criss-crossed with all kinds of tracks: the light scurries of mice and finches; the longer tread of a weasel. It occurred to Edit, as they walked silently on, that, in the snow, the stories of all the forest creatures coexisted – in space, even while not in time. The weasel had passed by much later than the mice; its tracks followed theirs. The mice had changed the weasel's story. How miraculous it was that all these journeys – which stored life-giving information, as well as being stories – persisted alongside each other, each to be followed and understood separately. Each traversed its own world, with its own time, yet connected with the others at converging moments. Her tracks and Zina's were part of this sprawling white book, and yet also a single story, of mother-and-daughter survival. All these journeys, theirs included, would remain intact until overlaid by a new page of snow.

Now – the tracks of a hare, fresh. Zina, forgetting her sorrow, immediately fell to her knees to peer at them, and then — Edit did not know why she did this — to sniff them. The hare had paused to nibble on a patch of lichen clinging to a birch tree. The track was sharp and deep, the edges of the print at the back blunted, not with fresh snowfall, but with newly tumbled grains of snow, dislodged by the hare's movement. If Zina gently lifted the fallen flakes, the print remained beneath, completely new. Probably, the hare had heard her coming and had run for it.

Excitement balled in Edit's stomach. Oh, if she should succeed at killing it, they would have food for days and this terrible turn of events would be forgotten, and all would be well.

The tracks went on, upland, still further. They crossed others — more weasels, an owl. Here, a clearing had been created by a tree falling, knocking others down with it. The trunk was coated in snow and looked like a huge white worm rising up from the ground. With the tree had come the vines that clung to it, and their treasure of remaining berries, leaves and insects. And, there, nibbling at the vine leaves, was the hare.

It had a knobbly, clever face, reaching almost as high as Edit's waist. Its coat was the colour of snow mixed with bark, and its immense ears lay neatly down its back, like twin fish.

Silently, Edit raised the rifle and sank carefully to her knees. The only sound was that of Edit's own bones, which seemed to creak and groan.

The rifle was a good accurate one, if old, now, and, for a heart-stopping second, she had the hare balanced in her sight.

But then – no! Something slipped. Was it her footing? Was it her concentration, her vision? Her body made a great *pah* in the snow, and the hare was gone.

Tears were pointless – they sapped energy, they froze – nevertheless, they came. Quickly, she wiped them away, so that Zina would not see and be disturbed. For there was nothing to cry about, in the forest. She dragged herself to her feet and they began their journey again.

'Next time, I will shoot,' said Zina, firmly. There was no point in Edit arguing. Not when she had bungled their last chance of food that day. Failure made Edit weak. Her shoulders slumped and her body ached.

Passing the tree felled at the start of the day, they gathered up the saw and the chopped sections. Wearily, Edit emptied the rifle at the door, leant it against the wall in the porch and got the fire started. Zina pored over the rifle, running her fingers down the barrel, lifting it to get a sense of the weight. She had a forensic stare that seemed to suck details out of a situation. She came alive over these details. Aiming the gun. Firing.

This was what children did, Edit realised. This was what new life was: devouring all you knew, everything you had to teach and to give. Then moving on to everything you did not have to give, taking it, anyway, because that is the direction of life. In the end, the child pulled everything to it, as if time itself were just fruit or rain, pouring down into their outstretched hands. And you were glad, even as your heart broke, that they surpassed you, leaving you kneeling in the snow.

Twenty-nine

MORE SNOW HAD FALLEN than in any previous winter Edit could remember. She and Zina had been imprisoned in the cabin for over a week as the sky closed in and snow engulfed the earth, wiping out all evidence of tracks. When at last the blizzard days passed, snow was piled as high as the window, and made a wall outside the door. They had enough wood for the stove, for Edit was meticulous about chopping and storing the wood all year. But they had nothing to eat, and it had passed beyond a situation that would be remedied before long, into a continuing state.

It was intolerable to Edit, not so much for herself, but for Zina. Her daughter had become tearful and listless. Mice scurried into the cabin with enraging audacity, and Zina devoted empty hours to catching them, laying trails of crumbs into tiny traps, and, when these did not work, simply sitting motionless until one should emerge for the bait, and then leaping on it with her great girl's foot. She had managed to catch one this way, but had had to peel it from her boot and it could hardly be described as meat. Simply, they boiled it with water to make a thin broth. Birch bark killed the appetite a little; *chunga* stewed in tea also helped to quell the pangs. But, as the days passed, it became apparent that the situation was dire.

Edit was weakening too, from the lack of food, but also from a near-constant blood loss. The monthly bleeding that she had learnt to manage, and had not been more than an inconvenience, had stuttered to a halt in recent years, which was a relief. But then, three weeks ago, it had returned, overwhelming in its sheer painful rush. She had been bleeding ever since and her usual methods of coping were woefully inadequate. She was growing afraid, not knowing what it meant. Trapped in the cabin, it was impossible to shield her daughter from what was happening, and it was becoming harder to reassure Zina that this was just a natural thing that would pass. The blood soaked through the pads she made from birch bark and cold ash, and drenched her clothes. It was, she now felt, draining her life away. She did not believe she had this amount of blood to spare, and did her body not know this? How she longed simply to lie down and sleep. Instead, she prowled the cabin, waiting for a break in the weather, turning over and over what she could possibly do to save them.

The camp. It was the last resort. Giving up and throwing

themselves on the mercy of strangers had always been a shadowy possibility, but it was rapidly becoming the only solution. Her whole body reacted against it, as if to an apprehension of death. Her teeth chattered, despite the warmth of the cabin, and sweat broke out across her forehead. To Edit, the camp was a kind of death. Her and Zina's life together would be immediately extinguished, the relationship between them altered forever. They would simply be woman and child, a unit no longer powerful, but vulnerable.

On the other hand, she was afraid of dying and leaving her child alone. Or of Zina herself dying of hunger, because of Edit's indecision. They had not been back to the camp in five years; who knew if it was even there? Two years ago, Edit and Zina had stumbled across a group of abandoned shelters, further into the mountains. It looked like an old Chinese hunting settlement, and inside the broken huts they found ammunition, tools and knives, and even rice. The rice was infested with weevils, but, still, when it was washed and dried out, there were days of starchy luxury to be had. They had gorged on it till they were bloated. The find of supplies had avoided the necessity of returning, for another stealing expedition, to the camp.

The other choice was the one Edit had consistently made in every other time of difficulty. Edit could see what tracks were on the white book that day, and attempt to find something to eat, anything. The forest went through phases of hardship and plenty. They just needed to pick their way through these terrible days by any means possible. She peered through the window into whiteness so complete you could believe yourself blind, or dead. Silence whistled in her ears.

Edit stoked up the stove and crouched beside her daughter, who was wrapped in a blanket. The girl's face was grey-tinged, bruises had appeared around her eyes and a sore on her lip. She was too weak to make the journey to the camp, now. Edit simply must find some food, any food, and then she could make a sensible decision about survival.

She forced a smile. 'Baby, you are to stay here by the warm fire, keep drinking the tea that's there on the stove, and I am going to go out and see what I can find.' She undid the lynx claw from around her neck and handed it to Zina, who smiled and, as she always did if mother and daughter were separated, wrapped it around Kimunka.

'Mummy, are you still bleeding?'

'You mustn't worry about that. It's much better. It will stop soon.'

'If I come with you, I can help.'

'No. You are to stay here, and catch mice, and rest. You promise me. You promise you won't try to leave the cabin?'

'I promise.'

'I think the snow will have brought the animals out.' This was nonsense, but Edit needed to sound optimistic, for herself as much as anything.

Zina's eyes fluttered closed. She was glad to sleep, she was glad at least to be warm. Edit kissed her sunken cheek and then attended to what must be done. As she stood, the cabin spun. She leant against the wall and breathed deeply till it passed.

With clumsy fingers, Edit pulled down the blood-soaked felt trousers and replaced the sodden pad in her underclothes, throwing it into the stove, where it incinerated. She was worried about the smell of this blood alerting every animal in the area to her presence. But there was nothing to be done. She changed her underclothes, but all the clean trousers were still damp. She was having to wash her clothes every day, now, hoping they would dry overnight, strung over the stove. For now, she resorted to Zina's deerskin leggings. It was exhausting.

She slung the rifle over her shoulder, checked the bullets, lifted her pack over her shoulder and pushed her way out of the cabin. This might be their last chance, but it was imperative that Edit did everything as though the stakes were not that high. Pausing at the first birch sapling she came to, she carefully cut into the bark, through to the sweet green cambium beneath. She cut several strips of this and chewed them, relishing the trace of sugar.

Progress through the drifts was slow. Her boots were not enough to prevent her sinking with each step, sometimes up to the thigh. She scanned the surface for tracks, ideally of boar or deer, but the snow was too new and its emptiness unfurled before her.

Then – crows, wheeling in the sky to the north. Edit stopped, panting. This could only mean one thing: a tiger kill.

Of course, she knew, right down inside her bones, that no one ever moves towards a tiger. Interrupting a tiger with its kill is simply inviting death upon oneself. But Edit was in a different world now. A grind of pain in her belly sent sticky warmth into her underclothes, and she felt the blood turning to ice on her legs. It chilled like metal.

Thoughts whirled like crows in her head. Perhaps there would be something left of the kill. Perhaps she could even shoot a crow. Her daughter's face rose in her mind. Today was their last chance. She had no choice. For the first time in her life, she turned towards the greatest danger in the forest and trudged towards it.

Tiger tracks burst across her path, like a blast of asteroid trails. The tracks swept beyond her, deep into the trees. Edit stopped to study them. The tracks were no more than a day old. Edit knew immediately that these were the tracks of the big tigress. She was alone, and must, like Edit, have left her cubs in order to hunt. She was moving fast, at this point, hard on the trail of something. What?

Her answer came a few metres on, where the tracks mingled with bear prints. These were older, though not by much – at most, a few hours.

A woodpecker rattled through the trees. The crows were just out of hearing range, perhaps a kilometre away. Edit scanned the forest's sharp shadows. A tiger is invisible in the taiga. You never see it, until it is upon you, plunging its mouth over your throat.

Though Edit had not seen a tiger in all her years in the forest, she behaved as if one might be encountered at any moment. Not fearfully – to behave as prey was a fatal mistake – but in the manner of another predator, wishing not to waste energy on a battle that would be very costly. This was how bears and tigers coexisted in the forest, taking note of each other, avoiding each other where possible. Bears were occasionally hunted by tigers, but, as an encounter was never without cost to the tiger, both generally chose avoidance. There was mutual respect. To bring about this pursuit, against the animals' natural reluctance, there must be desperation on both sides.

The tracks weaved on beneath the great mattresses of branches created in the treetops by bears in the summer. These were used as a platform from which to reach fruit and berries. Some of them were twice the size of the bed in the cabin. They were testaments to forest labour, made anew each day, as all the work in the forest must be performed anew. A huge Korean pine loomed ahead, with a hole about three metres up; bears selected either firs, which were soft enough to gnaw, or trees already hollow, for winter hibernation. Perhaps a bear was asleep in the hole. It crossed Edit's starving mind that she could find a way to climb up to the hole and shoot into it, but there was no way to get quickly up the smooth pine trunk, nor to get the bear out, if indeed she killed it. It was a horrible, desperate idea. Was it as desperate as attempting to steal from a tiger kill? She tramped on, her breath smoking from her face.

Could she hear the crows, now? She couldn't be sure, over the rasp of her own breath. The tiger tracks broke away from the line of bear prints, veering off to the west. What could have driven the tiger to do this? The tracks followed a meandering line, and Edit wondered if the tiger was tired, too. Everything in the forest was hungry and tired.

The grind in her belly began again. She paused to rest against a tree, and saw that blood had seeped from her clothes, leaving a trail in the snow. She stared in horror; blood was a marker, and it was a weakness. It left a trace of her for any animal to follow. But, she told herself again, there was nothing to be done, she had to continue. She elected to follow the tigress, sensing that the beast was executing a plan. She realised she had made the right choice when the hyperactive plaintiveness of the crows swelled through the air.

A break in the trees. The sky above, a whirlpool of crows. And, beneath a cedar – a bloodbath. Fur and blood flung everywhere, the snow churned crimson. Edit bent to pick up some of the hair scattered in clumps around the site. Bear. The blood was not yet frozen. This was the kill site. Edit cocked the rifle, scrutinised the forest around her.

Disrupted snow went off in a bloody trail, into the trees. The tiger would have eaten and drunk from the carcass urgently and then sought to drag her kill to a better location, where she could see all around and defend it, and where feasting could continue. Heart pounding, Edit gripped the rifle.

Placing her feet into the trail left by the tigress, she sought to disturb as little as possible. She checked around herself after each step, taking particular care behind. There seemed to be a tiger in every shadow; she flinched with each fall of snow from a branch.

Lumps of black fur clung to twigs poking from the snow. A tiger can drag something greater than its own body weight for many kilometres. More crows signalled the drag site ahead. Edit stopped, cocked the rifle, and fired twice into the sky. The crows evaporated and there was silence. Edit crept forward. Her gut clenched. She had never been so frightened as now.

Beneath a fallen trunk sprawled a hollowed-out bear carcass. Though there was no tiger at it, it was clear from the freshness of the churned-up snow and the gleam of blood not yet frozen, that this had happened recently. Tigers often returned to kills over several days, if, like this one, they were too big to demolish in one go.

Was the tiger still here? When the hairs on your skin flick upright; when the faintest crack of a twig or brush of snow seems to have been moved by an animal force; when shadows play at the corner of your vision, shadows that, when you blink, coalesce into stripes: these are facts not to be ignored. To do so is to be fatally ignorant, a thug crashing about in a carefully communicating world.

At her feet was the bear's heart. Two hands big, it was untouched, having simply rolled from the bear's body. How had the tiger not eaten it? It was one of the first organs a tiger would go for. Edit checked around her. Having dragged the bear to this spot, the tigress had probably returned for her cubs.

Edit slipped the heart into her pack. It was still warm.

She called out, 'I'm sorry. I'm so hungry.' Her voice clattered through the trunks, causing snow to tumble from a branch. In such unobstructed air, sound had muscle.

She picked her way towards the carcass. The bear was rather thin and mangy; for some reason, it had not begun to hibernate. A scrawny bear was still a big meal for a tiger. Even a tigress with cubs. Surely she could spare a little.

Edit drew out her knife and knelt by the carcass. Fresh meat assaulted her senses. She could not help herself: she sliced a little off and plunged it into her mouth. It was not quite frozen and, in her mouth, became livid again, flooding her tongue with blood. There was no time to eat more. Edit cut off a haunch, expertly detaching it from the joint. Blood squeezed thickly on to her hands and she licked it off. She put the haunch into her pack.

Do not take from a tiger's kill.

The tiger will come to find its property.

The old teachings pounded in her head.

She remembered the tiger, long ago, that saw her in the forest and spared her. And here she was, stealing from one of its descendants.

'But we are so hungry,' Edit mumbled.

326

She backed away from the carcass. 'Thank you,' she called out into the trees, gripping the rifle.

The haunch and heart would keep them going for a week. Perhaps the weather would ease, in that time.

Her own heart battered like a panicking jay in a bag. Surely the tigress could hear it.

Snow thumped to the ground, to her right. She spun round, convinced she saw a flash of orange. She shot the gun into the silent sky. The echo died into nothingness.

Edit was giddy with the exhilaration that comes with breaking a law. Her fingers around the gun were first slimy, then icy with sweat. Salty perspiration froze on her lip. Edit hoped that the fact the tiger had not simply attacked her, there and then, perhaps signalled some kind of forgiveness, some kind of kinship between mothers. After all, we will do what we must to feed our cubs. Every sense alive to her surroundings, she retraced her steps towards home.

The day was fading by the time she reached the cabin. Smoke was pouring from the chimney, and the glow from the stove lit the little window.

She took the remaining bullets from the rifle, left it propped outside and went in.

Her daughter was asleep, a heap beneath the blankets. It seemed she had not moved all day, except to stoke the stove. The smell of urine came from the bowl under the cot. She had not even been outside for that. Edit swiftly emptied the bowl, and returned to the stove, warming her hands and feet, the sodden boots pulled off. She dragged off the leggings, and steeped them straight away in the pot on the stove. The hot water swarmed red.

Worry stung the edges of her relief. Quickly pulling off the sodden undergarments and adding them to the pot, she wrapped some birch bark around some cool ash and replaced the pad. The clothes washed yesterday were at last dry. It felt good to pull on warm, clean clothes.

'Zina? Mummy is home. We have meat.'

Her daughter's pale face lifted from sleep, the almost-white lips parted. 'Oh!' she whispered, and opened her eyes. Mother and daughter gazed at each other, and Edit knew this catch had come not a moment too soon.

Invigorated by her success, Edit took out the heart from the pack, cut it into slices and placed the slices in a pan on the stove. From the haunch, she cut some fat and threw that in too, then she wrapped the haunch in birch bark and stowed it, under snow, beneath the porch.

In minutes, the smell of rich, frying meat filled the cabin. Zina found the strength to sit up, her long crinkly hair falling over her broad shoulders. While the meat fried, Edit heated water with *chunga* and berry jam, to make the stinging, medicinal tea that seemed to fortify them.

They chewed the strong, gamey meat in silent abandon, the juice of it dribbling down chin and fingers. Edit felt strength returning to her; while she lost blood, she gained blood. The Mother Taiga was just that – a mother who had saved them both from death.

Colour peeped in her daughter's cheeks. Edit told Zina of the trip, though she played down the proximity of the tiger. The good hunter took only what she needed, and said thank you.

'Did you see it?' her daughter asked.

'No. And that is good. It is unlucky to see a tiger.' Edit did not mention the flash of orange, the way that every cell in her body had experienced the tiger.

She shut out what she had done. It was just hunting. She looked upon her daughter, chewing her meat, examining it in her fingers, like a squirrel might examine a nut. She was unselfconscious, large and – what was it? Herself. Yes, that was it. Zina seemed neither girl nor woman, but a creature possessed of a mysterious and strange power that was all her own. There was only one other creature that struck Edit this way, that was simply what it was, in all its beauty and physicality, and that was a tigress.

Edit smiled and shook her head. There were things she could not explain to herself, let alone a ten-year-old. She sucked on the last of her meat, noting that the larger portion, which she had given to Zina, was all gone, and Zina was licking her lips uninhibitedly, like a satisfied cat.

She remembered, then, how the older women in the village had gone through some kind of slow transformation that demanded struggle, that, now she looked back on it, had been a kind of spiritual and physical writhing. The result was an absolute change in them, and their place in the village.

They, too, became *themselves*. Freed from childbearing, and from the expectations applied to young women, they were considered wise. They administered medicines. They were consulted on important matters. And more, they were much freer, in expression and in what they did.

Was this what was happening? Was Edit transforming into something authentically herself? A different kind of woman?

Edit's own mother had died before she could explain any of this to her daughter, or indeed before it happened to her.

Of course, the excessive bleeding could be, not a signal of positive change, but a disease. She did not know.

Edit wondered, as she often did when the possibility of her being ill arose, if they should have found a way to the city, all those hundreds of miles away. But how to survive there, friendless, penniless, the skills she had worthless? Would it have meant opportunity for Zina? Or a slow, desperate deportation back to the village, where Edit would have to witness the end of any dreams for her daughter?

Clearing the bowls away, Edit returned to the troubling questions. What about tomorrow, and the day after? Should they go to the camp? Where would Zina best be able to continue being the magical beast she had turned out to be?

Zina paused in licking her fingers. 'What?' she asked her mother.

'Do you want to go to the camp? Remember, the camp with the men? Where we got the supplies, years ago?'

'You said they would kill us.'

'I was trying to protect you. I know you don't believe it, but I was,' Edit said.

'You said I'm a forest girl,' Zina said, turning her big eyes away. 'And humans won't like me.'

'Zina . . .' Edit reached for her daughter's hand. 'I'm worried about my bleeding. I'm worried that I may get ill and not be able to do what I did today. I can't steal from a tiger again.'

Zina blinked. 'I can hunt. I can hunt and look after us.'

'But, if we go to the camp, perhaps . . .'

'Perhaps what?'

'Perhaps you'll be happy.'

Zina rolled her eyes. 'Oh, yes, like you said. I'll get married and have lots of babies.' One of her incisors caught her bottom lip, a sharp point. It was almost a smile.

'If you want to go, we will go,' Edit said, firmly. 'You should start to make the decisions.'

Zina sat back on her haunches and considered her mother. She said, 'Not yet. This is my home.' Seeing there was a point of tenderness opening up in their conversation, she seized an opportunity. 'My *father* . . .' she began.

Edit gave up the information gladly now. 'His name was Valery.'

'Did you . . . love him? Valery.'

Hearing Valery's name from the lips of his child was a shock. It seemed almost to be a different word. Until now, it had been Edit's word for a cluster of memories that still reeled with life. From Zina, it was a word without memories, a word that meant *father*.

Why had she never told Zina his name before? This suddenly seemed like a kind of theft, and Edit flushed with guilt.

Zina was thoughtfully turning the word over. 'Valery,' she whispered. 'Valery.'

Had Edit loved him? It was, of course, an impossible question to answer. It was a child's question, devastating in its simplicity. How could what she had experienced with Valery, and without him, be put into a single word? This was a Russian thing to do: use a single word to hammer out the paradox, the ambiguity at the heart of everything. She needed an Udeghe fable, her own story, that would express two worlds, split forever, longing for each other. One word was poor and savage.

'Yes, I did,' she said, firmly, looking into her daughter's eyes. If this was a lie, and she did not know for sure that it was, what did it matter? Her child needed to know that her mother had loved her father. A tentative smile began on Zina's lips.

'And we wanted you more than anything. Do you know we were married for ten years before you came along? We longed for you, all through it.'

Zina's eyes grew red at the edges. She said nothing, bowed her beautiful, shimmering head. Edit saw clearly what she had denied her daughter all these years.

'Zina, do you forgive me?' Edit gasped.

In answer, Zina pulled out her *khomus*, the little musical instrument Edit had fashioned from a flexible sliver of birch. She began a low accompaniment, to which they knew some words, and Edit began to sing through her tears. And, in the cosy firelight, mother and daughter sang the old songs. They needed nothing and no one else; Mother Taiga had provided, and they had, after all these years, stumbled into the essential truth of the forest. They could survive here, together, free.

Thirty

WAS SHE DREAMING? THE night took a shuddering breath, just as before a storm. At those moments, every bird fell silent and the animals fled, anticipating the chaos of spirits to come, boiling the air with their fury, lacerating it with ice.

The hairs on Zina's arms prickled upright.

A sound, like a crust breaking.

Her eyes snapped open. Every muscle tensed. The world had breathed in, but had not yet breathed out, as if all oxygen had been sucked from the cabin. Zina gulped like a fish on a hook. She looked round wildly for her mother. Edit was lying by the stove, fast asleep in its glow.

Did Zina imagine it, a shadow flicking past the window?

She slipped out of bed and stared at the pristine snow, lit by moon and stars. Her pulse seemed to fill the forest.

An owl, funnelling through the black.

The sky, a jewelled cloak. One day, the cloak would sweep aside and she'd know another world. That was what her mother had told her.

Unease clung with little talons, wouldn't shift.

Zina climbed back under her blankets and sleep sank its mouth over her face.

A few hours later, the thin winter dawn ran chilly fingers over her. Zina sprang awake, the unease insistent, like hunger or thirst. Her mother was still asleep. They had sung long into the night. They had been so happy.

Zina looked down at her mother as she slept by the stove. Edit's hair was grey, a wiry halo. Her face had the look of the moon when the air has cracked round it, like a shining plate dropped on to ice.

How strange it was that everything was like everything else, and yet also completely new. Her mother's lips were the colour of a deerskin tunic rubbed to a shine by the body. When her mother kissed her, which was not so often now, the kiss was a papery stamp, like the toe of a racoon dog. Zina liked those kisses.

Edit had grown very pale. Sweat beaded at her silvery hairline. Zina was distracted from her unease by her realisation that she carried so much of her mother in herself. She had her mother's cheekbones; her own wiry hair carried the youthful glow of her mother's hair. She wondered what she had of her father, or had the forest replaced his gifts? Perhaps her hands; she looked at them now, in the thin light. The palms were wide and traversed with creases, like the foot pads of a large carnivore. Her nails were thick, like claws.

The fire glowed, its heat like a fragment of the sun, captured in their cabin, as if the fire was a baby of the sun.

Edit's breath rushed, as if she was dreaming of a chase. Zina hoped her mother was the pursuer; surely, in her dreams, she was the tiger, with everything she wanted easily in her sights. They often dreamed about food, when it was short, and would discuss in great detail the meat they would have. It was a torture, if they were hungry, but less tormenting than fighting the pangs silently. Zina hoped that, behind her mother's frantic eyelids, she was sinking her teeth into warm, dripping flesh. She hoped they would eat the bear haunch today. Rest. Eat. Sing.

Everything her mother had said about her father the previous night stuck in her mind. She pictured him as one of the strong, gleaming men from the camp, still clear in her memory, after all these years. In her imagination, he bent over her mother to kiss her, and Zina felt a throb of jealousy. It was jealousy of both of them.

There was the faint tang of blood around her mother. Surely the bleeding must be, as Zina had been told, something natural, that would cease. Edit looked as if her very spirit had risen to the surface of her skin. Zina was frightened, for her mother was, in that moment, not the all-knowing place of safety she had always been, but a sleeping woman, feverish and bleeding. Zina banished the thought.

She stood and went to the window. In the pale light, the snow was perfect, like young skin.

Zina cut some *chunga* and steeped it for a few moments in a cup of water scooped from the pot of melted snow on the stove. She lifted the cup to her lips.

It soared from her fingers. Scalding water splashed her leg, but she did not feel it. She rushed back to the window, only now seeing in her mind what had been right before her eyes.

A tiger.

Tail flick-flick.

Lying down, at the edge of the trees.

Waiting.

A whimper escaped Zina. She backed away from the window, her body catching up to the terror now, almost knocking her to the floor with its trembling.

'Mummy,' she whispered. '*Mummy . . .*'

'Yes, good morning—'

'*Tiger.*' Zina pointed to the window, then turned and was violently sick over the bed. The hot remains of yesterday's meat roiled over the blanket.

Edit got to her feet. Her hand clasped her belly. 'Stay back,' she said, and rushed to the window. Her gasp told Zina she had not imagined it.

Edit said, 'It's the tigress. You know, the one whose prints we saw, with cubs? I wonder where the cubs are.' Her voice was bright and shut, like a lock.

Zina said, 'Has she come for her meat?'

Edit rubbed her eyes, as if the image might disappear. 'Yes,' she said, quietly.

Zina forced herself to look outside again.

It was as if all the light and dark of the forest, every flicker of gold, brown and white, and every magic thing had been sculpted together and brought to life, right in front of them. Nose to tail, the tigress was the same length as the cabin.

The beast yawned. Her teeth were like icicles.

'She doesn't seem angry,' Zina said, hopefully. 'Maybe if we just give her the meat, she will go away.'

Edit turned to her daughter. 'Stay back. Right back.'

'What are you doing?' Zina asked.

'The rifle is outside. I am going to bring it in here and load it up.'

'Mummy, don't open the door.'

'Zina, that tiger is not going to leave until she gets what she wants. We will starve to death, waiting for her to go. No, she . . .' At this, Edit gave a trembling gasp. 'I have to deal with it.'

With a deep breath, Edit pulled open the door. Icy sunlight rushed in, dusting the earthen floor with snow.

The tigress turned the huge lens of her face. Her lips drew back in a great hiss. An almost-movement rippled down her ribs, as if she was going to get to her feet. Her enormous tail flipped like a snake. Edit stepped smartly along the side of the building, beneath the narrow porch, and grabbed the rifle.

She snapped back into the room, slamming the door shut and dragging the bolt across. Then she sat heavily on the bed. Her hands shook around the rifle.

Zina had never seen a tiger, and this one was bigger than she had imagined, even in her nightmares. It seemed impossible that a tiger could be outside their cabin. Waiting. She knew, of course, from her mother, how a tiger never forgot a wrong done to them. But this one seemed to have leapt out of a dream or a story. It was beyond real, a conjuring, like the images of her father that she brought to life behind her eyes at night.

Edit grabbed her daughter's arm. 'A tiger is not a normal beast, Zina – you can see that, can't you? We know, the Udeghe know, it is the spirit of the forest, and I stole from it. It's me she wants, and I have to settle it. I thought . . . I thought perhaps she would forgive me. We were so hungry. I thought she could spare it.'

Zina was terrified, but of a different creature than her mother was. 'Mum, we can defend ourselves against an animal, can't we? But not a god.'

Edit pressed one of the warm kisses on her daughter's cheek. 'There is only one rifle. You *must* stay inside. Do you promise me?'

Zina smiled. 'I promise,' she said.

Edit had broken promises. For instance, she had promised

to stay married to Valery, Zina's father, and she hadn't. She had promised to find the other tribe and changed her mind. Like the cheekbones, and the hair, Zina decided that she had inherited her mother's view of promises as undertakings to be *assessed*. Fearsome change was about to deluge their little unit, and it was clear to Zina that the promises a child made to her mother could no longer be binding in all circumstances.

Edit looked even thinner and more fragile than she had yesterday. Bending to pull on clean deerskin leggings that she had washed and dried the night before, she stumbled and nearly fell. Zina grabbed her arm.

'I'm all right, just moving too quickly,' Edit said. 'Here, clever daughter, tie on my belt.'

Zina tied on the ammunition belt. While her mother filled the pouches with bullets, Zina went to the window to check where the tiger was.

'She's gone!' Zina cried.

'What?'

The tigress had vanished. The snow was disturbed at the spot where she had lain, but of the beast herself there was no sign.

'I can still feel her, though. Can you?' Edit said. Her eyes were wide.

Zina nodded, the hairs standing up on her neck and arms again. Nausea tightened in her gut.

Edit filled the barrel with ammunition and spoke commandingly to her daughter.

'As long as you stay in here, everything will be all right. I am going to use the cabin as cover and wait for her outside. When she comes, I will shoot her. I will be right outside – right there. Just stay where you are, all right?' She forced a smile, met with one from Zina, equally fixed and inauthentic. Then she pulled the door shut behind her. Zina stood, stunned, by the window.

Everything about the shining, beautiful day said, *No tiger, here. No danger.*

Pressed against the cabin wall for cover, Edit sidled to the corner and peered round. She scanned the forest edge. Then she moved to the other side and peered round there. There was nothing, not even tracks. Silence hung like a bowl over the clearing. Her heart echoed inside it; she thought she might die of panic.

The minutes stretched on. She would have to go indoors before too long, to warm up. Maybe the tigress had, after all, returned to her cubs for now. The unease remained, growing stronger. It penetrated mother and daughter both, to a cellular level.

Zina grew convinced that, if it came down to a silent stand-off between them, the tigress would win. She had the endurance and the ruthlessly patient nature. Edit and Zina could not wait forever without action. An idea seized Zina.

She grabbed some brushwood from the floor and tied it to the branch they used for a poker. With a taper, she lifted a flame from the stove and lit the top. Grabbing the bottle of diesel, which they had barely touched in five years, she pulled open the cabin door and strode out into the snow.

'Zina! What are you doing?' Edit cried.

'Fire!' Zina snarled. 'All animals, even tigers, are afraid of fire!'

'No! Zina, you promised!' Edit stared helplessly as her daughter crossed the untouched snow to the border of the forest, the torch blazing above her head. Edit's own plan had been to circle the cabin, observe the signs, await the tiger's reappearance, which would surely come. But, now that her child was out in the snow, she must abandon that plan and cover her with the rifle. Terror flashed in her veins as she watched Zina draw near to where the tigress had lain down, and set her torch to the base of a birch tree. The flames ripped up the bark, like squirrels running for their lives. On to the next, the torch sparking around her, a splash of petrol on the base and then fire dancing along the flags of loose bark, catching the leafless canopy above, seizing the dead remains of a bear's nest. A deafening cracking filled the air, drowning out all other sound, and smoke began to swill across the snow.

Zina panted with excitement. A wall of fire – that would drive away *Amba*. They'd have time to work out what to do. On she ran, stumbling in the deep snow, air knifing the inside of her lungs. Soon, the whole line of trees in front of the clearing was ablaze.

Her mother swept the rifle back and forth, scanning

desperately for any sign of the tigress. Her eyes were screwed up with a hunter's intense focus down the rifle's barrel. As Zina had abandoned her promise, now Edit had abandoned her plan. Edit would do everything to protect her daughter; it was now her only thought.

To scan effectively, she stepped forward, *away from the cabin wall.*

She stepped away from the cabin wall.

Flames roared through the branches, eclipsing all sound, and the tiger's decisive move.

A moan, or a shriek, or an actual writhing spirit split Zina's mouth to its limit. The mouth moved, trying to shape the scream into sound.

For the tigress was on the cabin roof.

Zina vainly launched her torch at the cabin. The cracking of the fire behind her was like shrapnel hitting her brain.

She dragged herself towards her mother, through the gobbling, ghoulish snow. Her face was a hole of fear.

Edit understood, and turned, just as the tigress leapt, with the greatest leisure, as if this were not a physical world where time and gravity applied at all.

Zina paddled in the drift, as if struggling to consciousness. Her mother fired, cocked again, fired, cocked again, fired, cocked again —

the tigress's body reverberated as she sailed across the sun, claws unsheathed bursts of blood from the tiger's head, like a hot spring

fired, cocked again, *click, click, click*

Edit, tiny as a child beneath a great cloud

the rifle dropped in the snow, because the rifle was empty

Edit holding up her two hands to hide her face –

'Mummy!' Zina screamed, crawling towards her, like a new-born, up the great belly of the earth, to the breast that would save her.

But now there was only a tigress, roaring and scraping in the snow, a great hole in her head, blood dripping from her jaws.

Smoke swept across them.

Through the scalding murk, Zina saw another tiger, a cub, creep round the cabin and stand frozen, watching its mother.

Part Four

TIGERS

Thirty-one

I F THE COUNTESS'S TRACKS could be followed backwards through her journey after the bear, back through the loss of her cub, back from her own death, through the impossible overlayings of snow and the change of the seasons, they would lead eventually to this nameless beginning, in a cave on high ground, on a clear night in early summer.

It was a few months before the footage of the Countess with her cubs, which Ivan and Tomas so loved to watch, was captured. The Countess was resting at the entrance of the cave she had selected to give birth to the cubs. She was far away from all camera traps. There were no people, and she was far beyond all human storytelling.

Something swept by in the cool darkness. It was silent, but the Countess felt the flutter on her cheek. Her face, in repose, was a great satellite dish of reception, which detected changes in air pressure caused by movement many metres away.

The pressure change was like a streak of bubbles, *pop, pop, pop*, down the right-hand side of her face. Her eyes snapped open. The darkness was not total; stars punctured the night sky so completely that it might seem to the human eye as if it would break apart under the strain of all the holes, revealing the unutterable brilliance behind.

With this amount of illumination, almost any movement was detectable. Only movement, though – detail was lost to her. But who needs detail? Who needs to see colours, the round of a creature's eye? If the creature was breathing, in range, the Countess would see it. If it dared to lick its lips, if it thought to raise its snout, she would see it.

She orientated her right ear towards the shift in air pressure. She heard, some ten lengths away, a breath. Not a creature's breath: it was the breath of the atmosphere when it sets a creature down.

Bird. Coming in to land.

Her head followed her ear, and now every sense was attuned forwards and concentrated in the miraculous dish of her face. She opened her mouth and sucked the air in through the flap at the back of her throat, which allowed her to taste and smell simultaneously. But the disturbance was not something big enough, near enough, nor necessary enough to alert her sense of smell – less sensitive than a dog's and more for communicating with her own kind than aiding her attack.

Apart from the delicate pant, drawing the cold air in, she was motionless. The Countess had been sleeping with her head at the mouth of the cave. In her belly, the cubs shifted, as if she was carrying a flock of birds. It sometimes felt like hunger. It sometimes was hunger, their hunger transmitting itself to her, becoming hers. But, now, a bolt of pain accompanied their movement.

Information came thick and fast.

A burst of grass.

Stars on an outstretched talon.

An eye, round and glowing as her own. An owl. The tiger observed the owl, but the owl did not see the tiger. She was so still, she could not be detected. The owl was, anyway, focused on a mouse, which it had now caught, with not even a squeak, the dispatch being instantaneous.

A scoop of darkness, a black scrap dangling.

Then gone. The pearly night swept over again. The Countess's ears turned independently, scanning the area for sound. Her third eyelids skimmed her eyes and her tongue slipped out, tasting again.

At this moment, she resembled nothing so much as a monstrous snake. A human observer would understand immediately why the Udeghe shaman drum has a snake-like tiger painted across its membrane. The Udeghe understand that all natural things are simply incarnations of each other. Observing with her deadly calm, the Countess embodied this factual magic.

It had been a week, now. When the dawn arrived, the tiger would need to catch something. She was ravenous. She'd dragged the last kill, a sizeable boar, back to this cave and gorged on it for days. But, now – more.

The territory must also be checked, marked out again. The Countess's life was a constant patrol of her territory, spraying and clawing the reminders of her supremacy on the trees. Performing either of these vital tasks was going to be hampered by the impending birth of her cubs.

This tigress was an enormous, sleek beast, who maintained her enormity and sleekness through judicious rest. In the summer, when food was plentiful and the temperature high, and the humid air rested in great foggy clouds, she would often sleep for fifteen hours at a stretch, her ears maintaining contact with all frequencies, but the blood of her vast body slowed to the river's slack meandering. At rest, her heart pumped with a languorous beat, like an immense sturgeon in the lake, keeping still against the current. And when hunger made its slow rumble, it could be attended to with grace because it was likely that one evening's hunting would satisfy it. The Countess might make ten or even twenty failed attempts to catch prey; in the summer, when game was plentiful, this was not so tiring a prospect. There could be alternative pleasures that overrode hunger – like sleep, like play.

But, as soon as winter began its approach, the supply of acorns and nuts dwindled; the boar and deer began to move further and further afield, and the ten or twenty attempts could have days between them. In addition, the Countess would have less comfortable nights – even with the layers of fur, and the long hairs trapping meagre warmth, even with the rolling layer of fat she'd managed to build up. Before the rivers froze completely solid, there was the chance to catch fish, but they were not so sluggish when the water grew cold, and ten or twenty attempts was exhausting.

Each season was incarnated from the last, and the Countess's history was written in the cubs she produced every two or three years. She was unusually successful as a mother: at least one from each litter had survived, often more. Her unusual size was a factor in this success, as was her ferocity in maintaining her prime territory. There were several female territories adjoining hers – including, until recently, that of her own mother, killed by a snare. The only tiger allowed to trespass into her territory was the king tiger, and this was because he didn't recognise it as separate from his own. There were five female tigers within his territory, and he spent his life circumnavigating this space spanning several hundred kilometres.

But, a month ago, there was a rupture in the established order.

The king tiger was dead. The Countess came across his body at the far reach of her own territory. He had been caught by a rifle snare, a huge hole blown in his side. It was some time ago, and the crows had already reduced him to bones.

After sitting for a while, hidden near the body, she had moved off into the king's wider territory. Though pregnant, she had begun to follow his trail, marking where he had marked, crossing into the other female territories, where she won every skirmish.

It had become the case that the king's territory was now hers, although it was progressively exhausting to police it. The Countess's son, from the litter two years ago, was a complicating factor. He had shown great resistance to moving out of the area as young males are supposed to do, to set up a king territory of his own, far away. Young males often resisted this challenge, and stayed near their mothers until forcibly driven away. The king tiger would only tolerate females within his territory, and, at a certain point, would fight his male offspring as rivals.

But, when her son realised the king tiger was dead, he immediately began spraying and scratching around the perimeter, often following his mother and spraying over her own mark. He was much smaller than she, but more aggressive, and also not afflicted with a burgeoning pregnancy. The delayed banishment was going to have to happen now, and so there had been a fight, right there on the earth beneath the arching trunk, where the king male always made his mark. The son was consumed with fury for his mother, which drove him to mount her, slashing at her eyes with his claws unretracted and clamping on her neck as if she were a sika deer he had caught.

Heavy with her pregnancy, the Countess had to be cautious. She could not allow an injury that would prevent her hunting. But her son's ferocity threatened to overwhelm her. She clouted him with her great paws and roared as he clambered on her back. Her son yowled and snarled, dragging at her sides with his claws. The Countess set off at an awkward bound, her son still clinging, biting into her neck. She headed into the thickest part of the forest, where low-slung branches and saplings crowded the way. Her son was soon dislodged; he rolled from her, hit himself hard on a branch, but sprang back on his feet with the seeming invincibility of youth.

Panting heavily, she headed downland to where the trees parted a little to allow soft growth and grasses, to which the deer flocked in season.

There lay abandoned pit-traps, set by Chinese hunters, years before. They comprised a distance of now-tumbledown fence, blocking the track taken by the deer, with gaps along the route. Just beyond each gap, a deep pit, which, when it was used, was covered with brushwood. The deer would go through the gaps and fall into the pits. When the Chinese moved on, they did not fill the pits nor dismantle the fence, and so they had continued to trap beasts until all had finally learnt.

The Countess knew this area; her son did not. She bounded through a gap, with her son close on her tail, and leapt over the pit. Of course, her son did not leap, so fixed was he on gaining his hold once again on his mother, and he crashed into the hole. The tigress did not look back as his outrage echoed through the trees. The Countess made her return to the cave at the top of the mountain, far from where he lay. There was every chance he would manage to get out, but, if so, he would not challenge her again for a long time, not until he was big enough to kill her outright.

Dawn came slowly in the forest. It had to make its way up from an invisible horizon, and then penetrate the thick leaf cover. The cubs turned again and pain ruptured through her.

The Countess retreated into the cave, hungry, thirsty, growling.

Thirty-two

NEARLY A YEAR AND a half passed, taking the cubs deep into their second winter, the harshest one in memory.

The Countess paused to sniff the heavy oval print of a bear. She was alone, her cubs left in a den beneath a log while she hunted. The tracks, made by an animal moving slowly, were heading upland. No blood. So there was no injury, but this was no time of year for a bear to be wandering. A bear should be hibernating, deep in the hollow of a tree. The bear must be hungry, like she was – hungry too long.

She changed direction to follow the trail. Passing a tree where both tigers and bears liked to scratch and spray, she stiffened as she tasted him. Hairs, caught on the rough cedar bark, wafted beneath her breath like anemones. She paused to listen. He was too far in front for her to hear. She picked up speed.

In winter, time became as hotly corporeal on the tongue as

blood. It haemorrhaged down the frozen, barren rivers; it crept like a life-snuffing vine over the empty trees. Time was the only real danger to the Countess in the winter forest: time without food; time away from cubs; time taken to hunt a starving bear.

Time's only weakness was that it left a trail. Time could be followed – backwards, forwards – in the snow. It held no secrets from her in winter. The bear was too far ahead, but he could not hide from her.

The only other bear the tigress had caught was a young one, making a nest in the treetops, a few seasons ago. The bear was noisy in the canopy, snapping branches in her eagerness to construct a nest that reached all the richest berries. The tigress was following a boar herd as the herd followed the acorns. But then a branch fell practically on her face, and, her success being in part down to her ability to evaluate opportunities, she paused in her hunt and looked upwards, to the source of the disturbance. The bear had not seen her, nor heard her; she crashed about in the treetop as if nothing existed but the engineering feat of her nest. The tigress selected a comfortable spot a few metres away, lay down, and waited.

Towards evening, the bear finished gorging on the berries and began her descent. Some five metres from the forest floor, she sensed change. A strange silence – a tiger makes every creature in the vicinity run for its life – made her freeze. She could see nothing, nor hear anything, but knew better than to come down. She retreated back to the nest, slept in the treetop.

The Countess now curled beneath a fallen log, where she could not be seen from above, and slept. A little rain fell; she licked the rain from the bark and waited.

The next day, the bear crept down as night fell; again, the terrible silence drove her back up.

By the third day, the Countess did not even attempt to hide. The air was soporific. She sprawled out on the log, her ears tuned in to the tree. She yawned.

On the fourth day, the bear began to whine.

On the fifth day, the bear ran down the tree just before dawn, her eyes wide stamps of fear, and leapt in a direction she thought the tigress was not facing.

The Countess was there, of course.

But that was summer, when time doesn't bleed and harden. This would be different.

At least the tracks were not hard to follow and there were hours of daylight left. The trail drew her further upland. Sometimes, her tracks inserted into the bear's, her trail obliterating his. Somewhere, a woodpecker hammered a trunk, echoes fluttering at the edge of the sky. The Countess paused to lick some snow, her sides heaving. Her ears scanned; on the screen of her retinas, details came together like iron filings around a magnet. Far away, a crow rose, like a tiny rip in the sky. She tasted, panting. Something . . . Something . . .

Time to leave the tracks.

She turned away and bore west along the contour of the

357

slope. This was part of the newly claimed king territory that was now hers. The bear would be heading to the furthest stand of oaks, in the hope of acorns. The tigress knew the boar had already devoured what there was and moved on. It was a further clue to the bear's desperation. The Countess could feel him, now, a shiver down her body, the prospect of satisfaction. Saliva dripped from her jaws, disappearing into the snow in little drills of desire.

Something, a flicker in her brain, made her tilt back and begin to conclude her loop. She jogged from the broken area of trees, not recovered from a forest fire after many years, into the thick stand of virgin forest, coming to a rest beneath an enormous cedar. Curled at its roots, she blended perfectly with the sharply contrasted light and dark of bark and shadow.

She waited. Not with the languor of that summer hunt, but with starvation's drooling tightness. There was no question that he would come to her.

Soon enough, his snuffling approach. He pushed the snow urgently with his forepaws, pressing his snout into the frozen nothingness beneath each tree. He did not notice the tigress, barely five metres away. He could see nothing but possibility and impossibility, rolling over each other, making his sides heave.

The Countess blinked. The bear's shoulder was scarred, his ribs poked.

She exploded against his back, smashing him against a tree. She squirmed on him, shifting her weight so that she had him pinned. Eyes closed, she opened her huge mouth to its fullest extent to bite his neck at the spine. The air was blown out of him, but he wasn't finished yet. He roared in outrage and reached with his paw, slashing her ribs. In response, she wrapped her forelegs around him as they fell, sending snow in constellations, upwards. There it was, the soft throat. If only he would stop moving. She was so hungry. The struggle was so tiring. All she wanted to do was eat.

And down went the great meaty lips, almost delicately turned to the side, as if for a kiss. Her teeth enveloped the bear's windpipe and one nicked his carotid artery, spurting blood over them both. His struggle intensified, while her body seemed to gather into itself, become more still. His pulse battered down the length of her whiskers, and his worried bear-eyes began to roll. The Countess kept her jaws quietly clamped around his throat, occasionally shaking him from side to side as the great bear-claws paddled him away from his life. At last, she felt time melting in delectable warmth all over her face.

Thirty-three

THE SNOW WAS ARMPIT deep, but the Countess negotiated the drifts powerfully, limbs scything through the white. It was the female cub who struggled: she leapt like a puppy, trying to stay in her mother's wake, failing and tumbling into the drifts. It looked like play, but both were exhausted. Stopping was not permitted.

Ahead, the line of trees thickened, snow borne on outstretched branches, like ghostly white bundles in the arms of travellers. Ahead, too, the remains of the bear carcass. All the forest knew the tigress was on her way to reclaim it.

The sky bulged over the trees. More snow would soon fall. Mother and cub must reach the food soon or – and here she steadfastly refused to look behind her – the cub would fail. They had left the dead male cub behind. Losing her remaining offspring meant total failure, and failure could not be her concern.

Her one goal was to get them back to the food that was theirs. It was just mother and daughter, now, and they were not far away.

Softness drifted from the sky. She quickened her pace, the full force of her mind trained on the line of trees. The snow wheezed and creaked as she drew near.

Silence is made solid by the snow. You must know what you are listening for, you must know to tilt the head, the brain, into the silence, taking account somehow of the tilt and magnetism of the earth, applying the mind with absolute precision to the unseen. This was how the tigress discerned if they were being followed and what lay ahead in the trees.

The Countess tasted the air, sneezing as she inhaled a snow-flake. It was hard to smell anything; as well as being solid silence, the snow was solid absence: the manifestation of no-thing. Then, a crash far away – sweeping through her skin like a flock of birds, ending with a jolt in her gut. The crash was, she knew, a branch giving way beneath the weight of snow, ice galloping exponentially from the impact. There were countless such creaks and breaks, and it took a lifetime of these conditions to under-stand them, so as not to be underneath when the fall came.

The cub had made a circle in the snow, with walls created by whirling round and round. She was nestled in the hollow, as if this was over, as if they might have some real rest. The Countess backtracked and peered down at her. She could not play, nor even now urge action upon her cub. So much of survival was turning away, keeping going, no matter what. The Countess had abandoned the body of her other cub in the snow – a cub whom she had fed and protected, and with whom she had played. Nevertheless, she had known the moment at which staying with him served no purpose. Knowing this moment in any situation was perhaps the great secret of her domination. The Countess could leave anything, anything at all, in order to survive.

This was a lesson her cub was absorbing. Obediently, she clambered out of the hole she had created. Her mother was moving on and she must follow.

Not far, now. Trailing glittering dust from its wing tips, an owl lifted. Two planetary gazes met. Two intelligences: one of air and night; one of snow and dawn.

The air was so cold that the bodies of mother and cub were not particularly wet. Nothing melted here in winter without force applied to it.

Hunger ground in their bellies. Fatigue clawed at their muscles. The Countess had dragged the bear somewhere safe, giving her time to collect the cubs and bring them to it. Here was the trail along which she had dragged it. The furrow had softened and the snow glowed red.

Something else.

Dots of unfamiliar blood along the trail – not hers, not the bear's.

She paused and sniffed it. Human blood. *Female*.

Nothing but crows would dare to approach her kill. She knew this, because she was the king of the forest.

But something was pressing at the margins of her understanding

– if the food *was* gone (though this was unthinkable), then hunting more would take time, and the Countess simply did not have the strength to keep time at bay again. This consideration, never breaking into fear, never crossing the line between the present and the future, did not settle on her mind as it would in the human mind. Extremity was in her nature. From her outsize muscles and impenetrable snake-eyes, to the way she jogged inside her coat, like an army of limbs inside a trophy fur, she was a physical specimen to take your breath away. She expected no joy, no rest, no peace. Her advantage was that she knew this hostile place intimately and knew it did not change much.

And so to the clearing, and the hiding place, and – for this is in the nature of the inhospitable place – the bear carcass which, while not demolished, was *reduced*. The crows had been, that was to be expected, but great lumps had been sliced away.

The Countess growled and paced back and forth in front of the carcass. Her cub hesitated, starving, but deferring to her mother. All round the carcass were spatters of blood, with their female human smell.

The Countess performed her analysis of the air, collecting in her nose and on her tongue the fragments of scent, licking the snow to impress the taste further. She knew, now, who had taken the food. It was the hunter she had seen many times, deep in the forest, the one who lately was bloodied, who smelled of blood. The cold leached scent and taste, but there was enough for her to lay down in her brain the unbreakable synapse that would lead her to the thief.

But now, there was no time to do anything but eat. The Countess nudged her cub towards the meat, grown slightly crisp as it half-froze, and then she sank down herself. Mother and daughter fed desperately in a cloud of crimson.

Hours later, when every scrap of meat that could be eaten had been consumed, the Countess attended to what needed to be done. Temporarily fortified, the cub bounded after her mother as she followed the trail of blood spots, and, later, the hunter's tracks. Where the tracks blurred beneath new snow, the scent of that hunter's blood still reached her, fragmented like light through pines.

The Countess was going to reclaim her food and kill the hunter who took it. The tigress undertook the journey like the start of any hunting expedition, with ruthless and methodical calm. Her cub sprang around her, and the tigress paused to lift the cub by her scruff and carry her on her back, to roll her off and bat her playfully with her huge paws. When hunger was satisfied and there was certainty of purpose, even the tigress could play. After a while, the cub fell back into her mother's wake, focusing on the waving tail tip, with its smooth upturn at the end.

The Countess knew their destination. The whys were not part of it, but the whys don't matter that much, in the end. Her world was composed of facts and consequences. The hunter would be expecting a consequence. It was a law of the forest: you never steal from the king. And so, on they journeyed, the tigress the acknowledged lord of the forest, nevertheless stolen from, always just a tail tip away from catastrophe.

Thirty-four

THE CHILD'S FINGER SHOOK violently against the trigger. The rifle was one of the World War Two Ka-lashnikovs that were the only weapons available for many years. They were unpredictable, and also heavy and stiff. Tomas prayed it wouldn't go off. The child's gaze was fierce, even as her lips trembled. His arms ached, but he kept them as high as he could, palms facing in a way that he hoped was pacifying, as well as showing surrender.

With a nod, she indicated the forest behind him, where he had come from. Desperation had drawn lines in her face, and the smoke sank into them, making her look older. Behind her, the treetops were still alight. Ash blew around her like flies, the snow tumbling, as if the sky were being shaken empty.

'Go away!' she cried, jabbing the gun nearer. 'Go!'

It flashed before Tomas that, if he were to do as she

commanded, if he were to leave this child alone, with a fire still burning behind her and what must be her mother dead, then he was worth nothing; he deserved every sorrow and desolation that would surely come his way. If she shot him for staying, it would be better than that. If the gun went off by accident, that would still be better. In some ways, it would right a balance. This thought gave him courage.

'Don't shoot!' he called through the muffling snow. 'My name is Tomas. The fire – we must put it out.' Defiance clouded her expression and instinctively he took a step back, babbling what came suddenly into his head. 'Do you want to see a mermaid?'

She frowned down the barrel. 'What's a mermaid?'

'It's a lady who is half a fish. The bottom half is a big fish tail.'

She said nothing, shifting a little on her feet.

'I'm going to use my hands to take off my jacket, now. I will do it very slowly. You will see my hands all the time. I'm going to prove to you how much I want to help you. Showing you a mermaid means I may freeze to death.'

Keeping eye contact, he slowly lowered his pack and took off his coat. The cold bored through his clothes, like an invisible drill. The girl's eyes widened as he reached the final layer, a worn wool T-shirt, and pulled it off over his head. He could not suppress a moan as the air descended like locusts. With the little breath remaining to him, he gasped, 'I'm going to turn around, now. You'll see the mermaid. Please, don't shoot. And, please, don't look too long. It's very cold.'

He turned to reveal the mermaid curled around his back. He flexed his muscles so that her body moved, beneath flakes of snow, in a way that was almost like white water whipping from her flesh. 'Do you like her?' he asked over his shoulder. 'They live in the sea, and they sing to the sailors to keep them away from rocks.'

There was silence. Very carefully, Tomas turned around. The cold was so great that it circumvented even shivering. His body had barely realised how low its temperature had plummeted. His nipples were like rotten berries. His skin was bruised.

The rifle was still pointing at him, but shaking almost comically in her grip. She was longing to put it down, the weight too much. Her eyes were red-rimmed, the eyelashes a frosted frame of white.

'The mermaid's name ...' Tomas stammered through freezing lips, his sluggish brain turning. His mother's name. 'Her name is Natasha. The mermaid's name is Natasha. What is your name?'

'Zina,' the girl whispered.

'Zina, may I put my clothes back on? Natasha is very cold.'

She nodded. With limbs like frozen lumps of meat, Tomas yanked on his clothes. The fire hissed in the trees beneath the snow's onslaught. It was like a mirage: the air rippled, but the heat barely reached him; only the smoke carried an acrid, dying warmth, like a leakage from an underworld.

'Your cabin, Zina. What do you have? A shovel?'

Zina nodded. She pointed with the gun. 'In there.'

'Good. We have to make a bank of snow in front, as high as we can. You take the shovel. I will use what I can find inside. Let's stand the rifles here, by the door.' He reached out to take the rifle from her.

Zina's eyes flickered over the bodies in the snow. There was a fragment of hope in her expression, which wrenched at Tomas. She did not understand yet. She looked lost, a sapling stranded in daylight.

'Will my mummy be cold?' she asked, looking him full in the face for the first time. How he answered mattered: the right answer would allow her to know that her mother was dead, without hearing the word, the fact hurled upon her like a rock.

Tomas said, as calmly as he could, 'Your mummy is warm in the spirit world. She is watching you, making sure you are safe.'

Zina bit her lip, but her gaze did not waver. Then she nodded and said, 'There is a plank at the back of the cabin. When I clear the snow with my mummy, it's what I use.' She lowered the gun and relief slackened her face, quickly followed by a defiant screwing-up of her features.

'Give me your rifle,' she said.

'But it's better—'

Zina lifted her gun once more and Tomas raised his hands.

'Here. Yes. Here is my rifle.' He nudged it towards her with his boot.

'I will keep them,' said Zina.

'It's just . . .' said Tomas. 'A tiger may come. This tigress has a cub—'

'I know. It was here.'

'Here?' Tomas looked round wildly. 'Where did it go?'

'It ran away. When you came. We both . . . We both saw . . .'

'Zina, the cub will come back, and when it does, we need to be ready. We need to catch it – somehow, I don't know how yet. I must take it back with me. It won't survive, out here.' He did not add, *and nor will you*, though he realised now what this journey had turned into. 'We need to have the guns near. But not inside, or the mechanism will jam from condensation. We must have them near where we sleep.'

'Hurt that cub and I will kill you,' said Zina. Gathering up both rifles, laying one on each shoulder, she strode towards the cabin with unconvincing arrogance.

IT TOOK TWO HOURS to create a bank of snow in front of the cabin. As they worked silently, at opposite ends, Tomas kept checking the fire. It was moving away from them, but, still, the direction of the wind could change at any time. Zina worked with fierce diligence. She had hidden his rifle somewhere in the trees and wore her own strapped round her shoulder. It kept slipping on her thin frame; with no sign of irritation or impatience, she would stand and adjust it, before returning to her shovelling.

In the few hours since the deaths of Edit and the Countess, the bodies had hardened and fused together. Tomas had to push the plank between them to prise them apart. It was hard to take in that such a beast as the Countess was dead. The pity he felt on looking at her was not for the tigress herself, so much as for the abomination that had been perpetrated by dragging such a creature into the real world. It was, he suddenly thought, as if he had found a mermaid out in the ocean and had carried her back to live upon the earth, where of course she did not belong, and she'd died. And only then, when she was dead, having suffered, was the enormity of the loss – and the crime – apparent. He understood, now, why the Udeghes believed that to see a tiger in the flesh was unlucky. To cause such a manifestation . . . There had to be consequences. It could not go unpunished.

Though the Countess was the reason he had undertaken this whole journey, and it was a deep shock to see her dead, Tomas was desperate to look at the face of the woman he had imagined so thoroughly, the clever woman who made the best sable traps he had ever seen, the woman whose footprints had burned his lips.

He pulled and levered the tiger from her body, dragged it to one side.

He gasped at her injuries. Although her neck was intact, with just a bite at her windpipe, her chest was a cavern, her collarbone and ribs splintered. Her eyes were open and they stared beyond Tomas, towards where Zina was working. Tomas reached out and touched the greying hair, wiry like his own. When he looked down the body, he saw a small frozen foot poking out – confirmation, though none were needed, that it was she who had made the prints.

How he hoped she had not had time to mourn that she was leaving her child behind. This, Tomas thought, must be the hard part of dying, worse than any fear of a monster descending: abandoning someone who needed you, your own flesh and blood, whom you loved more than yourself. Dying held no fear for Tomas. All his abandonments were done. There was no one to mourn him, not as this girl would mourn, for the rest of her days.

The clever woman – as he thought of her – was not the lovely young sylph of his imaginings, but what she was moved him far more. How had she done it – raised a child, alone, in the forest? Her eyes, in life, would have been sharp and knowing – like the finches it was impossible ever to capture. She had narrow lips, with a slight bow, heavy eyebrows that almost met in the middle. She was about his age, he thought, and he felt, then, inadequate before her suffering. He wished he had found her sooner. He wished he might have saved her.

He realised he was kneeling beside her.

What a clash this must have been, between the cleverest, most courageous human and the most ferocious predator in the taiga.

Tomas began to cover the bodies with snow. It would have to do, until he could melt the ground for a grave or build a pyre to burn them. Neither of these trophies of the forest must become carrion.

ZINA'S EYELIDS KEPT DROOPING, and she drove them open. The stove glowed and the cabin was humid with cooking. Tomas had sawn the remains of the bear meat into pieces and fried it from frozen. He had found some herbs that Edit had dried. He insisted that Zina rested while he cooked. She sat on the bed with the rifle on her lap, pointed at him. She felt dead and excited at the same time, like a stone in a lightning storm.

Having Tomas here was like having a bear in the cabin. He occupied twice the space her mother did. His head almost brushed the cobwebs hanging down from the ceiling. He smelled different. It was the smell of a bear den, or the glades where the boar lay down, the vast male leaving a dip the size of a pond. A male smell, dry and bloodless. She wanted to see the mermaid again, but did not want to ask.

His massive movements, the smell of the food, the sheer novelty of a man in the cabin crackled over the top of her horror at what had happened that day, that her mother lay outside in the snow. From time to time, she longed to get up and run out, and simply lie beside her. Guarding this man was preventing her from doing that, but every part of her body ached and exhaustion pulled at her brain. Tomas seemed unperturbed that a gun was pointing at him. He asked, simply, that she did not rest her finger on the actual trigger, because that might mean she shot him without meaning to, and he really wanted to make this meal, and he really wanted to talk to her about what to do next. She was at liberty to shoot him at any time – just, please, not by accident? That would mean she was left all alone. This seemed an odd request – why was he not more frightened? – but she had obeyed, mostly because the gun was simply too heavy to hold properly at all times, and her finger, indeed, too trembling to rest on a live trigger.

She must have dropped off because, when she opened her eyes, he was standing before her with the fried bear meat in a dish. She grabbed at the gun with a gasp and he darted to one side, but she realised that he had not attempted to move the gun while she slept and that he was doing nothing more than bringing her food. She took the dish, and used the little knife in her belt to skewer pieces to eat. It was dreamlike to be eating something so delicious by the warm stove with this stranger, when her mother was dead. The image of the tigress blocking the sun was seared into her mind, but somehow it did not yet connect to her gut. It was like a bad dream, one from which she would wake. And when she did, this man would be gone, and it would be her mother sitting there, eating the meat.

Tomas sat on the floor at her feet. The rifle was now upside down across her lap. Her hands were full, hunger had overtaken her, she had forgotten the gun, for now.

He said, 'Zina, you know I was following that tigress because we are trying to look after the tigers. My father and I . . . we are trying to build a reserve for the tigers. The President of Russia – do you know who that is?'

She shook her head.

'Of course not. Well, President Putin is interested in our reserve. The cub that you saw? I need to capture it, take it back with me, and take it to the Rehabilitation Centre. It can never survive here, with no mother. I have to build a crate. And I must build it from your cabin.'

Zina's eyes widened. 'The cabin is mine!' she cried. She swallowed another piece of meat, her hunger unaffected by outrage. 'I will look after the cub. I will live here, just like my mother did. I can hunt. And I can shoot.' She said this last with emphasis. 'You can just go home to your camp.'

'You won't help me?'

Zina stuffed the last of the meat in her mouth and shook the rifle at him. It made an ominous rattling noise and instinctively his hands went up. 'You do what I say!' she said. 'What I say is go away!' She stared at him wildly, her face a chaos of starved need, indignation and utter exhaustion.

Tomas was used to resolving disputes between drunk comrades at the camp. He was often a buffer between them and his father: they moaned to him about this or that and he made the first overtures to Ivan for them. For matters to do with himself, he knew to keep silent with Ivan. But none of these conflicts prepared him for how to negotiate with a forest girl with a gun.

The fact was he must capture this cub and take it back, and he must rescue this girl from the forest. And key to it all was this little cabin they were both sitting in.

Were all children like this, at heart? Stubborn, lacking in sense? The girl had just lost her mother, but, even so, could she not see that he was right? And yet, if he were to insist on any of these *musts*, there seemed every chance that she would follow through on her determination to kill him. In addition, she was simply too big to force her to do anything she didn't want to do. And he needed her help. Even if he were able to build a crate alone, and somehow capture the cub alone, he could not carry it, and her, to the camp alone.

It was a conundrum. His exasperation must have shown on his face.

'I know your camp,' Zina said, unexpectedly. 'Why would I go there? My mother says it's full of dangerous men, who will hurt me and then drink themselves to death.'

Tomas gave a yelp of laughter. 'How can you know my camp?'

'We went there when I was a little girl. We . . . took some things. Bullets. Our little window. I can't remember now.' Realising that she was confessing to thieving from this man, she moved on. 'I stood on a stool and looked inside, and lots of men were sitting round a table. My mother said we had to leave, quickly. That you would kill us.'

'You got round the dogs?'

'Mummy checked everything, and we went round the outside, at dark. It was a long time ago.'

Tomas looked at her doubtfully. 'We wouldn't have hurt you, Zina. We'd have looked after you. Well, I would have, at any rate.'

'Don't you have a wife and child?'

'No, I don't. And I don't drink vodka, either. I think I know why your mother said those things, but they're not true. Zina, you will die out here. I am a stranger, but you have to trust me.'

Zina shook her head fiercely. But, moments later, the life drained from her face and she slid sideways on to the bed, deep in an exhausted sleep. Tomas did not take the gun, for he wanted her to wake with it in her grasp and feel safe. But, carefully, he put the catch on it and pointed it into the corner of the room, away from where he leant against the wall, looking round the cabin, considering how the planks could be dismantled and put together again to save something from this disaster.

WHEN DAWN CAME, THE cub came back to get her mother.

The wind had blown the flames away from the clearing, and the blizzard, now exhausted, had crippled their fury. Flames still smouldered angrily against the deadening needles and smothering snow. There would be embers and smoke for a long time.

Firelight glowed inside the cabin, reflecting on to the snow like orange dancers in a shadowy cage.

The cub paused at the edge of the clearing, ears turning, mouth open to taste. Voices drifted from the cabin.

Smoke rolled in her mouth, like earth, and she coughed.

There were two mounds in the snow, and the cub went to one and sniffed it.

It was her mother. The cub scraped at the snow and uncovered her mother's head. It was devastated by gunshot, but the amber eyes gazed.

The young tiger's rough tongue scraped away the frosted blood. Her whiskers brushed the Countess's neck, where she had felt her mother's pulse so many times. Once, the Countess had caught a racoon dog and brought it to her cubs almost dead, and the cub bit its throat and felt the heartbeat quiver through her whiskers.

She paced round the mound, scraping at the legs. They were frozen rigid.

Her brother became like this.

Meat.

They had been left together, brother and sister, in order for their mother to hunt. The cub had skipped around her brother, trying to get him to play, but he had been slowing all day, trickling blood into the snow. Finally, the cold had grown worse and they huddled together in the den beneath a fallen tree and awaited their mother's return. The cub felt the warmth drift from her brother's body. She slept beside him and, when she woke, he was cold meat, like this. No amount of licking would wake him.

She had remained beside her brother, waiting for their

mother, who finally arrived to lead them to the kill. She, too, had poked the brother with her snout, rolled his stiff body with her great paw, nuzzled him with her whiskers. Mother and daughter lay down with the brother between them, to warm him. The Countess licked her son, especially the wound on his foot. In the morning, she had carried him by the scruff and laid him in the snow beneath the tree, nudged him a final time, and, when he did not move, made her decision. Turning, she led her daughter away. The cub did not want to leave her brother, but her mother was moving with total determination and she would become meat like him if she did not keep up.

The other mound was the human, whose trail they followed, whose strange blood gave her no hiding place. The cub could still smell that femaleness. It etched itself on her memory. Tigers do not detect human scent well; it must be impressed on the senses, thoroughly encountered.

The human, also, was meat.

The young tigress was ravenous. She had eaten nothing since the bear. She scraped the snow away from the thighs of the woman, fleshy and sweet-stenched with the blood smell. She licked Edit's leg, tasting for a place to bite.

The door opened, and the cub was pinned in the sudden light. She snarled, her ears flat back, the full length of her juvenile incisors bared. She backed away, not too far, intent on returning to finish what she had started.

The girl stood motionless in the beam of the doorway. She was holding a rifle. A man appeared behind her, but she swung round and pointed it at him. Voices, strange human yelps. The man's arms shot up and he backed slowly inside. When the door closed, the girl lay the gun down, clearly, carefully, where the cub could see it, and then she advanced on the two mounds in the snow.

The two youngsters stared at each other for a long time. No cat likes to break a stare, and it seemed the girl did not like to either. Between them, the bodies of their mothers. At last, the girl dropped to her knees, and, as the cub had done, she scraped away the snow at the corner of the mound. Her mother's hair pooled in the snow. The girl touched it with bare fingers. She brought out a knife and sliced off a handful of it. It hung like a tail in her hand, twitching, almost as if with life.

The cub hissed. Her claws sprang out. Around her neck, the fur bristled, as if she had a great mane to terrify. She crept closer, as if stalking, as her mother had taught her.

The girl opened her jaws and made an enormous noise, like a boar caught by surprise. Boar fight back, if they possibly can, which is why correct stalking is of the utmost importance. The girl leapt to her feet, towering over the cub. The wailing continued, becoming a crescendo. Something sparked momentarily in the cub. Fear? Not fear. Never fear. Proper apprehension of the situation, perhaps. The tigress stepped back, a tiny concession. She bared her teeth in a silent hiss.

The girl fell to her knees once more and scraped away the snow from her mother's face. With the knife, she cut something free from the woman's neck. The pale light illuminated a claw on a leather thong. The girl put the necklace in her pocket and stood carefully, her eyes on the cub the whole time.

The cub crept forward again, a growl vibrating in her throat. There was no point in attacking, they were too evenly matched. It would mean injury for the tiger, even if she killed the girl. It would likely play out as the encounter between the mothers had: a fight to the death, in which each dealt the fatal blow on the other. But there were plenty of ways to drive this human away. Then she could eat.

The door opened again, and the man strode out. He grabbed the rifle and, before she could react, leapt at the girl and dragged her away towards the cabin. He held her, writhing to one side, and, with his other arm, orientated the rifle at the cub.

A shot ringing across the clearing. A thud, like a rock, in the cub's back leg, flinging her across the snow.

The girl screaming, and the man screaming back, shaking her. Two of them running towards the young tiger, their faces open, like boar fleeing. Rope flung around the cub's neck, the girl screaming and screaming, like she did when her mother was killed.

The cub howled in pain and fury. Ropes around her legs, two ropes about her neck, the girl snarling at the man as though she was the one caught, but holding on, nevertheless, obeying the terse commands he gave her.

And, later, a wooden platform for the cub to lie on, tied to a stake.

And, after that, the man gouging the metal from her leg, stuffing the wound with something, while she roared and twisted against the ropes.

And, after that, a dark box with a brushwood floor and meat, which she could not eat, and a descent that must be dying. She roared in the box so that her mother and her brother would hear her.

This tiger left no more tracks in her homeland.

In a few days, snowfall erased her forever from the forest.

Human tracks took over where hers left off, leading down through the forest. Then the human tracks became vehicle tracks, crushed into the snow. The cub's life became a life without mark, borne from crate to pen to crate. On from the camp to a Moscow yard, bound with a chain and baited by dogs, fighting over and over, until her flesh was torn and her eye ripped out. Then, sold on for a rock-bottom price, back into a crate and a pen.

There would be crates and cages for the rest of her life. She was a lost scroll, a torn-out chapter from the last great tiger dynasty on earth.

Her wild kingdom would remain only in the ice field of her gaze, the white book unscrolling, pristine, behind her eye.

It would take a human female on the other side of the world to see what she truly was. Stumblingly, from the alien landscape of another species, this human would understand. And, in the way of the truest and most dreamlike of the Udeghe fables, the forest would have its presiding spirit returned.

Thirty-five

AT FIRST, TOMAS DID not recognise the woman advancing on him at Moscow airport, gloved hand outstretched, as his British counterpart, Frieda. She was dressed entirely in black and more than anything resembled the military security guards bristling around arrivals. She wore wrap-around sunglasses, and, as she drew close, he saw that the clothes were high-end Western-style snow-proof thermals. Only the hat was incongruous. It was embroidered with tigers.

Tomas straightened his felt jacket and cleared his throat. He had had a haircut and shaved off his moustache, believing this look to be more appropriate for the director of Ivanovich Reserve. His mouth felt very exposed and chilly without the moustache, and he was considering growing it back. He would ask Zina what she thought, when they got back. He had come to Moscow airport — for the first time in his life — to oversee with Frieda the transfer of Luna's cubs to another plane, for the longest leg of the flight, to Khabarovsk. He and Frieda would fly there together.

He had emailed Frieda to tell her that she should wear felt, as far as possible; it was silent in the snow, which was vital for tracking and hunting, and also it was in colours that were suited to the forest and aided camouflage. Underneath, it was good to wear wool, because it breathes. And a fur hat with flaps was the best thing to have – not this rather flimsy feminine item she was wearing. Admittedly, the effect of Frieda's outfit was superficially impressive. People were turning to look. She held herself very straight, and her movements had a suppleness that made an image pop into his mind, of the skin beneath the functional black. The boots were like nothing he had ever seen in Khabarovsk. She looked like she could traverse the moon in them. She looked like she was going to be highly effective at everything. He was confused.

'Tomas,' she said. Huge smile. She took off her glove to shake his hand. Her skin was so cold, the touch shimmered up his arm. Then she said, in excellent, if peculiarly accented Russian, 'The vet is waiting for us. Over at the other terminal. We have to check the cubs and turn them over before we set off, for their circulation. Shall we go?'

'OW!' FRIEDA FLEW ACROSS the back of Petrov's shitty van, straight into Zina, who had been consulting her English phrase book and mouthing words to herself. The two of them landed on the floor. This was the fourth time in an hour that Frieda had been thrown from her seat. It was not a seat. It was a packing case upside down, upon which Tomas had laid a bristly blanket. There was nothing to hold on to and the road was no longer a road but a series of craters at which Tomas drove the van as though it were a horse in a steeplechase. Calmly, Zina disentangled herself and clambered back on to the case. She grinned at Frieda and said, in English, through her magnificent teeth, 'My dad likes to drive fast!'

They were one hour into a six-hour journey, from the airport to the camp, and Tomas was hoping to get to the reserve by nightfall. Frieda checked the grimy rear window – was the Hilux, carrying the cubs in special heated crates on the back, still behind them? It was just visible; Ivan was clearly trying to negotiate the craters a little more gently for their benefit. Ivan's voice blasted from the radio into the van, a stream of Russian that made Tomas clench the wheel with knuckle-whitening force. He yelled at his father and tossed the radio to one side, then slowed down almost imperceptibly. Zina and Frieda raised their eyebrows at each other.

Outside, the world was endlessly striped, with a white underbelly. Where most people would see emptiness, silence, the hostility of nature, Frieda saw a blank page. The earth was full of possibility, just the same as after the first snowfalls, hundreds of thousands of years ago. It was as if time itself had been obliterated. The only other way she had managed to escape time was by taking morphine. It was the hardest part of the craving to resist; it had enabled her to step outside consequences, to rest on the margin of her own life. Nothing – until, now, this boundless pristine snow – had given her even a hint of that possibility. Frieda could barely sit still for the desire to be out in it. She would be like the cubs, stepping for the first time into the snow they were born for; she might go mad with the joy of it. No amount of being thrown about the cabin could dislodge her exhilaration.

A lorry was approaching, stacked with logs. There was only room for one vehicle on the trail. Tomas stopped the van, barked into the radio and clambered out. Ice swirled in a freezing vice around Frieda's calves, chomping like starving weevils through the expensive boots and wool socks she had bought. She wriggled her toes and pain curled through her bones. The floor of the truck was rusted through in places, sending jets of caustic air on to her soles.

But the sensation was so new, so physical and profound, that she found herself observing it, noting it, making sure she would cover this or that gap in her defence next time. The cold was like a predator one must live alongside, she realised: it must be respected; she must never expect mercy. And this Frieda, this new Frieda – tiger keeper, reintroduction leader, Russian speaker – did not expect mercy. She expected nothing at all.

It was two years since Luna had attacked Frieda, and she

could hardly believe the course events had taken. Tomas had traced Luna's journey to Torbet Zoo, and a relationship between the two organisations had resulted in this – the reintroduction of Luna and Lyric's cubs into the wild. Frieda rubbed her breath mist from the window so as not to miss the endless march of the forest. This was where Luna, her Luna, had lived. *Wild*. Her cubs were coming home. Frieda longed for the journey to end so that they could take their first steps into the snow and fill their lungs with the oxygen of Siberia. It made tears sting at her eyes to think of it. Coming *home*.

Tomas gesticulated in clouds of breath mist as he negotiated with the driver of the logging truck, an egg-faced man in sunglasses and an enormous fur hat. The flaps wiggled vigorously over the man's ears as he nodded an affirmative. It seemed that Ivan might join them – the door shrieked open – but then Tomas waved at his father and it swung shut again.

The lorry reversed to a point where the trail widened slightly, enabling Tomas to squeeze past. The radio rattled with Petrov's cursing as trees scraped the side of his van. It took fifteen minutes for both trucks to pass the lorry. Frieda craned behind them, hoping the cubs were not being tilted and jolted. They were sedated, but, still, this was a long and difficult journey. They would pass four more such logging trucks, and, each time, an amicable arrangement would be made to get them both past.

Zina had slipped down on the packing case and her face was upturned on Frieda's lap, slack with sleep. Frieda had never had a teenager rest her head upon her like this – had never held any child at all. Zina had clearly decided she was someone suitable to be slept upon, and, among all the other wonders occurring between being hurled across the cabin, this was another. She gazed down at the girl. It was miraculous how the young could just simply sleep like that, like animals.

Frieda pulled a photograph in a small frame out of her pocket. This was Luna, turned to the camera, good side prominent. Frieda loved the bad side, with its great dark bowl of secrets. She had not taken this photograph. It was a gift from Gabriel.

A few days before leaving Torbet Zoo, Frieda was cleaning out the indoor tiger enclosure, headphones clamped over her ears as she listened to Russian-language recordings. She had set to learning Russian, like a research project, as soon as the link with the Ivanovich Reserve was established. She was voracious in seeking out new things to listen to. Sometimes it was audio books, sometimes news. Sometimes it was a course. She had, by immersing herself in these methods, become very proficient, although she had no one to practise her speaking with. It was her own private Russian world, tending to the tigers and listening to Russian as she worked.

The cool of Gabriel's shadow startled her. She pulled off the headphones. In the two years since the attack, they had not stood face to face. For most of the first year, Gabriel had been in and out of hospital for operations on his chest, arms and legs where Luna had torn the flesh from him. Then there had been extensive rehabilitation, for which he had moved back in with Torbet, in the main house. Most days, he could be seen pacing the zoo grounds, building up the damaged muscle, and, later, he volunteered on any section that needed help – except cats – doing whatever work his weakened state would allow.

He'd done the avoiding so effectively that Frieda began to relax. She neither expected to meet him, nor wanted to. Meanwhile, the association with the Ivanovich Reserve had developed, and her work with Luna and Lyric had taken on new importance. Leyland had pushed for her to lead the reintroduction project and was thrilled at the possibilities that were unfolding for his tigers, only regretful that it would mean he lost her as a keeper. She was completely swept up in what was happening, and then there was Russian itself, a language so densely packed and majestic, it absorbed any remaining attention.

Shock. She couldn't get past it, not yet. Livid and deep, the channels of the skin grafts disappeared under the collar of Gabriel's overalls. His face was untouched. His eyes met hers from beneath the baseball cap.

'They're all off in Lyric's side,' she said, by way of explanation for the empty enclosure. Tinny Russian leaked from the headphones round her neck.

'I've come to see you.'

'Oh.' She wished they would be interrupted. His shape in the doorway was blocking the light. He was taking all the air. It was as if a fully prepared syringe of morphine had been presented on an open palm, just when she wasn't expecting it, just when she was over all that.

'Here.' He held out the photo of Luna. 'I thought you'd like it. So you can remember her.'

'Thank you.' Frieda took the photo from his hand and smiled. 'I can take Luna back home, too, now. In a way.'

'So, what's happening?' he asked.

'With the cubs? Well, we all leave mid-week. Specialist animal transport. Then, at the other end . . . Well, it's trucks into the forest. Tomas says they've built an enclosure in the right place. Where they can acclimatise, you know. I'll be living in a camp . . . Minus thirty-five degrees . . .' She trailed off.

'Well, look at you,' he said quietly.

'What do you mean?' she said.

'You practically get eaten by a tiger, and now – here you are, doing a reintroduction.' He grinned. 'Do they know . . . ? I mean, about your uselessness?'

'I'm not useless anymore.'

He drew closer to her. Even in his weakened state, he drove her to step back. He sighed. 'You're a bloody good shot. I wanted to say. And good call choosing the tranquilliser gun. Useless Frieda would have just sent a load of bullets in there. Luna would have carried on fighting . . . and I'd be dead.'

'Thank you for . . . you know. Rushing in. Saving me.'

He nodded, and turned to go. And what possessed her, in a rush that was almost a morphine rush, was the realisation that what she felt could be resisted. It was morphine in a drawer, the drawer closing. Her own hand pressing it closed.

Gabriel raised a hand, without turning back. 'Good luck, bonobo girl,' he said.

DARKNESS SWELLED AMONG THE trunks and she imagined tigers creeping to the roadside, ready to spring out, into their path. The cold had turned her bones to tortured metal and she was desperate for the toilet and for a hot drink. Zina woke and checked the window. Where the landscape seemed featureless to the outsider, she knew exactly where they were. 'Nearly home,' she said.

'I have something for you,' said Frieda, in Russian.

The girl shook her head. 'I need to practise my English,' she said. 'Let's talk English.'

'All right then.' Frieda held out the photograph.

The sight of the tiger snatched all expression from the girl's face. Then a drop of colour spread over each cheek, like ink in water. 'Oh,' she said. Then some whispering in Russian that was too quick for Frieda to pick up. Her finger touched the tiger's face.

'I'm sorry it's not Luna coming back, Zina. I know you two have a bond. But she's just not fit enough now, after all she has been through.'

Frieda had sent photographs of Luna and the zoo, during

the preceding year, and Luna's loss of an eye had been much bemoaned, and the understanding that it wasn't right for her to come back took a long time to be agreed.

'Yes,' said the girl, her lip trembling a little.

'But, these cubs . . . We are bringing them home. And Luna is very happy at Torbet Zoo. She will live a long time – and I am sure, one day, you will come and see her. I know how much you love her. I do, too.'

Zina put the photo in her pocket, and her hand curled around Frieda's and stayed there.

At last, the trail opened out into a wide area of snow, illuminated by the moon and solitary floodlight. Cabins were arranged among the shadows. A group of waiting men jostled inside their silhouettes. The two trucks, with their precious cargo, grumbled up to the group, and, through the window, Frieda saw the men's tired faces light up in excitement, peering, chattering, laughing, their breath rising in great white clouds.

She stepped down into snow and shook their hands.

DAWN SEEPED ROUND THE rough blankets pinned over the windows. The warmth of Frieda's cabin had dissipated in the night and she counted to ten to brace herself before leaping from the rough mattress and into the clothes she had laid out the night before. The outer wings of a dead beetle were stuck to her leg and she flicked them off.

According to Ivan, the camp was improved beyond all imaginings from what it was before, due to the funding from the government, but sanitation was not considered an essential. A bucket had been provided for her by Petrov, with a sullen flourish. The alternative was crossing the entire camp to a row of newly constructed shitters, of which Ivan was inexplicably proud. She had tried one of them that first night, placing herself gingerly on the freezing plank, feeling unknowable crusts against her skin, and she'd gradually become aware of a man on each side. Their cigarette smoke leached through the cracks in the walls and torchlight drooled yellow between the planks as they turned the pages of who knew what publication. She couldn't face it in daylight.

When she got to the enclosure, she found the snow inside completely churned up from where the cubs had sprung into their new world. The previous night, they had been lifted, sleepy, into the enclosure, and laid in the inside area to recover. It was heated by means of a pipe, laid underneath, attached to a wood burner. Over the weeks that followed, the heat would be reduced, acclimatising them to the cold nights.

As the tigers were installed, Petrov and Erik commented wearily that the entire previous year had been spent making tiger enclosures. A detail of them had spent the summer at Zina's cabin, creating a large compound and workable temporary settlement for the tiger introduction. At the same time, this cage at the camp had been constructed for the cubs to see out the remains of the winter, before introduction to the forest in the spring.

The cage was a fortress, with entire logs for struts, and hardwood planks for the internal accommodation. It made no concessions to aesthetics. The cage wire, which was clearly some kind of Gulag-grade military mesh, was dispiritingly ugly, but adequate to the security required, curving over at a height of fifteen feet, and, it seemed, buried to required depth, too. The men had been instructed to build a prison, and they had built one.

Frieda was glad to see they had incorporated her suggestions of platforms and hidden areas. The inner area could be sealed from the outer by means of a slide, which meant the men could go into the enclosure to clean it, without being seen.

The generator snarled into life. Electricity, Ivan had informed her, was provided for one hour in the morning and two hours in the evening. The camp might be funded, but diesel was extremely expensive and President Putin's money was going on essentials: tigers and high-class accommodation for Putin, when he finally came to visit.

With at least an hour until breakfast, there was time to explore a little. Frieda left the cubs to their pacing and set off along the Hilux tracks, down into the trees, where they had come from last night.

Within a few hundred yards, it was as if there had never been people at all. A wide, snowy trail, laced with animal tracks, branched off into the taiga. She did not recognise all the tracks, but mostly they barely broke the surface crust of the snow. Larger animals – she guessed, deer – left scrapes behind each print, which made the track seem bigger, but was really just an indication of the animal's weight. The snow gleamed like the white of an eye. Every wrinkle of bark carried a cocaine-like line, transforming the surface into a glittering maze. Her boots swooshed through the snow, which was so dry that it flew about her like dust. When she looked back, her trail looked like that of the first person, walking in the Garden of Eden, among the animals.

There was no birdsong, and there would have been total silence, were it not for the rustle of her clothes, as if she was clambering out of a vat full of steel wool. A crow launched itself, alone, from a treetop. Something moved in the corner of her vision: a squirrel, the exact colour of the tree bark, belted up into the branches. She peered into the unending trees. It was strange that the combination of the reflective snow, the bright sky and the lack of leaf cover meant the forest never disappeared into gloom. On the contrary, it went on forever, a pattern that defied patterning, limited only by the acuity of her vision. Did she think she saw a flash of something in the distance? She'd read somewhere that, while it was extremely unlikely that she would ever see a tiger in the wild, it was a certainty that she would be observed by one.

A shot ricocheted faintly in the distance and Frieda stopped.

'Frieda!' Far behind her, a man. She squinted at the shape,

not clear for a while who it was, because of the camouflage of the felt. Finally, she recognised its powerful lumbering as that of Tomas. He waved at her. Something was in his hand – not a gun, something else, like a stick. 'Frieda!'

At last, he reached her. She noticed how his approach was almost silent. It was true that her high-tech layers were very rustly.

'You shouldn't be out here!' he said angrily. 'Ivan just fired a gun to scare off the tigers. You don't even have a flare!' He waved the stick-like object in front of her.

'But . . . I am just having a walk.'

'Frieda,' he said, slowly, in Russian, as if she might not understand. 'This is a wild place. You can't . . . wander about! Tigers come right up to the camp. You will be dead if one crosses you here. You could cause an international incident. Come back, please. With me.'

'I'm not a child!' Frieda exclaimed, nevertheless stomping after his back. 'I'm the consultant on the reintroduction. You can't keep me prisoner in the camp.'

Tomas sighed. 'You're not a prisoner, Frieda,' he said. 'But, look.' He pointed into the forest as he walked. 'This probably looks barren to you . . . nothing, all deadness . . . but it tricks you. You think you can see everything, but a tiger is perfectly camouflaged. It could be ten metres away and you won't see it. How do you think they are so successful when food is so hard to find?'

'I'll take a flare next time. Or give me a rifle. I can shoot!'

He stopped to face her. 'Frieda, there can be no next time. If you want to go for a walk, I will go with you, or one of the men. What if you meet a tiger and you shoot it? Even if your life is saved – which it won't be – that is a disaster for us!' He grabbed her arm. 'You are not at the zoo, now. This is the Russian taiga, and it is full of wild animals!'

As he stamped back, he lit a cigarette, blew the smoke into the pristine air to calm himself. Mute with rage, Frieda followed.

She caught up with him just as they arrived at the kitchen. This time, she grabbed his arm and turned him to face her. She saw that his eyes were not angry so much as weary.

So that she would be understood, she spoke slowly. 'Tomas, I should have said where I was going. I apologise. But I can shoot. I understand tigers. I am your *partner* on this reintroduction. We are equals! Teach me what I need to know. But don't ever, *ever* tell me off like that again.'

She did not stomp off to her cabin to cry, though she wanted to, but instead walked on ahead of him into the kitchen cabin to have breakfast. She greeted Ivan and Zina with a cheery hello and thanked Petrov for the coffee, which he held out to her with a smirk.

THAT NIGHT, THE MEN insisted she go first in the *banya*. Tomas rolled his eyes as Ivan whispered something to him.

'My father says, of course, he will wear something to beat you with birch branches. And you can wear something, too. If you want.' Ivan snorted with laughter in the corner.

'I will be fine, but thank you,' Frieda said. She smiled at them from behind the sad realisation that this was probably her fate, now: to be treated with either exaggerated decorum, or innuendo. Being able to understand their language made it even worse. It was as if taking away the linguistic separation threw into relief her difference as a woman. After she had her sauna, the men all went in together. She heard their laughter from her cabin, and came out to watch them run into the snow. This was the second time she had been almost the only woman in her job, and she was sorry that it would mean, as before, being always left outside the camaraderie. But something was different, here: they did not know what to do with her, but they did not hate her. Perhaps, one day, they would even forget she was female.

Something else was different, this time, she thought later, in the scratchy bed. Something buzzed in the dark by her ear, brought to life by the heat of the stove. She batted it away, unperturbed. Frieda herself was different. She could resist anything, and she needed nothing. Poor Tomas, Frieda thought, he had no idea about life, living out here, in the forest, with his men, his little Russian heart never tested.

Thirty-six

THERE WAS SO MUCH to understand. Each day was a thrill of new information, either from Frieda to the men, about how to care for a captive tiger, or from the men to her, about the complexities of the forest, how it was even possible for it to be a home. Daily, she and Tomas pored over the map of this region of the taiga, with its neighbouring logging and hunting reserves, and its narrow, life-giving channel into the unspoilt wilderness beyond. The map bristled with pins and lines in different colours, showing which tigers had been tracked or captured on film, and where. There was the logbook, which Ivan proudly showed her, detailing the measurements and markings of each tiger that passed through the reserve. And there was the footage to watch, the Countess playing with her cubs. Frieda struggled not to weep as Luna was batted and rolled by her mother, her little cat mouth open in a yowl. All four of them – Ivan, Tomas,

Zina and she – watched the footage on a loop, Ivan and Tomas quietly mourning the Countess, she and Zina silently united in their amazement at Luna. After a while, all four often found themselves gravitating out to the enclosure, where the cubs were growing steadily more at home. How miraculous it was that the chain had been so shattered, and, now, these two were here, linking it all back together. Ivan set up camera traps in the enclosure to make sure every detail of the cubs was preserved.

There were many photos of the reintroduction enclosure, and Frieda familiarised herself with its dimensions, materials and conditions.

'Why are you in all these fucking photos, Petrov?' Tomas asked him as they were looking through them on the laptop. 'You're spoiling them, you ugly bastard.'

'I built that thing!' Petrov said. 'When you're boasting to Putin about this reintroduction, you're not going to fucking forget me! The President is going to know who I am!'

'Yep, he's going to say, "Who is this ugly bastard in the forest?" What the fuck? These aren't supposed to be your holiday snaps.'

Petrov gesticulated. Honour was satisfied, and the men returned to pointing out to Frieda the way the enclosure would work. It had a main front gate, and then a number of openings into which animals could be released or other items put into the enclosure. The cubs would grow properly wild there, among the wild sounds, right at the edge of the territory it was intended would be theirs. The enclosure included a rock face and a stream. The tigers would be trained to hunt, by animals being released into the enclosure for them to chase and kill. The forest's tigers would come to know they were there. The settlement was built on the site of Edit and Zina's cabin, some distance away, so as to keep disturbance to a minimum.

As the date approached for the cubs' release into the rein-troduction enclosure, everyone began to get excited. Frieda took her own photos of the cubs, watching them unobserved whenever she could, and she emailed the pictures to Leyland, who wrote her terse two-line replies, bursting with emotion.

Tomas could stare at her all he wanted with those intense hazel eyes of his. And he could top up her vodka – which she rarely refused, because a drink was the last subversive pleasure she enjoyed – while never drinking himself and observe her pink-cheeked slide into relaxation. He could spend afternoons shooting with her (and admiring her unexpected skill), and take her on trips to Khabarovsk with Zina, for the girl's English lessons and meals in restaurants, which were clearly a torment to him. He could teach her about tracks, and show her all the trees of the forest and their various properties, while amusing her with his genuine but vain attempts at English. He could devote himself to her acclimatisation to this place, attend to her every comfort, but she would never, ever respond in any way that was not friendly, polite and distant. Frieda's inner world was a frozen land, and now, at last, she held dominion over it.

One evening, after dinner, after Zina's bedtime, after the card playing and the drinking, when the men had all gone to bed, Tomas stayed behind and, when she made to leave, asked her to stay a while longer. He had lit candles and arranged some torches around the room to have light after the generator was switched off. He realised only after he had done this that it looked romantic in a way he had not intended.

'Just a little while,' said Tomas. He topped up her vodka glass.

'I'm tired,' said Frieda, nervously. Vodka softened her, and she didn't want to be softened. She liked this new Frieda. It was as if the Frieda always trapped in the mirror had managed to escape and was having a turn.

Tomas said the carefully rehearsed opening statement, which was professional and yet indicative of a wish to talk on a deeper level: 'It is good for colleagues to relax together after the day's work.'

Shit! He sounded creepy! He wanted to take the words back and to announce that he was not creepy, that he was not trying to obtain sex. Sex was something men dreamed about in the forest. They didn't expect it. Or have it. With actual women. There were no women. Fuck. It was just . . . It was just he wanted to talk to her, that was all. He rubbed forlornly at the space where his moustache used to be, thick and reassuring. There was something he wanted to say to her.

'Have a drink, if you want to relax,' Frieda said, in Russian. She raised her glass. 'Vashye Zdorovye!' she said, and downed it.

Tomas shook his head. 'If I have a single drink, I will have to finish the bottle. And all will be lost for me. I am all or nothing. In this, and everything.'

Frieda poured another. 'Is every Russian as intense as you are?'

'I don't know.' He looked confused. 'Are English girls all like you?'

'Like what?'

'Cold,' he said, in English.

'You think I'm cold?'

'Like *ice*,' he said proudly.

She considered this. Frieda had always been the emotional, passionate one. It was true, she did not feel this way anymore. And with this came freedom. Invulnerability. She said, 'Just because I am not in love with you, it doesn't mean I'm cold.'

'Who said anything about love?' Tomas said, returning to Russian. He needed his own language for this conversation.

'Tomas, I don't think about you at all, except as a partner on this project. You know that, don't you?'

'Hmm.'

'And, also,' Frieda continued, 'I think that a man who has lived his whole life in a forest camp with a bunch of . . . *bandits* . . . I don't think he should lecture me about feelings.'

She was like a boxer, Tomas thought, parrying until his concentration faltered, then *wham!* No wonder she didn't have a boyfriend.

'I'm sorry, that was rude. I've drunk a bit too much,' Frieda said.

'I think we are alike,' Tomas said.

'What, cold?'

'All or nothing.'

'I'm tired.'

'Is it true?'

'Is what true?'

'Are you all or nothing?'

'How can I be all or nothing, and yet cold? They cancel each other out!' She jabbed at the dictionary on the table.

Tomas sighed, gripping the dictionary, marshalling his mental forces to traverse the battlefield of their language gap. 'You *are* cold, because, at present, you are deciding *nothing*. But I am interested to know what will make you decide to give *all*.'

Frieda stared at him. This was a surprise, and not a pleasant one. Beneath her hat, her hair tingled like hackles. She felt like a dog, tethered in a yard, with a stranger circling. She could feel a growl nudging her lip. Who did he think he was?

'Frieda, I have to tell you something. You have an idea about me, and it's wrong. You think I'm like these other men, here – don't know how to care for anyone, don't know how to love anyone. You think I've just been hunting all my life, listening to football, wanking in the *banya*. Don't you?'

Tomas ran his hands anxiously through his hair. The words tumbled urgently out of him.

'I can't hide what my life is now. But I want you to know, I regret it. I regret the mistake I made, and I'm trying to be different. Zina . . . You know about Zina. She is my second chance. I grabbed it with both hands. I haven't given up. The men, here – they have all given up. Every last one of them. I want you to know, I'm not like that. And something else –' he eyed the vodka bottle, now. How hard it was to talk honestly without a drink. 'Frieda, since I met you, I've been watching you, and thinking about why you seem so sad. I think you did as I did. You didn't give all when you could have done, and then you resigned yourself to nothing.'

'What do you mean?'

'You seem so alone. Are you alone?' He looked at her directly then, the hazel eyes open and questioning.

Frieda's face flamed. 'Tomas, I am here to *work*. I am the only woman to visit this camp in God knows how long, so don't think I flatter myself with being in any way special. I'm just *woman*, like Petrov would say. Don't dress it up. You don't know me or what I have been through. I'm here for my tiger cubs, and it is going to be a success, and *you* are not going to fuck it up for me.'

She sat back, eyes brimming.

'Frieda, of course I am not going to fuck it up for you.' How could she have thought he was? 'This reintroduction means everything to both of us! For this reserve. For Russian tiger conservation. We are on the same side.'

She looked at him with her hard blue eyes.

Tomas said, 'What happened to you, Frieda? To make you like this?'

She stood violently and gripped the chair to steady the room. She said, 'You're right, I'm cold. I *do* feel nothing. I *like* feeling nothing. I love it here, with the cold blank snow and the tigers and the simple rules of survival. Luna taught me everything I need to know — about here, and about life! But you are wrong about *everything else*. My mistake was not that I didn't try to give my all, myself . . . whatever the fuck way you just put it. It's that . . . It's that . . .' She put her fists to her temples in frustration. 'It's that I *did*!'

She hated him for pushing and pushing until he got a response. There he sat, carelessly flinging rocks against the beautiful ice field she was comfortable living beneath.

'I've had enough of this.'

She slammed the door, and each of the subsequent three doors, on her way back to her cabin.

Thirty-seven

THOUGH THE WINTER WAS so harsh it was hard to imagine spring ever coming to the taiga, it finally did. As soon as the temperature climbed at night, the tiger cubs were to be sedated, put into crates, loaded on to the Hilux and then driven to where the trail ended and their journey into the deep forest began.

Tomas had made the cages from steel, so they were light and narrow, lined with thin planks and canvas. They had long carrying poles, designed for one man each end. Two of the men had gone ahead to prepare camp, to make sure the enclosure, built the previous summer, had survived the worst of the winter. Tomas pressed Zina to go ahead with them, as it would be safer and less work, but she would not leave the cubs. Their voices in argument had carried over the camp for several evenings. Used to these clashes of will, everyone kept out of it, until finally

Tomas gave in. Hardly able to contain his excitement, Ivan took pictures constantly in the days leading up to the exodus, and filled a sack with camera traps, saying to his son, 'Footage, Tomas!' Ivan would be staying behind, to keep the camp ticking over while they were away.

In the six weeks since their arrival, the cubs had grown, and something else: Frieda described it to Tomas as 'perking up'. There seemed no other way to express it. They were shedding, like a winter coat, the languid quality of captive tigers. As if they knew freedom was coming, they had become remote and lean, and Frieda glimpsed the empty depths she had seen in Luna's eye. It both chilled and delighted her. She had run to get Zina and Tomas, and had excitedly explained the absence in a tiger's eyes that signified their wildness.

Frieda found it almost unbearable to put the cubs through a second punishing journey. They groaned as the tranquilliser took effect, tottering to the ground, their immense strength flattened by simple gravity. Their flesh seemed sucked out, like a reverse taxidermy. She was grateful for Tomas working effi-ciently by her side to get the indignity over as quickly as possible.

Tomas had not tried to talk to Frieda alone since their con-versation of a few weeks ago, but what was wonderful, what she wished she could express to him as they worked, and couldn't, was that he did not change how he was towards her at all. He had decided to grow his moustache back, as Zina had commented that he didn't seem to smile as much without it, and, also, in the deep forest, shaving was pointless. He still practised his English with Frieda, he still showed her everything he knew about tracks, and, most of all, he was still warm towards her, smiling at her just as before. She wondered, in the scratchy bed, as she squeezed the roaming beetles to death with barely a look, why this lack of change made her happy, but it did. She looked forward to seeing him in the morning, checking the tigers or chopping wood, his cigarette dangling. Lately, she had taken to sitting with him in the kitchen as he cooked. Sometimes she read her Russian texts as he worked; sometimes she helped him, although she truly hated to cook and didn't do it with any enthusiasm. What he seemed to like best was when she read aloud to him as he cooked, extracts from the few Russian novels they had.

At last, the tigers were installed and ready, and everything for the camp was packed. Tomas and his father shook hands, hesitated, then embraced. Ivan waved at the convoy until it had completely disappeared. Frieda watched him growing smaller, waving like an old man in a film.

She and Zina were squashed in the front with Tomas, who revved the Hilux and hit the soggy ruts in the road at full tilt. The thaw of an entire winter's snow made the trail soggy with mud, and Tomas decided the best thing to do was to get the whole thing over with as quickly as possible. Behind them, Petrov yelled down the radio for them to slow down, as the shitty van wasn't built for racing.

In her hands, Zina held the photograph of Luna, along with

her lynx-claw necklace. She ran her fingers over them absently. These were all she possessed of the home she was returning to.

She had no photograph of her mother, of course. It moved Frieda that she had no such visual memento, but, in a world without photographs, Zina had not so far missed the fact that she did not have one of her mother. The lynx claw, as she told Frieda, made her see her mother when she slept. In response to gentle questions from Frieda, Zina happily chattered about her childhood in the forest – in Russian, and so fast and vivid, Frieda struggled to keep up – until, suddenly, she stopped mid-sentence.

The photo dropped from her hands and she turned to Frieda with a completely open expression in her eyes. 'I don't remember what she looked like anymore,' she said, seeming to check with Frieda exactly what her reaction should be to the fact that her mother had vanished from her imagination. Frieda was spun right back to the moment, years ago, when she had received the photograph of Zaire, looking out from herself with that same openness. She reached down and picked up the photo of Luna, and pressed it back into the girl's hands.

Frieda could not remember her mother, either, nor her father. In fact, she struggled to remember the faces of almost everyone who had been important: Charlie, Zaire, Gabriel. She had been away for nearly two months and they were already fading, like prints beneath new snow.

'What about the village you came from?' Frieda asked. 'Won't they remember your mother, there? Perhaps they will have a picture.' She looked enquiringly at Tomas. He, too, waited for Zina to continue. He and Zina had not talked about the village much. Tomas hated its association with Marta's abortion, and, if he was honest with himself, which was hard, he was jealous of the blood connection Zina had there, and afraid of the pain it would cause them both to unearth it.

Zina said, 'My mother said we would be punished if we went back. She escaped. She left to give me a better life. My grandfather was a shaman. My . . . My father . . .' She glanced at Tomas when she said this. 'My father, before Dad, he drank too much vodka. My mother said . . . they will all be dead.'

'Oh, Zina.' Frieda clasped the girl's hands. 'Tomas . . . surely . . . When the tigers are settled . . . can't we go? I'm sure no one will punish you, Zina; it's a long time ago now.'

Tomas reached over and clasped Zina's other hand. 'Of course,' he said. 'If that's what you want.' The girl's father, who might not be dead, flashed behind his eyes. And then, Marta leaving in the van that last time. She had sat there, right where Frieda and Zina sat now, carrying his child, his future.

The Hilux hit a rut and jolted violently forward.

'Dad, slow down!' Zina squealed in excitement.

The images vanished, leaving just the two of them, smiling at him.

*

EXHAUSTED AFTER THREE DAYS of walking through the forest – camping as little as possible, for the tigers' sake – they finally reached the line of frazzled trees. Zina swung off her pack and tore through the charred trunks into the clearing. She spun in the middle and gazed open-mouthed. Swathes of wispy pink fireweed lit the forest floor, and pale green ferns unfurled delicately at the foot of the trees. The forest had recovered, green shoots pushing from the snapped and charred trunks. The air flickered with birds, and Frieda suddenly noticed the presence of birdsong, trilling, shrieking, tapping, as life returned to the forest.

The cabin had been completely rebuilt and extended from where Tomas had used the wood for Luna's transport, and had then pulled the bodies of Edit and the Countess on to the remains, creating a pyre. It was solid and steeply pitched, with a proper porch on which to stand the rifles. Smoke drifted from the chimney. Even a shitter had been built, at the back.

Tomas embraced Zina, and they stood together on the spot where they had stood two years before, where they had captured the cub that would become Luna. 'Your mother and your home are inside all this. This will always be your place. Wherever we go.'

Men appeared from where they were gathering wood, preparing food, checking the enclosure, and there were greetings and slapping of backs. The crates were heaved into the enclosure, their fronts opened. Everyone retreated, before the tigers came to themselves.

'NO, YOU KNEEL LIKE this . . . and hold your hands still in the water, like this . . .' Tomas demonstrated to Zina how to tickle the fish. Her giggling at the very idea made her squirm in the water and frighten them away. His patience was endless, and his joy when he looked at Zina was something Frieda had never seen in anyone's face. Except perhaps Gabriel's, when he had his arms about a tiger's neck. She sat on a log beside them, dipped her finger in the freezing water.

How lovely Zina was becoming. She had big hands and feet that seemed made for any natural eventuality: running at speed, climbing, making. Puberty had arrived and her female body was developing so spectacularly that Tomas seemed to spend a lot of his time at the camp growling at the men to stop staring at her. When her periods started, it was Frieda to whom she turned to explain what was happening. This had led to the revelation that it was Edit's trail of exactly this special kind of blood that had drawn the Countess to find her. At last, Luna's violent reaction to Frieda's own sudden return to fertility made sense. Would this mean that tigers would come to find her when she had a period? Zina had asked Frieda this, wide-eyed. Frieda shook her head, thoughtfully. 'It must be a one-off. Luna associated losing her mother with the way that Edit was bleeding at the time,' she said.

Frieda had emailed Leyland excitedly after this exchange, picturing his phlegmatic receipt of this information, and his attempt to respond to it. She could see the frown deepening on his wrinkled face as he tried to integrate it into his pantheon of knowledge about his tigers. There wasn't really a place for female things. Leyland was as trapped as everyone involved with tigers in the language of the masculine ideal – the nobility, courage, majesty, and so on, exhibited by the king. There was, after all, no queen, simply the emperor-like patriarch with his harem of females. At least, that was how it used to be. He was, these days, interested in seeing beyond this narrow attribution of qualities, to the messier, non-ideal and, in the end, more wondrous real beast, with its social structures that could well prove to be more complex and flexible than previously imagined. Nevertheless, it had taken him a few days to reply. He wrote, *Don't know how to verify that this end, but have discussed with Torbet.*

'GOT ONE!' ZINA CRIED, holding up a small, flapping fish. Exhilaration flashed across her face like a kingfisher. There was a great babble of Russian as Tomas helped her get it on to the ground and dispatch it swiftly with a rock.

'Take it back with the others, Zina,' said Tomas. There was a net with several other fish from the morning. 'Petrov will cook them all up.'

Frieda watched them work, the sun dappling across Tomas's

back, that ridiculous mermaid flexing her tail. When Zina had trotted off with the bag on her back, Tomas sat beside Frieda on the log and yawned.

And why she did this, she did not know, but Frieda reached out and covered his hand with hers.

She reddened, expecting that he would snatch it away, that he would be angry, that it was a transgression, that it would require an explanation that she could not possibly give. The breath stopped in her throat, fluttered there like a moth. She felt her body grow rigid with fear.

Tomas did not snatch his hand away. He covered her hand with his.

'My mother and father . . . they died. When I was a child,' Frieda said. She did not know why she said this. It was not related to anything. It was not a conversation opener. It was not a happy statement.

Tomas led her by the hand a little further into the glade. He indicated a towering tree, festooned with pale spring leaves. It had a broad trunk, with deep striations, like an ancient palm.

'It's a cork tree. Touch it.'

Frieda laid her fingers on the trunk.

'In an emergency, you can use the bark to keep warm,' he said.

'Is this an emergency?'

'Frieda, take your clothes off and lean against the tree.'

·'What?'

He didn't say anything, just stood in front of her, with his arms folded. The expression on his face wasn't angry. It wasn't contemptuous. She could not tell what it was.

'I can't . . . I . . .'

He still didn't say anything. Why didn't he say anything?

'Why aren't you saying anything?'

He smiled a little, but still did not speak.

Had she heard him right?

Of course she had. The command took away the need to reason the moment away.

Frieda pulled off her jacket and the T-shirt beneath, reached round herself to release her bra, then endured a mortifying eternity while she realised that she could not take off her leggings without unlacing her boots. She was reduced to kneeling, topless, fiddling with her laces. She was too embarrassed even to look at him. Finally, the boots were loose enough to remove, and she hopped about, getting them off.

The socks, the leggings. The underwear. Her eyes were scrunched shut and she was shivering. She pressed herself against the tree. It was not actual heat coming from the trunk, but a rough absence of chill.

'The hat,' she heard him say.

'No,' she said.

His body was against hers, an enveloping warmth that stopped her shivering immediately. In her ear, he murmured, 'Frieda, take the hat off.'

'You don't understand,' she whispered. Her pulse banged against him. The problem was, if she did not take the hat off, she was now afraid this would stop, this warmth. And she wasn't sure she could bear it, if it stopped. Although, it might stop if she *did* take the hat off and he saw what was there.

She slipped off the hat. It dropped from her fingers on to the earth. Her hair fell about her shoulders, but on one side it was still thin, and a scar could still be seen on the pale shiny skin of her scalp. Frieda began to cry.

'I was attacked by someone. He hit me here. I can't get it to grow back.'

She wished he would say something. But, instead, he ran his fingers through the thin side and kissed the scar.

She could not keep hold of all the thoughts that were unspooling in her head. It was as if she were on a horse, galloping, in a herd of them, running wild, so that she could not tell which was running beneath her, or if indeed she had become one of them. She grabbed his head and kissed him hard on the mouth. He tasted of cigarettes and something else, something comforting. It was a kind of anger she felt now – why wasn't he saying anything? Why did her tears not affect him? – but she was sure that she did not want this to stop. What did a person do with that paradox?

They leant back against the cork tree, as requested.

Tomas moved down her body and knelt on the ground in front of her. She began to say, 'No, I—' but pleasure sliced through her, decapitating her sentence.

She wished she could tell someone how terrible it was to have her thin hair revealed, to be so exposed that an eagle could land and pick out her heart or her eyes, and yet to be at the mercy of a sensation that split her into constituent gasps. To want to run away as fast as she could from this person, while begging him not to stop. It was a boiling conflict that rose inside her, and met the final icy barrier in herself. The deepest sorrow she possessed, which pressed like a coffin lid on the surge of feeling.

'Tomas,' she whispered. There was a desperation in her voice that stopped him. He looked up at her. She struggled to form the words. 'Tomas, I can never . . . I can never have a child.' Tears fell down her cheeks.

'Hush, Frieda,' he said. He squeezed her hand gently. Then he said nothing else, and continued where he had left off, and Frieda realised that there was nothing left in her to resist the feeling he was sending through her body, on which she rose and rose, on which she became completely new.

Thirty-eight

THEY ARE SISTER AND brother. They have names given to them by Ivan — Zina, for the female; Vladimir, for the male — but, of course, they have never heard these names and know nothing of them.

The sister has the heft of her grandmother, a goliath in the making, with a magnificent slab of snout, like smouldering wood. It is derived, though she cannot know, from the king tiger. She is, at present, the same size as her brother, some six feet, nose to tail. She carries her head, framed by a white crescent at her throat, high and dead centre, making sure to gather all the information that comes her way into the miraculous dish.

Beneath his black stripes, her brother is a burnished orange. He is probably, soon, going to outstrip the sister in size, also expressing the bulk that made his grandparents so successful. He, too, has the white crescent of his mother, Luna, and the large black ears with a white spot of his father, Lyric. And yet, to those who might know the lineage of these beasts, it is wondrous to see both the familiar woven into their bodies, and also how utterly new they are.

Camera traps have been set. The camp has been cleared of all the human traces it is possible to remove. One end of the enclosure has been left open. At a later date, the whole thing will be removed, as it is potentially a hazard to animals who might get trapped in there, but not yet. The people have gone.

And so they do not see the terrible grace with which the sister approaches the open fencing, stopping dead with the inbuilt caution of a wild creature when it encounters change. The brother, a little more cautious, opens his mouth wide to taste the space.

Two pairs of enormous, clear amber eyes, with the pupils caught like a primeval insect in tree sap. There is nothing, in those eyes, of the dull fury of the captive tiger. They are pure wild attention. Then, the sister lifts her great head and gives a ravaging roar, which warns every creature in hearing that everything has changed, now, and she tenses her great body and springs, like an enormous bird from the shoulder of the earth.

She lands some ten feet on, and does not break stride, bounding into the forest like a ball of flame. Stems crack beneath her great feet; the petals of the ground flowers are crushed, and spring back gratefully when she has passed. Her brother is right behind; they are a unit, for now, which makes them more successful. Although, this will not last forever: one will turn on the other, in the end.

This natural wonder of two wild tigers bounding into their home territory passes in miniature over the corneas of birds launching themselves in terror, and the carapaces of tiny, vital insects clinging to the leaves. The trees bow a little to make room. On and on they go, far beyond the reach of the camera traps, invisible beneath the canopy to the sky's eye, heading instinctively to where they will know to rest, where they will find something to kill, where they will try and fail, and then succeed.

And if, in the far distance, from time to time, can be heard the shrill grind of the logging saws, and if the shocking peal of a rifle – so faint, only a tiger could hear it – signals that poachers are coming one day, then what of it? And if they do not know about snares, and have had no mother to teach them about these dangers, does it change this moment of tearing wild freedom? Mile after mile of teeming life, where people are never seen?

Acknowledgements

Two outstanding works of non-fiction ignited my obsession with the Siberian tiger and transported me with their prose: *The Tiger* by John Vaillant and *The Great Soul of Siberia* by Sooyong Park. When I knew that I needed to undertake a trip to the remote taiga, one classic of travel literature gave me courage: *In Siberia*, by Colin Thubron. I owe much to these books and their authors. Thank you.

I am very grateful to Creative Scotland and the Society of Authors for grants which helped to fund my research trip to track tigers in the snow.

Thank you to Martin Royle of Royle Safaris and Alexander Balatov of the Durminskoye reserve for their passion and expertise. The tigers are in safe hands with you.

Thank you also to: Frank Sayi, whose advice about police

reports was indispensable; my cheerleading friend Annalena McAfee; Jennie Erdal for both the Russian drinking song and the joy of her company; Alexia Holt and my colleagues at Cove Park for their kindness and understanding; and Julian Forrester, who has kept home fires burning so magnificently.

I am so grateful for the brilliance of Jon Riley and the team at riverrun. It's a privilege to work with people who love literature as they do. Special thanks to Rose Tomaszewska for shepherding *Tiger* with such flair.

And thank you, for everything, superlative Jenny Brown, agent and literary tigress.